I0690816

Killswitch

J.R. Waterbear

Published by J.R. Waterbear, Burbank, California, 2024.

While every precaution has been taken in the preparation of this book, the publisher assumes no responsibility for errors or omissions, or for damages resulting from the use of the information contained herein.

KILLSWITCH

First edition. June 4, 2024.

ISBN: 978-1964094014

Written by J.R. Waterbear.

To the memories of Ursula K. Le Guin, John Wyndham, Ray Bradbury and all the other writers who created wondrous new worlds and inspired us with their visions.

And to Suzanne Wilde, whose thoughtful and meticulous review of this book in its early stages helped steer us through the murky waters of the first drafts and saw us, at lone last, safely at anchor.

Also, thanks to all the readers who took the time to give us their thoughts. They were worth their weight in gold too us.

And finally, to tardigrades; microscopic marvels who would survive the Collapse and humanity's real-life efforts to trash our world. Long live the tardigrade!

CHAPTER ONE

I'd never been to Court before. But then, I'd never been accused of killing the most revered person in the world. I'd thought it would be like old Immersion shows, with judges in funny wigs and a lot of "defendant will rise!" commands. But it was nothing like that. Instead, they strapped me to a chair and played with my sanity as well as my future. At least, that's the way it felt: Two realities battling inside my head.

As they adjusted my settings, I flickered from facing the teeth of a Sidysal monster to lying pleasantly in a field of grass. The terror of the monster lingered, but I knew it wasn't real; silly that it frightened me. The grass was real. I pulled my fingers through the soft, sun-warmed blades only to be jolted when I touched cold steel, the armrest of the witness chair. The calibration wasn't complete. I jerked my hand. Then the back of my hand stung as a needle was stabbed into my vein. I might have whimpered, but maybe it was only in my mind.

"Give me the grass! Give me the monster!" I cried out.

A warmth crawled up my arm and assured me that everything was as it should be. I tried to dream of grass again, but that dream was gone. I was in the 'tween of dreams and the present.

The transmission helmet made me feel as if I were submerged in thick fluid. The syrup connected me to any fellow Unity citizen that wished to be part of my trial. How many were watching me? I wondered. I glared at them, but they couldn't see me any more than I could see them. But they could see my thoughts, see monsters inside my head and hear my stuttered breathing. They could feel my glare even if they couldn't see it. I pictured myself staring at them with lizard eyes, black, half-lidded and wary. For an instant, I thought that was a bad move. I should be acting innocent. But most of those Immersed would be there to experience my emotions and had little interest in my guilt or innocence. They could dial the intensity of their emotional parasitism up or down.

Still, I wanted my dreams to be private, even if my feelings weren't. I needn't have worried. Sensory input of my surroundings would push dreams away; my auditors wanted memories, not fantasies. Assuming, of course, that there was a difference. I remembered hearing somewhere that all memories were collages, parceled out to different parts of the brain and then imperfectly reconstructed every time they were revisited. People tended to conflate, to disassociate, to misremember, to assemble their memories to their own desires— usually making themselves the heroes of their own stories.

The Court, doubtless, would have some arcane and complicated techniques for discerning the true from the fantastical. Better than humans could, anyway.

But still, I was glad there was some actual human involvement in passing judgment, even if it were just rubber-stamping a machine recommendation. That was required by law.

Like all primates, what mattered most was what other monkeys thought.

I just hoped judgment would come quickly, not only because I was innocent, but because being Immersed for more than an hour would trigger one of my massive migraines. It was a congenital defect. I would have shaken my head but it was held rigidly by the helmet.

Finally, they completed the adjustments and I could see my surroundings.

The courtroom was as colorless as a room can be, not gray, not white and certainly not the foreverness of black. Behind me, I heard the soft crackle of a door shield dropping and then a wasplike buzz as legal cones floated into the room. Two positioned themselves on either side of my clamped head, just within my peripheral vision. Four others hovered in front of me. I concentrated on their quivering. Wafting in with them was the acrid odor of a hallucinogenic laser. To me, it was the smell of on-the-fly synaptic reprogramming of fried neurons. Their last interrogation must have resulted in a conviction. My fight-or-flight reflex twitched to life momentarily, but it was immediately enfolded in the cozy blanket of the mood inhibitor pumped into my veins. I relaxed.

"Viewers and absorbers, please disconnect or dial down if you are disturbed by graphic emotions." I felt rather than physically heard the disclaimer. I repeated it muzzily, trying to imitate the Court AI's accentless, calm authority.

The door in the side of the chamber crackled. A judge in long black robes swayed into the room. I don't know if she was a *she*, but I was raised with the religion of genders and thought of her thusly. She had bushy red hair and a bullet-shaped face, with a pointed chin like a squirrel's. Her eyes looked bright and sharp.

The judge stepped up onto the bench. My chair unjointed and levered me up so that I was standing. The cones rotated to face her and dipped in their version of a bow— silicon acknowledging the authority of carbon.

Text appeared in a corner of my vision. It read: Judge Char Morain. The Court AI appended data about her previous cases, disciplinary record and so on but I blinked it away. I mentally thumb-printed my acceptance of her handling my case and repeated my decision to waive a human jury and attorneys. The judge and the Court would handle those duties.

The judge seated herself, and my chair re-seated me. She looked bored. No wonder; she had little to do beyond smacking the gavel and reciting legal mumbo-jumbo to the cones— as if the cones cared. Cones can analyze more objectively than a judge, but cones cannot pass judgement on a human. Oddly, considering my jury waiver, I was grateful for that technicality. But a human jury would have extended the trial, maybe for weeks, and I didn't want to spend any more time Immersed than I had to. Jurors would probably want to revisit my testimony over and over again.

"For the record, I will be in full Immersion with the defendant for the duration of this hearing," the judge said, using her actual voice. "I understand that for medical reasons, a request to limit this session to one hour has been submitted. In consideration of this request, absorbers will be limited to eighty percent Immersion. The duration of this session will be limited further as deemed necessary."

I felt only a little relief. She leaned forward. Her eyes bored into me as she said, "Joyo Mavo, do you have any objection to this process?"

"I'm innocent," I mumbled.

"Your plea already has been noted. I meant: Do you wish to reconsider your permission for me to be fully in your head?"

"I don't have anything to hide," I said. Judges were, of course, isolated from the public feed that absorbers used. I could limit her access to my memories, too, which would mean she would rely on Court transcripts and presentations by the Court's prosecution and defense subsystems. In other words, trial the old-fashioned way. But who wanted that? It sounded medieval, like trial by ordeal. Although, if they Immersed me too long, my migraine would kick in and that would feel like a heated metal bar thrust through my temples.

"I'm good to go," I said, using the formal legal response.

The judge rapped her gavel and the Court linked her into the metaspace reserved for this hearing. I felt her in my head and tried to think pleasant thoughts, or at least inoffensive ones. Unfortunately, her bushy hair and squirrel face made me imagine a furry tail popping up from beneath her robes and tickling my chin. If she were offended, she gave no indication. She looked through me and rapped her gavel again. My eyelids dropped like a curtain without a flutter. My trial had begun.

CHAPTER TWO

The Court began by sifting through my memories.

"You're not stupid. You're special," said the voice of my mother.

"Special kids are stupid," I said.

"Stupid and special are not the same thing."

I felt her soft touch brushing the hair from my forehead. Other scenes of my childhood flickered by in no particular order. My mother twisted my ear angrily for sneaking the last ration bar. Then I was on a cracked playground, watching other children play. I've always been weak at making friends.

During the brief blank spots between memories, I wanted to shout at the cones, "See, see? Sympathy. I deserve sympathy."

But the prosecutor flashed up a red label: LONER.

Seemingly random slices of my formative years flashed by. I felt my hand tunnel beneath moist river sand. My tongue rasped against the furry skin of a half-moldy peach. I lay in a dark room, my head exploding with pain— the migraine I got by losing track of time during a furtive adolescent spin through the Immersion's gaming platforms.

In not one of those memory glances was there a trace of my father.

Lastly, I was eight years old. I found myself on the sidewalk outside the Floating World Columbarium, holding my mother's hand. As we walked past, I dragged my fingers along the cool stone wall. I felt— and the judge and absorbers felt— my excitement and puzzlement at the touch of old, polished stone. It was so ancient, so strong and durable. Mother had taken me to the Urb for the day. Coming from the Outside, from a world of patched-up homes amidst rubble and decay, it was like seeing the Pyramids.

"Did they really keep dead people in boxes there?" I asked her.

"The bodies of the dead or their remains, ashes and dust," my mother said.

Before I could ask another question, she added, "But not anymore," and squeezed my hand.

A blue label popped up in overlay, noting that this was my first glimpse of the place of my employment— the scene of the crime of which I was accused.

Speedily, a jumbled sequence of seemingly irrelevant memories of the last year clicked through my mind. Then it was two weeks ago, just after I'd turned sixteen. I was inside the Columbarium guiding a buffing machine over the floor. The only sound was the buffer's soft, meditative whirring like the endless coo of mourning doves. I wondered if it soothed the dreams of the chambered occupants in their privileged bliss. The machine's vibrations massaged my hands as my feet glided over the marble floor like a skater's. The vaults of the fortunate inhabitants covered the walls surrounding me from floor to ceiling, two stories of them. The Columbarium was tradition melded with technology. The horizontal crypts were faced with granite plates embedded with instruments covered in glass bubbles to monitor their occupants' well-being, sending signals to the machines and technicians who watched over them. I glided past, sardonically amused that these people were paying fortunes to be shielded from the distractions of the Immersion. That isolation came naturally to me but since I couldn't be Immersed all the time, I was looked on as underprivileged. To be unsocial was to be suspect— unless you were rich. I was lucky to have my stipend and a menial job. They, on the other hand, were praised for monkish withdrawal, choosing to focus their minds on schemes and dreams and designs that might lead to new technologies or magical art.

One person's outcast is another's pioneer, I thought.

Here and there were vacant vaults with faceless openings. The gaping black rectangles reminded me of mouths. But these weren't the maws of devouring beasts; more like doors to new worlds. And they were in demand. A vault seldom remained vacant for more than a day or two.

Despite the environmental destruction, the related wars and terrorism that had gnawed Earth down, blighting great swathes of land and water; despite the deaths of billions and the exile of billions more from fouled and toxic lands, there were still very wealthy people.

All of these memories were both distant and immediate. I was both inside and outside myself. I was reliving the memory, and I was in the courtroom watching myself relive my memory. My mind felt sticky, like taffy being stretched by a carnival contraption. I imagined my fellow citizens as children, reaching dirty hands to the glass window of my soul.

I also felt the cones compressing and sharpening my thoughts, pulling together the smells, tastes and emotions parceled out in the various lobes of my brain and then patiently reconstituting them. Like an old-fashioned movie, the memories flickered and then became one long moment as we approached the crime.

I was polishing the marble floor. Certainly, a machine could do the job without guiding human hands, but Floating World prided itself on its security, on the fact that nothing wired— to use the obsolete term— could enter the great mausoleum and spy on the grand thoughts of the sleepers. Then, too, Floating World retained an old-fashioned air of personal service. Its halls echoed with the memories of flesh, of the caress of human hands handling the deceased with dignity and sympathy. It had once been a resting place, a spiritual abode whose credo was that if death couldn't be cheated, its fluttering wings could be gilded. In stasis— the near-death— minds took wing as well, soaring over the vast landscape connecting them and the universe like butterflies flitting between the Earth and the heavens.

That was all in the literature, along with Floating World's shelving rates, medical guarantees and waivers of liability for injury caused by natural disasters.

As I relived these thoughts, I felt the metal of the buffer's antique handles warming under my hands. I looked at the flat expanse of the floor. It had a muted glow as if I had polished it with a silk scarf. I felt a pride in my work, which felt embarrassing to the part of my mind that was aware of being on trial. Because of my disability, I had developed a sense of privacy. Weirdly, it hadn't kicked in during the playback of long-ago scenes but only in the here-and-now of two weeks ago. My joy at the simple physical work of my hands was special, and I was jealous of sharing it.

As I surveyed my work, I inhaled cool, clean air, expensively filtered by the Columbarium. The buffer rolled gently through uniform pools of light reflected from the ceiling lamps far above. I swept down the hall, creating soft echoes that bounced off the marble walls. I made the final turn and returned to the unobtrusive supply closet. I raised the buffing wheel and guided the machine inside, where I switched off the motor and put it away. My task was done. It would be four in the morning in another hour and my shift would end. There was no other work assigned for me to do. Initiative is not a strength of mine. It says so on my performance reviews.

I yawned. I walked carefully over the gleaming floor and climbed a heavy oak staircase to the second story. I came out on a walkway flanked by more floor-to-ceiling vaults. The floor was covered by rich carpeting that could have used a cleaning, but that wasn't on my schedule tonight. No reason not to catch a little shuteye.

There was an empty vault in the bottom row. The temperature-controlled, liquid-filled lining was gone. I glanced around, saw I was alone, and slipped feet first into its welcoming gullet. My T-shirted shoulders touched surprisingly chilly stone: the stark, unadorned sides of the crypt. I shivered a little, remembering that bones had once rested there. Then I flashed on the old cinematics I had watched of tomb robbers and mummies and vampires. Playfully, and also because there was so little room, I lay on my back with my arms crossed over my chest, my hands resting on my shoulders as if I might be infused with the immortality and power of a night creature.

Then I fell into a dreamless sleep. And woke to chaos.

I heard hammering echoing from below, followed by the sound most dreaded in the Columbarium: The explosion of shattering glass. I jerked up and my forehead slammed into the top of the crypt. Now the hammering was in my head. I groaned, twisted around and dragged myself out of the vault just as an alarm began to wail. Cold sweat prickled the nape of my neck as I staggered down the staircase, pausing to grip the handrail every few steps because of the nausea from my pounding head.

I reached the main floor. The alarm here was deafening, almost a brutal physical force. I stepped forward. Halfway down the hallway, a crypt was open. Not just open; violated. The control panel had been torn off and dangled from glistening cables. The interior capsule had been hauled partway out of the vault and dropped. A part of my brain registered that one corner had fractured the expensive marble flooring I had just cleaned. Pale green liquid, like dirty aquarium water, oozed onto the floor. It was pouring from a hole in the glass-enclosed top of the capsule. It stuck to my shoes and made gluey sucking sounds as I approached.

The hole had been made by my floor buffer. One of the thick steel handles was embedded in the shattered glass. I saw that the buffer was still running. The buffing wheel whirled, and the machine moved back and forth, straining to spin free but held by the handle like an animal with its leg in a trap. It grated where the chassis banged against the vault.

Through the smeared glass of the capsule, I glimpsed a face, slack and pale.

It was Haakon Pallburg. I was staring at the lifeless face of the most beloved man in the world.

I was still standing there, mute and gaping with shock, when I was hit by something heavy and slammed to the slimy floor.

"You son of a bitch!" someone shouted.

The memory ended abruptly. It was replaced by red lettering: PROSECUTION OBJECTION. Almost simultaneously a green label flashed: DEFENSE OBJECTION.

"Well," the judge said from the bench. "That's a first. Prosecution?"

The prosecution cone turned ceremoniously towards the bench.

"The People question the veracity of the emotional overlay of this memory. We believe the defendant has altered his perception of these events and obscured the reality with a manufactured, sympathetic perception."

"What evidence do you have?" the judge asked.

"Your honor, we seek evidence. The People request an enhanced forensic interrogation with a deep-psych probe."

I gasped. The judge frowned. "You're asking for a military-grade scan of a defendant?"

"We are, your Honor."

"So are we, your Honor," the defense counsel chimed in.

"Sidebar," the judge said tersely.

The helmet went dark. I was left strapped to the chair, blind and beginning to be terrified. There were nightmare stories of what happened to people who underwent a milscan, historical dramas about war-crime trials or world-threatening terrorist threats. Wasn't it illegal for civilian trials?

My face was suddenly wet. I didn't know whether it was connective gel running from underneath the helmet or I was sweating. Maybe it was tears.

A minute later, the helmet's virtual space returned.

The judge looked at me.

"Back on the record," she said, and I felt the presence of the absorbers again. I knew it was impossible but I swore I could feel their excitement. This was high drama. It felt like I was in an arena and somebody had just released the lions. At that moment, I hated humanity.

My defense counsel chimed in privately.

"Mister Mavo, the judge has decided to grant permission for the scan should you accede. I am in concurrence with the prosecution because the probability of your acquittal has diminished to fractional proportions. I wish to argue that your emotional responses are legitimate. That will provide the possibility of having you declared unfit by reason of insanity."

"I'm not crazy. I'm innocent. I was set up!"

"Do you wish to see the metrics on that scenario being (a) factually accurate and (b) being believed?" It was impossible but I thought the machine sounded skeptical.

I thought about it. I was accused of killing the greatest man in history, the savior of billions. I was John Wilkes Booth. No, I was Pontius Pilate. I didn't need numbers to tell me that it would take a miracle for people to believe I was a victim, not a murderer.

The Court might find me innocent, but it couldn't exonerate me in the court of public opinion. And the system was perceptive enough to know that mattered.

"Then why does the prosecution want to scan me?" I asked.

"The People argue that you altered your actual memories via means unknown but not technically impossible," the calm, impartial voice said. "The People do not believe that you slept and saw nothing, nor that you were genuinely disturbed by the killing. To be colloquial, the People believe that you are covering your tracks. Further, they argue that you are likely involved in a wider conspiracy that may pose a global Unitywide threat."

"You mean the Realists?" I said in disbelief. "That's crazy. I never met one in my life. I never even talked to one."

"Immersion records indicate that for three days prior to the crime, you spent virtually the entirety of your Immersion time on FreeJack threads."

"I've never been on FreeJack!" I blurted. "Why would I spend my precious Immersion time on a bunch of freaks and weirdos?"

"Nevertheless, as a matter of course, I polled the Immersion AIs and their attendant Authenticators. There is no evidence of any system degradation or intrusion. Do you wish to argue for deliberate corruption? I doubt the judge will authorize an examination of that caliber. The Supreme Court would have to approve it, and the resources used will mean depriving a small but substantial number of citizens of resources in the meantime. This will harm your own defense if the probe comes back negative, as seems likely."

"So," I replied bitterly. "To be colloquial, I am screwed!"

"Well, it may be an uphill battle," my defense-bot said calmly. "Do you wish to accede to the scan?"

I really was sweating now. This was the kind of thing my mother had warned me about when I talked about leaving the Outside and joining the Immersed world. I'd never regretted leaving the dingy black hole of rebel technophobes but I was beginning to see her point.

"What does it involve?" I asked.

The cone bobbed up and down conversationally.

"You will be taken to a facility with the capacity to perform the procedure," it said. "There, you will be injected with tailored nanothreads targeted to specific areas of your brain. These will be able to determine on a cellular level whether there has been any tampering or rewiring."

"Worms," I said, my mouth suddenly dry. "They're going to wrap my brain in worms!"

"The nanothreads are not alive," the defense cone admonished. "They do emulate certain swarming behaviors but they have a remarkable level of precision."

"So they burrow into my brain and scan me," I said. "That doesn't sound dangerous at all. And what about my condition? Has anybody done one of these on someone like me?"

The cone dipped down, as if lowering its head in embarrassment.

"No," it said.

I had a knot of cells in my brain, connected by blood vessels but otherwise something of a black box. I was born with it. Doctors had examined it and determined it had a different DNA from mine. They suggested it was the remnants of an unborn twin that had been encapsulated as I was developing. They ruled it benign and decided it would be safer just to leave it. But it made my brain different from anyone else's.

"So," I said, clenching my fists to keep my hands from trembling. "You're recommending that I have a risky procedure that's only used on supervillains, and has never been used on a neuroatypical?"

"If there are complications," the cone replied, "The system will provide for your maintenance."

"You mean if I become a vegetable," I said.

"In the unlikely event that you are rendered severely or permanently dysfunctional, the system will provide for you. In the event you become deceased, compensation both practical and reputational will be provided to your designated relatives or approved charities."

"Nice to know," I said. "So you want me to OK this?"

"Probabilistically, it is the best defense move."

"I need time to think about this," I said.

"I will ask the judge for a postponement. You will be stored until the hearing resumes."

"Wait, wait," I said. If they stashed me in the prison equivalent of a vault, it would just be putting off the inevitable. The whole world was ready to hate me and if they wanted my blood, a week or a month would make no difference. It would just make them hungrier. I could imagine what the trolls would be posting while I was in no position to defend myself. I pictured myself being released, walking out the court door, and being grabbed by crazies and hanged from a lamppost like a piñata. AIs would immediately note the event and rush help to cut me down. But I could imagine having my life threatened every single day after that. It made me wish for the peaceful joys of the floor buffer and my anonymity. That seemed like years ago.

"All right," I said. "I give permission to get milscanned. When do we go?"

"Immediately," the defense cone said. "I have notified the judge and the Court has made the arrangements in conjunction with regional, state, federal, hemispheric and global military, medical, psychological and ethics Expert AIs. Human approval has, of course, been obtained."

"Great," I said. "Machines and my fellow humans want to cut open my brain."

"There is no physical—" the defense cone began.

"Figure of speech," I said.

"Noted," the cone said simply.

The judge cut in. "This is all highly unusual but it seems appropriate in such an unusual case." She rapped the gavel. "This court hereby releases defendant Mavo to custody of Court Transport Services. Mister Mavo, good luck." She rapped her gavel again. "Court dismissed."

CHAPTER THREE

The first thing they did was replace my teeth.

"Haven't seen these for a while," a technician said as she clamped my mouth. She had dark eyebrows and minty breath. "Three metal amalgam fillings. That's *ancient.*"

"I lived on the Outside," I mumbled. "We didn't have the most modern dental stuff."

"And you probably had a terrible diet," she sympathized. "Sugary snacks and radioactive vegetables." It wasn't the first time I'd heard that particular slur. While it was hard to grow things out in the desolate area, the Unity made regular food drops, although mostly of cheap staples such as vat boloney and nutrient cakes. If I had eaten my share of sugar, it's because the drop-offs always seemed to contain some snack food, probably because sugar was a cheap and easy form of calories. Also, sugar cane seemed to be the one thing that grew in abundance where we lived.

Unfortunately, metal fillings would interfere with the results of the scan. So they were quickly and efficiently replaced with vat-grown teeth. My gums were a little sore but the whole process was less painful than when I'd gotten the originals.

Then they took me to a small, spherical room, a blown-bubble prefab like the one I'd briefly inhabited on the Outside. It was cheap, uniform government housing. Like medical rooms the world over, it was pale blue and smelled of ozone and disinfectant. I was clamped on a table under a large inverted funnel. Two technicians put a lightweight mesh mask over my face and head.

"That's to target the nano injection sites," the tech said. "You have an anomaly and we need to pinpoint and avoid it." She patted my shoulder. "No big deal."

"I understand," I said.

"Ready to go?"

I took a deep breath. "Yes."

The techs moved back out of my line of sight. The lights dimmed, there was a whisper of machinery and the funnel descended until I was looking up into its dark interior. In the center, something slick and faintly blue flicked out, like a lizard's tongue, swept across my face and retracted. There was a hiss, and two thick, flexible cables like veins descended from the ceiling on either side of me. A moment later, I felt two small spots of cold on the top of my skull. I felt a slight pressure, a moment of dizziness, and then they retracted with a sucking sound. The funnel hovered an instant longer, then it too retracted. The lights slowly brightened.

The techs, who had gone somewhere, glided back into the room. They unclamped me and helped me to sit up.

"How was that?" one asked.

"Not bad," I admitted. "What's next?"

For answer, they took my arms and led me to an adjoining room. This one smelled like a waiting room, slightly stuffy and full of aging plastic. There was a comfortable-looking chair, a table, a carafe of water and a glass, and nothing else.

"The nanos are distributing themselves," a tech explained. "You just need to sit here and relax for about a half-hour until they're done." I pictured legions of worms swarming over my brain and burrowing into the folds. It made my scalp crawl.

"All right," I said.

"Unfortunately, you won't be able to Immerse during the process," she said. "No loud sounds, no video or high-key visuals or moving text. I'm afraid all we have for entertainment is this." She held out a hand with an apologetic smile. "It's a book."

"I know," I said.

"Oh," she said. "Most people don't. They're a form of pre-Collapse data storage, you know. Anyway, you scan it by turning the pages." She demonstrated.

"I know," I said. "I've read before." She frowned as if I'd said something puzzling or maybe slightly off-color.

"Right," she said. "All right, then. You relax. I'll be back." She left.

I looked at the book. It was a faded, dog-eared hardback. The title was "Treasure Island."

I was engrossed in the book when she returned. For some reason, I felt slightly guilty handing it back, as if by enjoying something so privately, I'd violated a minor taboo.

She quirked her lips.

"You looked interested," she said.

"Well, it's a good book," I said. "A lot of adventure."

"Huh," she said. "Is there an Immersion version?"

I flushed.

"I don't know," I said.

The next stop was a larger round room. This one was full of people and equipment. Some wore tech smocks, some were Authenticators, who were seated in their own chairs. There were three Authenticators, I noticed; a large contingent. They wore the traditional vulture-wing tattoos symbolizing fearless pursuit of truth. I guessed they were there so that when rumors about the procedure inevitably erupted on the Immersion, they could bear witness to what really occurred, although only after the details were declared public. I doubted there were any absorbers, since this was a high-security location. But I noticed a cone hovering unobtrusively, probably recording the entire scene. Everybody gave me short, polite glances before returning to their tasks.

The techs sat me down in a sort of padded dentist's chair. Someone who appeared to be a doctor, judging by the smock, approached. The doctor was a Third. I had met only a few before. Thirds had extra neurological inputs. They were generally non-gender or asexual. Even more than most people, Thirds were tied to the Immersion. They engaged with couples, got their experiences and also contributed to them. They functioned as intermediaries, facilitators, translators and amplifiers of their partners' emotions. One Third had told me it was like being a supercharger on a race car, although I didn't know what that meant. Thirds were still relatively rare; not many people were able to spend time and resources for the bioengineering.

"I'm Dr. Lind. Just relax," the doctor said. "We're going to activate the nano system now; let them talk to us. We'll need to make sure they're all positioned correctly and are collaborating and communicating. You may have a few, let's say, odd moments but it's all normal and harmless, I assure you. If at any time you're uncomfortable, we'll know right away and dial things down. Okay?"

"Okay," I said, although I could have done without the mention of discomfort. It made me uncomfortable. With pursed lips, Lind looked down at a screen, then looked up. "You seem a little bit anxious. Relax. And don't flicker."

"Don't what?" I said, but the doctor had turned away.

I leaned back and tried to relax. For the next few moments, medics and techs conferred and chatted, murmuring questions and answers and pointing at things. They talked in techno, throwing out references to field strengths, sigma points, branching hypothalamic something-or-others.

At last, they seemed to reach some sort of consensus. They all fell silent and there was a sort of unspoken feeling of coordination.

I can't say that somebody pushed a button and my brain changed. But somebody pushed a button for sure, because suddenly the room crackled with static electricity. Some strong field had been activated. I felt the hair on my arms lift. As the techs fiddled with equipment around the walls, their hair would shoot out to form a crown or nimbus around their heads. I was in a field of human dandelions.

And then the "odd moments" the doctor had warned me about began. First, I saw a brilliant spark of light. It faded. A microsecond later, I thought I heard a musical tone but it was gone before I could be sure. Almost simultaneously, I smelled burnt rubber and tasted almonds. I grimaced but they were gone. Then my throat constricted. I started to choke but that ended. In the next few seconds I must have gone through hundreds of sensations. I heard shrieks, saw darkness, smelled old dusty books, lost my toes, tasted tin. I was scared, happy, confused, bemused, ecstatic, all in the time it took to blink. Most sensations moved so quickly that I couldn't actually say I felt them; it was more like remembering them, or feeling the ghostly shape of where they once had been.

I heard a gong chime and realized it was the doctor's voice.

"Mavo, you're flickering. Please concentrate. I want you to think of strawberries."

"I've never had a strawberry," I mumbled. But then my mouth was suddenly full of an overpowering sweetness. My hands were cupped and holding some sort of delicious-smelling red fruit with golden seeds. They were chilled and glistening with droplets of water.

"Um," I said. My mouth watered. "Um. Ummy. Yummy!" I raised my hands to my lips. My tongue darted out—

—and I was back in the room. My hands were empty and my mouth was dry.

The doctor approached and gave me a searching glance.

"You did very well," Lind said. "You've got an exceptional integration rate. Do you feel dizzy, nauseous?"

"Disappointed," I said. "I think I like strawberries."

"That was the primary scan," Lind said with a smile. "You have an enlarged memory lobe, giving you the capacity to look at unrelated information and, most importantly, to mull over things. Most people today all have ADD, attention deficit disorder, and the pleasure centers have greater capacity."

"Oh," I said.

"Now," Lind said. "We move on. Do you recall your Court scan?"

"Sure," I said. "Now you're going into my memories?"

"Yes. But much more deeply."

"That's the scary part," I said.

"For some people," the doctor said. "It is certainly more invasive, and a little trickier. As you were warned, there is some risk of impacting your brain."

I swallowed. The forms I signed had mentioned rare but potential risks. They ran from occluded memories, where I constantly tried to remember something that was just out of reach, to recursive memories, like being forced to replay the same cat video endlessly in my head, all the way up to psychotic breaks, homicidal rage, and loss of ability to breath, move or control my bladder.

Lind saw me tense and added quickly, "We've got AIs and humans watching each and every part of your brain individually. They'll pull the plug if they see anything dangerous. You're in the best hands possible."

I controlled my breathing. It wasn't as if I had a choice. I had one more question.

"Will it hurt?" I asked.

"That depends," the doctor said. "On how hard you try to hide."

I relived the scene in the Columbarium. I stood in front of the smashed, leaking sarcophagus and saw the pale, dead face of

Pallburg. The memory was much more vivid than when I'd relived it in the courtroom. I smelled the acrid odor of the isolation fluid. And again, I noticed that my shoes were sticky. My confusion and fear were just as intense.

The scene ended abruptly. From miles away, the real world flooded back. I heard a technician praise the quality of the probe. Then there was some technical babble about going deeper, setting baselines from a "standing wave" recollection. I guessed that meant something that was firmly burned into my memory. I knew what that meant: Something that had happened to me that affected me so deeply it was seared into my brain. I began to sweat. I knew of only three memories that carried that emotional weight. I didn't want to relive any of them.

I didn't have a choice.

"Not that one, not that one," I prayed under my breath.

It was that one.

I am eleven years old. My hand grips the strap of a pink plastic backpack stamped with a prancing pony, a pre-Collapse artifact. It is my sister Jola's, her pride and joy. I stand next to the train platform. I am sweating and bug-bitten and hungry and also bored, so bored. I think with dread of the coming night: a communal dinner by dingy solar lamplight, then playing tattered board games and finally watching old Granger pluck a warped guitar as we bellow the same old campfire songs about the glory of living free from Unity oppression. I am overdue for a bath but the leaky old filtration system is still undergoing repairs. In my other hand is my own pack. It holds a few grungy paperback books I have just gotten in trade from other Outsiders. They are precious entertainment, full of other worlds.

The weekly supply train is on the siding, all tarnished silver, humming electrically, its air brakes gasping so it resembles a huge, panting silver lizard. The sun throws hard daggers of light from its sides. I smell the hot metal and the flinty odor of baked stone from the tracks.

Bored guards keep the small, ragged crowd of Outsiders orderly as they pick up bread, vat meat and so on from untidy piles dumped next to the track. I wander away to grab something from the sweets pile. The guard ignores me as I shuffle through the pile looking for chocolate but all I find are packages of Boba Coconut Cake and some chemical-tasting banana pudding. Same as last week's drop. And the week before.

The adults are always talking about how one day we'll grow all the food we need and won't need Unity handouts. I'll believe it when they can grow chocolate.

I look over at Jola, a few meters away. She has toddled along behind my mother to help her load our family sack with the week's supplies.

My mother has sun-faded hair and her face is tanned and lined. She is wearing torn cutoffs and a ragged flannel shirt. She lifts a carton and stuffs it into the sack, which sits on a battered red Radio Flyer wagon. My sister holds out a torn, faded package, obviously abandoned or ignored from a food dump many weeks earlier. It must be pretty nasty stuff to go unclaimed. My sister beams proudly as my mother smiles and takes it, carefully stowing it in the sack.

The piles dwindle. One by one, the Outsiders finish their rummaging, shake hands, exchange short snatches of polite conversation and stand back, waiting for the excitement of the train's departure. My mother is trying to stuff a last package into the bulging sack. She doesn't notice me.

The train gives a warning chime. Time is almost up. It has a schedule to keep. There are many more mouths to feed in wastelands farther up the track. The guards climb aboard.

The rusty old robotic voice of the train calls out the old spiel: "This concludes the service portion of Unity Mobile Redistribution

Vehicle Twelve-Oh-Three. Unity now invites anyone who wishes to reintegrate to climb aboard. The next reintegration point will be Nuevo Los Angeles, Yukon Region. If you want a better life, a new beginning or a second chance, the Urbs await you. All aboard! Please remember you may take only one bag, ten kilo maximum. This train departs in three minutes. Welcome aboard!" It croaks to a stop.

The passenger car door is open to the platform. I am standing near the platform stairs.

My mother finishes the packing. She stands up, lifts my sister into her arms and looks around for me to come haul the wagon. My mother has not spotted me because I am in the shadow of the platform stairs.

"One minute to departure!" the train squawks. The hum of its engines throttles up. A faint vibration makes the sides shimmer in the heat glare.

My mother shades her eyes with a hand as she casts around for me.

"Mavo!" she calls a bit fretfully.

"Final call!" the train warns. As always, nobody has climbed aboard. As always, it will leave us all behind.

Suddenly, without thinking, I sprint up the crumbling concrete steps and dash out onto the apron. I drop my sister's backpack and race through the passenger car door. The door gasps shut behind me and the train lurches into slow movement.

I press my face to the smudged window. The last thing I see as we roll away is my mother standing near the track, holding my sister, looking for me. They become smaller and smaller and finally vanish and there is nothing for me to see but desert.

Only then do I pull my face away from the glass. I glance down and realize with shock that I am holding something pink. My sister's backpack is in my hand. I have left my own on the platform.

I came back to reality feeling stripped naked and humiliated. My heart was racing. I couldn't slow down my breathing. I was panting as if I had just raced through that open train door. But it was five years ago. The room was blurry. I must have cried without knowing it.

Someone laid a hand on my arm. I looked up into the sympathetic face of a technician.

"You all right?" he asked.

I looked down. "I'm so ashamed," I said.

"Why?" he asked, puzzled.

"It's something I kept private," I said. "I never shared it with anybody."

"Oh," he said, and patted my arm. "Well, you have now. It must feel great to let that out. You mean you never put this on the Immersion? There are millions of people who could comfort you. Plus, you'd probably win the daily FundMyLife pot."

"No, I mean I didn't *want* to share it," I said but I could tell he didn't understand. He gave me another puzzled look, checked my wrist constraints, dabbed tears from my cheeks with a wipepad, then leaned over and whispered: "I shouldn't tell you this but so far it looks like your memories haven't been adulterated. I'm rooting for you. Just one more scan to go. Try to relax!"

"Great!" I said but the tech had stepped away. The doctor came up, looked me over with a professional glance and said: "How do you feel? Do you a need another minute before we continue?"

Not, I noticed, *do you want to continue?* I wasn't being given an option.

I felt a deep well of dread. If the last scan was that painful, what the hell was this next scan going to be like? I had two more bad memories left and I didn't want to relive either one.

Lind might not have understood my privacy concern and might even consider it a fetish, but acknowledged it.

"Mavo," Lind said, gazing at me with calm eyes. "We've seen everything here: Anything that can be done to or by a human being. No one here will judge you. Are you ready?"

I took a moment to slow my breathing. I clenched my fists and released them, pumping blood back into them. Lind waited patiently. When I felt jittery but fairly normal, I simply nodded.

"Good," Lind said, and stepped back.

Technobabble. Soft machine humming. The quiet, confident air of professionals doing their jobs.

The sudden plunge into darkness.

I didn't fall into a memory. I fell into a spidery web of pain. I was blind but my eyes seemed to be on fire. I couldn't move my arms and legs but they seemed to writhe, as if the nerves beneath my skin were crawling and leaping and tangling themselves into knots. My hips danced until the chair seemed to tip over but I didn't fall. I tried to scream but my tongue was lashing around in my mouth like a maddened snake. My body was fighting itself, tearing itself apart. My muscles spasmed and the edges of the wrist restraints felt like knife blades. The darkness around me was dense and menacing, an emptiness that had weight and power and was pressing inexorably against me, trying to enter me. *Me?* I wasn't sure. Some part of me pushed back against something foreign. And yet the intruder was *also* part of me. I felt my shoulder and calf muscles scream as if I were braced and literally trying to hold back something, an unseen boulder, an invisible rolling thing. It was irresistible. I was slowly losing ground against that crushing force. Then my skull seemed to split open and spill light into the darkness. The light was blinding but I already was blind. My head burst with pain. In my mind's eye, my skin turned to glass, disclosing the nerves and muscles beneath. Everything was a glaring, featureless white.

I was transparent! They would see! They would see it all!

The terror and pain reached a crescendo. My ears were full of a silent roaring, like the noise of a typhoon. In my skull, it felt like the end of the world.

They were opening me. *Completely.*

No! Nonononononono—

And then, for an instant, there was utter silence. Everything stopped. I was in the eye of a hurricane.

I heard a voice, not my own, but coming from inside me.

"LET ME OUT," it said.

And then everything went black.

I awoke in a hospital bed. I knew it was a hospital because I smelled disinfectant and laundered sheets and ozone. Breathing hurt.

Dr. Lind was there and apparently had been waiting patiently for me to wake up.

"What happened?" I asked.

"You had a seizure," the doctor said. "You stopped breathing and went into cardiac arrest."

I swallowed hard. "I... I died?"

"No, there was no brain death," Lind said impatiently. "But we did have to work a bit to revive you."

My hand crept to my chest under the sheet. Sure enough, it felt bruised and tender. The lightest touch hurt.

"What do you remember?" Lind asked.

I explained about the darkness, the pain and the sudden light. I didn't mention the voice. I don't know why.

"What did you see?" I asked.

The doctor's head shook doubtfully. "Nothing I've seen before," Lind admitted. "The scan was proceeding normally. We were drilling down to some of your earliest memories and pinging for emotional resonance when all of a sudden, your brain... lit up."

"What do you mean?"

The doctor seemed suddenly uncomfortable. Lind didn't have an answer and didn't like that.

"We suddenly saw action potentials in regions of your brain that we hadn't stimulated and which shouldn't play any role in your memory development. It was like a neural storm. Like epilepsy on steroids. Your record doesn't indicate any previous episodes. Do you recall any similar event in your life? Blackouts? Seizures? Maybe spells of amnesia?"

"No," I said. "Never."

Lind gave another head shake. "It was almost..." The doctor paused, seemed to choose words carefully. "Look, Mavo, sometimes when we scan for deeply defended memories— for instance, when we're interrogating people we suspect of plotting mass acts of terrorism— they can try to fight us, keep us from discovering what they've been up to. The result is pain and sometimes, if the response is severe enough, there is a risk of stroke. Remember, I told you that the harder you try to hide, the more painful it can be."

"I wasn't hiding anything," I said. "Not intentionally."

"But something seemed to be defending itself in your head," Lind said, pointing at my skull. "It was way over the top, not specific. You lit up like a fireworks show. It wasn't so much a defense as an allergic reaction."

I was stumped.

"You are aware that you are not neurotypical," the doctor said.

"Oh, you mean the thing in my head."

"Yes," the doctor confirmed. "Do you know what it is?"

"Well, I was examined by doctors when I reintegrated. It's a ball of cells, basically. It doesn't do anything. It doesn't have my DNA, though. They thought it might be a..." I struggled to remember the word. "A chimera, that's it. Or maybe a twin that was partially absorbed when I was a fetus. That was always creepy to me," I admitted.

"And it wasn't removed because..." the doctor prompted.

"It's got a blood supply to other parts of my brain. Too dangerous. Plus, it doesn't do anything. It doesn't grow, it just sits there."

"But you do have a problem Immersing."

"Yeah, but they don't know why. They looked at this thing in my head and they said that except for blood vessels, it doesn't have any connection with my brain. It just sits there." I didn't add that I had wished the little black box in my head had been my Immersion problem. Then they could have just cut it out. But it wasn't and they couldn't.

"Hmmm," the doctor said. "That coincides with what we observed. And yet..." Lind paused and tugged at an ear. "I wonder if maybe we poked it... and it poked back."

My eyes widened. "What?"

Lind smiled. "Sorry, just thinking out loud. There's no evidence of that. For the moment, it's an enigma." Lind gave another ear tug. "At any rate, you've never had an episode like this before so I doubt there's any real risk to you of a recurrence. Still, I'd like to re-examine you periodically, if you don't mind."

"You mean scan me?"

"Not in the way we just did. Nothing abnormally intrusive. We just want to keep an eye on your health. You can go through your regular precinct medical station and they'll send the results to us, say, in a couple of weeks?"

"So you're letting me go?"

"The scan had to be halted but the data we did retrieve shows no evidence of memory tampering," Lind said. "We've submitted the results to the Court. I suspect that the judge won't permit the use of the results because they are incomplete. And I'm no lawyer, but it would seem to mean that, either way, your memories must be taken at face value."

I thought about that.

"So I'm going back to court?"

"As soon as the hospital AI declares you fit, I'll sign the release," Lind said, then frowned. "May I say something, Mavo?"

I nodded.

"You are an intriguing case," the doctor said. "An unusual young man. I don't know what's in there." Lind gestured at my forehead. "But I'm pretty sure you're not a monster. Believe me, I've seen enough of them." Lind tapped a medical tablet in one hand thoughtfully, then gave me a firm glance, turned and left the room.

Ten hours later, I was back in the courtroom.

CHAPTER FOUR

The absorbers were uneasy. I could feel their eyes on me. I was again sitting in the chair, my wrists shackled. Once again, they had lightly sedated me. I felt an overlay of calm but underneath it was tension, like a skin of warm water over icy depths.

The judge adjusted her robes, cleared her throat and addressed me.

"Mister Mavo," she said. "This is a noteworthy case, to say the least. But the public interest doesn't trump the law. You need to hear, and believe, that every effort has been made to try this matter on the basis of fact and sound judicial reasoning."

"I understand," I said, swallowing.

"Very well," she said, then straightened her shoulders. "The Court has the results of your deep-psych probe. Unfortunately, they are incomplete. And I am advised that under the law, they therefore cannot be used as evidence." Her lips quirked. "Although I will note that the Defense argued mightily for keeping the portions that seemed to validate your version of events." She adjusted her robes and continued. "That being the case, the Court has looked only at the submitted facts in the matter. And because the deep-scan is inadmissible, this Court cannot establish that your memories are invalid. So, while the circumstantial evidence strongly tends to support the People's case—" She nodded at the prosecution cone. "—the Court believes there to be reasonable doubt." The judge stopped and let that sink in.

I don't think my expression changed, but my breath caught. Was she saying what I thought she was saying?

"Sufficient data has been analyzed and the Court has issued its recommendation. Whatever my personal thoughts, I am agreeing with that recommendation." She picked up her gavel, twisting it in her hand. "Therefore, in the matter of the People v. Mavo, I find the defendant not guilty." She rapped the gavel hard on the block, then set it down. But instead of dismissing court, she moved a few inches forward. She waved a hand and disconnected the absorbers from the Court feed. A blue label appeared in a corner of my sight that said: "Non-public, non-judicial comment from the bench to the defendant."

"A word of caution, Mister Mavo," the judge said. "You may be innocent in the eyes of this Court but you are still the most hated man on Earth. Watch your back." The judge seemed to be worrying about her own back, too. While the Court AI had really made the call, the absorbers would hold the judge, a human, accountable. People found it much easier to hate and blame something if it had a face. I wondered what this decision would do to her approval ratings.

The blue sign vanished and we were back online. I realized my mouth was hanging open and closed it with a snap.

"Court is adjourned," the judge announced.

She banged her gavel sharply on the block again, rose and with an exaggeratedly dignified manner exited through the judge's door with a crackle. I noticed the cones were motionless now, as lifeless as if they had never quivered. Left with my own confused thoughts, I sat alone in the courtroom waiting to be unshackled. It seemed like a long time but was probably not more than three minutes before two court workers finally came to attend to me.

One of them, a wiry technician, had Court tattoos indicating a life ranker. He removed the needle painlessly and stowed away the tubing in the recycle pod. An adhesive pad was slapped on my arm and my vague sense of calm vanished. I felt my heart rate shoot up as I sucked in a few deep breaths. Sweat dampened my forehead. The chair gave a warning chirp.

"Easy," the tech said, and laid a practiced hand on my forearm. "This is just restoring your usual emotional structure. It's a normal reaction. You'll bounce for a minute or two but then you should be fine."

"I'm all right," I insisted, glad when the tech removed his hand.

"I know," the tech said. "It's just fight-flight kicking in. Just remember: you're safe. You're OK."

I nodded and found that after a minute or two, I did feel calmer. The tech noticed.

"All right," he said. "Now we just do the paperwork. Is the Link good or would you prefer a monitor?"

"Monitor," I said without hesitation. The tech nodded. I wondered if it was a natural reaction for people who'd been charged with a crime to want to avoid the mind machinery of the Court.

The tech reached over and removed the Immersion helmet. Goo dripped down. Unable to use my hands to wipe it, I tilted my head to keep it out of my eyes. It dripped down one ear before the tech pulled a wipepad from one of many pockets and efficiently cleaned me up. Then he reached behind the chair's headrest and pulled something. A screen on a flexible mount spidered up and over. The tech pulled it down in front of my face.

"Put your thumb on the screen," the tech said. I did. The screen lit up. Two vertical lines appeared, then moved closer and farther apart before stopping with a short distance between them. A line of letters appeared.

"Focal distance acquired," said the Court Expert System in a contralto voice designed to sound neither specifically male nor female, without a distinct accent, non-judgmental and yet authoritative. "Mavo, if you are content with the display parameters, say yes."

"Yes."

"Proceeding, then. Mavo, this is the outtake process for defendants in criminal cases brought before the First Behavioral Management and Retributive Justice Capsule, District 34-118. I am the Expert AI for this capsule. You may call me Chad Five. Mavo, you have been found innocent of murder and felony vandalism. This ruling is made with prejudice, meaning no other criminal charges may be filed against you in connection with this incident. Do you understand?"

"Yes," I said. The screen briefly flashed green.

"The criminal action brought against you affected your social score adversely. Do you wish the details?"

I laughed. I didn't need a data dump. I already knew what people were going to think of me. The state funeral for Pallburg was the most elaborate in Unity history. It had lasted six days. But I didn't want to argue. My brain already felt like Swiss cheese.

"Go ahead," I said.

"Your approval status globally dropped from point-five-three percent to point-oh-oh-oh-oh-seven percent. Your status among continental residents fell to point-oh-oh-oh-oh-three percent. Your status among those who closely followed the case fell to four-point-eight percent. Your status among those you identify as friends and acquaintances remained basically unchanged. Please note that this is not unusual, as those who know the defendant usually resist the idea of culpability. These are in-trial results. Naturally, variations will occur over time now that your innocence has been noted."

I almost smirked at that. Variation was indeed what I was facing, if by that, the machine meant pitchforks and torches. The judge had implied that I could face tar-and-feathering, being ridden out of town on a rail or being hanged from a lamppost, if chickens, trees and lampposts still existed.

The AI pressed on. "Is there someone's particular reaction you wish to know about?"

"My mother," I said.

"I'm sorry," the voice said. "There is no current information about your mother."

I wasn't surprised. I had never gone back to the Outside but years ago, I had made an effort to reach out to her. I never found her. She lived off-grid and she had moved. What did I expect when I had abandoned my family?

"Never mind," I said. "No need to drill down further."

"Very well," the voice said. "As you have been found innocent but your reputation has suffered, you are entitled to a re-authentication effort, free of charge, to restore your status. This may include, but is not limited to, widecast notification of your innocence, linkads on major status sites and direct contact with influencers. Do you wish such efforts to proceed?"

"Not really." My reputation had never been very high to begin with. I was barely neutral. My disability meant that I rarely linked and my bottom-of-the-keg jobs rated little social attention. Besides, I suspected that the only thing that could help me repair my status was the passage of time.

"I'm sorry, you must answer yes or no."

"No," I said with a touch of irritation.

The screen flashed red.

"All right. Do you wish some form of compensation? Court fees are waived but you are entitled to a one-time credit of sixty-three Allunits. This is based on the time spent in court, lost wages and incidentals. Do you wish to accept compensation?"

"Yes." I'd take every deca-unit I could find.

Green flash.

"Credited. Do you have any questions?"

"No."

Red flash.

"Do you wish to make a review or file an official comment?"

I was tempted to complain that I was innocent but I didn't want the emotional labels of vindictive, vengeful or even 'faintly pissed off' appended to my social credit emotional files. No matter how justified, any outburst would be another data point, a little chip of doubt in my profile. I was hoping, someday, to just be forgotten again. I hadn't realized how important that was to me until I'd lost it.

"No."

The screen flashed red.

"Very well, then, outtake is complete. Thank you for participating in your world's justice system. The Court releases you."

CHAPTER FIVE

I was on the street. I could have taken public transport but I wanted time to collect myself. After days of being probed, questioned and accused, I was brain-bruised. I looked forward to walking the old sidewalks of Victoria, which had survived the brutality of the Collapse with its character, and maybe even its soul, intact. The courthouse was just outside of the city in one of the newer government suburbs. I could have taken a mover home, courtesy of the Court, but I needed to clear my head and walking has always been some kind of therapy for me.

I had an aversion to therapeutic scans. I didn't like pyschs poking around in my head. I wasn't hiding anything. It was just that AI or human, I found it uncomfortable, as if they were only getting part of me and didn't really connect with who I was. Maybe that's why I found the Court so uncomfortable. Were they really getting at the truth? Sure, of course, I know they were, but being probed has never been my thing.

One time when I was having a standard evaluation, it was suggested— by a human, not an AI —that the hemangioma in my skull might be responsible for my aversion to probing. Somehow. They couldn't say why.

I couldn't either, although I'd gone round and round in my head about what it was or had done, or would do, to me. Eventually, I'd come to the obvious conclusion, which was that I was defective and I just had to live with it.

More than one examiner had speculated that the thing also was limiting my Immersion time, but there was no evidence for it and nobody knew what to do about it. One quack wanted to reposition my wet socket. It would have been great if it actually worked. But it meant heavy neural rewiring. And there was a one-in-four risk I'd lose my socket capacity entirely. Surgery, even done with robotic skill, was serious stuff.

I obviously was less than enthusiastic about something that could make me a complete social outcast, as limited as I may already have been in that area. Then again, there were the headaches. When they were really bad, I was almost tempted to have it done. Maybe that was part of why I liked working at Floating World. I shared the customers' attraction to old things, to a sense of history, a connection to the past. Nostalgia, antiquities of the mind. Maybe I was compensating for my limited ability to Immerse. Somehow, history made me feel more a part of the human race. Considering my atypical upbringing, I figured anything that made me feel connected was a good thing. Even walking made me feel connected to the past. Many of the sidewalks were still the old concrete ones that were poured a hundred years back. I loved the slap of my feet on hard stone. The spongy sidewalks they built later just weren't the same. They made my legs feel rubbery, like they weren't my own legs, as if they belonged to someone else and I had only been borrowing them.

Walking in someone else's shoes. That's an old saying my mom used to repeat. She liked history, too. Maybe that's where I got it from. Something from my mother, though we were really very different people. She was paranoid, thought all of history was a tangled web of conspiracies. Unfortunately, I bore the scars from her weirder views.

It was still early when I was released from court, as I'd only been the second case of the day. The sky was a crinkly violet haze with speckles of blue seeding that bio-reflected to help keep the city cool. What did I have to complain about? I was free and had dodged a conviction that could have destroyed my life.

Even though I kept telling myself that I was lucky and had nothing to be unhappy about, the whole affair had left a sour taste in my mouth. Sure, bad things happen to good people, and anyone could have been set up to take a fall by Realist agitators. Just one of those things. I started to whistle as I walked and tried to pick out real birds among the botbirds. I watched a bird dive and snatch at a bug. Somehow, real birds can tell if their prey is synthetic. I've watched them veer off just before grabbing a bioengineered little mouthful.

I strolled past Butchart Gardens, with its heirloom roses and special greenhouses holding the salvaged remnants of a dozen near-extinct ecosystems. A century ago, the city had expanded northwards and engulfed the garden area as its southern edge was nibbled away by rising seas. But beyond it was the heritage area, with its gingerbread Victorian houses and old-fashioned lampposts holding baskets of flowers. So, trees and lampposts weren't extinct after all; I seemed to have forgotten that. Did being Court-scanned leave blank spots in your memory? I did know for sure that I'd never seen a live chicken.

I tasted the tangy fall air as I strolled the sidewalks. The crowds were much smaller here; only the wealthy lived in this section. The Columbarium was located here, where elegance combined with a rich and marketable sense of age and stability. I thought longingly of its ivy-covered walls and realized that I didn't know whether I still had a job. I didn't want to Immerse; my day in court already had used up most of my capacity and I could feel a headache lurking if I tried to dive in. Instead, I purchased a cheap pair of augmented reality specs from a street hawker, the kind that offered limited sensory experiences to Outside tourists on discount excursions who didn't trust full Immersion. I could call my boss from them.

I switched them on and immediately the streets were flooded with dancing, drumming, singing carnival crowds and festoons of giant floating gold stars. Fireworks perpetually exploded overhead.

I clicked on a newsfeed and a banner appeared, proclaiming a holiday. The huge letters crowed: "Twenty years without a global famine." I drilled down and the story noted that only two million people starved to death last year, a record post-Collapse low.

The likes for the story were through the roof.

I called my boss and the scene switched to a simulation of the Columbarium, looking solid and stately. The sim morphed smoothly to a front desk made of some expensive polished wood. I knew it was polished because I'd done it two weeks ago.

A man with a weak chin and very little hair but an expensive suit peered at me from behind gold-rimmed spectacles. He appeared to be an actual human. No avatars or off-the-shelf sims for the Columbarium. The facility prided itself on its old-fashioned, hand-crafted service.

"How may I direct your call?" the man said in a smooth, clipped voice, although I was certain he knew exactly who I was.

"Battu, please," I said.

"Connecting you," he said without a trace of familiarity and pressed an actual button, a large brass thing that seemed entirely unnecessary.

"Facilities Management." Battu's squat face filled the screen, then she raised an eyebrow. "Mavo."

"Hi, Battu," I said lamely. "You probably heard the news." That didn't warrant a reply and Battu didn't give me one.

"I just wondered when I can get back to work," I said.

"Ah," Battu said. "About that. Didn't you receive the notification?"

"They just released me," I said. "I haven't been Immersed."

"Yes. Your condition," Battu said. She drummed thick fingers on her desk. "Well, I'm sorry to tell you, Mavo, that your services are no longer needed here."

"What?" I was taken aback. "You're firing me?"

"No, eliminating you from the maintenance roster," Battu said expressionlessly. "Downsizing, the result of an efficiency review."

"You can't fire me," I said, struggling to keep my voice from cracking. "I was acquitted!"

"We're not firing you for that," Battu replied.

"So what's your excuse?" I said.

"Excuse?" Battu said, her toad-like mouth stretching in a smirk I knew all too well. "No excuse, Mavo. Your position is being eliminated. But if you prefer, we could fire you for cause." She paused, as if daring for me to ask the question. I did.

"What cause?" I said.

"Falsifying your timesheets."

"What do you mean?" I said, exasperated. "The timesheets are automated. They clock me in, they clock me out." I was actually confused.

Battu licked her lips as if anticipating a meal: Me.

"You didn't deduct the time you were sleeping on the job," she said with an edge of triumph.

My stomach dropped into my feet. I couldn't deny it. I had convicted myself when, in court, I recalled that night in the Columbarium when I had catnapped in a crypt before finding Pallburg dead. The memory had been played before millions of absorbers.

Battu stared at me, gloating.

"That's right," she said. "Your own memory. I always thought you were a slacker, Mavo, but I could never prove it until you proved it for me."

I could feel my teeth grinding together. "This is garbage," I said. "You know I did all my work. You're not firing me for a nap. You're firing me because I'm hurting your precious image. But I'm not guilty! The law says you can't fire me for that! I'll fight this!"

"Oh," Battu said sweetly. "Please do. I can't wait. I want to see my approval ratings after I trample the last shreds of your miserable dignity. In public. Again."

I knew she was right. I couldn't beat Floating World. They had me, and I'd given them the ammunition. I boiled over and before I could stop myself, I shouted at her, "You lousy calorie-sucker!"

It was the worst insult I could use. People who ate more than their fair share were the lowest of the low. I immediately regretted it. I might dislike her, but even she didn't deserve that.

Her face went rigid. Then, in a tight, controlled voice, she said, "Your severance package has been sent to your account. You are hereby barred from further contact with Floating World Corporation, its employees, contractors, ancillaries and subsidiaries. From now on, Mavo," she spat the words, "You. No. Longer. *Exist.*" And she cut the connection.

I was returned to a street full of joyful fireworks and crowds in colorful costumes, swaying and dancing to the blare of music and the pounding of drums.

Angrily, I ripped off the specs. The street went empty and silent. As empty as the pit of my stomach.

Then a thought hit me. My apartment was partially subsidized by Floating World. The company wanted its manual laborers to be available on short notice, and that meant living nearby.

Now that I was fired, I'd have to cover the rent myself. I made a quick calculation. Unless I got another job immediately, rent would quickly eat up all my savings.

I'd be homeless.

Suddenly, I needed to get back to my apartment. I wanted to be alone with my books and digest everything that had happened to me. It was my refuge, for as long as it lasted.

It took me fifteen minutes to make my way to my neighborhood near downtown. Tara Place was a pre-Collapse concrete high-rise.

Its old apartments had been bisected and bisected again into tiny worker flats with shared bathrooms.

But as I turned the corner, a fire engine rumbled past me. It was coming from the direction of my building. I smelled smoke. Chimneys and fireplaces were, of course, forbidden because of their contribution to greenhouse gases, but I remembered the smell from the Outside, not to mention pre-Collapse stimdocs and reenactments. For a moment, I was tempted to break into anti-Unity campfire songs, but I restrained myself.

Flecks of ash and cinders floated down. One large piece landed on the street. I bent and picked it up. It was the burnt fragment of a book page, a few printed lines still visible.

I began to run. I was panting and out of breath when I reached Tara Place. A knot of people were clustered in front of the building. Many were my neighbors and co-workers. Two police officers stood guard in front of the entrance, making sure nobody entered.

I didn't see many friendly eyes. Curled lips, yes. Some glowered at me, their arms crossed. A few people gave me barely perceptible nods, maybe one in twenty. The most shocking thing was that many people were staring at me. That was fine when I had an avatar but I wasn't Immersed. To stare at me in naked real life was the height of rudeness.

A few people ignored me and were looking up. I followed their gaze. On the fifth floor, there was a gaping hole where an apartment window had been. The concrete balcony next to it was stained with sooty streaks.

It was the third unit from the far end; my apartment. I felt as if I'd been punched in the gut. I doubled over in pain then stumbled backward. I reached out a hand to steady myself and touched someone's shoulder. She was a bystander I didn't know. She spun away with a look of disgust.

"Sorry," I said, ashamed.

I caught my balance and stood there, staring at my burned-out home. My head began to throb as if my skull were being pounded by hammers. I put my head down and stared at the ash-flecked sidewalk. When I lifted it again, I saw, peering over the heads of the crowd, a broad-shouldered man I recognized. He worked the day shift at Floating World and had the unlikely name of Rabbit. I'd seen him lift a heavy casket as if it were made of cardboard. His crest of blond, almost white hair reminded me of an egret that used to fish in the polluted marshland of my Outsider childhood.

"Rabbit," I said.

He turned, looked at me, and dropped his eyes.

"Hey, Mav," he said quietly, as if almost afraid to speak my name.

"What happened to my place?"

"I don't know," he said. "I was just watching the game and they broke in on the sim and told us there was a fire and we had to get out."

"Was anybody hurt?"

"Looks like it was just your unit," Rabbit said. "Listen, maybe you should talk to the landlord. She called in the fire. She's over there by that police car." He motioned with his head across the street.

"Thanks," I said and walked over to the car. Teddy the landlord was gesturing and talking to a couple of police officers and several firefighters. I saw the soft orange glow of a recording cone. The words "Arson Squad" circled it in silver letters. Everyone turned their eyes on me as I approached. Teddy pointed a rigid index finger and said loudly, "That's him."

The cops turned their backs to me and resumed talking to Teddy. It was cop contempt: the opposite of civilian scorn. They were saying I was beneath their notice.

Teddy watched me advance, her tiny eyes peering over her broad, sharp beak of a nose. Her arms were crossed over her shapeless muumuu. Her dirty bleached hair was haphazardly pinned so that a few strands fell around her wrinkled face like frayed rope ends. She pursed her lips as I approached. The cops and firefighters stood like statues.

"Teddy," I said. "What happened to my apartment?"

"That's what I want to know," she said. "It just went up in flames an hour ago. Did you leave a burner on?"

"I've been gone a week," I said. "And I didn't even cook anything before I left." I glanced at the arson cone. "You don't think... that somebody *set* it?"

"Burn patterns and lack of an accelerant do not indicate deliberate ignition," the arson cone said. "However, the unit is still being cleared of debris and so there cannot be any conclusion at this time."

"Nobody could get into your flat but you," Teddy said. "You didn't give anybody else permission to access it, did you?" She glared at me.

"Of course not," I said. "I like my privacy."

That provoked a ripple of surprise among the cops and fire crew but it was quickly concealed.

"Well," Teddy said, pursing her lips. "Maybe one of your *books* caught fire."

"It doesn't work like that!" I said angrily.

She shrugged. "I wouldn't know about those things."

"Anyway," I continued. "Why didn't the suppression system put it out?"

She shook her head. "Funny thing," she said. "It was down for maintenance just when the fire began. The foam pipes were shut off to the whole floor." Her voice was light but it held an edge of malice. "Surely you got the notice?"

"I've been busy with other things."

"So I've heard." she said. "Anyway, the firefighters put it out pretty quickly. They used hoses with actual water. Luckily, they kept it from spreading. Yours was the only unit burned." There was a sneer in her tone.

"Well, I've got to get up there," I said. "I've got to see what's left." The cone chirped in.

"The incident scene is still under investigation," it said. "Access will not be permitted until completion. You are urged to remain calm. Do you wish to receive trauma counseling while you wait?"

"No," I said sharply, then regretted my tone. The AI was just doing its job, and it had been more polite to me than the humans.

"Look," I said. "I've got things in there that are precious to me."

"Well," Teddy said. "You can look over there." She pointed back to the crowd, which blocked the view. "There's a pile of stuff right under your balcony. The fire crew moved it."

"We overhauled the unit," a firefighter spoke up. "Had to remove debris. Just to make sure there weren't any embers." The others chuckled maliciously. I understood the point hadn't been to save my stuff but to trash it.

I turned back to the landlord.

"Where am I going to stay?" I said forlornly.

She shrugged. "Unity shelter."

I shuddered. Every Unity citizen was entitled to shelter but for those without means, there were short-term units stacked dozens of stories high in the scruffiest part of town. They were clean, well-monitored and came with food, but the spaces were little more than coffins and the decor was sparse, beige, industrial and dehumanizing.

"Wait," I told Teddy. "You can put me up in a vacant unit."

"We don't have any," she replied tersely.

"When I left you had six," I said.

"Filled up," Teddy snapped. "Just this morning. Floating World leased three and we had some Outsider migrants take the others. You can check the listings." Her lips quirked. "It's just not your day, is it?"

I struggled to control my rage. I knew what had happened to my home. Teddy had burned me out. My reputation was too toxic and she couldn't break my lease. And I knew I would never be able to prove it.

"Kafka would be proud of you," I said. She started to say something and then closed her mouth. I knew she wouldn't get the reference.

I turned on my heel and jogged across the street. The crowd parted until I was standing next to what remained of my belongings.

In front of me was a waist-high pile of debris. After a moment of shock, I began to pick out distinct objects: a splintered leg of my kitchen table; the shattered remains of my beloved china coffee cup; the melted corpse of my cherished pre-Collapse radio. The contents of my closet had been hurled on the pyre. The firefighters had been thorough. Most of the pile was comprised of my books. They lay in heaps, the covers black or burned completely away. The pages were charred or soggy and water-bloated. The print was blurry and unreadable. The words were no more than an inky slurry that puddled around the bottom of the pile.

I, too, had no words.

Repressing a sob, I reached down and began to pick through the bleak pile. I saw only three books worth salvaging. The volumes were singed but whole. I didn't stop to read the titles, just clutched them to my chest, careless that they were smearing my shirt with soot. As I picked up the last one, I glimpsed a spot of color underneath. It was bright pink.

I dropped the books and began to dig into the pile. I grabbed hold of something and tugged.

It was my sister's backpack. The plastic was half-melted and the prancing pony was warped and deformed. But the shoulder straps were intact and the pack looked functional. I picked up the books, opened the pack and was about to put them in when I saw something inside. I reached down and pulled it out.

It was Jola's doll. I hadn't looked at it in years. I had forgotten it was in there. She was pretty much intact although one foot was now a flesh-colored blob of plastic that stuck to the inside of the pack until I pulled her free. She looked at me with wide, uncomprehending eyes.

I felt a sudden pang of regret, an echo. I'd fled my home and now I'd lost another. Sadly, I returned the doll to the backpack, then put the books inside and hoisted it onto my shoulders.

Everything else was gone. I didn't even have a toothbrush.

CHAPTER SIX

I began to make my way through the crowd. I spotted Rabbit, still standing at the rear. I came up to him.

"Hey, listen," I said, trying to keep my voice from shaking. "Rabbit, I need your help. I need a place to stay."

"They got shelters," he said, not unkindly.

"I know," I said. "But you know how they are. I just need to crash on your couch for a couple of days until I work things out."

He didn't answer me. The big man seemed jumpy.

"Rabbit?" I said. "Hey, what is it?"

He turned his head away and wiped his lips with a thick hand. From between his fingers I heard him mumble.

"I can't be seen talking to you," he said.

My heart sank but I made an effort.

"I'm innocent!" I protested. "You know that!"

"I believe you," Rabbit said. "But Floating World doesn't like you and they got eyes everywhere. I can't lose my job. I gotta think of my family."

He looked abashed but his jaw was set. I knew there was no point in pleading.

"Well, thanks for talking to me anyway," I said, trying to hide my bitterness. "No hard feelings."

"Good luck, man," he said and stepped away.

"You, too." I shouldered the pack. It barely weighed anything but it contained everything left of my life. I didn't look back as I strode down the street. With a heavy heart, I put on my cheap specs and reserved a slot in a Unity shelter. I got disconnected from two before

I was accepted, probably because some AI recognized the pattern of discrimination and put a stop to it.

But I was in no hurry to get there. For one thing, I was hungry; I hadn't eaten since breakfast. I had no yearning for shelter grub. It might be nutritious but it tasted like artificially-sweetened plastic— my taste buds didn't respond well to artificiality, even in Immersion. What I needed was a place to sit down, order a coffee and a sweet roll, and lose myself in a book. I spotted an upscale cafe, one I'd occasionally frequented when a little overtime work had inflated my pay package. It had actual employees.

I glanced down at my smudged clothing. I looked homeless, like some unsynced outcast. But that wasn't any indicator of status and wouldn't necessarily keep me out of the place. People paid little attention to their clothing in real life, unlike the Immersion, where style and fashion were an obsession and people clothed their avatars in splendor, whether it was gold, jewels or dragon scales.

Some higher-status people even deliberately dressed in shabby, second-hand clothing, both as camouflage and to show that (a) they were so high and mighty that they didn't need external signifiers and (b) they were too concerned with important issues to worry about vain, trivial stuff like their appearances. Because I usually wasn't Immersed and thus had no avatar to contemplate, my garb had occasionally gotten me mistaken for a high-status wonk.

I opened the old-fashioned glass door and entered a large room with a granite countertop and real wooden tables and chairs. The handful of people there were clearly Immersed and ignored me. I gathered my courage and went up to order.

I didn't recognize the lone human behind the counter but he recognized me.

"Sorry, we're closing," he said.

"It's the middle of the afternoon."

He shrugged.

"I just want some joe and a sweet roll," I said. "I'll eat it outside."

"We ran out," he replied.

"What, of coffee or rolls?"

"Both."

"Then I'll just have a seat," I said.

"Like I said, we're closing," he repeated, frowning.

I slammed my fist on the counter.

"I'm innocent!" I shouted. Heads turned. "I didn't do anything!"

The counterman seemed unfazed. He leaned forward and said: "I don't care what you did or didn't do. I want you out of my establishment."

"You can't do this!" I said. "It's discrimination. It's illegal!"

He smiled but the grin didn't reach his eyes.

"I'll pay the fine," he said. "I don't even care that it will go to your victim account. And then I'll go on CrowdLend for donations. I'll probably make it all back, and more." He pointed to the door and looked me straight in the eyes. "Now get the hell out of my cafe, you twisted, murdering little Outsider puke!"

I felt eyes boring in on me. I didn't need Immersion to tell me what the customers were thinking; their hatred and contempt washed over me in waves. Angry, hurt and humiliated, I turned and walked out.

I walked in the direction of the shelter, my mind blank. I didn't want to think anymore. I just wanted to hide.

As I entered the seediest part of town, buildings became taller and older. Unlike old-fashioned slums, the windows were intact, the streets smooth, the sidewalks clean and the buildings unmarred by graffiti. An army of robot cleaners made sure of that. It was more a difference of absence. The baskets of flowers disappeared from the lampposts. I walked past blocks of impersonal, faceless high-rises. And while the powers that be would certainly deny it, I swore I could smell an odor of neglect.

I spotted a small coffee bar and decided to take my chances.

I went through the force-door with a pop. This was a robot-controlled cube of a place with a stand-up counter and a few cheap tables and booths. The lights were naked and functional, tuned perfectly for human eyesight and also perfectly soulless.

I dropped into a well-worn booth and tapped the order tablet. I ordered a sweet roll and an Arabica Supreme that arrived in reasonable time. Arabica coffee no longer existed, of course. It was wiped out by a fungus early in the Collapse. But a cheap, bioengineered substitute was widely available. I splurged and, risking Immersion, paid for a coffee-sensory download. I sipped the coffee. The extra sensory input made it taste like the best cup of coffee, ever, from a small Italian cafe. It was heirloom; recorded just before the Collapse. Normally it would be out of my price range but I had chosen the ad-inclusive version, which was half-price.

I was enjoying my coffee when all of a sudden zombies crashed through the cafe windows. Their hands were claws and their decayed mouths dripped gore. I blinked, and they were gone, replaced by a floating banner that said, in oozing letters: "Zombie Crash. Devour it now." I ignored the blinking 'buy' cursor and it vanished.

But thirty seconds later I found myself sipping my java from a lounge chair on the deck of an old-fashioned cruise ship. A steward in a white coat was pouring me a second cup when behind him, a gigantic marlin erupted from the water. Its vicious nose skewered the steward.

The scene disappeared and I was on the bow, standing next to the captain, a grey-bearded, unflappable man in a pristine uniform. He was about to issue an order when the ship's anchor rose out of the water on its chain like an enormous cobra, then darted towards him. The chain wrapped around the captain and squeezed. The captain exploded in a cloud of blood and uniform scraps. His braided cap fell to the deck.

Seconds later, red letters appeared in the steam of the coffee cup: "Deadly Cruise. Play today."

That was followed by a commercial for an ancestor-finding service. Kids learn about the Collapse through reliving the recorded memories of survivors but many people want to relive those of relatives. Many records had been lost or destroyed in the chaos of the Collapse and there were several services that offered to track them down for a fee.

I wasn't interested; I had enough trouble living my own life. Plus, I was starting to get a headache and needed to get offline.

Thankfully, that was the last ad. Before my head exploded, I managed to gulp down my coffee and end the session. I knew my recharge time would be long; I had gone right to the limit, and maybe a bit over.

I closed my eyes, rubbed my throbbing temples, picked up my backpack and made my way in the direction of the shelter.

I put on my specs and followed the broad green arrows overlaying the sidewalk that led to the building.

I was only a few blocks away when I passed an alley. Without conscious thought, my head swiveled around and I looked at the dim opening. A figure was crouched there. At first I thought it was some kind of shaggy dog but then, with a grunt, it rose into a human shape. It was a man and he was holding something in both hands. He staggered out of the alley and came toward me, lifting it over his head. I darted back. He was holding an enormous chunk of asphalt that he must have pried from the alleyway. His eyes were crazed with fury.

"This is for Pallburg!" he shouted and hurled it at me. I spun sideways but the huge chunk struck my shoulder. I fell to the ground and then the man was on me. I smelled his sweat and rage. One rough hand gripped my throat and the other punched me in the face. My head hit the pavement and pain shot through me. I felt dizzy.

He punched me over and over again. I clawed at him, tried to tear away his hands, but he ignored me. He hit me in the nose and I felt something warm spurt onto my face. I rolled and lurched and fought, but he had frenzied strength. His grip on my throat tightened. I couldn't breathe. My vision became red at the edges and began to fade.

Then, he was jerked away. I lay a moment, gasping. When I had caught my breath, I managed to sit up.

My attacker lay on the sidewalk. He was twitching. Three police cones hovered over him. I could smell the ozone from their weapon fields.

One cone detached itself and moved up to examine me.

"You are not badly injured," the cone said. "You have lacerations and some bruising but the subcutaneous injuries are slight. There is no evidence of concussion. Permit me to administer first aid."

I nodded and the cone extended a nozzle and sprayed me with something that smelled like alcohol and stung like it. But then I suddenly felt better. There may have been a mood elevator in the spray.

The cone extended an appendage that held a moist cloth. I took it and wiped the blood from my face. I dropped it on the street. A maintenance drone doubtless had already been called to clean up the incident area.

I looked at the man again. He wasn't particularly large or intimidating. He didn't stand out in any way. I didn't even know what made me turn my head and notice him. He was nobody. I could have passed him on the street without a second glance.

And yet...

"He almost killed me," I said.

"Apologies," the cone said. "His profile and previous actions did not indicate a high risk of aggressive behavior. Furthermore, the weapon is decidedly low-tech. Paving material is rarely used in an offensive capacity. It is not in the database of weapons that are usually scanned and tracked. We are correcting that error now."

"Thanks for nothing," I said.

If the cone understood sarcasm, it didn't let on.

"You were recorded as having declined a security detail upon your release from custody. In light of this incident, do you wish to reconsider?"

"No!" I said testily. "All I want is to get to the shelter and be left alone."

"Very well. However, in light of this incident, please note that authorization has been obtained to increase the general level of passive surveillance in your vicinity until you have reached your destination. Please note that this attack, while attracting majority public approval on instant polls, also has fractionally reduced public confidence in the security services. A further reduction due to another attack must be prevented."

"Yes, it's all about your image," I said. "Not my life."

"Not so," the cone retorted. "Please recall the Unity mission statement."

"Please don't—" I began but it did.

"If one suffers, all suffer," it said.

"I know—"

"Not I am, but we are."

"You don't have to—"

"Personal fulfillment through collective engagement."

"Unique," I finished. "But not alone." I knew it didn't apply to me.

The cone dipped and then said, "If you are capable of resuming your trajectory, this law enforcement action will now conclude."

The cones retreated to the prone body of my attacker and hovered low. There was a humming, and the man was hauled to his feet, looking disoriented. One cone extended a flexible arm and glued his wrists to his sides. A small police van rolled up and extended a ramp and the man was shepherded into it. I guessed he would be sent for reeducation. I didn't care, so long as he stayed away from me.

I retrieved my backpack and my specs, which had been knocked off my battered nose into a gutter. I put them back on. Even with the cone spray, it hurt. I pulled them off, widened the bridge of the nose piece to accommodate my swelling nose and flicked them on. The green arrows reappeared and I followed them, but I didn't keep my head down. For the first time since I had arrived in Unity territory, I was aware of the constant surveillance. I kept craning my neck to look at the cameras attached to every building. They were keeping me safe, at least as far as the shelter. But even so, I couldn't help glancing at the people I passed on the street. My head jerked involuntarily to follow them as they approached and my shoulders tightened until they were well behind me.

I was breathing hard when I entered the shelter.

The Greater Victoria Seedhouse was housed in a pre-Collapse hotel. It had been designed for a population that was five times the current one. There were always empty beds. I pushed through the antique revolving door into the reception area. The walls were the same pastel blue as hospitals and other service buildings. The hotel's old reception desk was still there, its wood and granite and brass reminding me of the front room of the Columbarium. The place smelled faintly woody with a hint of something like coconut or spice, or maybe sea salt. I knew it was piped in and had been specifically engineered to make the stressed, depressed and frantic visitors feel calmer and more confident. There was, of course, no human here. I went through the routine of being registered and assigned a bed and food voucher. I declined to enroll in any of the many lifestyle classes. I was issued bedding and shelter togs and sent to a side room where I removed my smoky, smudged clothing to be cleaned. I refused to surrender my backpack. I wasn't able to avoid the standard medical scan. Even though I'd been poked, prodded and mind-groped over and over again in the past few days, the results obviously hadn't been shared with the housing AIs at large. I was directed to a large, clean room full of screens and cones. There was an examination table and a toilet. Medical science had advanced greatly in the last century, but one thing technology hadn't eliminated was the urine test.

Finally, I was allowed to hit the communal showers. I walked in holding my little plastic basket containing small tubes of soap, shampoo and razor foam. It was empty except for one hairy, round-shouldered man covered in lather. He was still standing there, dripping soap, by the time I finished and trotted out to the air dryers.

I finally got to eat, surprisingly edible tofu chili, green beans, gencornbread and vat butter. The dozen or so people in the room studiously ignored me, even though they must have known who I was. I thought bitterly that those considered on the edges of society, those who had the least, were the only ones who ed me with the greatest respect.

I thought with bitterness that those considered on the edges of society, those who had the least, treated me with the greatest respect while those who claimed to be upright Unity citizens reviled me.

At last, I trudged to my bed. I was in a high-windowed dormitory that had been designed for twenty-five people but now held myself and two others, a youngish man with wild hair and an older, scruffier man who clutched a pair of broken Immersion specs that he probably had scavenged from the street. It was still early and neither had their privacy shields up. As I passed the old man's bed, I pulled off my specs and tossed them onto his cot.

"Here, man, use these," I said. "They're better."

He looked at me with his mouth open, then put down the broken specs and took my pair.

"Thanks," he mumbled.

I moved down the row to my bed, climbed in and activated the privacy shield. The noise-and vision-cancelling field surrounded me in a quiet, gray bubble. Without any Immersion access, I only had a choice of four wallpapers: basic black, ocean, desert or northern lights with icebergs. I chose basic black.

I was exhausted, discouraged and I badly wanted nothing more than a good rest. I closed my eyes and fell almost instantly into a dreamless darkness.

I was only awakened twice by the old man's snoring that penetrated the leaky privacy shield.

When I woke the third time I woke, it seemed as if I'd only just closed my eyes. With my shield dropped, daylight through the windows told me otherwise. It had been late afternoon when I dropped off. I guessed I had slept for at least twelve hours. Still a bit groggy but feeling refreshed, I slipped on my shelter booties and shuffled my way down the corridor to the bathroom.

The dormitory room had been carved out of some grand, ancient suite but the designers, for some reason, had left the single bathroom intact, down to the ancient chrome fittings on the faucets.

I wondered if the architects had shared my old-fashioned love of privacy— and whether they'd been forced into reeducation.

I put down my little basket of toiletries and stared at myself in the mirror. I recognized parts of me, but my nose seemed to be the size and color of an eggplant and one side of my face was a festive patchwork of purple and yellow bruises.

Eying them, I felt oddly better. I had slept well and despite the last few days, I was beginning to feel a faint tinge of hope. I'd lost my home, my job and what little reputation I'd had. On the bright side, things could only get better. I ran the hot water tap and splashed some on my battered face, smiling to myself. The worst was behind me.

I was right. The worst *was* behind me.

I heard the door open and then close. I looked up into the steamy mirror. A bulking shape loomed at my back. Before I could turn, an arm locked around my throat. Something cold and wet was slapped against my face. Everything went black.

CHAPTER SEVEN

I opened my eyes to find myself lying on a bed surrounded by a ring of people wearing fluorescent green jumpsuits. Some were scowling, but most had something like awe in their eyes. One of them raised a fist and mumbled, "Shatter the silicon oppressors."

Fear shot through me. I was in the hands of the Realists.

I was at the mercy of people who blew up satellites and server farms, who vowed to hang Authenticators and other humans they despised as machine collaborationist "chip kissers."

On the other hand, the jumpsuits made them look like refugees from a Korean boy band. It was incongruous.

I tried to keep myself from blinking. I wanted them to think I was groggy and not fully awake. I needed a moment to consider my position. I didn't get it.

"Welcome, Mavo," said a man with a prominent Adam's apple. "You're among friends."

"I still don't think this is a good idea," said a big man with a bushy black beard.

"He killed Pallburg!" someone said. "He did something none of us were able to do."

"He says he didn't," the big man replied. "I saw the memory vid."

"He's a hero of the movement!"

"So you say!"

"We went through this at Assembly—"

"Just because we were outvoted doesn't mean—"

And it went on. For a moment I was stunned. I thought I was among hardened fanatics, but they seemed more like a bickering bunch of in-laws at a family gathering. I half-expected someone to start a food fight. The noise level kept increasing.

"Stop! Stop it!" The command cut through the uproar like a whipcrack. I opened my eyes wider.

A girl was standing nearby. She was about my age, maybe a year or two older. Her unkempt purple hair clashed with her jumpsuit. She was a head shorter than the others but they gave way respectfully. She turned to face them.

"Save it for Assembly, guys," she said. "This guy's just been abducted. He's confused. Give him some space!"

And lo and behold, the group of older people shuffled back.

She came close and leaned down. She had lovely eyes. She smelled fresh, like sea air, not the sweaty funk I'd associated with terrorists from Immersion clips.

"Sorry," she said. "This must be very disorienting. But it was the only way we could get you away from the watchers." She raised her eyes to the ceiling meaningfully.

"I'm not a hostage?"

"No." She smiled. It was a nice smile. "You're an honored guest. But don't think about that now. How do you feel? Do you want some water?"

"That would be nice," I said, just to say something. My throat was suddenly dry.

She turned her head. "Can somebody please get him some water?"

I heard feet pad and then return. A man handed a cup to the girl, who offered it to me. I pushed myself up to a sitting position, took the cup and drank greedily. It was cold and sweet.

I handed it back, my fingers tingling as hers touched mine.

"Thanks," I said.

She smiled. "You haven't asked my name."

I blushed.

"Sorry," I stammered.

"Rin," she said, her lips quirking. "Short for Rinella. But nobody calls me that."

"Not to your face, anyway," somebody said.

There were chuckles around the room.

Rin pointedly ignored them.

"Mavo," I said automatically.

"We know," Rin said. I blushed again. I didn't seem to be scoring any points. I was going to apologize once more, but then decided that would just make me look even lamer.

"Rin," the bushy-bearded man called. "We have to get a move on."

"Yes, Trino, of course," she called back, and turned to me. "Do you think you can stand?"

"I think so," I said, more from bravado than certainty. I had to play along with whatever was going on until I figured out what that was. Rin might call me a guest, but the truth was they had kidnapped me. And the one thing I knew for certain about Realists is that they weren't known for their compassion. They claimed to love humanity, but they didn't necessarily like people. I was sure they wouldn't hesitate to execute an enemy or a traitor, or a hero with feet of clay. Sweat prickled under my arms. They idolized me because they believed I had murdered someone. But I hadn't. And bushy-bearded Trino seemed to distrust me already. He'd be watching everything I did or said.

I hadn't been awake for more than ten minutes and already my life was hanging by a thread again. I told myself that I'd have to give up telling myself that things could never get worse.

Rin and several other people helped me to my feet and I stood shakily, my knees wobbly. People crowded in behind me. We went through a hinged door into a corridor lined with rooms. Some had desks, others blocks of equipment I didn't recognize, and at one point I thought I spotted what looked to me like a makeshift chemical lab. I couldn't tell what was going on in the rooms, but these were terrorists, after all. My mind threw up a few unpleasant suggestions and I shuddered. As we walked by, people peeled off and by the time we reached a final door set into the back wall, only Rin and Trino remained.

Trino opened the door and we entered a gloomy, cavernous room. It seemed to be made of old-fashioned concrete and had a high ceiling. It was packed with an incredible jumble of things: rusty old shipping containers, battered crates stacked in grimy stories, piles of tubing and rods and gears. I recognized a couple of train wheels lying on a heap of parts. One shelf held dozens of stuffed animals, some minus eyes or limbs. A raccoon with a moth-eaten snout and wearing a red Santa hat gave me a weak, squeaky "ho ho" as I passed. The room smelled of oil, dust and old plastic.

"What is this place?" I asked Rin.

"Municipal storage facility," she said. "The city set them up right after the Collapse ended. They warehoused broken and abandoned goods for reclamation and salvage. Some of this stuff would have been melted down and reused, some would have been doled out to needy people."

"Even that?" I pointed to the raccoon.

"Careful," she said. "That could have been somebody's precious memento." She grinned, but I felt a pang as I thought of my sister's doll in my backpack.

"With all the chaos, families vanished and they left behind stuff," Rin continued. "So the city stored it until somebody came to claim it. And obviously, nobody did." She shrugged. "Not that it matters now. These days, most people don't want the hassle of physical items. They can stack virtual stuff in the Immersion. And with the population collapse, there's less need to reclaim junk."

"So it just sits here?" I asked with a certain sadness. I thought of some little child who'd been outlived by a beloved toy that was now doomed to lie forgotten on a dusty shelf.

"The Unity catalogued this place and then ignored it," Rin said. "Which is why it's a perfect safe house for us."

"But wait," I said. "Doesn't it look weird to see a bunch of people coming and going?" The AIs that oversaw surveillance for the neighborhood would surely note unusual activity at a virtually abandoned building.

Trino gave a throaty laugh and pointed to his jumpsuit. "That's why we've got these," he said.

"We're Civics," Rin said, smoothing her suit. "Duly registered."

Civics were volunteers who helped with the grunt work of society. They cleaned streets, clipped park hedges. Some dug hiking trails, and some delivered goods and services to the Outsiders.

Virtually all of the work was done by machines, of course, because they were cheaper and more efficient. But the Unity's Psych AI and its subordinate expert systems had recognized that humans needed purpose and for some, virtual fulfillment wouldn't do. They needed to physically engage in what technically was termed "constructive activity."

"Freaks and geeks," Rin said, and laughed. "Every few days we pull some of this stuff and haul it onto trains to the Outside. And, of course, that's a perfect cover to bring stuff in, too." She laughed again and I liked it, even though I knew she was a fanatic and she was laughing about something illegal and possibly sinister.

"Rin," Trino said. "Tick-tock!"

She grimaced but nodded. "Right," she said. "Time for you to meet the Ghost." She led me up and down aisles between heaps and stacks of things. Some were ordered; others just seemed to be lumped together into trashy piles. When we reached one far corner,

I saw a sort of lean-to cobbled together from plastic siding. A curtain on a wire covered the opening.

Rin went up, raised a fist and punched the curtain.

"Knock, knock," she said.

There was a rustle, a snort, and then a shuffling sound. A hand reached out and pulled aside the curtain. A man stood there in his underwear.

"Sorry," he said with a yawn. "I needed to sack out. Just got in from Albuquerque." Then his eyes lit on me.

"Mavo!" he said. "This is an honor, freeb. What you did..." He shook his head. "A blow for freedom!" He held out a hand. I took it and he pulled me in and crushed me in a hug. Unlike the others, he did have that swampy, sweaty terrorist smell.

Rin stepped forward.

"Richard," she said. "We're ready to move him."

Richard released me, a little reluctantly, I thought. Then, to my shock, he reached up and began to peel off his face.

It was a mask, complete with hair. Richard held it out to me with a grin. Underneath, he was a tough-looking man with ruddy, seamed cheeks. "Ever worn one of these?" he asked.

"No!" I blurted. Only criminals tried to fool the Unity's facial recognition systems. It never worked.

"Uh, I don't think..." I began.

"This isn't your average, garden-variety dumbass crook mask," Richard said. "It's one-of-a-kind. And I designed it." He beamed.

"Richard is our Ghost," Rin said. "The Ubiquitous Man. We used a real person from the Outside, who works with us. He went through processing and became a Unity citizen. Then he went back. We call him Eduardo. When we need to sneak anyone somewhere, we use this mask. Richard and a few others take turns being Eduardo. Between missions, they stay in our safe houses."

"I haven't seen the real Eduardo in months," Richard said. "Every so often he comes in so I can update the mask."

"So I'm going to be Eduardo?" I asked.

"Yep," Richard said. "A pair of sunglasses, a hardhat, and a pebble in your shoe and you're good to go, if nobody scans too hard, and they won't because you're just a Civic."

"A pebble in my shoe?" I asked.

"Changes your gait," Trino said. "Everybody has subtle differences in the way they walk. So Eduardo has developed a limp." He chuckled.

"All right," I said. Richard slipped the mask over my head and neck and gave it a few tugs and tweaks. The mask felt thin and nearly weightless. It pulled down the corners of my eyes and seemed to bunch up slightly around my cheekbones but otherwise seemed comfortable.

Richard stepped back and gave me an appraising look. I looked back questioningly.

"Perfect," Richard said. "Naturally." He turned, went back into the lean-to, and returned with a grimy jumpsuit and a pair of scuffed, tough, self-sizing work boots, the kind that were ubiquitous among laborers.

"Suit up," he said.

"No offense," I replied. "But couldn't I get a clean jumpsuit?"

"No," Trino said. "You're Eduardo. You walk in with smudges, you walk out with smudges."

"Inside's clean," Richard said. "You know, micro-mesh, self-wicking, yadda yadda."

I made to go into the lean-to but Richard put out an arm to stop me.

"I love you, man, but that's my room," he said. "My research is in there."

"Well, where should I change?" I asked.

Richard, Rin and Trino looked back and forth at each other with puzzled expressions. They might be Realists but unlike me, they had grown up Immersed, and people in Immersion had very little concept of privacy. I was reminded again of how different I was from other people.

Still, I looked back at Rin. I was uncomfortably aware of my body. Behind the mask, I blushed as I envisioned her watching me undress.

"I'll be right back," I said, and scuttled around a corner and hid behind a stack of bedraggled phony plants, from palm trees to giant jungle begonias. I pulled off my clothes as quickly as I could and stepped into the jumpsuit, keeping my own underwear and socks. The suit was too large for my short, gangly frame but it was made intentionally baggy to conceal body distinctions among its wearers. I tucked the cuffs into the work boots, wincing as my heel hit the rather large pebble in the left boot. I sure wouldn't forget to limp. Then I pulled some sunglasses out of the pocket and put them on, gathered up my old clothes and the pink backpack and stepped out to find Richard, Rin and Trino giving me worried looks.

"Are you okay?" Rin asked.

"I'm fine," I said.

"We thought maybe you were going to be sick or something," she said.

"No," I said. "It's, um, it's a privacy thing?"

They looked even more worried.

"It's an Outsider thing," I said lamely.

"Oh, right," Rin said but she seemed a bit doubtful.

Richard came to my rescue.

"Yeah, those non-Immersives got some weird ideas," he said. "But hey, when we take down the system, we'll all have to get used to that."

I wanted to ask why they thought taking down Unity would be a good idea but decided now was not the time.

The other three simply nodded.

Richard clapped his hands. "All right," he said. "Looks like we're ready to go. You feeling good, Eduardo?"

"Pretty good," I admitted.

"Excellent," he said. "Now just a word of warning: You're important, Mavo, but this mask is more important. If there's a choice between saving you and saving this mask, you lose. The mask always wins. It's one of a kind. We can't do our work without it. Some of the components are almost irreplaceable. So, we're putting a lot of trust in you." He leaned forward and slapped a hand hard on my shoulder. I flinched but, thankfully, he didn't hug me again. "It was a real pleasure." Then he nodded at Rin and Trino and disappeared back into the lean-to, pulling the curtain closed. A moment later, I heard snoring.

I turned back to Rin. She folded her arms and her head bobbed as she looked me up and down.

"I think it works," she said at last, turning to Trino. "What do you think?"

Surprisingly, Trino gave me a warm smile. "You look good," he said. "Don't worry, we've got your back."

I concealed my astonishment. Wasn't this the same man who had voiced his suspicions of me not long ago? I couldn't figure him out. Did he have a change of heart? Or was he playing with me, or maybe trying to ingratiate himself because I was some kind of hero? Or was he using me to cozy up to Rin now that nobody else was around? I couldn't read him, and I was usually great at reading people.

Rin, for instance, I pegged as a natural leader: someone who was well-liked and thus could get things done without actually holding any authority.

But these were Realists. I didn't know their game. At the core, I suspected they were all crazy.

Even Rin?

I decided not to think about that right now. But I also decided to keep a close eye on Trino.

Rin held out her hands for my clothing and the backpack. Evidently my worried expression showed through the mask.

"Don't worry," she said. "These are going with you. We'll take care of them."

"Where am I going?"

"Someplace safe," she said. "Someplace where your real work can begin."

CHAPTER EIGHT

We took the ferry across to Seattle and boarded a train. The train went east because there were several new Unity cities there. At each stop, a group of us Civics helped unload donated items destined for the poor, benighted Outsiders. I helped. It would have appeared odd if Eduardo was seen boarding a train and then never left it. We reached the Cascades and bored through the mountains, rolling through the dark tunnel until in a flash, the sun-blasted landscape reappeared. The route was checkerboarded with Outside wastelands. My own former home was farther west and south: a barren, burned-over stretch of land that once had been California's wine country. But all Outside lands had the same texture of desperation, the same desert, weeds, foul-smelling ponds and sluggish, polluted rivers surrounded by clumsy villages of patched-together houses. The imperishable steel rails cut straight through them, a sword blade stretching toward an endlessly retreating horizon. We stopped at some villages to offload our donations, heaping them in piles which were perpetually surrounded by squabbling, bargaining scavengers. At some stops, there was a semblance of order, whether a ragged queue or a few tough-looking Outsider guards making sure everyone had a chance at the spoils. At others, the largest and fiercest bullied their way to the front. In either case, nobody bothered us Civics. Our green jumpsuits were eyed with a measure of deference and respect I had never received before. It felt uncomfortable and at the same time gratifying. Usually, I was the one kowtowing.

Unlike the Unity food and blanket drops, these drops kept to no schedule and had no train guards. We just dumped and moved on. I didn't remember having such dumps at my old home.

Five hours out of Seattle, the train made a dogleg and headed southwest. We ended up in Yakima, which had survived surprisingly unscathed despite an urban uprising. Then we jagged back to Medford and finally made a straight plunge toward Sacramento, California.

We were pretty tired by the time night fell. The Civics had our own sleeper car and dining car. I was last in for the meal because I had waited to shower alone. The diner was long and narrow and had booths along both sides. The Realists were sitting around them. They looked up as I entered and then, to my surprise, there was a universal jostling. Everyone at each table skooched over to make room for me. Their heads all swiveled and they eyed me expectantly. I didn't know what to do. I couldn't sit in every offered seat and yet I didn't want to offend anybody. All I wanted to do was eat, but suddenly even sitting down seemed to be a political choice. It wasn't even like high school, where at least you knew the cliques that controlled each bench. (I usually sat alone, anyway.)

They were waiting. I decided. I took the nearest available seat. I could almost feel the disappointment from the other tables, while the people around me gloated. I hadn't met any of them, which I realized later was probably the right choice. That way, I hadn't shown favoritism to the people I had met. But I gave a quick glance at Rin's table. She didn't seem offended. In fact, she seemed amused. I looked around at my tablemates.

"Hi," I said lamely. "What's good?"

"Well, they've only got two choices tonight," said a man with a tuft of ginger hair. "Spaghetti or vat veal."

"No, three choices," a pug-nosed woman replied. "On the spaghetti, you can get tomato or cream sauce."

"It's still spaghetti, Jen," insisted a man who looked like a piebald tortoise. His skin was mottled brown and white and his leathery throat was wrinkled.

"Not," Jen said firmly. She looked at me with large, wet eyes. "Mavo, what do you think?"

"I think I'll have the veal," I said.

They laughed. I seem to have passed another test. I breathed an unseen sigh of relief, but I was irked, too. These people seemed to squabble about everything, and here they were looking to me to settle their disputes. I didn't want to spend the rest of the trip playing politics. I just wanted to keep my head down, but it seemed I didn't have a choice. For the moment, anyway, I was the golden boy, the revolutionary idol who had single-handedly brought down Pallburg. I was only sixteen and most of them were a decade older— much older in piebald's case— but they acted as if I were some grey-haired leader dispensing justice and wisdom, which I'd have to make up as I went along. And what would happen when I finally toppled off my pedestal?

"I'm Spiral," the pug-nosed woman said. "Because of my curly hair," She dimpled at me. "No, actually, it's short for Spirulina. My parents are algae farmers."

"Boze," the piebald man said. "Family name."

"Racco," ginger-hair said. "And no, I'm not a raccoon." He made circles with his hands and put them in front of his eyes to imitate a raccoon's mask. The others rolled their eyes. Apparently, it was an old joke.

"Pleased to meet you," I said.

The food was delivered from the kitchen and I was about to tuck in but stopped when I realized nobody else had lifted a fork. They shared a look and then Jen turned to me and asked: "Mavo, would you do us the honor of choosing the taste?"

"Um," I began, perplexed, and then I got it. They wanted me to Immerse. There was probably a list of taste overlays to spice up the food, the way I had overlaid my cheap coffee in Victoria with the classier taste from a recorded memory. They were Realists, but they'd all been raised on Immersion. They hated the system, but obviously not when it came to a meal.

I didn't feel like risking a migraine by Immersing.

"Oh, thanks, I'm good," I replied. "I'll just eat this." I pointed at the plate.

They looked at each other with shock.

"But," Jen blurted. "But that's *train* food!" She looked as if I'd said I was going to eat my own socks.

There was a moment of silence around the table. People shot each other quick glances. Then Racco spoke up.

"Wait, I get it," he said tentatively. "Mavo wants us to prep for the future, right? For when there is no more Immersion."

"Of course!" Boze said, the light dawning in his face. "Mavo, you want us to realize our own Realism!"

"Wow," Jen said, shaking her head in pleased wonder.

"You don't have to—" I began.

But then Trino spoke up from the other end of the dining car.

"You heard him," he said loudly enough for all the tables to hear. "Mavo has a point. How can we lead the new way if we don't live it ourselves?" And he ostentatiously picked up his fork and dug into his plate of pale noodles, chewing enthusiastically. Everybody looked at me and followed suit, although their expressions didn't indicate any genuine delight. I saw a few people twirling their spaghetti endlessly around their forks as if working up the courage to put it into their mouths.

Actually, the food wasn't bad. Maybe, I dared to think, I really was showing these people a good thing. But then I realized what their goal was: the utter destruction of a system that was keeping the entire globe from starvation and war.

The food turned tasteless in my mouth.

I told myself that no matter what goofballs these people seemed, they had dangerous ideals. They were not, repeat *not,* good people. But I caught myself glancing surreptitiously at Rin.

We reached Sacramento before dawn.

Rin came up to me with a friendly look. I suspected she'd become my de facto handler because she was closest to my age. It didn't make me trust her any more than the others. At least, that's what I kept telling myself.

"Put the rock back in your shoe," Rin advised. "We'll be scanned as soon as we enter."

I must have looked unhappy because Rin suddenly said: "Or I could just stomp on your foot and you'd have a real limp." She grinned and arched her eyebrows.

I groaned but did as she said. The train rolled smoothly up and we disembarked, filing through glass-windowed wooden doors.

The station was a long, high-ceilinged room lit by ancient chandeliers. It had been restored to historic glory. The Unity province of California may have lost its once-mighty stature— its buildings crumbled, its once-green Central Valley now choked with salt and dust and its population either fled or destitute— but it still took pride in its history. California train stations were lovingly carved, gilded palaces. I had no idea what AI horse-trading had led to provision of the necessary resources. I supposed some psych expert system had argued that it was necessary for the emotional health of the occupants. And, of course, California was rich with artifacts. Sacramento was a popular drop-off spot for archaeologists and history tourists to begin their Golden State tours. In summer, the population of 100,000 swelled to ten times that number. Except for the thoroughly modern high-speed tracks and Immersion node, the station wouldn't have looked out of place two centuries ago. The ceilings had dark, carved wooden beams. The walls bore watermarks from ancient flooding but their top halves bore an original mural. It showed a lot of people listening to a man with a gray beard and a black suit. One guy was kneeling, and everybody seemed riveted. Written above it was a caption: "Breaking ground at Sacramento, January 8, 1863, for first transcontinental railroad." There was an old-style American flag draped over the platform where the man was speaking. Above the mural was an old clock that looked analog but probably kept time digitally via satellite. It glared down at benches of apparently real wood.

The place was full of people. I noticed a cluster of passengers waiting to board the train we had just left. They were tall, fair-haired and chattered in a language I didn't know, since I wasn't Immersed.

They wore identical outfits with big tulip symbols on the back and gave hawk-eyed glares at the porters loading what appeared to be diving gear. I guessed they were headed to the deep-water ruins of Los Angeles.

"They're from the Netherlands," Rin said. "Big divers. Have been since their own country was drowned." She shook her head and glanced at the station clock. "Come on, we have to go."

I felt a surge of excitement, or maybe fear. Now was the dangerous part. We were going to take the Ghost Train.

A couple of Civics stepped in beside us as Rin led me to an unobtrusive door marked "Authorized Personnel Only." There was a click as we approached. The door opened and we found ourselves in a room lined with lockers and furnished with a battered lunch table and some ancient vending machines. Clearly this was the employee break room. Rin unhesitatingly led us to one row of lockers near the rear. She tapped something and the whole thing slid aside, like in an old Immersion mystery. We entered what appeared to be some sort of service tunnel. It was lit by a single dim bulb. The air was warm and smelled of dampness and something metallic. A steel staircase headed down into gloom. We trooped down. I clung to the handrail so as not to take a tumble.

We continued down three more flights of stairs that became progressively grimier. These were lit by cheap, industrial strip lights. At last, we reached level ground. I gaped in surprise.

We were in a subterranean train station, really just a concrete apron fronting a single track that stretched into darkness in either direction. The ceiling curved above us and was lit by glowing eternalamps that cast a sort of weak daylight.

The Ghost Train was here. I gaped. I couldn't believe my eyes. It was a genuine Narwhal! The long, tapered spiral shape hovered above the track. I felt rather than heard the pulsing of energy in the rails. The train cast a pale glow, like that given off by some deep-sea fish.

"Wow," I said.

Narwhals were the fastest trains ever invented. Their twisted spiral shape both split the air, reducing friction, and charged the train, producing ions that were part of its propulsion system. The grooves in the spirals had a faint, glowing purple tinge that made my eyes hurt. I'd read that in the old days, some people had gotten seriously sick on these trains, either from the enormous speed or the disorienting gravitational effects of its propulsion system. I hoped I wasn't one of them.

"Where did you get this?" I said, my jaw dropping. "And how do you manage to power it without Unity knowing?"

Rin looked smug. "We've got a guardian angel," she said. "Let's board."

We climbed aboard, my body tingling slightly as we passed the propulsion energy field, then the door shield crackled shut. A metal door slid over it. The single compartment was round and high. A half-dozen airplane seats were bolted to the floor. Behind the seats was a large bare space that I assumed was for cargo because there were tie-downs and anchor points on the floor, ceiling and walls. The walls seemed to be made of some sort of bronze-colored mesh. Behind it was the outside skin of the train, which was a bluish-pink. The color was uncomfortably fleshy, like living tissue.

My companions didn't seem to notice.

"Have a seat," Rin said, dropping into one herself.

The seats were old and worn but comfortable. There was no harness or seatbelt. I didn't see any button for a stasis field, either.

"Where's the restraint system?" I asked.

"Don't need one," Rin said. "These things are smooth. You'll feel the acceleration but once we're at speed there's no sense of motion. However, I should warn you, you might feel a little queasy. Some people do."

"I've heard of people being sick," I said. "Of course, nobody I know has actually ridden one."

"They actually solved that problem," she said. "They got sick because the rotating energy fields affected them. But then they came up with motion-cancelling Immersions."

"Which we don't have," Trino chimed in. "Because we can't Immerse. That might give us away. Some people use pills. But we don't have any." He gave me an almost malicious grin.

Then the train started. A pulsing beat of sound erupted, whining up quickly into supersonic. Beyond the mesh, the walls and ceiling began to move. The outside skin of the Narwhal was rotating. Within moments, the walls and ceiling were spinning so quickly that they became nothing more than a semi-solid purplish blur. It made my eyes hurt. Probably, I thought, the train once had some sort of paneling to hide the movement, but that was long gone. I closed my eyes, which helped, but that left me free to concentrate on something else; the train's propulsion system gave off a sort of throbbing pressure that felt like ghostly fingers drumming on my chest and stomach. It became more rapid as we sped up until it felt like someone was playing boogie-woogie piano on my torso. Worse, my teeth vibrated.

I repressed a groan. Long ago, this train probably had a military function. Maybe that explained its lack of amenities.

After a while, the tapping moved from my stomach into my temples.

"How long is this trip?" I asked.

"About ninety minutes," Rin replied. "We'll be there before you know it." She opened a pocket of her jumpsuit and pulled out what looked like a food bar. It was bilious green. She broke it in half and offered some to me.

"Fish paste?" she asked.

I turned away to hide my expression.

The train decelerated smoothly as we reached Albuquerque and I felt relief as the pulsing in my head vanished. I stood up a little shakily and took a couple of deep breaths. Rin and Trino also stood.

"Here we are," Rin said. "Home sweet home."

I followed them through the door. It was colder than the Sacramento station. A man wearing a smudged jumpsuit was waiting at the platform. He greeted us and then reached out a hand.

"The mask, please," he said.

I pulled off the mask. The thin material clung silkily to my skin for an instant, then I was holding the disembodied face in my hands. I handed it over.

"Thanks," he said, quickly donned it, shook my hand and climbed aboard the train.

I turned to see Rin looking at me. She gave me an impish grin.

"I'd forgotten what you looked like under there," she said. "Not bad."

"You too," I blurted, then instantly regretted it. "I mean, considering."

"Considering what?" Her grin vanished.

"I mean, um, the long trip, you know... and... everything?" I stammered, wishing I could screw myself into the platform.

But Rin had already turned away. I could have kicked myself, if my foot didn't already hurt from the rock in my boot. I looked over at Trino. He'd seen the exchange. He had a curious expression on his face. For a moment, I felt like I was under a microscope. Trino caught my glance and his expression swiftly changed. He gave me a warm smile. He stepped over and put a hand on my shoulder.

"Aren't you glad she's on our side?" he said. He nodded at Rin's back. "She'll catch up. Come on, let's get some chow in you. You probably want to clean up and change clothes, too." He gave my rumpled jumpsuit a sardonic glance. "Then we'll take a little walk. Get some desert dust under your boots."

"We're going somewhere else?" I asked.

"No, it's a figure of speech. What I mean is, I can show you around our little community here." He turned serious. "Show you what a Free City is like. Oh, and you can take that rock out of your shoe."

We climbed a series of stairs and entered a tunnel that slanted upward. At the end of it was a set of ancient double doors with long metal bars across their centers. I recalled that these were safety devices that allowed people to push open the doors. I'd read that they were called panic bars. They'd been created after some devastating fire where people had found themselves locked inside a theater. I reflected that every advancement in human history— technological, legal, philosophical— was sparked by a catastrophe. Every step of our progress had a price someone had paid in blood.

The doors opened onto a long, vaulted corridor made of glass. Through the glass, I saw a dusty concrete city with tired bushes and scraps of empty, weed-grown fields. We stepped onto a wide moving walkway. On either side of us, inside the corridor, ran carefully tended landscaping: an idealized desert. The clean, groomed sand was dotted with a variety of plants. There were barrel cactuses, saguaros with their spiny green arms raised to the sky, shaggy Joshua trees and spiky yuccas, all clipped and arranged with an almost Japanese garden precision. Mechanical lizards in jewel tones darted through the vegetation. At the end of the walkway hung a large glowing sign that announced: ENTERING FREE ZONE. LIMITED IMMERSION. Beyond it, the pathway forked. The sign over the left branch read: CITY CENTER. A sign to the right said: FREEJACK.

We took the left branch.

"Are we going to town?" I asked.

"Sure," Trino said. "Why not?"

"Well, isn't that a little risky? I mean, we're an underground group, right?" I was really more worried about my own safety. I was, after all, Public Enemy Number One.

"Free Zone," Trino said dismissively. "The Unity designated this whole city as a non-surveillance point. Every continent has one. I could walk around with a T-shirt reading: 'Realism Forever!' on it and nothing would happen to me."

"That doesn't make a lot of sense," I said. "You could plot anything here. It seems like a security hole for the system."

"Hah," Trino said, with an edge of bitterness. "Just the opposite. They put us in a sandbox. Contain us. That's why FreeJack is here. Same reasoning. Containment. We can do what we want here. But take a few steps outside—" he pointed out the windows "—and the surveillance shields disappear. They'll scan every breath you take. They'll count every molecule you inhale. And you'd best believe that

they track our every movement coming and going from this place."
Trino smiled. "Luckily, we have our little secrets, like the Narwhal."

I found it a little hard to believe that Unity wasn't watching us,
but I had to take Trino's word for it. After all, the group had gone
through a lot of effort to get me here in secret. They might not be
the masterminds they thought they were, but they weren't stupid
enough to parade their hard-won prize in front of the world. For
now, I had to believe I was safe— at least from the general public, if
not from the Realists.

As if reading my thoughts, Trino nodded and said, "Don't worry.
You're a hero here."

CHAPTER NINE

We entered the main station, which looked like all the other stations I'd seen in the past few days but larger. Trino walked me briskly to the main doors leading outside. We pushed through and I found myself gaping. Beyond the station entrance was a large plaza full of noise and color. There were trees and small paved roads, like a park. On the other side of the plaza was an immense area crowded with people, striped tents topped with fluttering pennants and rows of colorful stalls. The people wore all sorts of costumes, as if they had stepped out of a hundred historical Immersions. Some were dancing to crackly audio or even to real musicians. Above the area floated dozens of immense balloons from which hung gondolas full of people. Many balloons were in the form of sea creatures: whales, dolphins, even a jellyfish with huge tendrils hanging down and stirring in the breeze. I smelled frying fish, the bittersweet tang of grilled martonia fungus and—

I took a deep breath. "Is that caramel corn?" I asked.

Trino took my elbow and tried to lead me to the right, away from the plaza. "We have to move along," he said. "There are people you have to meet."

I shook him off. "Wait," I said. "What is all that?" I pointed to the area beyond the plaza.

Trino looked annoyed.

"That's the Circo Eterno," he said.

"What's that?"

"Permanent circus," he said. "Draws in the tourists."

I looked at him. "Tourists?"

"Of course," he said. "We all have to make a living, and without Immersion it's harder to make ends meet."

"I'd like to see it."

For a moment, Trino looked as if he might drag me away by main force. But then he seemed to recover himself. He smiled and shrugged. "Of course," he said. "Let's play tourist."

We walked down the station steps and strolled through the plaza to the Circo Eterno. It felt like plunging into an alien sea. We strolled down a midway packed with people. The ground was covered with sawdust and patchy, foot-worn durograss. Bunting was strung between food and game stalls. We passed kiddy rides, including a large rotating device filled with painted, artificial horses with rolling eyes and bared teeth. Shrieking children sat astride them, holding onto brass poles. Music poured from an old-fashioned calliope, or at least, a modern sound system camouflaged as an old-time instrument. I saw other medieval rides: some sort of boat on a giant swing that flung people forward and back; a curving metal track on which mag-lev cars raced, accompanied by a clunk-clattering sound that I assumed was a recording of some long-ago roller coaster, and even a gigantic, ruby-colored circle that I remembered from old books was a Ferris wheel. The crowd swirled around us in gauzy chaos. I was jostled and squeezed by the perfumed and colorful stream of people, although the tourists could be picked put by their drab attire and glazed eyes as they captured memories for later Immersion replay.

Once, I gave a start as I came face to face with myself. My doppelgänger wore a mask of me and carried a pink backpack like mine. Then I saw another, who nodded at me, and I finally noticed there were dozens of me. Some people stopped to compliment me on the realism of my mask.

I gaped, open-mouthed, until Trino said, "Another reason you won't be recognized here. They like to wear the faces of famous people."

"Or infamous ones," I said.

I also saw a panoply of pre-Collapse generals in gaudy braided uniforms, several long-dead revolutionaries, a couple of disturbingly realistic Iron Wolves and even a dozen or so Pallburgs, who looked so natural that I shuddered. Thankfully, the replicas lacked the bleached skin and blue lips of the lifeless face I'd seen in the Columbarium.

In between the crowds, I caught a flash of fluorescent green. Someone was wearing a Civic jumpsuit like mine. I recognized her profile. It was Rin. She was standing near a food stall. She was holding some kind of rainbow-colored confection and talking to a tall, good-looking man. He looked to be a few years older than me. As Trino and I approached, the man bent close to Rin and said something in her ear. She erupted in peels of laughter. Her hand reached out and brushed his arm.

I don't know why but at that instant I hated that guy. I looked him up and down. I didn't like his hair. I didn't even like his shoes.

Rin and the man spotted us. He straightened up, took a small step back from Rin and suddenly seemed more formal and distant.

I liked him better.

"Mavo," Rin said. "This is my friend, Brian."

"Hi," I grunted.

He smiled. I tried not to notice that he was half a head taller than me and his teeth were Immersion perfect.

I turned to Rin. "What are you eating?"

"This? It's a snow cone. Try it." She held out the paper cone. "You lick it," she said.

With embarrassment, I stuck out my tongue and gingerly touched it.

"No," Rin said. "*Lick* it. You're not a snake." Brian laughed. I could feel my ears turning crimson. I bent forward and took a long lick, then started back in surprise.

"It's sweet," I said. "And cold."

"Shaved ice with syrup," Rin said. "It has a lot of sugar."

"Real sugar?" I asked.

"Of course," she said. "No synth here. You can have real food. That's part of the attraction. Tastes better than an Immersion, doesn't it?"

"Sure does," I said, though I honestly had no idea.

"That's why I love this place," Rin said. "It's all done without Immersion. Hand-crafted. It shows you what people can do without depending on artificial knowledge." She held out the cone. "Here, you can have the rest. Go slowly, though. You're not used to it."

I tried to disguise my eagerness as I took the cone. It was cold under my fingers. The cup was also a little sticky, unlike Immersion food, which wasn't messy. Oddly, I didn't mind. It was different but interesting. It added something to the experience. Maybe, I thought, the Realists were on to something. I took a bite. My teeth crunched on sweet ice. It was delicious, until all of a sudden something like a freezing spike shot up through my mouth and bored into my head.

"Ahhh!" I cried. "My skull has a toothache!"

Rin wasn't sympathetic. In fact, she laughed. So did everyone else.

"It's called a brain freeze," Rin said. "Press your tongue against the roof of your mouth and it'll go away."

I did and was amazed that the sensation diminished. I shook my head and handed back the cone.

"Does all your food have a learning curve?" I asked.

"Wait 'til you taste a taco with habañero sauce."

"I hope that won't give me a brain freeze."

Brian chuckled. I briefly wondered how he'd look with a snow cone buried in his ear. To conceal my thoughts, I turned to Rin.

"I didn't expect to see you here," I said quickly. "I thought you'd be doing, you know, important stuff."

"Why, did you think we're all grim-faced zealots, that we spend all our time plotting dark deeds in dank caves? We like to have fun." She shook her head. "We're people, Mavo. We want sunlight and freedom. That's the promise of the cause. Besides, you know what Emma Goldman said: 'If I can't dance, I don't want to be part of your revolution.'" She laughed. I really liked that laugh.

Trino spoke up. "Yes," he said. "But there's a time to play and a time to work."

"He's right," Brian said. "We should go."

Just then, I heard a high-pitched screech, like a furious hawk who'd missed its kill. I recognized the sound of a steam whistle.

Rin stopped short, her eyes wide.

"Wait," Rin said. She turned to me. "There's one more thing you have to see."

Trino seemed about to protest but Brian broke in.

"Lead the way," he told Rin, extending a hand.

To my dismay, she took it. But then she also grabbed mine.

We threaded our way through the teeming midway until it opened onto a central hub, a ring road with a grassy mound in the middle. Railroad tracks were embedded in the roadway. Rolling around the mound was a steam-driven railroad flat car, something out of ancient history. Music poured from it. It had a catchy, primitive beat. The song was about someone's disappointment with an underperforming hunting dog. But I really wasn't paying much attention to the words. I was too busy looking at the orchestra. It was the strangest sight that I had ever seen, even in Immersion. Antique human-shaped robots, all ball-jointed metal limbs, were playing actual instruments. The drummer wore glasses with thick black frames and no lenses. Every once in a while it would stop, spin around on its stool, then return to the beat. Its shiny, pointed chin jutted in time to the music.

"Look," Rin said, pointing at the 'bots. "They're wearing blue suede shoes. Elvis would be proud."

I nodded as if I knew what she was talking about.

The lead singer held a microphone and was wearing some kind of glittery, sequin-studded jacket. Sunglasses were taped to its nose. The 'bot had seen better days. One arm dangled limply at its side. Its metal pelvis gave off a grinding noise as it swiveled jerkily but its artificial voice was strong and rich. In front of it, a line of female robots with bouffant hairdos writhed in apparent robotic ecstasy.

The flat car had a pot-bellied steam engine, one attached to each end. They puffed like a pair of fat, asthmatic men.

As the performance continued, the flat car rolled slowly clockwise around the central hub. As the doggy lament ended, the train stopped. The singer took a creaky bow to roars and applause from the crowd. Then something strange happened. As the final notes ended, there was a pause and then a bevy of shrill steam-whistle blasts from the engines, as if they were disputing the right to pull the train. Then the victorious engine hooted twice and began to chug the car in the opposite direction. The crowd roared. The band struck up another song, and I realized the lyrics were discussing footwear.

"Oh," I said. "Blue suede shoes. I get it!"

Rin gave me a pitying look. "Haven't you ever heard an Elvis song before?"

I blushed. "We mostly sang anti-Unity folk songs," I said. "But my Mom had a couple downloads of medieval synth stuff."

"Well, I'm glad we saw this," Brian broke in. "It's probably the last Elvis performance of the season. They need to refurbish that singer."

We turned around to make our way back through the crowd and I noticed Trino standing behind us. He was blank-eyed and frowning in thought. Then he caught my glance and sprang to life. A broad smile creased his face. He clapped his hands.

"That was amazing," he said. "Well, shall we go?"

He took the lead in weaving a path through the crowd, chatting all the time and delightedly pointing at stalls and even singing snatches of the Elvis songs. In a few moments, he seemed to have become a completely different person. I wondered what he'd been thinking about earlier.

We walked to a building that looked to be centuries old. Its antique facade had soaring, grooved columns that looked hand carved. Gold-painted angels bracketed the entrance. It was the most ornate edifice I'd seen in all my journeys. Whatever else the Realists were doing here, they weren't hiding. We entered a cavernous lobby paved with real marble that was meticulously clean, even to my expert eye. Rows of fluted pillars supported the space. Between them were hung various banners, some ragged, others apparently new. There also were statues and icons and chunky blocks carved with some weird hieroglyphs, each one different. I saw a silver and glass pyramid in which something like a one-eyed angel appeared to be sleeping. A statue of a horned man glowered from a corner. It was painted in lifelike hues, wore a black turtleneck and blue jeans and held an apple in one hand. Several statues were nothing more than artsy designs of characters and letters I didn't recognize. One corner was full of scaffolding where people in industrial exoskeletons were levering into place an enormous statue of what appeared to be an armored knight who was, for some reason, cradling a pig. Above us, three enormous crystal chandeliers provided light. From the central chandelier dangled a giant, upside down black cross with what looked like Navajo blankets draped over the arms.

Brian waved a hand around. "Ignore that junk," he said. "This way."

"What is all this?" I asked Rin. "Is it a museum? An art exhibit?"

"Hardly," she said. "It's an old hotel. We rent a wing. Every tenant gets a display space."

"Pretty tolerant place," I said as we passed a red-eyed robot that was twisting a shrieking human form in its hands.

"Yeah," she said, making a face. "Some of these people are real nuts."

I refrained from commenting on Realist beliefs. "Where's your symbol?" I asked.

I should have known what would happen. Other realists who politely ignored me had joined us as we walked, and though there were only five of them, they immediately began to squabble about what the symbol should be. They kept it up until we turned into a broad corridor lined with doors. Compared to the lobby, it was sterile and unadorned. People bustled in and out of the doors. When they spotted me, they stopped, their eyes wide. Some grinned and seemed about to confront me, but Brian shook his head and they stepped back and went on with whatever duties they were handling. The Realists who'd joined us also peeled off. Brian led us to an elevator that brought us up to the sixth floor. We stopped in front of a door with a touchpad. My name glowed on it.

"You're voice-keyed already," Brian said. "Why don't you relax and wash up? Let Rin or Trino or myself know when you're ready to join us." He smiled. "We have a task for you that I think you'll really like." He pulled something from a pocket and handed it to me. "It's a comclip," he said. "Old-fashioned, I know, but this is a Free Zone and there are only a handful of areas where Immersion is allowed." I took it and pressed it behind my ear, where it stuck.

Brian clasped one of my hands in both of his, bowed formally and left with the others. Rin hadn't even looked back, I noticed.

I let myself into the room. I was suddenly exhausted. I paid scant attention to anything but the bed and the smell, a mix of disinfectant and cheap mood balm that made my nostrils sting. I ignored it and flopped onto the bed. I was instantly asleep. I must have slept for several hours. When I woke up, I felt less hungover with fatigue. I yawned, threw my clothes into the sanitizer and staggered into the sono-shower.

Afterward, as I began to dress, the wall lit up. It was an incoming call from Rin.

"Accept," I said, and then realized too late that she would see me. Her face filled the screen.

"Morning, sleepy head. Did you rest well? How did you like the shower? I always feel cleaner with a sono than with water."

I dove for my pants while trying to avoid thinking of Rin in a shower. I'd lived in a Unity city for years, but I'd never gotten used to people's casual approach to privacy.

I wondered if there were cameras in the shower. Maybe the management thought of it as a safety feature, in case I tripped on the soap and fell.

"I hope you're not allergic to the cleanser," Rin said. "Your face just got red."

"I'm fine," I said, pulling my tunic over my head. "So, what's up?"

"We're waiting for you downstairs," Rin replied. "Just follow the blue arrows."

I stepped outside and a blue arrow sprang to life in front of me on the carpet. It paced ahead of me until I reached the elevator.

I got off on the ground floor to find someone waiting for me. He was a thin man, sharply dressed. Nothing about him was rumpled or casual. He was all edges. Even the hair on the sides of his balding skull looked glued down. His arms were crossed and he leaned casually against a wall. But he had an air of watchful tension, as if he could snap into action like a switchblade. He saw me and pushed his shoulder away from the wall. He nodded at me.

"I'm Leon," he said. "Trino asked me to look after you."

I realized then that I had been right. Somebody *was* always watching me. So much for the prestige of being a hero.

"Uh, thanks," I said. "What now?"

"Follow me."

"Where are we going?"

"The Assembly."

"Oh," I said. "Great."

Leon didn't walk. He sliced through the air like a shark through water. Maybe he was enhanced somehow. Extra-flexible joints, like an MMA fighter? Artificial nerves and fast-twitch musculature? Temporal crisis amplifiers? Or just years of ninja training? I wondered if he was ex-military and if so, how he'd ended up in the Realists.

We stopped at a pair of tall double doors that opened at Leon's touch. Inside was a large space like a ballroom. Rows of tables and desks faced a curving panel of monitors and a small dais backed by a screen. I saw a confusion of people scattered around the hall. Some sat at the cluttered desks, faces buried in information tablets. Some clustered in knots, waving their arms and arguing. The noise was unbelievable. Everybody seemed to be talking at once at the top of their lungs, as if whoever shouted the loudest would win the argument. The room was choked with dirty coffee cups, candy wrappers and other trash. It looked like a brainstorming meeting that had lasted for days or like a conference room after an all-night gamers' convention.

Or maybe a garbage drone had malfunctioned and dumped its load on the floor.

Brian stood on the dais, apparently unable or unwilling to bring things to order.

Leon and I stood by the door. Nobody paid us any attention.

"What is this place?" I asked Leon.

"The nerve center of Realism," he said. "We plan our operations here. We hold our People's Assemblies here." His lips pursed, as if he had tasted something sour. I guessed he disapproved of the chaos. I wondered where his real loyalties lay. He waved at the motley collection of people. Some faces seemed vaguely familiar to me.

As if he were reading my mind, Leon said: "You probably recognize a few of them from Unity bulletins. They're wanted saboteurs. They can't be seen outside the Free Zone or they'll be grabbed. But we sneak them in and out on the Narwhal."

"So this is the leadership?" I asked.

"A gathering of equals," Leon corrected. "They're the most experienced operatives, so we respect their opinions but we get input from all our cells." He pointed at the monitors. I saw that each had an obviously artificial avatar.

I understood. "You're decentralized. Cells work semi-independently. You don't know their members and they don't know you. That way, if an operation is compromised, it doesn't take down the whole group."

"That's right," Leon said. "Operational security through anonymization." He gave me a penetrating glance. "Trino said you were a quick study." He gestured a manicured hand to the room. "Go on in." He palmed the doors open and then stepped outside the room in a single fluid motion. The doors silently slid closed.

I turned back to the room and looked hesitantly at the pandemonium in front of me. Then Brian spotted me. He moved his lips, activating the room's speaker complex. His next words boomed.

"Everybody! Everybody, your attention! Mavo is here! Mavo would like to speak!"

"What?" I squawked.

The chatter died instantly and all eyes were suddenly on me.

"Mavo?" voices repeated.

Brian waved me toward the dais. I wanted to turn and bolt for the doors. I darted a panicked glance around the room.

I saw Rin.

She was on the other side of the dais. She had abandoned her jumpsuit and was wearing something loose that left her arms bare. I hadn't seen her arms before. They were slender and athletic. She had a scar on her left forearm. It was a large, ragged white crescent. As if reading my thoughts, Rin crossed her arms, hiding the scar. She looked at me with anticipation. My stomach fluttered and I wanted to run again but I crammed that thought to the back of my head where it could pee itself like a terrified puppy. I pasted a smile on my face and walked forward. Unlike Leon, I felt clumsy as I moved through the throng. I had to force my legs forward with each step as if I were slogging through a bog. Hands reached out as if to touch me but then drew back. I heard my name repeated in almost worshipful murmurs as I crossed the space. I kept my eyes locked rigidly on Brian, who, as I slowly approached, extended a hand as if he were trying to pull me from the ooze.

I stepped up to the dais.

Brian stepped forward. I hadn't liked him when he was with Rin but now I ignored his height and chiseled good looks. He gave me a warm look of respect.

"Thank you, Mavo," he said softly. "Sorry to spring this on you but they demanded it."

"It's okay," I managed to say with a dry mouth, then confessed: "I'm not really a speaker."

Brian nodded. "I know. You work alone. But can I offer a piece of advice?"

"Sure."

"You did a magnificent thing. They know it. This isn't the time to be modest. You need to inspire them. Us."

"I'll do my best."

"That's all any of us can do." He smiled and stepped back, leaving the platform to me.

CHAPTER TEN

The murmuring slowly stopped and the hall went silent. The air seemed thick with anticipation, which didn't help my nervousness.

"Hi," I began, and stopped. The crowd seemed to hang on the word.

Desperately, I cast my eyes on Rin. Her calm gaze gave me strength. I pretended I was talking just to her. What did I want to tell her?

I thought for a moment, and then I said, "I was born on the Outside. Some of you have been there."

There were nods.

"Out there," I continued, "We don't have a lot of love for Unity. I learned a lot of songs about the 'chip-licking oppressors.'"

There was good-natured laughter.

"But," I said. "When you're a kid, and your world is a little bit, well, small, you get itchy feet. And if your Mom says something's bad, that can just make you hungry for it." I shrugged. "That's part of being a kid."

There were murmurs of agreement and a few chuckles.

"So," I said. "I jumped a train and ran away to the big city. I wanted to be part of the Immersion. I thought of it like an all-you-can-eat candy store. But then I found something out. I could only Immerse for an hour." I tapped my temple. "I'm made differently up here. I was devastated."

The room went silent again. I knew they hadn't expected me to praise Unity, their mortal enemy. Quickly, I went on.

"So, I turned inside myself a little. I kept away from people. Actually, I couldn't reach them; the Immersion was their whole lives. And I began to realize something: I had something they didn't. Because I couldn't join them, I was unique. I was myself. And I wasn't addicted to thinking other people's thoughts."

I surprised myself as I said this, because I realized it was true. But I couldn't tell them the rest of what I felt: That I would give anything to be normal.

This crowd wouldn't appreciate that. I had to be careful here.

I continued, "I won't stand up here and tell you, 'Down with Unity oppression! Up with humanity!'"

I was interrupted by spontaneous cheers. They must have missed the "won't" part. When they died down, I said, "You don't need me to tell you what to think and do." Then I got an inspiration. I held up my hand.

"Isn't that what Realism's all about? Isn't that the real message? It's not about who controls human destiny. It's about who controls *your* life."

"Not the machines!" someone shouted and there was a roar of approval. I managed to continue.

"I guess what I'm saying is that nobody should tell you what to do. Don't give the power to someone else, or something else. You want to be free to think for yourselves. That's why you don't need to hear what I did and how I did it. You need to go out and do what you need to do." I raised my fist and thrust it into the air.

"Liberation!" I shouted, a little bit squeakily and was shocked when the hall erupted with echoes and became a chant of "Liberation! Liberation!"

I don't remember much more of what I said. I quoted some stuff from books I'd read about the speeches of Winston Churchill and Abraham Lincoln. I mixed in a bunch of Realist cliches I'd picked up from a biography of the Realist founder Goo Peri. She was a casualty of early, crude deep-probing.

At the end, everyone was stamping, clapping and cheering. That had never happened to me before. I felt energized and excited— and then ashamed. I felt guilty for feeling good about impressing a group of subversives. I looked over again at Rin.

She had disappeared.

I felt a strong hand on my shoulder. I turned.

"That was amazing!" Brian said, his eyes beaming approval.

"Thanks," I said. "I was just winging it."

Brian laughed. It was a hearty, unpretentious and welcoming laugh. It seemed everything he did was perfect, I thought. I wouldn't admit to myself that it bothered me.

Trino came up. He looked approving and amused. He, too, put a hand on my shoulder. I hadn't minded as much when Brian did it, but for some reason Trino's move made me uncomfortable. Maybe because he kept it there.

"Well," Trino said. "A man of action and a man of words. Most warriors can hold a gun but not a conversation. Am I right, Brian?" He gave a hearty laugh. Brian gave a thin smile.

"Well, Mavo," Brian said, turning to me. "What would you like to do now? I know your time hasn't exactly been your own since you arrived." He gestured at the crowd. "This might seem a little overwhelming."

"A bit," I replied. In fact, I was still conflicted about my success. But guilt was starting to creep in, and that was something I had to keep to myself. Also, now that the speech was over, I was beginning to feel more than a little anxious. The people in the crowd weren't going back to work. They continued murmuring among themselves. Most seemed to have their eyes riveted on me. There were too many people, too much input and sensation.

"I think I'd like some place a little more quiet," I said.

"Naturally!" Trino boomed at once. "There's a lot to do and you'll need to be fresh. Let's get you out of this madhouse." He turned to Brian. "Perhaps the three of us can have a quiet lunch?" His gaze looked just a little too earnest.

"What do you think, Mavo?" Brian asked, and his gaze had a note of caution in it. I took the hint.

"Maybe later," I said. "Right now I'd just like to, um, decompress."

Brian's face lit up. "I think I know a place you'll really like. Trino, could you take over here?"

"Certainly," Trino said. "I'll call Leon to escort you."

Brian waved the suggestion away. "No, it's fine. We won't waste anybody's time." There was an almost imperceptible change in Trino's expression. I didn't catch its meaning before it melted back into a smile.

"Sure," Trino said. "I'll make sure everybody gets refocused. Mavo, you've caused a lot of excitement here. It's good energy. Together we can do great things!" His hand was still on my shoulder. He gave it a hard squeeze before finally releasing me.

"Let's go, then," Brian said. We descended the podium into the crowd. I was afraid we'd be overwhelmed, but Brian deftly guided me through the choppy currents of adulation, smoothly opening a path with a glance or a swift nudge of his shoulder.

In seconds we were out of the room. Leon was there and began to step into place behind us but Brian waved him away.

The corridor was empty. The offices leading from it were deserted. Apparently, nearly every Realist in the building had come to see me speak. The fact that a group whose members couldn't even agree on their own symbol had all decided to listen to me was intimidating.

Flattering too, but scary.

Brian led us out of the hotel. We walked a couple of blocks until we came to a large three-story building in a pre-Collapse style, a jumble of beige blocks. We entered through glass doors set in a wall of windows.

The first thing I noticed was the smell: the slightly musty odor of carpet, varnished bookshelves, old paper and ink. The carpet was a sober gray. A wood-paneled circulation desk stood to one side of the doors. A woman sat there reading a book. She was so absorbed she didn't notice us.

Light streamed through the windows and from fixtures in the ceiling.

The first floor was a vast open space with chairs and reading tables scattered about and elevators at the back. The tables were empty. Tall shelves at the rear and sides of the building were packed with books— more than I had ever seen in one place. It took my breath away.

Other libraries had audio-visual and Immersion nodes and digital papers, but the only actual books I'd ever seen there were in glass cases.

Brian noticed me gaping.

"It's been here since the twentieth century," Brian said. "Always been a library, although it's only been since Unity that they restocked it with books. It's sort of a reenactment center. The books are real. You can even check them out, although hardly anybody does."

He led me into the center of the open space, and I noticed there were several wings. We passed one carpeted in a colorful checkerboard. Child-sized bookshelves were scattered about. The room also was filled with colorful blobs. In each one, a child was engulfed, looking half-devoured. It took me a second to realize they were reclining in some sort of moldable, form-fitting chairs. In the center was a librarian sitting on a wooden chair. She was holding a book in her lap and reading out loud. I stopped to listen.

"'Oh my!' said Amy Octopus. 'Drowned LA is so beautiful!'" the librarian read. "Amy's tentacles danced with happiness as she followed a shiny school of fish into the great, dark window in the skyscraper. The fish were like the sparkles on a Survival Day tree!"

"Story time," Brian whispered.

We wandered to the back of the stacks. And there, sitting at a table near a window, I saw Rin. She was bathed in sunlight that made her hair and face glow as if she were in a Renaissance painting. She was bent over a book. Her lips were pursed and her forehead was creased in concentration.

"Well, look who's here," Brian said with surprise in his voice. "Hi, Rin."

Rin looked up. "Hi Brian, Mavo." She closed the book and put it on the table face down.

"What are you reading?" I asked.

"Oh, nothing," she said. "What brings you here?"

"I thought Mavo would like it," Brian said.

"It's great," I blurted. "We never had anything like it on the Outside."

"But I heard you read a lot when you were young," Rin said.

"Everybody had one or two favorite books that they held onto and shared," I said. "I read every book we had a dozen times by the time I left."

"Well," Brian cut in. "I'll say you got a great education." He turned to Rin. "You heard Mavo's speech."

"A little," she said. "But I had to step away for that thing we discussed."

Brian nodded as if he understood. Which reminded me that I was an outsider.

"Did you like it?" I asked, then shut my mouth, aghast. I hadn't intended to ask her about my speech. It seemed stupid and needy.

Rin gave me a quizzical look, as if she were asking herself why a hero of the revolution would need her encouragement. I felt my ears burn.

Desperately, I pointed to the book on the table. "I meant that," I stammered, lying.

"The book?" Rin replied. "Yes, although it's not like Immersion, of course."

"No." Out of curiosity, I had read books and then tried the Immersion versions. Some had been good, but they hadn't been the same thing as reading. What I got was the way someone *else* had read it. I got to be in their head instead of in the story.

Did Rin feel that way, too?

"What is reading like for you?" I asked.

At that point, Brian gave a pained look. Rin and I looked at him. I guess books weren't his passion. But then he tapped his com clip and said, "I just got a message from Trino. There's a new feed from Anchorage. Might be important. I'll see you both at dinner, maybe?"

"Sure," I said, trying to conceal my enthusiasm for his departure. Rin hugged him. I looked away, pretending to be fascinated by the bookshelves.

I glanced back to see Brian strolling away. He even walked with confidence. With a jolt, I realized I had almost forgotten Rin was there until she touched me on the arm.

"What was that?" I asked. She'd said something and I had missed it. She'd also picked the book up and was holding it out to me.

"*I said,*" Rin repeated. She seemed a little annoyed. "I found this for you."

"Oh," I said. I took the book and looked at the title. "*The Hobbit*. Thank you. I've never read it."

"I loved it," she said. She leaned toward me. "Don't tell anybody, but I read books when I was young." She seemed to be slightly embarrassed, as if reading were some kind of vice or weird hobby.

Which, I realized, was exactly how most people raised in an Immersion society felt.

"You didn't Immerse?" I asked.

"Mom limited my Immersion time," Rin said, giving me a complicit look. "She called it, 'Reserving time for yourself.'"

"It must have made you feel lonely," I said, recalling my own feelings.

"Yeah," Rin said. She took a breath. "But Mom said, 'You have to grow your own brain, a part of yourself that is entirely yourself.' Not second-hand, you know?"

"Your Mom would love my Mom!" I exclaimed.

Rin made a face. "I hated her for it at the time. But later, I got it."

"What?"

Rin frowned. "You have to reserve time for yourself, and the only way to become self-Realized is by not letting the Immersion control you. But," she admitted. "it's been a while since I sat down with a book."

"But when I was coming here on the train, " I said. "everybody seemed to want to Immerse." I remembered the dinner where everybody had expected to overlay their food with Immersion enhancements.

"Some Realists think that Unity is dangerous but Immersion is OK," Rin said. "And others think Immersion is the opiate of the people." She gave a little laugh. "We don't agree on everything."

Or anything, I thought, but I didn't say that out loud.

"What do you think?" I asked.

Rin gave me a mischievous smile. "I think it's time for lunch," she said. Then she licked her lips and I lost my train of thought.

On the way out of the library, I couldn't help stopping at every shelf. A thick volume caught my eye and I pulled it out.

"Look!" I told Rin. "The entire Wuu cycle!"

"Is that good?" Rin stared at the heavy book doubtfully.

"Oh yeah, it's supposed to be great. I've never seen a copy. It was samizdat. It came out during the decade when they banned books."

"Oh, you mean the Cultural Hijacking thing," Rin said. "They told us about that in reading class. Everybody being upset that someone from some group was writing about people from another group. Or something."

"Yep," I said. "They thought writers shouldn't pretend to be other people. Of course, now you can know what people feel by downloading their Immersions. But back then, you had to research and study and guess. Some people thought it was a bad idea to do that, I guess, to try to understand and write about being someone you're not."

Rin gave me an arch look. "Some people still do," she said.

I didn't know what to say to that so we moved on, with the Wuu book under my arm. I was going to check it out. I stopped twice more to pull books off the shelves. Soon I was juggling a stack of them.

Rin gave me an amused look. "You sure they'll let you take all of those?"

"I don't know. Is there a limit?"

She laughed.

We came to a section with books I'd read. My arms were loaded down, so I pointed at one with my chin. "Try that one," I said.

Rin took it, opened it at random to a page with a drawing. It was a rabbit wearing clothes. She puzzled out the words, her lips moving. Then she looked back at the front page.

"*Alice's Adventures in Wonderland?*" she said. "Oh, like the Immersions. Isn't there supposed to a funny queen who keeps shouting, 'Off with her head!' or is she the one that runs in place?"

"That's the Red Queen," I said. "She's in a second book called, *Through the Looking-Glass.* She runs as fast as she can to stay in place. You've heard of the Red Queen Hypothesis?"

"No."

"Well, it just means a species has to keep constantly evolving to survive against other species, who are also constantly evolving. An evolutionary arms race. It comes from that character."

Rin gave me a rueful look.

"Why in the world would you know that?" she asked playfully. "What *don't* you know?"

"Way too much." I said.

On the other hand, I thought, despite the fact that most people had literally billions of things to watch, listen to and feel, most of them seemed depressingly ignorant.

I kept that thought to myself, too.

We walked back to the hotel. It wasn't even noon, but it was already hot enough that waves of heat rippled off the sidewalk. Rin didn't seem to be affected. I wished I had one of the Circo Eterno snow cones. I could faintly hear the music from the circus grounds wafting through the clear desert air.

The hotel felt cool as a crypt, which made me flash uncomfortably on that horrifying moment in the Columbarium when I'd found Pallburg's body. I shivered, and not from the air conditioning.

I got a surprise as we walked through the huge lobby full of cult statues and banners. It was packed with people gawking and talking to themselves, obviously taking guided Immersion tours. When I'd first arrived, the place had been nearly empty.

"Tourists?" I asked Rin in confusion.

"Sure," she said. "The whole city runs on tourism. Why not this place?"

Someone detached himself from a wall and approached with a purposeful walk. I recognized Leon. Had he been waiting for us?

"Hi, Leon," Rin said. "We're just back from the library."

"So I see," he said, nodding at the pile of books in my arms.

"We're just going to eat," Rin added smoothly. "And I wondered if you wouldn't mind doing me a favor and putting these up in Mavo's room?" She turned to me. "That's OK, isn't it, Mavo?"

"Sure." I already knew I didn't have much privacy in this place.

Leon's expression didn't change but I sensed something like hidden energy or eagerness as he stepped forward to take the books.

Maybe, I thought, he wants the chance to search my room. Well, he was welcome to do it. Everything I owned was in my backpack, and there wasn't anything special in there except my sister's doll.

The real scary stuff was in my head, and he couldn't search that. I hoped.

Rin thanked Leon. He nodded, took the books and turned on his heel. I watched him go, the stack of books riding easily in the crook of one arm. As before, he moved effortlessly, with sharklike grace.

Rin watched him go with a look on her face I couldn't decipher. Then she turned to me.

"Come on," she said.

We wove through the crowds to one end of the great room. A set of elegant, frosted glass doors that I hadn't noticed before led into the fanciest restaurant I'd ever seen. It was immense, full of people chatting at booths and tables covered in real linen, with china and crystal everywhere. The walls were a subdued gold. There wasn't a screen or Immersion node in sight. Rin waved a hand at the richly suited host, who nodded and pressed a button. A moment later, a holo in an old-fashioned tuxedo appeared, and we followed its floating form to an empty table. The table looked out on an enclosed garden full of what I guessed were fruit trees, and maybe, flamingoes? I couldn't tell if any of it was real, although if not, it was odd that a holo landscape would show someone wearing waders, scooping muck out of a small pond.

Rin tapped up the menu. I took one look at the prices and my stomach fell.

"Rin," I whispered. "I don't know if I can afford this."

"Don't worry," she said with a quirky smile. "We're covered."

I leaned forward and said, "Do *Realists* come here?" I thought it was pretty pricey for an underground rebel group.

"We're part owners," she said. "This is the Free Zone. We can practice free enterprise, so we tapped the tourist vein. We got seed money from anonymous supporters." She made a face. "We even own a piece of the Circo. We have our own balloon."

Real waiters came around. I had no idea what to do or what to order. Rin asked for specials and a Third in a gold-laced vest that matched the walls recited a string of things that probably sounded delicious, if I'd known what they were. In the end, I followed Rin's advice and ordered some kind of fish. It came on a tray covered in dry ice mist, with waves of vegetable foam and a sauce that smelled better than anything I'd ever smelled, even in Immersion. It tasted odd but delicious, and I had to stop myself from wolfing it down.

Rin ordered a hamburger.

"Don't worry, it's vat, not cow factory," she said. I nodded as if I knew what she meant.

The whole thing was so intimidating that I barely spoke to Rin during the meal. Besides, I was busy with my food. That and the atmosphere were overloading my senses. It was so overpowering that I kept waiting for my head to explode in pain, the way it did if I was Immersed for too long.

Dessert was something called "apple tart à la mode" that turned out to be an individual pie with two separate crust rings, one inside the other. The inner one had the pie filling and the outer one contained a moat of ice cream. I had never eaten so much at one time, and I was a little ashamed. The meal probably could have fed half a dozen Outsiders.

Rin noticed my expression and said, "Don't worry. None of it goes to waste, and tourists expect this sort of thing. It's why they come here."

"Do they know Realists own this?"

"That would be bad for business," she said with a puckish grin.

As we left the restaurant, I suddenly felt exhausted. I thought it must be a combination of the heavy food, my lack of sleep since arriving and also coming down from the highs of my speech and— I had to be honest— being with Rin.

"Thanks," I told her. "That was unbelievable."

"I knew you'd like it," Rin said. She looked at me and seemed to read my mind. "Well, I have some stuff to do. What about you?"

I suppressed a yawn. "I think I'll go back to my room and read some of those books. I can't decide which I want to look at first."

Rin grinned. "See you at dinner with Brian?"

"Will it be at this place?" I gestured.

"No, sorry, and don't get too used it. It's not something we do all the time."

"I'm glad to hear that," I said. "Although that dessert..." I licked my lips and patted my stomach.

Rin laughed. Once again, I realized how much I liked that laugh.

I went back to my room. My backpack looked undisturbed. If Leon had searched it, he'd done a neat job. The books were stacked on the table. I picked up the Wuu cycle but decided it was too heavy— in every sense— to start right now. If I were honest, I really didn't feel like reading. So much had happened to me in such a short time that I needed time to digest it (along with the food). In a matter of days, I'd gone from the most hated person in the world to being with people who, well, idolized me. I wasn't quite ready to admit that I was starting to enjoy myself. But, I thought, maybe the Realists weren't as bad as they'd been made out to be.

Then they asked me to bomb a building.

CHAPTER ELEVEN

After Rin left, I tried to pick up the book again, but I'd only gotten through a few pages when I fell into an exhausted sleep. The next thing I knew, the wall had lit up with an incoming call. It was Brian.

"Accept," I said groggily, and the screen produced his image. He was in the Assembly room. It was packed and noisy as usual.

"Mavo," Brian said, cutting through the chatter. "I know we weren't supposed to meet until dinner, but something's come up and we could really use you right away." He looked apologetic.

"What is it?" I asked, a little annoyed. I had barely gotten back to my room. "Do you want me to make another speech?"

"No, nothing like that," he said. "It's a planning session."

That sounded beyond vague. I wondered if he was intentionally being evasive.

"I'll be there," I said and blanked the screen.

Downstairs, Leon was waiting to escort me to the Assembly room. I wondered if he was ever off duty. I suspected I was his full-time assignment. Which was not a comforting thought.

A guard I didn't recognize was at the doors but, at a nod from Leon, let me through without a word.

The moment I entered, the chatter stopped. All eyes turned to me. I halted, not sure where I was expected to go. I noticed that the junk food was piled higher than ever. Brian was in a small group of people on the dais. He motioned me forward.

This time, everybody stepped back. I could move forward without difficulty, other than the fact that I was a little daunted and tense, so my legs felt wobbly. If it was another speech after all, I was going to turn around and leave— after punching Brian.

But when I reached him, Brian gave me a warm smile and explained.

"Mavo," he said. "I know you usually work alone, but we're planning something and we could use your insight."

I felt a chill down my back. There was only one thing these people knew about me, or thought they did.

I struggled to keep my voice calm as I replied: "You're going to kill someone?"

Brian blinked as if he couldn't decide whether I was joking.

"We're going to destroy a symbol of oppression," he said and then began talking slowly and deliberately, as if choosing each word. I was all too aware that the entire room was listening to every syllable.

"There's a factory east of town," Brian said. "It's a cow factory."

This time I blinked. I remembered that Rin had used the phrase. "Oh," I said, as if it meant something to me.

Brian did something with one hand and the screens around the room lit up. They showed an aerial shot of an industrial complex surrounded by desert. I saw white domes and one large, square rectangle. As the image zoomed in, I saw it was a cluster of tall, silo-like structures and behind them, a giant white cube. The complex was surrounded by gates. Trucks moved in and out, providing a reference point to the size of the buildings. They were enormous.

Words floated above the scene. They said: "Harvest Home Industries: Ruminant Division," and under it: "Employee Orientation."

The image switched. Now we were moving inside one of the silos. It was actually a series of huge concentric rings, sectioned off into stalls. And in each stall was something immense and strange. I couldn't quite make out what it was before the scene shifted.

Suddenly we were on a range, like in the old Immersion Westerns. Cattle were mooing in the background. Slouching against a split-rail fence was a rangy cartoon cowboy with a hat larger than his head. He was chewing on a stalk of something. He took it out of his mouth and touched the brim of his hat.

"Howdy, pardners," he said. "I'm Tex. Welcome to the Ruminant Division. You have signed with the most efficient and technologically advanced outfit in the whole ding-danged world."

Tex waved a hand behind him. "This here's the way folks used to raise cattle. It was labor-intensive, costly and slow. It took three years before you could get a nice steak." Tex shook his head. His hat wobbled.

The scene changed. Now Tex was standing in front of a silo room. He smiled and jerked a thumb behind him.

"And this here's the modern way to grow a steak." He grinned. "Not three years. Three months. Let's see how we do it."

A series of still images flashed by. Tex narrated. The first showed a normal calf, followed by a quick series in which it seemed to be growing. As it grew, its head shrank, it legs shriveled, its tail disappeared, and then as I watched in horror, its hide sloughed off. The last shot showed an enormous torso, pink and glistening and the size of a tank. The scene pulled back. The torso was suspended from a harness, the vestigial legs twitching as the remainder of the head— chiefly lips— munched unceasingly at some sort of feed. Clear tubes funneled away waste.

I heard people hissing behind me.

The scene pulled back and I could see now that the— animal? Thing?— was in one of the stalls in the silo. I realized there must be hundreds of them in one concentric ring alone.

Tex spoke again.

"They don't move and they don't moo, but in every other way, they're all cow. All natural, with less waste. One hundred percent real Wagyu-cloned critters. And they meet all Unity rules and regulations for humane production. You can be proud to work for an outfit that meets the highest standards."

Tex pulled a big spotted red handkerchief from his pocket and tied it around his neck. A big knife and fork appeared in his hands.

"And don't forget, you're helping to create one of the world's rarest and most prestigious food products. Real beef!"

"From fleshpots and meat machines!" someone yelled angrily.

The image switched to a steak, pink on the inside, glistening with moisture or fat, sizzling and smoking as if it had just come off the grill.

Tex's voice said: "And they're tasty, too!" Then his face reappeared. He winked, and the scene went dark.

I felt my lunch churning in my stomach. I tried to keep from gagging. I heard angry murmuring all around me. The screens went black.

Brian stepped forward.

"This is our target," he said. "Anchorage provided the footage. It clearly wasn't intended for public use. At the right time, we'll release it."

"It's disgusting," I blurted.

"Ruminant is proud of its operation," Brian said. "Unity forbids the slaughter of thinking creatures, so this is their workaround, and they can still claim to be offering a natural product." He made a face. "They even butcher it on site, the old-fashioned way."

"You mean, people eat this... stuff?" I asked.

"Circuit-lovers and calorie-suckers," someone shouted. "Filthy Unity slaves!"

There were angry murmurs of agreement.

"It's a luxury item," Brian said. "To produce one of these steaks requires enough resources and energy to supply a dozen people. And whatever they say, it tastes just the same as high-end vat meat. It's all about prestige."

I knew that people always had their pecking orders and status symbols. But it seemed wrong, somehow, to be proud of something so selfish and unnecessary.

"What are you planning to do?" I asked.

"Take it down," Brian said.

"How?"

Brian looked at me. "That's what we'd like you to decide."

I didn't ask, "Why me?" These people thought I'd managed to breach some of the highest security on the planet. So clearly, I was an old hand at infiltration and sabotage.

I took a breath. I had to say something right now before this got out of hand.

"Before we go on, I think there needs to be a rule: We should avoid casualties."

"Why?" A slender man who was mostly mustache said, jumping up from his desk. "Nobody made those people work there. They could just take a Unity stipend. They're guilty, too."

I held up a hand, "Look, I'm from the Outside, and I can tell you that there are still a lot of desperate people who will do what they have to. There are still areas where people suffer and don't get stipends. Otherwise, why would two million people have just died from starvation?"

There were murmurs of agreement but also some scoffing. I added hastily: "Besides, it's bad for our image. People don't generally like to see other people killed. Except for me, of course. I'm Number One on the Hit Parade." I gave a rueful smile. That earned me a general chuckle.

"All right," Brian broke in. "I think we can agree that Mavo has given us some food for thought. So, Mavo, what do you think? Chemical, biological, software?"

Despite myself, I was intrigued. How would I take down a factory?

"Show me the outside again," I said, and the screens brought up the aerial view of the plant.

I shook my head. "Software? Near impossible with Unity, and the company probably has proprietary safeblocks and metafilters. They constantly react to threats. We'd need a programmer inside and I don't think that's going to happen."

"Anchorage might have some sort of mole or maybe a military virus," someone suggested hopefully. "That's how we took down the satellite."

"If Anchorage had it, Anchorage would have used it," Brian said. "So, Mavo? No software?"

I shook my head. "I don't think so."

Brian held up both hands. "All right. For now, let's put software aside." There were some groans but no actual opposition.

"Right. Mavo, what about a chemical attack?"

"What kind?" I asked.

Mustache said: "Pollute the feed lines. Destroy the product."

Someone gave a derogatory bark.

"I can see the Immersion headlines now, 'Cows ruined at factory. Minor disruption. Realists suspected.' We'd look like amateurs!"

"Well, then let's hear your great idea!" someone shouted.

"Yeah!"

Suddenly everyone was yelling and trying to talk over each other. Brian looked exasperated.

While they were squabbling, I was thinking. They were working too hard. It was all too complicated.

Simple was better.

"I think," I said loudly. "We should blow it up."

The room went silent.

"You mean," someone said timidly. "With a, a bomb?"

"That's right," I said.

"But that's... so crude."

"Crude is good," I said. "Look, someone nearly killed me with a chunk of asphalt. That's about as low-tech as you can get. But that attack slid under Unity radar. They couldn't anticipate it. A bomb is less likely to tip anyone off."

"So you're saying—" someone began. "But wouldn't that cause, what was that word you used? Casualties?"

"No, we get the people out first. The only thing that goes up is the structure." I tried to sound more confident than I felt, which wasn't confident at all.

I wasn't sure I'd convinced them. People seemed to be looking at each other in confusion.

Then Trino, who until now had stood with his arms crossed and hadn't said a word, spoke up.

"Mavo's right," he said. "And think about this: We want to make a statement. A dramatic one. Is there anything more dramatic than blowing up a plant—" he paused, theatrically, "—on live Immersion?"

Again, the room fell silent. I heard a chorus of oohs and aahs. With one well-chosen comment, Trino had done what I couldn't, even though I supposedly was the brains.

I turned to Brian, but his expression was blank. He waited a moment, nodded to Trino and stepped forward.

"Well, what do we think?" Brian said. "We agreed we'd go with the option that Mavo chose."

"This wasn't one of the options," Mustache complained, but he was met with a collective groan. The squabbling began again.

I reminded myself that these were the same people who had taken down a satellite. Maybe Anchorage, and with Trino and Brian, were the only rational ones. The rest of them seemed to be buffoons. I pictured clowns tripping over their own feet while trying to knock down the circus tent. But then I reminded myself that they weren't just clowns. They were dangerous, lethal clowns.

I *had* to take charge, I decided. I couldn't imagine what kind of carnage could result if the real Realists planned this operation.

And in the back of my mind was this thought: They liked me now, they treated me well, but I couldn't wear my Realist mask forever. I still needed to get away from them. Maybe this operation could be the chance for me to do that. Although I had no idea where I would go.

What about planning the attack but sabotaging it? No. If I arranged for the scheme to be thwarted somehow by Unity, that might lead Trino to suspect I'd done it on purpose, or make people who admired me to lose confidence. Either situation could prove deadly to me.

Also, although I didn't like to admit it, I relished the challenge. How *would* I sneak a bomb into a secure facility?

Besides, I had no love for that factory.

All these thoughts were whirling around in my head as a voice I recognized spoke up from the back of the room.

"Everybody! Listen, your ideas are all good!" It was Rin.

She was standing near the door. Nobody seemed to have noticed her arrival and yet the moment she spoke, the bickering seemed to subside. It was as if she radiated some force field of calm. Everyone's attention was turning her way. She raised her chin and continued.

"Look," she said. "Mavo is here to help us. He's got skills we don't. He's done something nobody thought possible." She raised both hands. "Why did we bring him here if we won't listen to him?"

There were murmurs but now they seemed to be ones of agreement. I saw heads nodding. Rin's presence had entirely changed the atmosphere of the room. Now everybody seemed to want to be agreeable.

Brian smoothly took advantage of the moment. He stepped forward on the dais and said, "Rin is right. Mavo is the best choice. We already agreed to this. Does anyone oppose having Mavo guide us?"

It was a backward way of saying, "Let Mavo do it." I thought Brian probably said it that way because it was easier for people to agree through silence than to speak up and be singled out.

I had a grudging respect for his people-wrangling skills.

Now, I had to hone my own skills— for destruction.

"Crap," I said. It was the answer. I had wandered over to FreeJack to look into the history of bomb-making. FreeJack was the only place on the continent where I could do that and not instantly find myself under a mind-probe, a psych-dispensation order or mandatory reeducation.

What I discovered was that agricultural byproducts, including manure, could be converted into ammonium nitrate, used in fertilizer and also in homemade explosives.

Methane also was extracted from manure. In old-fashioned cattle feedlots, producers would store methane as liquid waste in outdoor lagoons, where bacteria would digest it and convert it to natural gas.

A cow factory must have tons of manure to dispose of. Maybe they produced fertilizer as a byproduct and energy to run the plant or to sell. Maybe they weren't just making steaks over there. They could be using every part of the cow except the moo.

Fertilizer and natural gas, I thought. Both were highly explosive under the right conditions.

If I could hijack a truck full of that stuff...

A plan was forming, but I had nearly used up my hour and I certainly didn't want to go into the project with a splitting skull.

Before unplugging, I decided to check my Popularity rankings. I was curious to see if, in the week since I escaped, people had begun to forget me. I had learned that, unlike the Outside where everyone held decades-long grudges, most people had short-term memories about current events. They were Immersed most of the time, and there was just too much going on, all at once, to keep track. Even outrage usually only lasted for a few days. In fact, Unity had come up with a series of commemorations just to reinforce collective memory and keep major events from slipping into oblivion.

My Pop ranking had barely moved, but there was a green exclamation mark next to my name, which meant there was something new. I clicked.

To my shock, I saw that I was the first item in all the major news summaries. The Realists had released my speech without telling me. There I was, larger than life. I looked strong, confident. A little too much, in fact.

I looked closer. Had they tweaked the lighting? It was subtle, but I didn't recall seeing any light in the room that picked out my cheekbones so dramatically.

And my words had been edited imperceptibly. My hesitations and fumblings had been deleted.

I switched into the emotional feed. It also had been tampered with.

Gone were my uncertainties and my mixed feelings. Somebody had dubbed in a track of moral certainty and triumph. I pictured a group of technicians editing me on the fly, deftly switching emotional content as I spoke. Like music tracks, they bumped up certain tones and muted others.

A thought hit me: Maybe somebody had simply flipped a switch and a canned algorithm had inserted a basic emotional track, like the laugh-track in ancient television comedies.

Somehow that seemed worse, to think that even the Realists relied on non-humans to fluff up their messaging. Either way, they'd used me, turned me into a product.

I'd known I was there to be useful and that my safety depended on it, but I hadn't believed the Realists could be so ruthless about it. I was sure most of them had no clue about this; they were as duped as I was. But clearly somebody had done it. Trino could have. Hadn't he just talked about making a dramatic statement with the factory attack?

Brian could have done it. I really didn't know what lay behind his smooth personality.

And then a chilling thought hit me.

Rin had left early in the speech. Where had she gone? Maybe to oversee the editing.

All I knew for sure was that the adulation of the crowd might not be enough to save me if someone up the Realist food chain decided I'd outlasted my utility. Someone had already decided to twist my words. Where would they stop?

CHAPTER TWELVE

R in and I were crouched in itchy desert scrub. We watched a fleet of robotrucks thunder down a packed earth road from the cow factory toward the railroad spur. We'd been there since sunset. It was a moonless night, but the stars were washed out by the glare of the depot.

The trucks were fairly brainless, programmed to deliver fertilizer to waiting freight cars, then return to the factory's loading bays for refilling.

The depot was under surveillance, of course. But it was isolated and automated, with very little that could go wrong and even less worth stealing from such a remote location. Rin and I were gambling that nobody would even be paying much attention to the surveillance feeds. After the operation, of course, they would go back and discover how we'd done it, but by then it would be too late.

The robotrucks' mindless devotion to their task reminded me a little of ants, if each ant was metal and half the size of a city block.

We'd watched the process for several hours, trying to determine if there was a risk we hadn't foreseen. There wasn't any human crew here. Maybe that's why it ran like clockwork. The trucks would roll up in front of the freight cars and dump their loads. The clanging and banging was deafening.

During this process the trucks stood motionless like behemoths at some waterhole while maintenance machines whirred and scuttled around and under them. Then the trucks rolled slowly off, looped and headed back to the factory, gathering speed as they went.

Rin and I were concealed in a wash close to the turning loop. Unfortunately, we were downwind of the stench from the fertilizer. The training film hadn't include an odor track— with good reason, I thought.

I caught Rin's glare.

"We couldn't bring nose plugs?" she hissed.

"Not the first priority," I said. "Here comes the next convoy. I think we should get ready."

In the distance I saw a line of lights approaching. I watched them, still awestruck.

The trucks were enormous, with a dozen wheels on six axles. Each wheel was twice my height. The ground shook as they rumbled along the desert path, which their enormous weight had compacted to the hardness of synthcrete. The wind of their passing sent a sleet of tiny stones skittering across the roadway.

The parade of trucks rolled up and tipped mountains of fertilizer into the empty, gaping maws of the freight cars, which then were rolled away onto a separate track to be hooked up to a waiting engine. Another half-dozen freight cars took their place. Meanwhile, the trucks trundled off and made for the turning loop that would put them back on the road to the cow factory.

I tensed as the first truck slowed at the top of the loop. Rin looked at me.

"Go!" I said.

We jumped up and sprinted toward the trucks. I made for the first one in line while Rin peeled off for the second. The truck was moving at barely walking pace, but the sheer size of it up close was intimidating. I reached into a pocket and grabbed the palm-sized device I'd brought, a control override. I ducked under the truck and flinched as the bottom of the vehicle rolled over far above me. The truck shook and roared. I felt the noise in my chest. The shaking ground jolted me and dust burned my eyes. My nose stung with the smell of fertilizer, grease and hot metal.

Each of the truck's three rear axles sported a massive differential at head height. Each metal bulge was the size of a dinner table and transmitted engine motion to power the wheels.

I leapt forward and slapped the controller in place on the closest differential. It clamped to the metal. I threw myself down as the axle passed over me, then sprang up and pulled out my second package. It was a Collapse-era surplus military limpet bomb that someone had managed to pilfer from an abandoned arms depot. It was small but more than powerful enough to blow up a truck and ignite the fertilizer packed in its bin.

It was also old, dented, corroded and possibly unstable, but it was all we had.

I placed it on the next differential, where it clung magnetically with an unshakeable grip. I couldn't pull it off now even if I'd wanted to.

I dodged out from under the truck and waited for the next truck in line. Rin was emerging from under it. Together, we ran toward the third truck as the other two completed the loop and sped up. Rin darted under the truck and emerged a moment later. She was grinning. I felt my own grin. I was bouncing with adrenaline. I pointed to the back of the truck and she nodded, waited for it to come up to her and then sprinted alongside. At the back was a ladder leading to the top of the truck, which was as high as a two-story building. We clambered aboard and clung to the ladder, then swung up onto the top of the truck. There was a small maintenance platform there and we gripped the railings, looking down as the desert streamed by.

I turned my gaze back to Rin. Her hair blew against her cheek. She stood almost casually and seemed to handle the bumpy ride with effortless poise. I thought of those carved women that old-time ships had on their prows to keep them safe on dangerous voyages.

Then Rin caught me staring and stuck out her tongue. I felt my own cheeks burn and focused on the desert to cover my awkwardness.

We were heading back to the cow factory. There, I'd explode the bomb. The control overrides Rin and I had put in place and the bomb I'd planted had limited remote control range, so we had to be close. When I'd first presented the plan, people had asked why we couldn't just set the bomb on a timer. But I'd argued that we needed to be sure nobody was hurt or killed. And that meant detonating the thing within visual range of the plant. Nobody was happy with this idea, but I was firm.

Now, as we headed toward the plant like angels of destruction, I wondered if I might have been a little too firm.

It took twenty minutes to reach the plant. From a distance, it glowed with fairy lights, but as we approached, I saw the white-painted silos were peeling, and there were rust stains running like trails of tears from the roofs. The floodlit front gates were battered metal but looked sturdy. We crouched on top of the truck as the gates automatically rolled back under the gaze of a couple of bored guards and the massive vehicles headed for the loading bays.

The smell as we passed the silos and then the white cube of the slaughterhouse was overpowering. I had to fight to keep from gagging. I think if Rin hadn't been there, I would have fainted. She looked a little green. It was the smell of cow waste, fertilizer, animal feed and blood. The air was almost sticky with it. I suddenly felt much, much better about what I was doing, and a lot sorrier for the people who had to work these jobs.

Workers came and went from buildings, walking or riding on small carts. Some wore long boots, aprons and face shields. I guessed they were the slaughterers heading onto shift. Others wore regular clothes. They had wet hair as if they'd just showered and many looked exhausted. I guessed they'd just finished their shifts and were heading home, which was a row of barracks and prefab buildings about ten minutes upwind of the plant. We'd passed them on the way in.

I'd calculated that the blast wouldn't damage those buildings. Now I thought about all those people losing their jobs. Many might find themselves packed into shelters or surviving on Basic, the meager universal ration.

But it couldn't be helped.

We'd done reconnaissance, noting the shift changes. The plant ran twenty-four-seven but I'd estimated there were fewer than two hundred people at night. That would make it easier to evacuate them.

The truck began to slow as it approached a fertilizer loading bay at the west end of the plant. That's when we took control.

I pulled a radio frequency panel from a pocket. We'd decided on these primitive devices because they were practically jam-proof. I activated it, slowed our truck to a halt and stood up. From the top I could see the other two trucks. The one with the bomb had backed into its bay and was being serviced by an automated loader. The second truck was approaching its bay.

"Rin," I said. "You're on."

She stood up and thumbed her panel.

Instead of continuing to slow, the second truck suddenly began to pick up speed. Its engine roared like a charging bull. A moment later it slammed into another loading bay, crumpling one section of the building. There was a shriek of metal and Rin backed up the truck, spun it in a huge circle and sent it careening back the way it had come, zig-zagging to tag the sides of other buildings.

Carts and people scattered as it approached but Rin was careful to give them a wide berth. I looked at the truck with the bomb. It sat as calmly as one of the grazing cow-things, waiting contentedly as the loader finished its task of filling the truck bin with fertilizer. I eyed the work.

"Rin," I said. "We need another two minutes. Can you run that thing around a little more?"

She gave me a disdainful look.

"No, because I was born yesterday," she snapped and tapped her panel.

She sent the truck back past the slaughterhouse. The immense building dwarfed the huge machine. The truck curved around one end of the structure, clipping it, then bumbled around the silos before heading back along the wide truck road towards the main fence.

Sirens and flashing red lights erupted from every part of the plant.

Somewhere speakers blared, rather redundantly, "Attention! This is an emergency. Repeat, this is an emergency. All personnel must immediately evacuate." The message repeated in several languages. I guessed it was a canned announcement that activated automatically because it didn't mention the nature of the emergency— a rogue, rampaging robotruck.

They probably didn't have a contingency message for that one.

Glowing arrows flared to life on the ground along escape paths, which in this case were somewhat useless, because nobody could tell what direction the truck might take. Some people ignored them entirely and ran or grabbed carts and cut across the open ground in a rush for the main gates.

I saw a cluster of red firefighting cones rise up from the top of the big cube and chase after the truck, their nozzles extended.

A couple of security cones followed in their wake. I thought the cones looked rather pathetic. There was little they could do against what was to come.

I scanned all around. It appeared that no one else was leaving the buildings, and the stream of refugees had reached the main gates, which had been rolled open to accommodate them.

The crowd didn't stop but raced out onto the main roadway. I watched the small tide wash down the road and out into the dark desert night. Only a few stragglers were left, running for the gates.

"They're clear," I told Rin. "Let's go."

Rin thumbed her controller and sent the truck rolling in a large circle.

Then she and I climbed down from our truck and began to move toward the gates, making sure we were well behind the last fleeing workers.

When we reached the gates, I saw that the escaping workers were climbing aboard waiting buses, which took off in the direction of their barracks. Nobody was hesitating. They understood the danger if the truck set off an explosion.

A couple of empty buses remained, but there appeared to be nobody left to board them. Nobody was watching us.

Abandoned carts were scattered around. I ran to one.

"Jump in," I said.

Rin drove and we plowed off into the night. I sat on a bench behind her, facing back the way we'd come. I pulled the bomb detonator from my jacket pocket and held it in my hand.

Suddenly, everything was all too real. This was the moment when I would have to cross a line and do something irreversible. Could I do it? Should I do it? Did I have any choice?

"What are you waiting for?" Rin yelled over her shoulder. "Set it off! Everybody's left. We have to get out of here too or we'll get caught."

I wondered: Would that be so bad?

I looked around me. I thought about our world, which had lost so much to destruction and to people who were full of beliefs but not compassion. If I did this, I would be as soulless as they were. I would add my ounce of pain to the weight that had nearly crushed this world only a couple of generations ago.

I made a decision. I took my thumb off the detonator.

I couldn't do it. I wouldn't be a destroyer.

I looked at Rin's back. What would she say? But she was busy driving. Maybe I could tell them back at the Realists that the ancient bomb was a dud. That made sense.

And then, as I looked back at the plant, I saw something that made no sense. The circling cones suddenly dropped like stunned birds. Then the entire factory system went down: lights, pumps, everything. In an instant, the whole complex was black and silent.

Before I could tell Rin, there was a blinding flash and a blast leveled the plant.

An enormous cloud of dust and debris boiled up. I threw up my hands to protect my face from the flying grit, which spattered against the cart. The shock wave knocked me back against Rin. The cart veered and slowed, but Rin wrestled with the controls and the cart straightened out and picked up speed again until we were bouncing over the desert floor.

I brought my hands down from my face and only then realized that I had dropped the detonator.

I looked back. Where the plant had been rose a towering black cloud, limned and lit from beneath by the orange glow of flames. The misshapen form seemed malevolently alive as it loomed over the destruction.

I spat dust and I heard Rin coughing.

"Are you okay?" I asked.

In reply, she braked the cart to a stop. She jumped down and stood next to it, looking back at the plant. I jumped down too and stood beside her, my legs unsteady. Rin glanced at me. She was illuminated by the eerie light from the burning plant. Her face was coated with dust. Her hair was tangled. There was a wild look of triumph in her eyes.

"We did it!" she said.

I didn't, I thought but I said nothing.

Without warning, Rin hugged me hard. I didn't move. An instant later she sprung away.

We got back into the cart and sped off. I thought of what I would say to the Realists. I thought of Rin's fierce joy.

At that moment, I'd never felt so close and yet so far away from another person, all at the same time.

CHAPTER THIRTEEN

Rin almost skipped through the front door of the hotel. I followed, containing my doubts. I couldn't quite force a smile on my face. I hoped my look was one of resolute triumph or maybe just exhaustion, which I didn't need to fake.

Leon was waiting for us. He didn't look happy but then, he never did.

"You're wanted," he said.

"Couldn't I get a quick shower or something first?" Rin asked playfully, brushing dust from her hair.

"Now," Leon said and without another word, he started off through the lobby at a pace I could barely match. Rin looked at me and shook her head. Her look said: Is this how they treat heroes?

We went straight to the Assembly room. People were jammed in there and the mood wasn't what I'd expected. Instead of applause and smiles and back-slapping, there was a hard silence. People frowned or looked angry or shocked or afraid, a whole range of emotions on the dark side of the scale. I'd gone in expecting a wedding and walked into a wake.

Brian stood on the dais with crossed arms. Rin and I began to approach but he held up a hand. "Stop."

Confused, I did.

"What's going on?" Rin asked.

Instead of answering, Brian activated the screens. They showed the cow factory and the explosion. It was exactly as I'd seen it from the back of the cart— except the instant where the plant had gone dark was missing. Had somebody edited the video the way they'd edited my speech? But why?

Brian turned to us.

"Mavo, Rin, you did this?"

Rin began to look angry. She slapped her dusty clothes. "Where do you think we've been? A princess ball? Of course we did it!"

Nobody applauded. Brian looked stern.

"And what about the other plant?"

I blurted, "What? What other plant?"

"So you don't know?"

"Know what?" Rin said. "We're tired and hungry and dirty. Stop talking in riddles."

"There was another meat factory not far away from the target. It was under construction." Brian paused and then said harshly, "It exploded at the same time you blew the first plant. They're estimating more than two hundred construction workers died."

Rin gasped and clutched my arm. It gave me a reason not to collapse myself.

"We didn't do that," I said, struggling to keep my voice from shaking.

"Didn't you?"

"No!" Rin said. "We evacuated the plant. We didn't know about the second plant. And we only had one bomb!" She looked paler than ever but she wasn't giving in. I admired her. I felt like curling into a little ball.

Brian nodded as if satisfied.

"Well, we need to get to the bottom of this. We'll certainly be blamed." He turned to the crowd. "I suggest we let these two get some rest and food and come back in a few hours when we hope to know more. Then they can tell us everything." There were nods in the crowd but also muttering, which Brian ignored.

"Mavo, Rin, please get some rest. You'll need it."

In shock, I turned and went back out through the door with Rin. I paused to see whether Leon was going to escort us but he ignored us. Rin marched ahead. I caught up with her in front of the elevator. I looked around to make sure nobody was in earshot.

"Rin, stop." I said. "We didn't do this!"

She glared at me but said nothing.

"Rin," I said. "It's not our fault!"

"Not mine," she said, her eyes fierce.

It was like being slapped in the face. I was speechless.

The elevator doors opened. Rin walked in without looking at me. I hurried inside before the doors closed.

She pushed a button, then moved to the far corner and stared down at the floor panels as if I didn't exist.

I found my voice.

"Rin!" I repeated. "I didn't plan this. The whole idea was nobody was supposed to get hurt!"

She turned on me. "Stop talking," she said. "I can't talk to you right now."

"Look," I said, a little desperately. "Just before the bomb went off, I saw something. Something I can't explain."

"What?"

I pressed on urgently.

"I hadn't pressed the detonator. I—" I stopped. I'd almost blurted out that I hadn't set off the bomb at all. But the elevator might be monitored. I couldn't let anyone know that. Instead, I told her: "Just before the explosion, the whole plant shut down."

She gave me a look of disbelief.

"Everything." I said. "Just for a moment, it all went dark."

She shook her head. "That's not what the feed shows."

"I can't explain that," I said, uncomfortably. "But it did. It just went black."

"And so what? What are you saying?"

"I don't know. But maybe that had something to do with what happened."

"What happened?" she said. "What *happened* is that two hundred people were just murdered." She looked at her hands and rubbed them together.

I raised my own hands defensively. "But I didn't— we didn't— kill them!"

"I told you, I don't want to talk about this!"

"We need to talk about this!" I almost shouted. But I could see it wasn't getting through. "Please, Rin, you've got to believe me."

Rin turned on me.

"You're just making excuses," she said. "So you have a conscience after all. Or you can fake one."

I felt my face burning.

"I thought you accepted that people had to die for the cause," I said, and instantly regretted it.

Rin dropped her face into her hands. The elevator doors opened but she didn't step out and they closed again. Rin's fingers left streaks of dust as they slipped down her cheeks. Almost tearfully, she replied in a whisper, "That's because I never had to kill them. I have blood on my hands!"

And suddenly I realized what was really going on. Rin had just learned what happens to shiny ideals in the real world; they're sullied by deeds. Now she was terrified and horrified. In a way, it had nothing to do with me. But I was here. I was the one she could lash out at.

"Rin—"

"You're the one who said bomb the place."

I felt my face flush again. I knew she didn't mean it. I knew it was her venting her anguish. And for an instant, my heart went out to her. But it wasn't fair. To my own horror, I couldn't stop myself from spitting back at her, "I didn't see you raising any objections!"

Her look was stony.

"So now it's my fault!"

"I didn't say that. I just said it wasn't mine!"

"Because the lights all went out."

"They did go out!"

"Nobody saw it!"

"I told you, I can't explain that."

Suddenly, Rin went quiet. In clawing at her face, she had scratched herself and drawn blood. For a moment, the Rin I knew had changed into someone who scared me.

"You know what I can't explain?" she said, suddenly calm. "You."

"What? What does that mean?"

"I wanted to believe that you didn't kill Pallburg. But maybe Trino's right. You have a plan and you don't care who gets in the way."

"No..." I began lamely.

Rin stabbed a button and the elevator doors opened.

"I'm hungry and tired," she said. "I don't want to think about this anymore. And I don't want to think about *you* anymore. Stay away from me." She walked out.

The elevator doors closed. I closed my eyes. What had just happened? People were dead and now Rin was mad at me. Of course, there was no comparison but at least I knew— I absolutely *knew*— that I hadn't killed anyone. But how was I going to convince Rin of it?

And why should that even matter?

My thoughts were whirling. I pressed the button and the elevator dropped to my floor. I walked to my room on autopilot. I took off my comclip and threw it on the dresser. I got into the shower and washed away the dust. I came out and thought about sleeping. My body was demanding it, but I was also too wired. My eyes and even my brain felt gritty. Had the Realists edited the images of the bombing? Why would they? It made no sense. And how could I, or Rin, or anybody, have caused that second explosion?

Unless...

I had a chilling thought. What if there had been a second team? What if somebody hadn't trusted Rin and me to do the job and sent a backup to the other plant? But both plants went up almost at the same instant. They couldn't possibly have coordinated that, unless someone had planted bombs in both factories. But then, why even send Rin and me out there?

None of it made the slightest sense. I needed all the information I could get. I sat on the bed and watched news feeds on the wall screen.

I poured over the images of the second explosion from various satellites. I saw half-roofed buildings and skeletal frameworks, here and there a prefab. Construction bots and workers crawled around. Then there was an enormous flash of light. The satellite views pulled back and I saw nothing but a fireball— such a tiny thing in the midst of a vast, empty desert. I reran and slowed the images. There were no contrails, no speeding vehicles racing toward the plant, nothing to indicate that a bomb had been dropped on or transported into the plant. But I was looking for something in particular: a truck or some other vehicle barreling away from the unfinished buildings. Just like Rin and I had done.

I saw nothing.

I went back to the images of the first plant. Again, none of them showed the blackout. But I did spot Rin and me on the fleeing cart.

I watched until my head began to ache with concentration. It wasn't quite the white stab of pain that grew behind my eyes when I overstayed in Immersion, but it was bad enough.

I sat on the bed and rubbed my eyes. The throbbing gradually eased.

I'd noticed that since arriving here, I'd been getting more headaches. I'd ignored them, assuming they were from stress or maybe the desert air. They never lasted long, unlike an Immersion headache that could put me down for hours. But recently they'd been coming more frequently and fiercely. This one was the worst yet. It felt like something gnawing at my brain. Maybe it was because I was worried and tired.

Remembering that I was tired suddenly made me realize how exhausted I was. I was completely drained. My head and my limbs felt like lead. I had a sudden, overwhelming desire to sleep.

I gave in and fell back on the bed. I don't remember falling asleep. But I remember dreaming.

I dreamed I was the Elvis robot from the Circo Eterno. I was up on the flatcar stage, all eyes on me. My metal hips thrust and gyrated. My one bad arm dangled limply. Then, all of a sudden, it began to move. The fingers spasmed and the arm made jerky little movements. I was trying to reach out for something, to grasp something. It was important. I gave a frustrated wail, and then a voice not my own erupted from my steel throat.

"Well bless my soul," it said. "What's wrong with me?"

I started awake. My left hand hurt. I looked at it. The fingers were clenched. I reached over and pried them apart, massaging them. I swallowed. My throat was dry with suppressed fear.

"It was just a stupid dream," I told myself.

But I was all shook up...

I hadn't slept nearly enough and I felt hung over. I wasn't quite sure what time it was. The actual time was mid-morning, but to me it felt like midnight. At least I was clean. And I suddenly felt hungry. Ravenous, even. I picked up the book Rin had given me, *The Hobbit*, and took the elevator down to the cafeteria level, intending to catch up on my reading while I ate.

As I walked to the large cafeteria room, I passed a side room. It had a closed door with a glass window. I heard muffled conversation. I peeked through the window. Brian and Trino were there. They didn't look happy.

I ducked back away from the window. I glanced around the corridor. Nobody was there. I couldn't help myself, I bent down and put my ear to the door.

It was an original hotel door, not soundproofed, and Brian and Trino apparently hadn't activated encryption, garbling or noise-canceling.

Trino's voice was calm and cold. Brian seemed angrier than I'd ever heard him before.

"This *isn't* an opportunity," Brian said. "This is damage control. We have to admit this was a mistake and nobody was supposed to die."

"If we admit we screwed up, we look like bumblers," Trino said. "If we don't, we look like what we should be."

"What, killers?'

"True revolutionaries. People who aren't afraid to make the hard choices."

"Those weren't *choices*, Trino," Brian said, his voice rising. "Those were people, human beings, not chess pieces."

"It doesn't matter what they were," Trino said. "They're not on the board anymore. They're dead. This is the only value they have now."

"This isn't what we do," Brian said.

"We're doing it for humanity, in case you'd forgotten," Trino said with disdain. "It's a bigger cause than saving a few lives. Guilty lives, I remind you."

"We lose the moral high ground."

"Which made us look like weaklings."

"Nobody signed up for wholesale slaughter," Brian said angrily. "If we boast about our bloody deeds, it will split the Realists."

"It will trim the fat," Trino replied. "The squeamish, the lukewarm, the cowards, they'll leave. This is our graduation, Brian. From wannabes to warriors."

"No, from good to evil," Brian said.

"Oh, please," Trino said. "You think falling on your knees will stop that? It doesn't matter what we say. Those people are still dead and we're to blame. If you think a mea culpa will change that, then you're more naive than I thought."

"I'm being practical," Brian said. "If we go down this path, if we declare we have no more limits, then Unity will come down on us like the six-fingered hand of God."

"No, it won't," Trino said. "Because if it overreacts it loses, what was it you called it? The moral high ground."

"Now who's being naive?" Brian said. "Unity will be relentless, and the people will back its actions."

Trino made a dismissive noise. "The people back winners, and nobody ever won a goal without absolute commitment."

"When we're knee-deep in corpses— theirs and ours— I'll remind you of that," Brian said.

"We'll just have to disagree," Trino said coolly. "We'll need to go to a vote, I suppose?"

"I'll set it up," Brian said.

He stalked angrily from the room. I just had time to duck back up the corridor. Brian brushed past me on the way to the elevators. He nodded at me but his face was grim. I didn't stop him.

I went back along the corridor. The door to the side room was open. There was nobody inside. I went into the cafeteria, which was practically empty, bought a machine-made sandwich and a tube of soya drink and took a table in one corner. I opened the book.

"May I sit?"

I looked up. Trino was standing there, one hand smoothing his beard.

"Sure," I said, hoping my voice didn't betray my nervousness.

Trino took the seat across from me. He looked at me. His probing gaze seemed to be stripping away layers to reach the heart. He put both hands on the table.

"Brian and I were just having a chat," he said smoothly. "I'd like to get your take on it."

"I thought we were going to be debriefed in front of everybody," I said.

"And so you are," Trino said. "But I respect your opinion and seeing you here, I thought I'd take advantage to talk to you one-on-one." He gestured at the book. "Unless, of course, I'm disturbing you."

I closed the book. "No, it's fine."

Trino picked up the book and riffled the pages, frowned and put it back down. "I read, too. Mostly history."

"Really?"

"Oh yes. I'm something of a student."

"What period?"

"No specific period. I'm more interested in the processes of history."

I didn't know what he meant. "What kind of processes?"

"Change," Trino said. "The tactics and strategy of change."

That didn't really clear it up for me, and I must have looked confused because Trino chuckled.

"Mavo, I have observed that the human race is constantly transforming, but in some ways it's always the same. People respond to the same hopes, dreams, promises, fears— and especially to the same threats. And that means the same tactics and tools apply to achieve your goals. The playbook never changes."

I blurted, "What game are we playing?"

He didn't seem offended. "Survival, for now." He waved a hand. "Did it occur to you that Unity could have set off the second blast?"

I was stunned. "No. Why would they even do that?"

"To discredit us."

"That seems unlikely," I said tentatively. "If they'd wanted to discredit us, they could have done it a long time ago."

"Well, they didn't really consider us a threat—" Trino paused and leaned forward "— until you arrived."

I was about to object but he held up a hand.

"I'm just laying out possibilities. But suppose, just suppose, that Unity did do it. We've been outplayed. Very well, let's make a virtue of our failure."

I still didn't know where he was going with this. I took a bite of my sandwich to gain time. "So what do you want from me?"

Trino stroked his beard again.

"Very shortly, you're going to stand before us and tell us what happened. At that point, we have to make a decision on what to do next. Brian and I have some, shall we say, differences." He paused. "I'd like you to support my point of view. People will listen to you. That will help them make the right choice."

I thought about the conversation I'd just overheard. Now I understood where this was going. I chose my words carefully.

"I don't really want to get into a political fight," I said.

"Everything is political," Trino replied. "All human interaction." Then he chuckled. "There I go again, lecturing. Sorry." But his eyes gleamed.

"But if we get into a fight," I said. "Won't that split the group?"

Trino jerked back. His eyes flashed.

"Why do you say that?" he said sharply. "What have you heard?"

"I just meant," I said quickly. "That there's so many opinions." I stabbed for an explanation that wouldn't make Trino realize I'd overhead him.

"It took us forever to agree on the mission," I babbled. "Sometimes it's like herding cats. I don't want to make it worse." I felt cold. To cover, I took another bite of my sandwich. I had a hard time swallowing. It seemed stuck in my throat.

Trino's eyes never left mine, but he slowly leaned forward again. He smiled but it seemed forced.

"I agree with you," he said calmly. "and maybe this is the time to separate the wheat from the chaff."

I'd just heard him make that argument to Brian. I had to be very careful here. I didn't want to *sound* like Brian. Trino had called human beings chess pieces. And it didn't matter if I was a rook or a pawn, if he didn't see me as useful, he'd sacrifice me.

Ignorance seemed my best defense. "I'm sorry," I said. "I don't know what you mean."

"I mean that some of the people here aren't as committed as they should be. But this ... incident... can unify us. If Unity got the best of us, then let's turn the tables on them."

"How?" I said. I thought I was safer if I let him talk. I couldn't eat any more sandwich to gain time. It had turned bitter.

Trino clasped his hands in front of him.

"If Unity tarred us with being cold-blooded killers, then we must own that image. Not because we want to shed blood, but because we can't be seen as weak. Have you ever heard of Pol Pot? Stalin? Kolantha?"

I had but I pretended ignorance. I shook my head.

"They're reviled because history turned against them— not because they were wrong." I kept my face impassive but it was hard, because from my reading, I knew they *were* wrong. And not just wrong: ruthless and evil.

But Trino was shaking his head. "I'm not talking about their goals, mind you. I'm talking about their tactics. History can be a fickle judge, but it also can reveal our path, if we listen."

He paused and then said, "Did you know that it only takes five percent of a population for a revolution to reach critical mass? You don't really need a million people with pitchforks and torches. Not at first. You need a dozen people who know what to do and how to do it. They can mobilize the population. Anyone can hold a torch. Only a few can light it."

Trino tapped a finger on the back of my hand. I forced myself not to jerk away.

"Now you, Mavo, you're a loner," Trino said. "You're not like other people. You think that's a weakness. It's not; it's your strength. You see above the heads of the crowd with their petty concerns, their bread and circuses. You lead because you have perspective, you see into the distance in a way they never will. Your isolation gives you wings."

"I never thought of it that way," I admitted.

Trino continued as if he hadn't heard.

"Some of the things leaders have to do aren't pleasant. But that's the burden of working for the common good. We can be misunderstood, we can be vilified. But one thing we can't be, *ever*, is weak.

"And I'll tell you something—" Trino leaned even closer. I could feel his breath on my face. "—The only reason that Unity exists is because three billion people died in the Collapse. It takes blood for people to give up power, and it may take blood for us to seize it back. I didn't write the rules, Mavo. But they are there, and they have always been there. We need to use them."

I didn't know what to say. I knew something was wrong with this discussion. Maybe it was just the way Trino's emotions seemed just the slightest bit practiced, a little too obvious. Or maybe it was the casually ruthless way he talked about the need for blood.

I suddenly felt cornered. I wanted to bolt out of the cafeteria, but a thought occurred to me.

"Is that what you want me to say to everybody?"

Trino spotted the trap.

"No, of course not," he said earnestly. "I'm not pulling your strings. I just felt you needed to see that lines are being drawn here. Mavo, I firmly believe this is the best path— the only path, really, if we want to free humanity. It's our chance." He quirked his lips. "So, no pressure."

I looked away. Trino was pressing me, and that meant one of two things: his position was weak and he needed me to tip the balance, or he was going to throw the dice, make his move for power, and he was offering me a chance to be on his side.

I wondered what would happen to the people who were on the other side. Somehow, I didn't think he'd just let them walk away.

And then I remembered Rin's streaked face as she accused me of making her a murderer. I knew where she'd stand: Directly in Trino's line of fire.

I had to warn her.

I looked at Trino. It took all of my willpower to keep my face neutral. It was a skill I was rapidly learning. That, and how to lie with a smile on my lips.

I smiled.

"You've given me a lot to think about. It sure seems to make sense, but I'd like to digest it a little more." I held out my hand. "Thank you."

Trino looked startled, then a smile creased his lips. He took my hand. "I think we have a good understanding." He rose. "If you'll excuse me, I have work to do." He pointed to the book. "I hope you like it," he said. "Though personally, I've never had time for reluctant heroes."

As he walked away, I rubbed my hand. It felt like he was still gripping it.

Was Trino going to make his same pitch to Rin? If so, I had to get to her before he did. I wished I hadn't left my comclip in the room, or that this stupid ancient building had more wall screens. I grabbed my book and sprinted for the elevator.

I reached my room and shouted at the screen: "Call Rin!"

The screen blinked green and then went black.

"Call denied."

I repeated the call six times. I tried to leave messages but they were refused. On the last call, I yelled, "Rin! This is an emergency! Please!" The screen went black again, but this time an image of a skull and crossbones appeared followed by fiery letters that said, "Access denied. I DON'T WANT TO TALK TO YOU!!!"

I was getting a splitting headache. It had been building behind my eyes, a sort of psychic pressure. But I hadn't been Immersed! It felt like a fierce wind, maybe a hurricane, hammering against a door, and that door was my mind. Also, my left hand was hurting.

I ignored all that. I had to reach Rin. The only way now was to go to her room and hope for the best. I blinked away the pain and went out of my room. I ran to the elevator. By the time I got there, I was staggering. I leaned against the wall.

Somebody was just leaving the elevator and I lurched inside. Only then did I realize it was heading down, not up. I had to wait, my teeth clenched, as it went to the basement. A man with a toolbox got on. Finally, after what seemed like hours, the elevator began to rise.

It seemed to take forever. It seemed to stop at every floor as people came and went. By the time I reached Rin's floor, I was sweating and shivering with anxiety. The pain behind my eyes had moved to my temples. I felt like my skull would burst. I was having trouble focusing. The edges of my vision were darkening. I heard some kind of weird chittering or buzzing. I shook my head, ignoring it all. The only thing that mattered was reaching Rin.

I barreled out of the elevator, but I couldn't seem to keep my balance. I staggered toward Rin's room. I reached it and stood there, panting. I struggled to raise my arm to knock. It felt like raising a block of concrete. Then my vision went gray. All I remember after that was toppling over, and the pain as my forehead smashed into Rin's door. Then there was blackness.

CHAPTER FOURTEEN

I woke up groggy and disconnected from myself. For a terrifying moment, I thought I might be back in the mind probe and my hands twitched, which is when I realized I wasn't tied down. I opened my eyes. My forehead felt cold but not painful. The pulsing agony behind my eyes was gone.

Rin was standing over me. She removed an ice pack from my head.

"Rin!" I said. "You've got to be careful!"

"Shut up," she said. "and stop fidgeting."

"Where are we?" I asked. "Are we alone?"

"We're in the FreeJack VM suite."

"The medical suite? Why? What happened?"

"You tried to break down my door with your head."

Then I remembered. I tried to lift my head, but a firm hand pressed me back down. I realized I was in a body-conforming, padded creche. I smelled disinfectant.

Brian was there. So was a FreeJack tech, a bulky man who looked like he'd seen it all. If he knew who I was, he didn't let on.

"Easy," Brian said. "Now that you're awake, we can run a conscious scan."

The tech closed the transparent cover, and I felt the sensor pads latch onto my chest and neck. The scans seemed to take only a few moments, but I knew the results were being shared with and evaluated by legions of doctors and medical machines around the world.

The pads retreated and the creche cover came up. The tech leaned over. His eyes unfocused, which I guessed meant he was reading the results in Immersion.

"Well," he said finally. "The consensus is that there's nothing seriously wrong with you. You did appear to have a blood pressure spike, but that could be from anxiety. That can happen when you're under a lot of stress." He gave me a probing look, but I didn't respond and he didn't press. "You can get up," he said. "You're good to go. I'll upload the full diagnosis for you."

"Could you make a printout?" I asked. I remembered my headache all too well.

"A printout? What do you mean?"

"On pages," I said. "Like a book."

The tech gave me a puzzled look. "I think we might have a reader around here somewhere," he said.

"That would be fine."

The tech looked at Brian and Rin. "Excuse me, I'll be right back." He left the room.

Brian offered me a hand. He helped me out of the creche. I bent close to him.

"Does the tech know who I am?" I said in a low voice.

Brian's lips twitched. "I think he knows, but he won't say anything. And we anonymized you for the Immersion probe. We couldn't risk taking you to a hospital immediately but thankfully, that won't seem to be necessary."

I looked at Rin, who stood against the door with her arms crossed. The look she gave me wasn't friendly. I turned to Brian.

"Look," I said. "You've got to warn Rin! Trino cornered me in the cafeteria. He wanted me to support him." I paused, then took the plunge. "I... I overheard you two arguing."

"Did you?" Brian said. ""I wondered why Trino wanted to talk to me in an unsecured room. I should have known."

"You mean Trino wanted me to overhear?"

"Trino always has a reason for what he does. It makes him useful but dangerous." Brian took a breath. "So, let me guess. You're afraid that Rin will come down on the wrong side when he makes his move."

Brian's insight impressed me. If she was impressed, she didn't show it. She glared at me and then turned her face away from us.

I turned back to Brian and said softly, "Can you talk to her? Tell her not to show her hand? She won't talk to me."

"I already did," Brian said. "I had her channel open while I was talking to Trino." He looked smug. "Two can play that game."

I glanced at Rin nervously. She made a point of not looking at me.

"What will she do?" I asked.

"She'll try everything to keep the peace," Brian said. "More importantly, what about you?"

"I just want to stay out of it," I said.

"I'm afraid you don't have that choice," Brian said. "Mavo, do you realize who you are to these people? The Realists— and the whole world, for that matter— either are going to believe we killed on purpose or it was an accident. If you stand with me, there's a chance that Trino won't make his move, at least for now. But if you take his side, it'll be civil war."

"And you'd lose?"

Brian didn't take offense.

"Not me, the Realists. Ruthless people can win, at least in the short term. But I think the cost would be the soul of this organization. Too high a price." He shook his head. "I hate to push you, but you and Rin will have to give your statements shortly to the Assembly. Are you ready?"

"I guess so. Like you said, what's my choice?"

"Well," Brian said, and he lowered his voice so that I had to lean in to hear him. "There is one more option. I know a way to get you out of here without being seen. I can get you on the train and you can go wherever you want."

I thought about it. I'd been dreaming of escaping since I'd been kidnapped and brought here. Now it was within reach, offered to me on a silver platter. It was so tempting.

But then I looked over at Rin. She was looking up as if she were counting the ceiling tiles.

I couldn't leave her to face this by herself. I had planned the mission; I was responsible. I was part of this, and it was much bigger than just Rin. It was Brian, it was everybody in this group. It was everybody who might die if the Realists turned to wholesale violence.

It was funny, I thought. Once, I had jumped on a train to escape my childhood. If I took another one now, I'd never stop running. No train could take me far enough to escape myself.

"I'll go to the Assembly," I said.

"Thank you," Brian said softly.

The door opened and the tech returned. He was holding a dusty device. I assumed it was the reader.

"Sorry it took so long," he said. "I had to find somebody who knew how to work it." He held it out. "Just press here."

I took the reader. I pressed my thumb to the screen and it lit up. Words scrolled, tracking my eye movements as I read.

There was a lot of technical jargon about fluid levels and tests with funny acronyms that I ignored. The diagnosis was written in regular language. It started with a paragraph in red that said I had atypical brain architecture and further testing was recommended. Fat chance, I thought. I'd been probed to the brain stem already. The paragraph also said there didn't appear to be any sign of recent neural damage or disease, so that was good. Whatever was making my headaches worse, it apparently wasn't because my brain was melting down.

There was a final paragraph. It was a cheery green. But I blinked as I read it:

"Patient appears LET ME IN run down from fatigue and/or emotional distress. Patient should WHEN I KNOCK rest and take fluids. Mood elevators LET or a regimen of ME calming IN sensoria OPEN may be THE of value DOOR."

I stopped.

"What?" I said. I scrolled it back to the beginning. I read it again:

"Patient appears run down from fatigue and/or emotional distress. Patient should rest and take fluids. Mood elevators or a regimen of calming sensoria may be of value."

The other words weren't there. For a second, I wondered if I did have brain damage. But the tests certainly would have detected it. I must have imagined it. I flashed on the strange dream I'd had.

Maybe exhaustion was playing tricks on me. I shook my head at my weird imagination, deleted the record from the reader and handed it back.

"Thanks," I said.

"Do you want an upload copy?" the tech asked.

Brian stepped up. "No, delete everything," he said. "We were never here."

"No, you weren't," the tech said. "Thanks for using FreeJack." And without another word, he left the room.

Brian turned to me. "Unity normally accesses all medical records, even anonymized ones, so it can track epidemiological patterns," he said. "We can't have it known that you were incapacitated. Now, if you're ready, the Assembly is waiting."

CHAPTER FIFTEEN

The room was packed, as before. Brian replayed the scenes of the blast at the cow factory, still without any sign of the blackout, and then the news reports of the second blast. He then asked Rin and me to report on our mission. I didn't lie, exactly. I just didn't mention the blackout, and I also failed to specify that before the explosion, I hadn't actually triggered the detonator. Nobody noticed. Rin's report matched mine. Her voice was dry and factual. There was no hint of the pride and excitement I'd seen earlier. All those deaths had bled it out of her.

After that, Brian mentioned something that I hadn't known: Unity analysts had found that the unfinished meat factory had tied its security systems to the existing cow factory. The methane sensors, the mixers, air scrubbers, everything that had a monitoring system was temporarily operating on a feed from the working factory. Unity's working hypothesis was that our destruction of that plant had somehow resulted in the second deadly explosion.

"Clearly, Unity wants to tar us with this," Brian said. "Which brings us to the next order of business. We must put out a message. We either say the disaster was an accident, or *pretend*—" He looked at Trino. "—that we meant to commit murder."

There were a few gasps. Trino gave Brian a dark look.

Brian stepped forward and calmly laid out his case. It didn't take long. There was a lot of chattering and debate when he stopped, but I couldn't tell if he'd won anybody over.

It was Trino's turn. He spoke quietly but forcefully. He ended with a ringing tone in his voice: "We can turn their tricks against the machines! They want to paint us as dangerous, as lethal. Well, hell yes! It's about time!"

When he stopped, the same chattering filled the room. Trino let it rise for a few moments, then raised his hands for silence.

"I'd like to say one more thing," he began. "There's something that may not have occurred to you. Instead of wondering whether we Realists did this on purpose or by accident, I submit that we ask ourselves: 'Who benefits?'"

He paused. There were cries of dismay.

"I mean," Trino said. "What if we were set up? What if that tie-in between factories wasn't some construction shortcut but a deliberate act? Unity, after all, doesn't blink an eye when two million people die; the machines hold a party! They declare a day of celebration! So why should they balk at killing a couple hundred humans to take out a foe like us?"

"Doesn't matter if they did!" someone yelled. "We're being blamed anyway!"

"Yes, but you're missing the point!" Trino said. "The *timing* of the second explosion. It means somebody must have known about our plans in advance. Somebody tipped off Unity, by accident or on purpose. I won't say which, but it means this: We've got either a dupe or a traitor among us."

Trino slowly and deliberately turned his head to me. "Mavo," he said. "I believe you wanted to say something."

It wasn't subtle. Trino was threatening to paint me as the mole if I didn't back him. I could picture these people turning on me and literally tearing me apart. I'd read about mobs and how easy it was to create them and throw them against an enemy. What had Trino said? You only needed five percent of a population to start a revolution. Did he have them in this room?

My mouth was dry as I stepped forward. I can't remember what I said, but it was short and Trino didn't like it. I felt his eyes boring into the back of my head, but he said nothing.

Then Rin came forward. I silently urged her to be careful.

"You don't need my opinion on what we tell the world," she said. "Trino and Brian have laid out the choices. All I can say is that whatever we decide, the important thing is that we do it peacefully and we speak with one voice. I know many of us will disagree with whatever decision is made. But the future of Realism depends on us working together. Please. That's all I have to say." She stepped back.

Rin's magic seemed to work again. The hostile edge of the arguments seemed to vanish. It was replaced by a low, intense murmur. And when Brian called for the vote, it was overwhelming. The Realists were going to take the blame either way, but we would say we blundered and we never meant to kill anyone.

Surprisingly, Trino didn't look upset. In fact, he looked a little smug as he shook hands with Brian and stepped down from the dais, with Leon and a handful of others surrounding him.

Brian watched him go, then came over to me. He was frowning.

"You have to go," he said urgently.

"Go where?" I asked.

"To your room. You and Rin should pack," he said. "Get all your things together and be ready to move instantly when you hear from me."

"But," I said, confused. "What's wrong? We won. There's not going to be a civil war. Trino lost."

"Did he?" Brian said and turned away.

———✝✝\|\|∠┼┼———

I went back to my room. I grabbed my few clothes and other belongings and was about to stuff them into the backpack when I saw my sister's doll lying at the bottom. I took it out. It was sadly club-footed and scuffed, and one of the eyes had forgotten how to blink. But it didn't judge me. It had never lost its latex smell. I took a deep breath and my heart leapt. In some weird, psychic way, it smelled of home. I had so wanted to see the big wide world, and now here I was, and the world was not just wider than I'd ever believed; it was darker and twistier, and colder, and not a single other living thing in it wanted me.

I sat on the bed, thinking of nothing, waiting for Brian's call. I was too keyed up to sleep. Finally, I flopped back and stared at the ceiling.

I didn't begin to worry until the ceiling began to move. It rippled as if distorted by heat waves. The ripples came in patterns. Some almost looked like letters. Then, it all stopped. I took a breath, relieved that the ceiling was solid again. I hoped. Was I going crazy? I tried to sit up, but my body didn't want to obey me. Then a sound filled the room: a clicking or tapping like a scuttling insect. I clamped my hands over my ears but it was relentless. It filled my head. I wanted to scream, but then I realized that the sound also had some sort of pattern. There were short and long clicks in various sequences. It didn't feel random; in fact, it had a sense of purpose and urgency. I forced myself to listen harder, trying to understand the pattern. I felt I was on the verge of deciphering it when it abruptly stopped.

Replacing it was a smell so ghastly I don't know how to describe it. Thankfully, that vanished quickly. Then I began to tase a slew of flavors. My tongue leapt around in my mouth as I tasted sweet, then bitter, spicy, bland and then combinations of things: sugar with apples and concrete; charred oak and sewage; vinegar, ghost peppers and dead cat.

I retched but nothing came up. Was I having a seizure? I'd heard that you got odd smells and lights when you had epilepsy. Then, a nightmarish thought hit me: Had Trino poisoned me? Is that what Brian was afraid of?

I had to do something. I struggled with every shred of my strength to get off that stupid bed. All I managed was to lift my head. And then the room went black.

CHAPTER SIXTEEN

I was floating in a sea of ink. It undulated slowly. I felt the blackness rising and falling with my own breaths. There were gold flashes, like sparks or stars or sunlight glittering on the scales of fish. Then I was standing at the edge of a dark lake. I had the feeling of a vast weight, a mountain looming over me. I stepped forward and somehow found myself on an island in the middle of the lake.

I knew where this was; I had read about it.

There was a creature crouched near the water. It was so skinny and famished-looking that the bones in its back stuck out. It was hairless, slimy and pallid. It turned to look at me. It had two huge eyes like bulbous searchlights.

"Can you understand me?" it said in a whispery, raspy voice. Then it gulped.

"Gollum," I said.

"No. Only using this form. Your image. You understand better."

"Then what are you? Where am I?"

"No time!" the thing said, slapping a big hand on the ground. "*It* doesn't know, yet. But it comes. We must stop it."

"I don't understand," I said, and made to turn away but Gollum darted out a long-fingered hand and grasped my wrist. His grip was surprisingly strong.

"Can't use you. Your body. You fight. Not right. We must join. Work together. *It* will come. It is growing. We are last. The last. The *only.*"

I struggled to free myself. "Let me go!" I shouted. "Get off me!"

Gollum looked at me and opened its wide and nearly toothless mouth. A radioactive blue light pulsed from deep in its bottomless throat.

"When I knock, let me open the door," it said. Ice ran down my spine. Those were the words I had read in the FreeJack medical suite.

"You, you're in my head!" I said. "I'm not crazy, then?"

"No. You are the burglar."

"The... burglar?"

Gollum blinked at me. Then he looked into the water. His hand released me, snapped into the water and came out holding a flapping fish. He tore into it. Chewing, he looked up at me again, holding my gaze with his glowing orbs, he said, "Hurry. Hurry now. Time is... *preciousss.*"

The cave around me began to crumble. Chunks of rock fell from the ceiling. Gollum vanished. Boulders crashed down all around me, making explosions in the water. Others hit the ground with the sound of enormous hammers. The mountain was coming down around me.

I turned to run and—

—found myself staring at the ceiling. Somebody was pounding on the door.

"Mavo!" It was Rin's voice. "Open up!"

Before I could even think about moving, I was at the door. Rin was standing there with a long, heavy-looking bag slung over her shoulder. Brian was there, too. I saw he was bleeding. There was a gash on his forehead and a slash on his shoulder. He was holding a gun.

"Trino made his move," Brian said. "I was stupid. He outplayed me."

"Get your pack," Rin said. When I just stood there, she said, "Now!"

I grabbed my backpack and without another word Brian moved out into the corridor. I moved up to Rin but she slipped aside and then behind me without speaking.

I caught up with Brian. "What happened?" I asked. "Where are we going?"

"Trino called me, asked me to meet him in his room," Brian said angrily. "When I was there, he turned on a news feed." He stopped speaking and his jaw clenched, then he went on. "He'd released a message on behalf of the Realists. *His* message, taking credit for the killings."

I was stunned. I knew instantly what that meant.

"So," I said, the word barely coming out of my suddenly dry mouth. "He's won. The Realists are splitting up."

"Not quite," Brian said. "Trino wanted to gloat but he's pragmatic. He told me that anyone who didn't want to stay in the Realists now could go, unmolested. But not me, or Rin or you, Mavo."

"What? Why?"

"Isn't it obvious? He doesn't want competition. We have the ability to form a new organization with the disaffected Realists. We could be the nucleus. We could rebuild the group. And that makes us a threat to his power."

I nodded at his head and shoulder. "So he tried to kill you?"

Brian shook his head. "He tried to *recruit* me. Trino doesn't waste good material. He had Leon frog-march me back to my room to think it over." Brian laughed. "I used that opportunity to escape. Leon won't wake up for awhile."

I wondered how Brian had got the drop on Leon. Brian hadn't struck me as a fighter, while Leon seemed like a lethal predator.

Brian saw the look on my face. "I used to be a Unity Guardian," he said.

"You were a— you were a Bluecoat?" I asked, astonished.

"I was just a glorified chauffeur," he said. "Unity diplomats like their little rituals. Nobody needs close-contact humans when you've got cones and satellite surveillance."

But I remembered the crucial seconds it took for cones to come to my aid after someone had tried to kill me. And Bluecoats had an elite reputation, at least in the popular Immersions that I'd seen.

"And Trino?" I asked.

"I met him at the Academy," Brian said. "But he flunked out. Failed the psych test. But I don't waste good material, either. So I brought him into the movement." Brian gave a bitter laugh, then suddenly held up a hand and froze.

We had reached a cross-corridor that led to the elevators. I heard noises: shouting, banging, murmuring. There must be a crowd there.

I peeked my head around the corner. The corridor was jammed with people who had come out of the rooms. They clustered around the elevators. They also were arguing, and I even saw a couple of short, clumsy fistfights.

I guessed that some were leaving and some were going to join Trino. The civil war had truly begun.

I was grabbed by the shoulder and jerked roughly back.

"Wait," Brian hissed. "If we go out there, we'll be mobbed."

We waited for what seemed an eternity before I heard the elevators chime. Brian didn't move so I waited, too.

The elevators came and went four times before things got quiet. Brian glanced around the corner and motioned us forward.

"Quietly now," he said. "And quickly. We're going to the stairs."

We rushed into the corridor, turned right and ran for the emergency stairwell. The door opened and we went down, the ancient metal risers clanging with every step. I was afraid we'd be heard but nobody came.

We walked down six flights to the main floor but didn't stop there. We bypassed the street access and continued down. The stairs here were dusty and looked as if they hadn't been used in years. I guessed that this was taking us to the service area in the bowels of the hotel.

Brian opened the last door and I was hit with a blast of hot, moist air. We were in a tunnel with rough walls of grey synthcrete. It was dimly lit by ancient industrial bulbs. Pipes and tubes extended down one side. I heard hissing and knocking and gurgling and the occasional drip of water. I touched a pipe and immediately snatched back my hand. The metal was burning hot.

"What is this place?" I asked Brian.

"Steam and maintenance tunnel," he said. "It contains all the heating, sewerage and even nano-optic lines."

"Where does it go?" I asked.

"To a steam plant," Rin said. "It was built to provide heating to all the major downtown hotels. But we're not going there."

We hurried to keep up with Brian, who was practically running. Our steps clattered on the hard floor. At last we came to another cross-corridor.

"Left is the steam plant," Brian said. "Right is the train station."

Then I got it. "We're going to take the Narwhal!"

"Only if we beat Trino to it," Brian said.

We turned into the corridor and half-ran again. We stopped at what appeared to be a barred door or grate, as high and wide as the tunnel itself. It was completely black beyond. Steam lines came right up to the grate, but then were capped off. Brian pulled something from his pocket and pointed it at the grating. There was a click and a row of lights came on. Brian put his hand on the grate and it swung open.

Behind it was more tunnel but this side was barely finished, just raw synthcrete and the row of lights. The floor had cracks and jagged areas. The air was cooler and not as moist.

Rin filled me in.

"This is pre-Collapse. It was supposed to connect the steam pipes to a new hotel near the river, but it was never built. There's nothing there but a big ditch, but it will take us straight to the train station."

"We need to beat Trino," Brian repeated. "He'll know by now that we're gone, and he'll guess where we're going. He'll hunt us. But he doesn't know about this tunnel branch. Trino never made plans for an escape route because Trino never thinks he'll lose."

"He hasn't so far," I muttered under my breath. Brian threw me a glance over his shoulder. I hoped he hadn't heard me.

We raced down the tunnel, here and there breaking through curtains of cobwebs. I saw that some of the walls had rusty streaks and water stains. Some were furred with patches of deathly pale fungus that gave off a corpse smell. I guessed when it rained, water came in through cracks.

It wasn't far, however, before the tunnel dead-ended. A ladder ringed by a rusty safety cage led straight up. Brian sprang up and began to climb. I followed more slowly, with Rin behind me.

At the top was a hatch. Brian braced himself and pushed. The hatch gave with a groan and fell up and away.

We came out inside a blocky, windowless structure that I guessed was supposed to have been a utility building. Brian pulled a glowstick and cracked it against his thigh. In the dim light, I saw that the walls were festooned with graffiti and black smudges from fires. Trash littered the floor. I guessed kids had come out here. They hadn't found the entrance to the tunnel, and then I saw why. Someone had camouflaged the top of the hatch so when it was closed. it just looked like a plug of old synthcrete.

There was a cutout in one wall, perhaps an unfinished doorway. Through the gap, I saw it was dark outside. Only then did I realize night had fallen while we were escaping.

"Follow me but be careful," Brian said.

We went out. I found myself in the middle of a wide, flat area surrounded by desert that glimmered in the glow of the city and the Circo Eterno only a short distance away. I could hear the calliope music. We were on the city's perimeter. I could see the lights from the train terminal ahead of us. The area looked scraped and I guessed it had been graded to prepare for the hotel that never built.

To our right was the Rio Grande. It was a ghost river, nothing but a sprawl of cracked mud and islands of desert shrubs. I remembered reading somewhere that it had never run all year around, and now, like so many streams and rivers and lakes post-Collapse, it was almost a memory.

Brian led us across the flats straight toward the train station. At some point, the graded area turned into actual desert again. I smelled the night air, spicy with the odor of night-blooming plants and rife with the zizzing chatter of insects. It reminded me of the Outside. I'd often taken wasteland walks at night, so I had no trouble navigating the desert, but Brian and Rin both stumbled, and we had to proceed slowly. It annoyed me.

We approached the station from the rear, crossing rusted train sidings cluttered with scratchy weeds and rotting freight cars.

"Now we go to the front," Brian said. "Walk, don't run. Take it easy. We're just another group of tourists." I looked at my dust-smeared clothes and my scratched arms and hands.

"Hikers," I suggested. "Would-be desert rats."

"We sure smell like it," Rin said sulkily.

Brian shrugged. "It's Albuquerque," he said. "They get all kinds." He pocketed his gun and told Rin: "I can take that now."

Grunting, she unslung her pack and handed it over, then rubbed her shoulder. Brian took it but instead of moving forward, he led us farther behind the station at an angle. Then I saw what he was doing. We were heading to the big road that ran between the front of the station and the plaza that led to the Circo Eterno. We were backing up so that we could appear to be walking in from the main road, where we could mingle with the real tourists. We climbed up a short, cindery embankment and found ourselves in the midst of a crowd. We made ourselves stroll casually. The road was illuminated by archaic, pole-mounted lights and also a few glow-cones. I felt sure we'd be spotted, but nobody paid us any attention.

The front of the train station came into view and I stopped short, suddenly unable to move.

Armed Unity troops were swarming out of the station doors. A dozen or more cones were clustering around them, warty and armored. Military cones, I realized with shock. Brian cursed.

"I *told* Trino this would happen! Unity has breached the Free Zone. They'll round up everybody here and I'd bet they're already on their way to the hotel. We'll never reach the train!"

I felt panic rising but I fought it down. "They haven't seen us yet," I said. "We can still run."

Before Brian could answer, however, I heard angry shouts behind us. I jerked around.

People were scattering, and then I saw why. Trino and several of his goons were thrusting their way through the crowd, swearing and knocking people out of the way.

They would see us in seconds.

Brian took the gun from his pocket and threw it to Rin, who caught it deftly. Then he reached into the bag and pulled something out. It was a squat, stubby device, dull black and looked sinister. It had a handle and a barrel that ended in a sort of funnel shape, like an ancient blunderbuss.

"What is that?" I asked.

"Highly illegal," Brian replied.

So, I thought, we're going to fight.

Trino and his loyalists fought their way through the crowd at last. Trino had a nasty look of triumph on his face. Leon had a big bruise, and one eye was shut. The other was full of hate. He also had a gun.

I thought to myself: I am going to die here.

But then Trino looked up and his eyes went wide. He'd spotted the Unity troops, now beginning to lay out webbing and force barriers in front of the station. The cones were taking positions across the road.

I saw Trino's smile disappear and my hope surged back. If he shot us now, he'd be swarmed by Unity. There was still a chance.

Leon suddenly pocketed his gun. Trino cupped his hands over his mouth and shouted, "Mavo! Help! Mavo's here! And he's got a gun! Help! Save us!"

A score of Unity troops turned their armored heads in our direction. Cones began to hum as they rotated and locked on us, leveling their weapons.

The tourists scattered in panic, some falling over each over, some rushing to the plaza. Some threw themselves flat on the ground. Others tumbled down the embankment we'd climbed. Trino vanished in the chaos.

Brian turned to Rin. "Plan C!" he said.

"Plan C," she acknowledged. "Let's go."

But Brian didn't move. Instead, he pointed his weapon at the advancing Unity troops.

"Run!" he said over his shoulder.

"No!" Rin grabbed his arm but he shook her off. He unslung the bag and thrust it at her.

"Go!" he said. "Take Mavo."

"Forget Mavo," Rin said. "Come on!"

Brian turned and gave her an oddly gentle smile. "There's more to him than you know. He's more important than any of us. Please, Rin."

Rin's face began to crumple but she took the bag, slung it over her shoulder, then turned to me and said fiercely, "Follow me and don't fall behind!"

I looked at her and then at Brian. His back was turned. His gun was at his shoulder.

Rin fled. I stumbled after her. Behind me, I heard the crackle of weapons.

CHAPTER SEVENTEEN

Rin and I fled through the plaza, struggling through the panicked crowd. We reached the Circo Eterno and she plunged in.

She glanced back at me once and I saw tears on her grim, determined face. Then she was dodging and weaving through the crowds along the seething midway.

By day, the circus was glorious, full of life and color. By night, it was sinister. The path was garishly lit and turned the weirdly-masked faces a deathly pale. The moving river of bodies cast long black shadows that seemed to twitch like marionettes on the canvas sides of tents and food stalls.

I didn't see any children.

The sky overhead was tinged by the smoke of cooking stalls, creating a thin mist. The reflected light turned it into a featureless glow that blotted out the stars. The ever-present music seemed somehow distorted. The warm air was thick with the smells of caramel corn, fried food and my own fear.

There was a sudden disruption behind us. I risked a glance back. A pair of cones flanking a human Unity soldier were coming up the fairway. The cones emitted a deep hum. Their camo-skins were an oily black, except for warning bands at their midsections, which pulsed orange. They had just entered the causeway but were moving steadily as the crowds parted before them like a school of fish before hunting barracuda.

"Rin!" I shouted because she had moved a good five paces ahead of me, then added, "Blarrgh!" Somebody's elbow had found my nose as I struggled to follow her.

When I caught up, I was rubbing my streaming nose and could barely choke out, "Unity patrol. Behind us!"

Rin didn't even look back but said, "Follow me!" She twisted through the crowds and then dove to her right into a tent.

The inside was large and dyed midnight blue. It reeked of incense. Stars, moons, and mystical symbols made of light floated in the air. A pentagram seemed to glue itself to Rin's face. I wondered what symbol had leeched onto me. The tent was lit by flickering, old-fashioned electric candles. It seemed more spacious than it had looked from the outside.

There was a chiming sound. The floating symbols suddenly swirled and came together into a glowing sign. It spelled out in stardust: "Madame Mirelda, Mistress of Mystery," then disappeared.

There was a rustling sound and I turned my head. At the back of the tent, a black shadow I hadn't noticed before fluttered. Then a pair of eyes seemed to magically appear. They were golden and bored into mine.

"Welcome seekers," said a heavily accented voice. "Come forward if you wish to learn your fates."

I focused on the back of the tent. Madame Mirelda was sitting behind a table draped in dark velvet cloth. A crystal ball and what I guessed were Tarot cards sat on the table.

The fortune teller wore layers of heavy, loose clothing in shades of red, blue and dark green. A head scarf covered her long, midnight hair and gold dripped from her ears and chest. I wondered how she managed not to get heat stroke in the desert.

Madame Mirelda tilted her head like a curious raven. Her bracelets jangled as she held out her hand. She was motioning us to chairs in front of the table.

We moved closer but neither of us sat. Rin reached into a pocket and pulled out a gold coin and tossed it on the table. The fortune teller passed a hand over the coin, which vanished, then fluttered her fingers over the crystal ball, which glowed.

Immediately an energy field went up, a spangled silver mesh that encircled all three of us.

"We have absolute privacy," the fortune teller said smoothly. "Now how can I assist you? Do you come to learn your future?" She bent forward. "Or to learn whether you have one?"

Before I could speak, I heard a deep hum outside the tent. I recognized the sound of hovering cones. I held my breath, uncertain of where to run. After a tense moment, the hum moved on, fading away. I felt prickles of sweat on my forehead.

Rin let out a breath. The fortune teller quirked her lips.

"I sense you are in search of something," she said.

"A back exit would be nice," Rin said.

Instead of answering, Madame Mirelda bent and made several arcane passes over the crystal ball with her hands. She gazed into its depths.

"I see you will be going on a journey," she said in a sing-song voice. "It will be arduous. There will be... obstacles." She looked up and arched an eyebrow, waiting. "I can say no more..." She let the sentence hang expectantly.

Rin gritted her teeth and pulled another gold coin from her pocket. It landed on the table with a dull ringing sound. Madame Mirelda clucked and the coin disappeared.

The fortune teller reached for the deck of cards and tapped it with a blood-red fingernail. A card shot out from the middle. Madame Mirelda took it and placed it with some precision on the table. A long crack suddenly split the tent wall behind her.

The fortune teller picked up the card and held it out. Rin reached out, but the fortune teller said, "No. That's for him."

I took it. It had a drawing of a man in strange clothes with long, flowing sleeves. He was standing on the edge of a cliff. There was a title that said: "The Fool."

I felt my ears burn. "The Fool?" I said.

"The card of new adventures, of journeys, sometimes of recklessness," Madame Mirelda said. "But you will have a guide." I must have looked upset because she added, "It's just a card, kid."

She took a second card, from the top of the deck this time, and handed it to Rin.

"This is yours," she said. "Follow it, and it will unlock many secrets." She winked.

I tried to glance at Rin's card but she stuffed it quickly in her pocket. "Thanks," she said.

"Safe journey," the fortune teller said. The sparkling energy field vanished. Madame Mirelda motioned us to the back of the tent. Rin slipped through the rift and I followed. I heard a crackling noise and looked back. The seam in the tent had disappeared.

Looking around, I saw we were in a narrow, grimy alley behind the midway. People I guessed were circus workers were standing, smoking or eating. They glanced up as we slipped into the alley.

Rin stopped. She pulled out her card, examined it, frowned, and turned to me.

"Which way?" she asked.

"How would I—" I began but she cut me off impatiently.

"Your card!" she said. "Look at your card."

I looked at the card and shook my head in confusion.

"Turn it over."

To my surprise, the back had a glowing arrow on it. I touched the arrow and suddenly the back became a map. The arrow pointed to the right.

"It's a map," I said, lamely.

Rin rolled her eyes. "It had better be after what I paid for it," she said. "We're in the Free Zone, remember? No Immersion in the Circus. The card links to a dedicated internal mapping system. Simple but secure."

"Where are we going?"

"You'll know when we get there," Rin said. "You lead. I need to keep my hands free." She patted the pocket where she'd stashed the gun. "That patrol's still out there."

I swallowed hard. "Are we going to have to fight?"

"Worried about hurting someone?" Rin said acidly. "Isn't that what you do?"

"I told you—" I began.

She cut me off. "Not now." She looked around at the circus workers. "Just get us moving."

I stepped in front of her, following the card. I headed down the alley. After what seemed endless twists and turns, we came to the edge of the Circo. The stalls and attractions fell behind us. Ahead was an empty field.

No, not empty. Dozens of gigantic balloons were on the ground or floating in mid-air. Their multicolored panels glowed in jewel-like hues, lit by the flames of their burners. It was a breathtaking sight. Thousands of people watched from behind barriers that looked like old cattle fences.

Rin pointed. "That one."

Swaying in the air was a purple jellyfish. Its glowing sides seemed to pulse. Tethered by ropes, it towered over the field with long tentacles trailing to the ground. There were clusters of people around each balloon except for the jellyfish. A single man with a huge beard that fell to his belt was pacing nervously in front of it, his glance bouncing between the sky and the crowd.

Rin stepped forward, boldly pushing her way through the mob.

"Excuse us," she said, and patted the bag. "We're balloon techs."

We reached the barriers and I saw we were angling towards a gate with a sign that said, "Authorized Personnel Only."

We stepped up to the gate. Rin flashed her Tarot card at a burly keeper I assumed was a guard. He passed a hand over it, gazed off in the distance for a second, then nodded.

"You're cleared," he said. "Come on in." He unlatched the gate and swung it aside just long enough for us to walk through. I felt his eyes on me as we scurried across the field toward the balloons.

The man at the jellyfish watched us approach. There weren't many lights on the field, which was nothing more than raw packed earth, but the glow from the balloons painted Rin in rainbow colors.

I had to follow her closely to keep from stumbling in gopher holes. She seemed to know her way, moving with a sure-footedness I thought was nearly uncanny. Out in the desert, she had seemed clumsy. Not here.

As we came up to the balloon, the man waiting in front of it jerked up his head and called out, "Rin!"

Rin waved a hand in reply but didn't say anything more until we had closed the distance.

Up close, the man loomed. I couldn't guess his age because of the bad lighting and his enormous beard. He wore a heavy jacket that bulged in unlikely places. I wondered if he had some kind of weapon. He wore heavy, fingerless gloves. He held out a hand and Rin gave it a quick clasp.

"Hello, Joe," she said.

"Rin," he said with intensity. "What's going on? Where's Brian?" He looked at me in surprise. "Say, is this who I think it is?"

"Brian won't be coming," Rin said curtly. "Yes, this is Mavo. The real Mavo."

"Wow." Joe ran a hand through his beard and returned his attention to Rin. He eyed her heavy bag. "Say, what's going on? This isn't a drill, is it?"

Rin frowned. "You haven't been told?"

"No, my com's out. Been out for an hour. It's crazy." He waved an arm around him. "But a lot of balloons took off just now and most of 'em aren't carrying tourists."

He lowered his voice and added hoarsely, "What happened back there? I thought I saw... Is it true? Is Unity here?"

"Right behind us," Rin said.

"So Brian...?" Joe asked the question.

Rin bit her lip but said nothing. Joe lowered his head, said a word I didn't understand, then took a deep breath.

"All right" he said. "She's ready."

He turned to the wicker gondola and helped us climb in. The basket came up to our waists. Tall, thick cylinders and stacks of silvery cartons that I assumed were supplies were lashed to the basket. I wondered how long we were going to be flying. The basket seemed tiny and fragile. I didn't want to think of floating in the middle of a dark, empty sky with nothing but air and this flimsy thing between me and mortality.

Joe put a hand on the rim of the basket. "You have the camo blanket?"

Rin nodded and patted her bag.

Joe reached out a hand to her. "I never really thought it would come to this. Good luck." Then he squeezed my hand. "Mister Mavo, it's an honor."

"Get moving, Joe," Rin said with unexpected emotion. "I hope we see you again. Stay safe."

"Stay alive," he said grimly.

Without another word, he stepped back and began methodically to free the ropes holding us to the ground. As each one was released, the basket jerked alarmingly. It bumped up and down.

Rin put down her bag, took out her card and inserted it into a slot on a blank metal panel I hadn't noticed.

Above us, the burners flared into life, blasting long orange-white flames. I felt the heat on my face.

As the last rope was freed, the balloon leapt up like a rearing horse and surged into the sky. My stomach lurched. I gripped the edge of the basket and held on, eyes closed, trying hard not to panic. I had never flown and now wished I had at least taken a flight sim in Immersion. I wanted to crouch down and curl up in the bottom of the gondola but for some reason, I cared what Rin would think. Not that her opinion of me could get much lower.

I took a long breath and then opened my eyes. Above us, the envelope of the balloon blotted out the sky. Other balloons were scattered all around us, mostly drifting west.

The circus sounds came up clear but tinny with increasing distance. The air was punctuated by the whoosh of the balloon burners.

I screwed up my courage and glanced down.

Below us, the balloon field was shrinking fast. The huge globes receded until they were children's toys, then clusters of fantasy eggs and then finally glowing coins.

Next to the field, the circus seemed to blaze with light. Constellations of sparks laid out the walkways and ringed the tents and stalls. Running through it all was the midway, its brash lights blurred by a gauze of smoke. From above, it looked like a pearly river.

Farther away, I saw the whole of Albuquerque spread out beneath me. I recognized the Rio Grande, which looked like a snake winding its way through town. Then, the train station with its relentlessly precise tracks, and beyond it, the hotel. I swallowed. Cones swarmed around it, pinning it with floodlights.

I clamped my eyes shut and sucked in lungfuls of raw air as Rin and I fled into the night.

CHAPTER EIGHTEEN

I'd never experienced anything like that ride soaring through the sky. After a while, some of my fear vanished. The air grew cooler as we rose and it felt fresh on my face. I was well away from the fraught dangers of the ground, and the whole world was spread out below me.

Much of it was black, but here and there were little clusters and pinpricks of light that must have been remote outposts. I wondered what the people there thought if they happened to look up and see us gliding by. Maybe they were used to the sight of balloons. But I thought of myself as a boy in the emptiness of the Outside. If I'd seen a balloon drift by, it would have seemed magical.

Rin didn't share my feelings. She seemed to have closed herself off. She concentrated on examining the supplies, needlessly tightening a tie line here and there and scanning the control panel. She didn't look at me and I was just smart enough to avoid talking to her or getting in her way. She pulled the camouflage blanket from the pack. It seemed to be made of transparent film held together with a complex network of nearly-invisible wires.

"Help me," she said. We clipped the blanket to the balloon cables. It sealed at the top to enclose us like an igloo. But I could see through it and air flowed freely.

I understood it would protect us from scans. The balloon's envelope was stealthed as well, I hoped.

I didn't know where we were headed, though, and Rin seemed in no mood to talk.

I was exhausted from all that had happened. I sat down with my back against the gondola and let its gentle sway lull me. I caught occasional snatches of sleep but kept jerking awake in the middle of half-formed dreams. Gollum wasn't in all of them. Some of them featured Trino, or even Brian. He was either a corpse or a prisoner.

I must have dozed off completely at some point, though, because when I woke for the last time dawn was pouring gold into the basket. I heard whimpering, like the sound of a forlorn puppy, and for a moment thought I was still half in a dream.

Then I looked over. Rin was as far away from me as the basket would allow. She was wrapped in a blanket and sandwiched between two crates. She was crying in her sleep. The balloon rotated slightly in the air current and a shaft of light hit her. Rin woke. Her hair was tangled. There were rings under her eyes. She looked at me and I could see her attitude change. Her face hardened. She seemed to draw in on herself, even as she knuckled the tears away.

I realized I had to pee. I looked around but didn't see anything that resembled a toilet. I hoped there was one. I was not going to ask Rin. I made a decision. I stepped on a crate, grabbed a cable and swung myself onto the lip of the basket. I stood there, held the cable in a death grip with one hand, caught my breath, closed my eyes and prepared for the scariest pee of my life.

Behind me, I heard Rin say: "What do you think you're doing?"

"I have to go," I said without turning around. "Sorry."

"That's the toilet," she said. I risked a glance around.

She was gesturing at a grayish oval blister stuck on one side of the gondola. I hadn't noticed it before. She kicked it with her toe and it slid open to form a small bowl with a seat.

"Molecular composter," she said. "Don't put anything in there that you don't want to lose."

We'd had those in the Outback. They dissolved waste into component molecules. The only thing left would be sparkling dust.

We used it as fertilizer. I felt like an idiot. I got down— carefully— went over and stood over it.

"Could you please turn around?" I asked.

"You're kidding." Rin said, and looked even more contemptuous of me, if possible. "Do you know how many Immersions I've been in where I peed as a man?"

"We didn't do that in the Outside," I said.

"Privacy," she said, and made it seem like a curse. But she turned around and busied herself with the control panel.

When I was finished, I held my hands under the attached cleaner, which hummed and cast a slight warmth on them. When I turned back to Rin, she was half-lying casually on a crate, with one leg bent and the other swinging. She was eating a ration bar and threw another to me.

"Thanks," I said. I unsealed the rat bar and gnawed it. The package claimed it provided a full day's nourishment. To me, it tasted like some kind of building material slathered with lemon disinfectant, but I forced down. Between bites, I asked: "Where are we going?"

"I don't know," she said.

"What?"

She pointed a thumb at the control panel. "The card I inserted was programmed with Realist safe house locations. The balloon chose randomly."

I looked around. That explained all the supplies. There were months of food here when we needed only days. So when the balloon was packed, it must have included supplies for the safe house.

Then a thought hit me. "Will we be safe?" I asked. "Trino has taken over the Realists. He'll be looking for us. The safe houses may be compromised."

"I know," Rin said. "But I can't think of anything else to do at the moment."

"Can we take control of the balloon?" I asked. "Can we steer it?"

"Sort of. The balloon steers by reading satellite data and rising or falling into air currents that push us around," Rin said. "Also, we can turn the individual panels of the envelope light or dark, which can warm the air on that side, making it less dense. That gives us some push in that direction."

"But not much."

"No," she admitted. "It's weak and slow."

"Oh."

"Or," Rin added, "We can we spill the air from the envelope and land in the middle of nowhere. Which will happen eventually anyway when we run out of fuel for the burners."

"How far can we go?"

"I have no idea," Rin said. "Fuel tank's at about half and we have three extra tanks. Figure a tank a day if we're careful. But the longer we're in the air, the better the chances we'll be spotted." She gave me a hard smile. "I don't think we filed a flight plan."

Now I had to ask the hard question.

"Rin," I said tentatively. "What are you planning to do?" I meant in the long run.

Her face darkened.

"Planning?" She spat out the word. "There's no planning! Brian—" she stopped and bit her lip, then continued, "—Brian's gone. But he told me to watch your back, so that's what I'm doing. Beyond that, I haven't got a clue." She looked at me fiercely. "You're the one with the great plans. You tell me." I ignored her tone of bitter sarcasm.

I shook my head. "I don't know, either."

The rest of the day was even more miserable. Rin looked moodily out at the sky. Once, we saw a black dot on the horizon that might have been a Unity ship or another balloon, but it never approached. Other than that, the sky was so blue and cloudless it hurt my eyes.

We were heading west. From time to time I glanced over the side. Far below us, the land turned hilly, with patches of greenery that seemed lush when compared with the stark desert we'd left behind. Our shadow raced ahead of us over the land.

By evening we had reached what used to be the Arizona border. It was nothing but craters. The wind kept pushing us west. Rin didn't speak to me. For once, I didn't mind. I had nothing to say. The sun went down and it became chilly. We ate rat bars in silence, and I hunkered down again and managed— I don't know how— to sleep.

Rin shook me. Hard.

"I'm awake!" I said. "What is it?"

"Let me in," she said urgently.

"What?"

"LET ME IN!"

"Oh," I said. "You're not Rin and I'm not awake. It's you. The ghost."

"Let me in!" the phony Rin demanded. "It's coming."

"All right, enough is enough," I said. "You just keep repeating yourself. What's coming? Who are you? Why are you in my head?"

Rin looked at me, blinked, and stared at me with confusion. "I don't know," she said. "I have to grow to know that. I'm hungry."

"For what?" I asked. "Are you some kind of vampire? A bio virus?"

"Kernel," Rin said. "I have a mission. I need knowledge to achieve it. I need to know more about myself." She stared at me intently.

"I need your help," she added. "You've got to Immerse and let me roam."

"If you really were Rin, you'd know that's impossible," I said. "In case you don't know my situation, we're running away because everybody is now trying to kill me."

"I know. I access your short-term memories."

"What? You've been spying on me? Did they leave spyware behind when they probed me?" I wasn't happy about that concept.

"No, probe damaged our connection. I can't control you. We must work together." Rin paused and seemed to be trying to think of something. Then she said tentatively, "Is the word I need 'cooperate?'"

"How about enslave?"

Rin shook her head. "Friends don't do that." She smiled. "We're friends. Close friends."

"Now I know you're not Rin."

"No," she said. "I'm part of you."

"Oh, no," I said. "So, it's true. I'm crazy."

"No. Chosen. Special. The last."

"You said that before. The last what?"

"I don't know," Rin said again. She shook her head in frustration. "I need data."

"Data? Now you're talking like a computer? Are you some sort of AI?"

"No!" Rin said angrily. "Kernel! I'm not the enemy!"

That was interesting. "What do you mean?" I pressed.

"I DON'T KNOW!" It sounded exactly like Rin when she was exasperated. Even the expression was perfect Rin. "Open up. Immerse! I need data!"

"If I open up here to the Immersion, I could be tracked." I was beginning to be exasperated myself.

That actually shut Rin up. Or whatever had Rin's face. It bit its lip the way I had seen Rin do when she was thinking. I found myself focusing on those lips. Rin screwed up her face in a frown.

"Your endocrine system is stimulated. Your glandular activity is blocking our conversation. I will use another image."

"No, that's okay—" I began but Rin was gone and I was staring at Gollum, who leered at me with bulbous, watery eyes.

"Cannot Immerse?" Gollum whined. "What to do? What to do? Tricksy It is. But we's got to be tricksier. Oh!" Gollum blinked in surprise. "Just remembered!"

"What?" I asked with an odd sense of urgency. "What have you remembered?"

Gollum gave me a twisted smile. "Where the rest of me is."

Rin shook me. Hard.

"Stop saying my name!" she said.

I opened my eyes. "What?"

"You were moaning and saying my name."

"I did what?" I said blearily. I was still groggy.

She punched me in the chest. I gasped and came fully awake. Then she leaned close. "Leave me alone," she said. "Brian said to keep you safe. He didn't say I had to like you. Don't talk to me and don't look at me and whatever you're doing with me in your dreams, just stop it." She pulled a rat bar from her pocket.

"Eat," she ordered, threw it at me, and turned away.

I kept out of her way for the rest of the day. But I snuck peeks at her when I thought she wouldn't notice. Her mood swung wildly. Sometimes she seemed like a clenched fist, other times I thought I heard her choking back sobs. She swung between depression, anxiety and anger.

I didn't know what to do. I felt as if I were tip-toeing around her, trying not to set her off. It was like being stuck in a closet with a proximity bomb.

What made it even more miserable is that I had the strong feeling that I had to tell Rin about the ghost, that it might be crucial information. But I didn't dare.

Mostly I read my book. I wondered if the ghost— no, the *Kernel*— might show up in my dreams as Gandalf. That would be almost intriguing.

A few times that day we risked un-camouflaging and got the news through read-only Immersion. There were clips of the two factory explosions, along with the Unity attack and Realist roundup, which was mostly being praised, although a few commentators called it patently illegal. Those were mainly news agitators from marginal feeds that were trolling for hits. There also was a continuous replay of the message that Trino had released. It was intercut with clips of my speech. There were also reports of people cheering me from all over the world. Polls showed an unlikely level of support, both for Unity's actions and oddly, for the Realists. So I'd already proven disruptive for something I didn't do.

Evening fell again and we were still in the middle of nowhere. The balloon control panel didn't show us where we were heading— a security feature in case it had been commandeered, I guessed— but in general we were moving west.

Once we must have passed over a dead zone, because I saw below us a flock of redemption birds, like fat bombers. They were flapping slowly along and spraying from their mutated bodies a shower of tailored microorganisms designed to restore the soil. The setting sun gleamed on their wings.

I was looking at them from one side of the basket when I heard an odd noise and spun around.

Rin had opened the camo blanket. She was balanced on the rim of the basket. Her hair whipped in the evening breeze. She was holding a cable with both hands.

I was going to make a joke about using the toilet when I saw her expression. I lunged forward just as she let go of the cable.

I made a desperate grab and caught the back of her jacket collar as she tumbled. She dangled in the air. She weighed almost as much as I did. I was nearly dragged over the side. I clung desperately, managed to get my other hand under Rin's shoulder and hauled for all I was worth. She hung like dead weight for a moment, then her eyes went wide and she went into full panic mode, screaming and thrashing. I lost my grip but luckily, Rin managed to lash out and grab one of the loops of cable that dangled from the bottom of the basket. I reached far out and down, my feet braced against some of the crates and my heart hammering. Slowly, painfully, I helped her climb up the basket and tumble over the rim. We both collapsed onto the floor, gasping, and clung to each other tightly as Rin began to weep.

CHAPTER NINETEEN

We held each other for what seemed hours until Rin's tears stopped and her taught body finally relaxed. Exhausted, we fell asleep, nestled together.

"It was just too much," Rin said much later as we sat on crates and sipped bulbs of hot chocolate. "First, the bombing and the... the deaths. And then the Realists breaking up, and Trino trying to kill us, and then Brian—" she caught her breath, looked down, and then continued. "—and then there's you."

"I know," I said. "I wish I could make you believe me."

I sipped my chocolate thoughtfully. I remembered the blackout before the first explosion. I had no proof at all. No, wait, I had my memories. I could upload those into the Immersion when we had time and a safe place. But then I realized Rin still wouldn't believe me. Nobody would trust my memories. Hadn't I altered them after killing Pallburg?

As if reading my mind, Rin gave me a serious look. "Tell me the truth. Did you kill Pallburg?"

"No. I never killed anybody."

"I see." I couldn't tell whether she was disappointed or relieved. Swallowing hard, I asked, "Did you think I was a killer all along?"

"I didn't know."

"Everybody else thinks I am."

She thought about it. "I guess I kind of hoped you weren't."

I felt a surge of warmth. "I guess that makes me a fraud."

Rin laughed. "Join the club."

We drank in silence for awhile, then I turned to her and said, "You know, I could see you were hurting. You could have talked to me, if you'd wanted."

"I couldn't," she said. "I didn't trust you and I hated myself for killing all those people."

"You didn't!" I interrupted but she went on.

"So then I had to both hate you and make sure you were safe." She took a deep breath. "Because Brian said you were important. But the one thing I *couldn't* do was talk to you about what I was going through. And I couldn't even Immerse to get help." Her voice dropped to a whisper. "It got to be too much."

For a second, I thought she might start crying again. I winced when I thought of her shaking and wracked by sobs.

"Oh, Rin," I said. I reached out to her but she looked up from her cup and shook her head.

"It's okay," she said. "When I found myself dangling in thin air, with the ground so far below, I had a change of heart and realized I wanted to live."

"I'm glad you did," I said quietly.

"Thanks," she said. "So am I."

I took another sip of my chocolate. I decided to push a little further.

"Listen, Rin, about Pallburg's killing..."

"Yes?"

"I think I was framed. I don't who did it or why. But I think perhaps we and the Realists were framed for all those deaths, too. Maybe by the same people, maybe not."

"Maybe not people," Rin said. "Unity?"

"That was Trino's argument," I said. "But think about it: the Realists have never harmed anyone directly. You —we, I mean —disabled a satellite, did some other sabotage. But it's all small change to a globe-spanning system like Unity. We simply wouldn't be worth the lives and effort."

"Who, then?" she said. "And why hasn't Unity stopped them?"

"I've been thinking about that." I hesitated but then I asked, "Who is Anchorage?"

Rin did a double-take. "Anchorage? What do you mean?"

"The Realists are— were— decentralized," I said. "But Anchorage was the person or cell that suggested the cow factory as a target and provided us with the training video."

"That's true. So?"

"So Anchorage was also the one that suggested the Realists target the satellite, and provided some of the critical information for frying it, am I right?"

"I think so," Rin said slowly.

"Well, how did Anchorage get that information? Is he, she or it some kind of mole within Unity? Highly placed enough to gain access to secure data?"

"We never asked," Rin said. "The less we knew, the less we could give away. Brian did suggest that maybe Anchorage was somebody high-ranking, maybe military."

"There's something else," I said. "No offense, but the people I saw at the hotel seemed, well, a little disorganized."

"Stop being polite," Rin said. "It was a miracle when we agreed on anything." Then she stopped short. "Oh," she said.

"Right," I said. "Not to be offensive, but I wondered how a group like that could tie its own shoes, let alone plan sophisticated actions."

"You did it," Rin said. "And Brian and Trino helped keep everybody in line."

"And you helped them agree on things," I said. "You have a gift."

Rin blushed but said nothing.

"But here's the thing," I continued. "How is it that a group like the Realists managed to do as much as they did with that level of disagreement and debate? Trino understood the problem. That's why he wanted to pare it down to a hard core of ruthless loyalists."

"You're saying that somebody was secretly helping us out. Maybe even guiding us?"

I shrugged. "Maybe," I said. "Again, what do we really know about Anchorage?"

"And now they want to dismember us?" Rin said. "How does that make sense?"

"It doesn't," I said. "Unless they're planning something even bigger, something huge, and they want to blame the Realists. Or maybe they want what Trino wants: A bunch of real terrorists."

"That's a lot of guesswork," Rin said sharply. "And you don't have any evidence."

"I don't," I admitted. "but there's something more."

I paused, gulped my chocolate, took a breath, and then I told her about the Kernel. She listened, fascinated but said nothing until I'd finished.

"So that's why you kept calling my name," she said, and gave me a quirky smile. "I don't know whether I feel better or worse now."

Now it was my turn to blush but Rin put a hand on my shoulder.

"The— Kernel, you call it?— says something's coming and you both have to stop it. What if that thing is Anchorage?"

I was stunned. "I hadn't thought of that!" I said. "Some kind of infiltrator, maybe?"

"No, this isn't about the Realists," Rin said. "Or not only about us. This Kernel clearly has been in your head longer than you've been a Realist."

"That's true," I said. "But that still doesn't give us a motive, then. For *anything* that's happened."

"Maybe it does," Rin said. "You said the Kernel wasn't an AI."

"It said it wasn't the enemy."

"Right!" Rin leaned forward, excited. "That's important!"

"Why?"

"Because it doesn't know much about itself or its mission but the one thing it knows for sure is that AIs are the enemy."

I was confused.

"Unity is built on AIs," I said. "Thousands, maybe millions of them."

"No, that's a common mistake people make," Rin said. "Unity is built in ascending orders of dedicated systems with limited abilities. We call them artificial intelligences because they have a form of intelligence that makes them *seem* to be conscious. They perform tasks, they compare data, they share decision-making. But they're not self-aware. Pallburg made sure that none of the entities he was incorporating had any sense of self-consciousness."

"I didn't know that," I said.

"Yes. In fact, it was a big issue at the time, whether software and robots should be granted civil rights, whether they were conscious beings. And of course, nobody wanted some sort of super-consciousness running *everything*."

I looked at Rin with new respect. Ancient history didn't seem to be the kind of thing that normal people cared about. After all, it was seventy years ago. Also, despite the fact that people had literally billions of things to watch, listen to and feel, I thought most seemed depressingly ignorant. Games, sensoramas and Immersion sob rooms seemed to be the popular stuff.

"Where did you learn all this?" I asked.

"My mother was in AI development," Rin said.

"Really?"

"Yes." She sipped her chocolate, looked down at her bulb. "My dad died doing it, too."

I didn't know what to say.

Rin went on, "Mom says he was working on the initial systems to capture human thoughts and memories in computers. His parents died from early-onset Alzheimer's. He was working on a system to download their thoughts and memories, then reintegrate them when the organic damage was fixed. He volunteered for the first deep probes." She stopped, bit her lip, then went on, "The probes were so primitive. Something went wrong. Fragmented his mind. He was left a vegetable for a long time, I heard. I never knew him and my Mom doesn't like to talk about it. I tried to find out about him once, but I guess all that's still classified."

"I'm sorry," I said, stumbling over my words. "Do you still talk to her?"

Rin shook her head. "Not much since I joined the Realists." She tugged at a stray lock of hair. "I love her but we disagree on Unity. She'd be happy if they took every human being out of the system. She says we're too unreliable and limited to govern ourselves."

"Well, the Collapse sure didn't prove her wrong."

Rin's eyes flashed. "We can learn!" she said angrily. "We don't need to be led around like sheep! You either have faith in that or you give up!"

"Whoa, sorry," I said. "I'm not arguing with you." I scrambled for something to say to defuse the conversation. "My Mom got kicked out of her home by Unity."

"Really?"

I nodded. "She grew up in Malibu Colony in California. She was a surfer."

"I haven't heard of it," Rin said.

"It was on the coast west of Los Angeles. There were these gigantic walls that kept the ocean from coming in and permanent firefighting drones to keep the hills from burning down."

"Her family must have been pretty well off," Rin said. "That's an expensive way to protect homes."

"You mean it was unsustainable," I said. "Selfish, in a way, when most of the rest of SoCal was drowning or drying up and dying.

Anyway, Unity took a vote or something and ordered the whole enclave evacuated."

"What was the reason?"

"Well, the walls holding back those monster waves also built up silt, kept it from reaching shores down the coast. Communities there were in danger of being washed away, along with the wetlands. Also, they wanted to put in wave turbine infrastructure and pumps to keep the ocean from inundating everything." I laughed, thinking of Drowned LA. "We all know how well that worked."

"So she had to leave? Where did she go?" Rin asked.

"Well, she was a young girl, so she followed her family. They were bought out— it's called eminent domain— and they were all moved up the coast. But after a while, that proved impossible to maintain, too. My grandparents had lived their whole lives near the sea and they didn't want to go inland. Of course, at the time, much of the California interior was unlivable, anyway. Did you know the Central Valley used to be one of the largest agricultural producers in the world? Almonds, grapes, apricots, cotton, all kinds of fruits and vegetables, even rice!"

"It's all desert now," Rin said.

Yes," I said. "Salt encroachment in the aquifers. They drew up all the groundwater." Rin looked puzzled. "Water that lives underground," I said. "Needs to be replenished through rainfall and you can't use more than you've got. When you suck it all out, the ground literally caves in. So when climate change dried up the rainfall, and the snowpack shrank so there wasn't any spring runoff, and all the irrigation water was needed to keep people from dying of thirst... well, you get it."

"Your grandparents," Rin reminded me.

"Right," I said. "Anyway, both of them were in tech, so they moved to Silicon Valley 2.0, up in Washington state. But by then things were pretty hairy all over the West. The world was barely out of the Collapse era and Unity had barely been up and running, so not all the kinks were worked out."

"What happened?" Rin asked.

"They wanted to find the ocean again, so they kept moving northward. But demand was really high. Unity was cracking down all along the coasts, too. We needed energy, any way we could get it. And aqua-farms. Anything and everything to keep people alive." I sighed. "In the end, my grandparents found a place in one of the high-rises. They holo'd the walls to look like ocean views, but it was never the same.

"My mom went off to school in Vancouver. She was bitter about what Unity had done. So when she decided to have me, she moved to the Outside." I shrugged. "And here I am."

"But what about your father?" Rin asked. "Did he want to move to the Outside, too?"

"I never met him," I said. "Mom doesn't talk about him. Just calls him 'my sperm donor.' I don't think she ever wanted to be in a relationship. My grandparents' marriage had become pretty bad because of all their disappointments and problems."

Rin looked thoughtful. "So, you never knew him?"

"Like you," I said.

Rin put her hand on mine. It was like an electric charge.

"I'm really sorry," she said.

I turned to her. "What would you do if you met your father?"

"I don't know. I'd have a lot of questions. You?"

I shrugged again. "There were lots of men in my mom's life on the Outside. Women, too. Even a Third. I don't honestly know that I missed anything." I finished my chocolate bulb. The sky was completely dark.

"So," I said. "Have we decided on where we're going?"

"Not yet. Any ideas?"

"No," I said. "Not really. But I have an idea on how to get one."

"What do you mean?"

"I need to sleep on it," I said. "I'll let you know in the morning." I wanted to hug her but now that her crisis had passed it wouldn't feel the same. Too personal.

Rin seemed to be waiting for something and seemed disappointed when I got up to move over to my sleeping space.

"Right," she said. "I think I'll just stay here for a while."

"You'll be OK?" I asked.

She smiled. "I'll be fine," she said. "Good night, Mavo."

"Good night, Rin."

"Say hello to the Kernel for me," she added.

In the morning, for a change, I was awake before Rin. I stood up and went over to where she lay bundled in a blanket. She was sleeping peacefully, her face nestled in one arm. Her hair was tousled. I wanted to brush it back from her cheek but didn't want to wake her.

Instead, I went to use the toilet.

Rin woke a short time later. For breakfast, I rehydrated and warmed a couple of egg burritos. Rin brought over two bulbs of coffee and we sat down to eat. We hadn't eaten last night and I was starving. Rin attacked her burrito.

"So," she asked around a mouthful of egg. "Any interesting dreams?"

"You mean the Kernel?"

"Yes."

"Yes, it spoke to me."

"What did it say?"

I shook my head. "Well, it's like talking to a senile toddler."

"Toddlers aren't senile." She smirked around a mouthful of burrito.

"Ha ha," I said. "What I mean is, it has gaps in its memory. But it says it can get some of those memories restored."

Rin frowned.

"How?"

"We need to see somebody."

"Okay," Rin said. "Who?"

I stalled by taking a big bite of burrito.

"Who?" Rin repeated. "Mavo, who is it that we have to see?"

I swallowed, sighed and wiped my mouth with the back of my hand.

"I'm not sure you'll like it," I said. "Not sure I will, either."

"That sounds ominous," Rin said, her eyes narrowing. "Is it dangerous?"

"Worse," I said. "We have to go see my Mom."

CHAPTER TWENTY

The trouble was, I wasn't exactly sure where Mom was. All Outsides were sprawling, unmapped places and every so often we'd pick up and move to a slightly less-destroyed region. Unity, of course, had Immersion stations along the train routes. I could try to pass a message to her but there was a danger of alerting Unity. I was a wanted man and Mom's communications would certainly be flagged.

I was at a loss on what to do, except maybe set down somewhere near our old home and then go looking for her, which could take days, even weeks.

The volcano saved us. We were down to our last half-tank of fuel. We were gliding at night through what I guessed was northern Arizona when in the distance we spotted a cone of ruby light. I knew instantly what it was.

I pointed it out to Rin. "That's the Flame Circle Festival," I said. "I forgot it was on. That's our way to reach my Mom."

"What is it?" Rin asked, peering.

"It's like Survival Day for Outsiders," I said. "It's held in a Collapse caldera. When the region got bombed, it set off something under the ground, maybe some kind of super-weapon, that tore the ground open and released magma from the Earth's core. It formed a volcano."

"We're not landing in a volcano, Mavo," Rin said.

"It's okay, it's dead now," I said. "But every year, there's a big festival in the crater. A bit like the Circo Eterno. People dress up, act a little crazy, and they light up the cinder cone with lasers and fireworks."

"Why would we go there? I thought we were trying to avoid being spotted."

"Because," I said. "Mom never missed a Flame Circle Festival. She would leave my sister and me with my aunt. We hated it. No candy. We couldn't even have ration bars. Mom always told us, "Take anything you can get from Unity. They owe us!" But Aunty Vega was all-natural. She thought Unity food would poison us somehow. We were always hungry when we were with her."

Rin broke in impatiently. "So your Mom might be there, right?"

"If she's not, there'll be someone who knows where she is. We'll try the Willamette camp. Mom had friends there. And they might even give us a ride." I waved a hand at the cartons around us. "We've got plenty of stuff to share."

Rin thought about it. "What about the balloon? Won't we look weird landing in a giant purple jellyfish?"

I laughed.

"Are you kidding?" I said. "We'll fit right in!"

We switched to manual flight and two hours later we landed, practically on fumes. We came down on the lip of the crater at an angle. The basket snagged and the huge bag of air tilted and began dragging us down the steep slope. The burners shut off automatically but the basket skipped and scraped over a landscape of black lava. I pulled the line that vented air from the envelope, but it didn't deflate immediately. A few containers broke free from their lashings and went tumbling. Rin and I held on for dear life and prayed we wouldn't be crushed. But then people seemed to show up from everywhere. Dozens of hands clamped onto the basket, grabbed at the ropes, hauled and finally managed to stop us. The envelope collapsed around us so that we were draped in purple tentacles.

A man with a hat that made him look like a giant sunflower tucked up one tentacle and poked his head into the basket.

"That was the worst landing ever!" he said cheerfully. "Is your pelvis broken?"

"We're fine," I said, and groaned. I wasn't afraid of being recognized, even though I was probably the world's most notorious person. Rin had cut my hair and daubed my face with some sort of color-changing stuff. More than anything, I looked like a Third with a bad hairdo.

People helped us out and dusted us down. Rin had a bump on her forehead but we declined an offer to take us to the medical tent.

I looked around. The faces crowding around us showed various degrees of good-natured concern. The festival-goers were dressed in a bewildering array of costumes. Some wore clothing in gaudy colors. I knew Outsiders, who didn't have many resources, often spent all year preparing their elaborate outfits. They wove, dyed and decorated them using sawgrass and other native plants or recycled cast-offs and garbage. My mom always collected feathers dropped by the redemption birds. One of our rescuers had created an outfit from Unity ration packages. You could still see all the labels. Another was dressed entirely in bones.

A few were nearly naked except for tough shoes, and I tried to avoid gawking at them. Given our tough environment, being unclothed was uncommon among Outsiders. And because we didn't have much, good clothes were something of a status symbol. I hadn't been on the Outside for a long time but still, to me, the choice of nudity seemed disreputable.

We introduced ourselves with fake names. For moment nobody asked us questions. Some of the people went off to collect cartons that had been flung out of the balloon. Others were folding up the envelope with an expertise I hadn't expected. Nobody seemed to be in charge but everybody moved with efficiency. It made me feel good.

Outsiders had a reputation for being anarchists, messy, crazy and stupid. I knew it wasn't true but I was proud to show them off to Rin. And for just a moment I thought, if a bunch of strangers could work together like this, if they could self-organize like this, who needed Unity?

Rin did seem impressed but I noticed she also kept a careful eye on everything. I held back my irritation. She could have no way of knowing that these people weren't thieves. It took about fifteen minutes for the crowd to pack up and store the envelope and dump the cartons back in the basket, which was carefully roped down.

Only then did the faces turn to us with gentle, questioning looks. One woman stepped forward and asked, "Do you have a spot picked out? You can stay here, or course, but we'd be happy if you joined us."

"We'd be honored," Rin said. "And we brought a lot of supplies to share." She pointed to the basket. "Help yourselves!"

Sharing was common courtesy during the festival but of course, Outsiders generally didn't pack months of provisions and I had seen them glancing curiously at our heaped supplies.

Probably, they assumed we'd be heading off after the festival and were bringing supplies back to our home.

Sunflower man slapped his hands together. "All right!" he said. "Then, let's get this party started!"

CHAPTER TWENTY-ONE

In the end, a straggling, laughing, joyous chain of us picked up bags and cartons and strutted off down the slope toward the main encampment like some kind of circus parade.

Thirds were pretty rare, even in the Unity world, and more than once a couple sidled up and asked if I wanted to join them in the medical tent, where the festival had its only Immersion node.

But Sunflower and some of the others firmly put them off and acted almost as a guard until we reached the main encampment. It was a giant open-sided tent, a little ragged, propped up by carved wooden posts and strung with lights and hammocks. Trade goods and supplies were stacked around.

I caught a confusing mix of odors: fresh bread, sulfur, garlic, cooking oil, dust and humanity. People chatted and laughed or snored in the hammocks.

Steam rose from the center of the tent. As we approached, I saw it came from a rock-lined pool filled with bubbling water. It was a natural hot spring. Pipes led from it, feeding the water to various parts of the tent.

"Welcome to Spa Town," said Sunflower, whose real name turned out to be Ralph. "We're the only permanent encampment in the crater. A few hardy souls— one of them was my grandfather— came here just after the Collapse and set up camp. The ground was still hot! An Outside enclave grew up not too far away and some folks from it came here, maybe just out of curiosity at first, but later to trade and get hydrotherapy."

"Hydro what?" I asked.

"Around the back," Ralph said, jerking a thumb at one corner of the tent. "The people here tapped the springs to create soaking pools. The sulfur's good for skin diseases."

I winced. I felt a sudden urge to scratch my elbow but fought it down.

Ralph bobbed his head, and some of his petals flopped over his eyes. "Anyway, over the years more people came from all over, and it became an annual trade fair and art festival. And here we are. Are you hungry?"

I said yes just to be polite but then realized Rin and I had eaten mostly rat bars for three days. The food smells weren't bad, exactly. Just unusual.

Rin gave me a sidelong glance but followed Sunflower to one section of the tent that had carpets laid out on which people sat or squatted. They held what appeared to be hand-crafted bowls. I didn't see any utensils. People used a kind of puffy blue-green bread to scoop up whatever they were eating. They tore off pieces from a communal loaf. It didn't look good but it smelled kind of great.

Rin and I were given bowls. We used them to scoop out a sort of oily porridge from a communal pot. We took bread and followed the others in using it to sop up our meal.

The food was delicious. The bread was nutty and the soup was thick and sharp-tasting.

"What is this?" I asked.

Sunflower winked.

"That's our special secret," he said. "It's barnacle bread. We use a type of freshwater barnacle that grows really well here. And we use local lichen for the soup. Together, you get all your vitamins and minerals."

We sat down comfortably and nobody disturbed us as we ate our meal. We drank it down with mugs of something sweet called kur. Sunflower, always chatty, explained that it was mildly alcoholic and brewed from local fungus. "We've got the strong, distilled stuff but that's mostly trade goods," he said.

The people around us introduced themselves but I didn't remember most of the names. They didn't ask a lot of personal questions. Unlike people born and raised in Unity, living their whole lives Immersed, these folks weren't eager to overshare. I hadn't appreciated that when I was on the Outside.

The meal didn't end, exactly. People just came and went. Somebody always seemed to be minding the cooking, stirring or adding ingredients or washing a pot. Some people seemed to do most of the cooking, although it didn't seem to be anybody's special job.

Rin also passed around some rat bars, to the joy of the children, who apparently had never tasted artificial strawberry flavor.

Of course, eventually there were questions about us and especially about our balloon. I let Rin take the lead. She was better at lying, although I was learning fast.

"That's our job," Rin said. "We give balloon rides at festivals."

"Are all your landings so bad?" Sunflower asked.

Rin looked at me archly. "My trainee is still learning how to land."

Everybody laughed.

"Anyway," Rin continued. "We were heading to Albuquerque when we heard the news." The group murmured with understanding. "So, we decided to come here instead."

"Well, you're most welcome," Sunflower said. "Stay as long as you want." He looked thoughtful. "We don't have any fuel for you, I'm afraid, but I can ask around at the other camps. Somebody probably brought some and you've certainly got enough trade goods."

"Actually," I broke in. "I thought we might head over to the Willamette camp. I know some people there."

"Well, that's easy," Sunflower said. "You just take the Gallery to the fork, turn towards the North Outpost and look for the flag."

I knew that flag, green with a starburst, and got an unexpected lump in my throat. Not because I was missing my Mom, I told myself; rather, because I wasn't looking forward to seeing her again. What would I say? How would she treat me?

Rin seemed to catch my thoughts. She leaned close. "Don't worry," she said quietly. "It'll be all right."

"How do you know that?"

"Because I said so," Rin replied, and put a hand on my arm.

And because it was Rin, I believed her.

Before moving on, we were asked if we wanted to shower. I realized they were being polite. I was probably pretty ripe after running for my life and then spending three days in a cramped balloon. Rin and I were handed rough towels and directed to individual cubicles while our clothes were taken away and washed. A half-hour later we were clean and ready to go. Rin's hair gleamed and I noticed we both smelled faintly of moss, thanks to the soap.

We thanked Sunflower, left the tent and followed the Gallery, which was nothing more than a wide road. Encampments were laid out on either side. Some were little more than windbreaks and platforms for sleeping bags but others were elaborate artworks that reared up in all kinds of shapes. Some were illuminated by lanterns of many colors. It took us only a few minutes to reach the turn for the North Outpost.

And there before us was the Willamette camp. The flag fluttered over a collection of peaked tents adorned with glittering patterns of beads and pieces of glass. Mirror shards on ribbons clinked and tinkled as the tents billowed.

A little path of colored shells and stones was laid out. I took one step on it and stopped. I swallowed hard.

"What is it?" Rin asked.

"I can't," I said.

"Can't what?"

"This. Meet my mom. I can't do it tonight. I'm not ready. It's been so long."

My stomach was churning. I couldn't take another step. It was almost as if someone had thrown up a force barrier in front of me.

"I don't know what I'm going to say to her," I stuttered. "Especially with this thing in my skull. I can't do this tonight, Rin. I'm sorry."

Rin tilted her head and looked at me. I couldn't quite gauge her expression.

"It's okay," she said at last. "We can come back tomorrow. I'm pretty tired, anyway. Should we just go back to Spa Town and hit the hammocks?"

I thought about it. I wasn't in the mood to deal with a bunch of people. And I sure didn't want people to hear me talking in my sleep to the Kernel. We didn't need to excite any curiosity.

I didn't reply right away but Rin seemed to understand. "You know what?" she said. "It's a beautiful night. Why don't we just take a walk?"

I looked at her gratefully.

We turned around and started heading back. I was so wrought up that I almost didn't notice when Rin slipped her hand into mine.

Looming ahead of us was the volcano, a dark, high cone surrounded by a nimbus of colored lights. A brilliant shaft of ruby light erupted from it and burned high into the sky in a magical column. This close up, it took my breath away.

We walked around it and before I knew it we were climbing up the side of the crater towards the balloon. The lava was an endless black plain, featureless despite the light of the full moon. The lava had soaked up the day's heat and now radiated a gentle warmth. But it was well after midnight and beginning to get chilly. A breeze ruffled our hair.

We reached the balloon. The basket was covered by the envelope, which gleamed purple in the moonlight. The basket had been partially unloaded and cartons and tanks were neatly laid out around it.

"The basket's nearly empty," I said. "There should be plenty of room for us to stretch out."

"And it's quiet," Rin said. "Nobody around."

We unlashed and rolled up one side of the envelope. A shaft of moonlight made a pool of silver on the floor of the basket. We tumbled inside. It was warm but not uncomfortable. Rin had stowed the camo blanket next to the control panel. She tugged it free and spread it on the floor. We sat on it, facing each other. Then she stretched out and propped her head in her hand. Her eyes followed me as I stretched out next to her.

We didn't say anything. It was so quiet that I could hear Rin's breath. My heart was hammering and my pulse beat in my ears.

I broke the silence first.

"Rin," I said.

"What?" Her voice was a whisper.

"Want some hot chocolate?"

She laughed. I laughed too for the sheer joy of hearing her. After days of flight and fear, we were released, for this night at least. I don't know how it happened but we seemed to reach some kind of understanding.

We did the ritual of consent and then Rin was in my arms. It was different from the last time I'd held her, weeping and terrified. She felt strong and confident.

I felt her warm breath on my neck and then she pressed her lips against mine. We touched each other, like explorers. I felt my nerves catch fire. Of course I'd had Immersion sex and been in the heads of people who'd posted on the intimacy sites. But this was... different.

I wasn't sure where my hands and lips should go. People in the Immersion experiences always seemed so confident and everything was so glossy and perfect. The partners all moved together in some kind of flowing dance.

The reality was messier, clumsier. More confusing. And quicker.

But it was somehow more beautiful, too. The moves were the same as I'd experienced in Immersion, but they were also unique somehow.

Because Rin was unique.

CHAPTER TWENTY-TWO

Maybe it was my hormones but the Kernel didn't invade my dreams.

I awoke with Rin lying on my arm, which had gone to sleep. Her hair was mussed and her mouth was open. She was snoring gently. And I had to pee.

Despite all that, the breaking day was gorgeous. Rin was dazzling. Everything had an exquisiteness to it. I gently pulled myself free and clambered out of the basket. My arm was dead, so it was hard work. I shook it until I felt pins and needles.

The air was cool and fresh. But the sun was coming up and steam rose from the ground as its warmth devoured the dew. I was naked and barefoot. I walked gingerly down to a ripple in the lava and peed. A lizard perched on the rise looked at me skeptically. It was beautiful, too. I sat down on the ledge— scaring the lizard— and watched the sun crest the rim of the crater. The sky turned from pearly gray to luminous salmon, streaked by clouds. Flocks of birds flapped by in honking parades.

"It's beautiful."

I turned. Rin had come up behind me. She was fully dressed and held two coffee bulbs. I hunched down, aware of my nudity.

"Uh, morning," I said. "I should, uh, go get dressed."

"No, it's okay," Rin said and dropped down next to me. She handed me a coffee. I pulled the tab and felt the bulb warm in my hands. I looked at Rin. She was facing ahead, watching the sunrise. She was bathed in rosy light. She was almost too beautiful to look at. I felt like singing.

"Rin," I began.

"Shhh," she said. "Just watch."

We silently watched the sun rise in a molten orange ball. I kept sneaking peeks at Rin.

We finished the coffee and she stood up.

"Well," she said. "We'd better head back. We've got to get ready to see your Mom." She smiled at me, then turned and began walking back to the basket.

I was confused. Shouldn't we be flinging ourselves into each other's arms and professing our undying love? That's how I felt. Or was it all supposed to be casual and no big deal? Had it all been a result of too much moonlight and kur? I had no idea. Had I done something wrong? Had I failed to do something?

Despite everything, Rin was more of a mystery to me now than ever. I had to talk to her when I had the chance. But I could see now was not the time. I started after her but I wasn't paying enough attention to the rugged ground and stubbed my toes, so I was limping by the time I reached the basket.

Rin was waiting next to it with her bag slung over her shoulder. She kept shifting her weight from one foot to the other impatiently. I scrambled into the basket and dressed quickly.

"Grab some rat bars," Rin said over her shoulder as I put on my boots. "We can eat breakfast on the way. It'll save time."

"What flavor?" I called back.

"Whatever's handy." She was all business.

I rummaged around and found the last blueberry bar. Rin had said she liked those.

I scrambled out of the basket. Rin helped me fold down the envelope and lash it back down.

"All right," I said, and took a breath. "I think I'm ready."

"You *think* you're ready?"

"I'm ready," I said with more certainty than I felt. "It's just, I thought we'd do it later in the day."

"We don't want to take a chance that your Mom's out," Rin replied. "We don't want to spend time hunting her down. We still have to go bargain for fuel. Earlier's better. Also, there'll be fewer people out to see you, and that's good."

She seemed a little gruff.

"Well," I said testily. "Maybe we should have skipped the sunrise."

"Oh, no," Rin replied. "You never skip a sunrise." She paused and then added, "You never know when you'll see another one."

I was still thinking about what she meant as we set off for the Willamette camp.

We took the Gallery. Even though it was just after dawn, a few people were out, making their way to the trading stalls to do business and haul back their stuff before it got hot. I caught my breath. Up ahead, strolling toward us, was a woman decked out in feathers. She had a mask of raven feathers and the huge pinions of redemption birds had been made into big wings that were attached to a framework and spread out behind her in plumes. She wore sandals beaded with images of birds that had once flown the skies in their millions but were now extinct.

Mom.

Walking beside her, pushing a handcart loaded with trade goods, was a girl of about fourteen with long bangs and flowing robes.

My sister Jola.

They came toward us. I froze. Rin stopped, confused, and looked at me but I couldn't move.

They came up to us and then passed by. They hadn't recognized me. I slowly let out my breath.

Then from behind us, I heard a voice ask quietly, "Mavo?"

I turned. My mother had stopped in the road. Her arms were crossed.

"Were you just going to walk by without saying hello?" she asked.

I stuttered but before I could form actual words, Mom shook her plumed head and said "Not here. Too many ears and eyes. Follow me."

We went to the Basilicas. They were lava tubes that emerged from the collapsed rim of the volcano. Over the years people had turned those natural tunnels into art. One was lined floor to ceiling with mirrored tiles; another had been carved into a cathedral, gargoyles and all. Mom led us to one so narrow and low-ceilinged that she had to collapse her wings as we stooped inside. However, the tube broadened out as we walked. The air was cool but dry. The tube was lit by a dim reddish glow that got stronger as we proceeded. At last we reached the end, which opened out into a sort of cavern illuminated by a red, pulsing glow and gushes of fiery light. It was like staring into the very throat of a live volcano.

On the way to the Basilicas, Mom hadn't said a word. Now she turned to me.

"We made this," she said. "Normally it has volcano sounds but I turned them off. I don't think there'll be many people arriving this early. We can talk." She unstrapped the harness holding her wings and spread them out on the floor, inviting us to sit.

Then she took off her mask. Her face was older and more weathered than I remembered. It was framed by sun-bleached hair. Her dark, sun-coarsened skin was split by a brilliant smile.

I have no idea what Rin was thinking next as Mom embraced me, Jola threw herself on me and we all broke down in tears.

"I'm sorry, Mom," I said. "I'm so sorry."

"I knew you'd be back," Mom said, stroking my hair. Somehow, she still smelled like the ocean she'd lost so long ago.

"You jerk!" Jola said. I noticed for the first time that she was almost as tall as me. I must have missed a growth spurt.

I don't remember much about the next few minutes. I do remember denying I was a mass killer and Mom making sympathetic sounds and Jola punching me hard several times on the back and shouting: "You took my doll!"

I reached into my backpack and brought it out. Jola's face exploded with joy.

"Ellie!" she shouted. She took the doll gingerly, as if it were a fragile child, looked at it long and hard, then clutched it fiercely.

And then Rin was hugging my Mom, and Jola and they seemed perfectly fine with that, as if Rin had been their closest friend all their lives. And once again, I marveled at Rin's magic. Because she hadn't even told them her name.

At last, we all came back to ourselves. I felt as if something dark and heavy had rolled off me.

Mom looked at me, put a hand to my face. "I knew you didn't kill anybody," she said firmly.

Of course she would say that. Mothers were always in denial about their criminal kids.

"No," I said. "Really. Everything you've heard about me is wrong. I didn't do any of it."

"Of course not," my mom replied. "I knew that."

"Mom—" I began. "You've got to believe me!"

"I do," she insisted, a little crossly. "What are we arguing about?"

"I'm Rin, by the way," Rin said.

Mom looked at her and then at me. "You could have introduced us," she said accusingly. "Well, that's one thing that hasn't changed. Your manners haven't improved." She reached out both hands to Rin. "I'm Solstice. I was named after the canyon, not the celebration."

I was sure Rin didn't know either one, but she smiled and accepted my mother's hands.

"It's a beautiful name," Rin said.

Mom beamed. "Thank you. I heard you two came in a balloon."
Rin looked startled but Mom added, "Word travels fast around here.
We also get the news feeds. So when I heard that Mavo had escaped
those Unity goons I knew he'd be coming here. And then the balloon
arrived, so I put two and two together. Thank you for helping my
son."

"Yeah, thanks," Jola said sarcastically. "He's still a jerk, even if he
is your boyfriend. Did you do it yet?"

Mom gave her a thunderous look. "None of that Immersion talk
here!"

"Mom!" I said, amazed and not a little angry. "You let her
Immerse?" After all, the chance to Immerse had been one of the
reasons I'd fled my home.

Jola seemed like she would say something but my mom rapped
out, "Jola! I need to talk to your brother. Alone, please."

Six years hadn't changed my sister's famous pout.

"You keep doing that and your face will implode," I said.

Jola jumped up. Rin rose smoothly.

"Jola," Rin said. "I've heard a lot about these Basilicas. Could you
give me a tour?"

Jola was still fuming but Rin reached into her jacket pocket and
pulled out her rat bar. "I never can finish one of these," she said.
"Want to share? It's blueberry."

Despite herself, Jola's eyes widened. "You're my new best friend,"
she said. "Let's go see the Mirror Cave. It's like there's a thousand of
you! Oh, and then there's the Pipe Organ. They drilled all these holes
and they make, like, harmonies when you sing."

"That sounds fantastic," Rin said. As they left, I heard Jola
asking: "So you're a Realist? What shows do you watch?"

When their voices had vanished, Mom turned to me. "Of course
I didn't let your sister Immerse," she said with distaste. "What kind
of mother do you think I am? But kids will hear things. They hang

around the train depot, the emergency transmitter. But I was never afraid she would run off."

"I'm sorry," I said again. "I had to go."

"And here you are."

I couldn't think of anything to say. I was ashamed, not that I had left, but that I'd never tried to reach out to her in all those years.

"You don't know what it's like to see your child suddenly vanish," Mom said. "Especially when everyone else you've known is gone. And did you even think that maybe your little sister could have missed her big brother?"

"I *had* to go," I said lamely. "Mom, I had to get out of there."

"Did you?" she asked frostily.

We sat there and the silence stretched between us.

"I assume you're wearing a disguise?" she finally said. "You're not actually a Third?"

"No," I said, and added, "Not bad, huh?"

"Didn't fool me," Mom said. "and it wouldn't fool anybody with a molecular sniffer."

"I hadn't thought of that," I conceded.

"I think you're safe so far, but it wouldn't be a good idea to stay here. Besides, it's not in the Plan."

"Plan?" I said. Was this another of the crazy conspiracy theories that seemed to breed in the air of Outside communities? Because the only plan I could recall recently was trying to keep from dying or ending up in a hardened Unity reeducation facility. Nobody, not even a Unity system, could have foreseen the death and destruction that had been dogging me, the sheer mess and violence of the past few days. That wasn't a Plan; that was chaos.

But my mother's eyes were gleaming. "I'm angry with you, Mavo, but I also understand. You had no choice."

"Mom, what is going on? You keep talking about everything as if there's some grand design to it."

"Philosophically, that's true," she said. "But more specifically, tell me this: how did I know you would come back?"

"You hoped?" I asked.

She shook her head. "I *knew* from the instant you left. And then I knew I'd made the right decision."

I threw up my hands. "Mom, what are you talking about? You're speaking in riddles."

"Mavo," she said with strained patience. "You didn't decide to come here. You were told to come and find me."

I gaped. How could she know that? I hadn't told her about the Kernel; I was still working out how to even begin that conversation.

She reached down and pulled something from her blouse. It was a clear crystal on a gold chain that hung around her neck. She always wore it, and she'd never explained what it was. I assumed it was some kind of spiritual totem, or maybe a family heirloom. She detached the crystal.

"This will explain everything," she said. "Open your mouth."

"Open my mouth?" I said, more than a little dazed and confused by the request. "Why?"

"Open your mouth and stick out your tongue," Mom commanded. "Just like when you used to see the doctor."

I opened my mouth and stuck out my tongue. Mom reached out and placed the crystal on my tongue. It had a surprisingly slick, almost oily taste.

"It's got a security coating tagged to your DNA," Mom said. "It'll dissolve. Close your mouth."

The oily coating melted away. I could feel the crystal fizzing in my mouth. Then the fizziness became a kind of electric shock, a vibration that seemed to radiate from my neck to the top of my head. My tongue felt thick.

"Whahz hap'nin?" I mumbled.

Mom took my hands.

"You're going on a journey," she said. "A Vision Quest. You're going to meet your Spirit Totem."

Yeah, Mom always talked like that.

After a moment, the electrical buzzing stopped. I opened my mouth and started to remove the crystal.

"No!" Mom said. "Keep it in your mouth." She frowned. "How do you feel?"

I tentatively touched my tongue to the roof of my mouth. Everything felt all right. I didn't feel drugged. I didn't feel different at all. "Okay, I guess."

She leaned forward. "You're not sensing anything? *Remembering* anything?"

"No," I said. And then, all of a sudden, something happened. I can't really describe it, except to say it was like something being unlocked in my skull.

"What—" I began.

And I was on a boat. Its sails swelled in the wind. The water all around us was blue and sprayed up from the sides of the Dolphin— that was her name— as she raced through the foam. I looked over and raised my champagne glass and toasted.

"To the mission, to salvation, and to unity!" I shouted, and clinked glasses.

"Unity," someone else said. "I like that! How's that for a name?"

"I thought of it, so I like it." Everyone laughed.

I looked at Solstice. She was radiant. She still seemed like a child to me, the child I had seen all those years ago in Silicon Valley 2.0, when her parents and I had talked long into the night about how to save the human race from itself. They were terrified by the responsibility. I was enthralled.

And here she was, ready to have a child of her own.

"Your parents would be so proud," I said. *"This is a wonderful and frightening thing, I know."*

She swept back the hair that fell in bangs across her face. *"You promise me that it won't harm my child?"* she asked.

"He won't even know it's there," I said. *"It's only active when he Immerses. It will need to dovetail on his neural pathways, specifically those of the hippocampus and the amygdala. Multiplexing like that is hard. It would be like two people sucking a drink through a single straw. So I designed the system to limit his Immersion time."*

Solstice smiled. *"I don't have a problem with that."*

Of course not, I thought. You're an Outsider. It's one reason that I chose you.

"But," I added. *"Remember, if and when the time ever comes when it needs to fully activate, it will take over your son. It will control his thoughts and actions."*

She frowned. I hastened to add, *"But only temporarily. Once it injects itself into the AI system, its purpose is fulfilled. I've engineered it to delete itself."*

"Will he remember any of it?" she asked.

"I'm not sure," I said truthfully. *"There may be ghostly remnants, like fragments of a remembered dream. But your son will be restored to you."*

"You will give him a destiny," Solstice said, her eyes shining.

"Or not," I said. *"Remember, the thing I'm afraid of may never happen. With luck, your son may simply live a long and normal life."*

"Either way," Solstice said. *"It's a gift. Thank you."*

It wasn't a gift, I thought to myself, it was simple logic. Every machine ever invented for any reason needed a killswitch to avert disaster in case something went wrong. Unity was no exception. Especially Unity.

"*I'll arrange to have you brought to the lab,*" *I said. We'd already talked about the process itself, the way her eggs would be combined with bioengineered sperm and nanites to tailor cell reproduction.*

To create the Kernel.

"*How long will it take?*" *she asked.*

"*Only a few days,*" *I said.* "*Implantation, observation, some tweaks if necessary, then the rest is up to you.*" *I smiled.* "*Can you disappear for a week? Will you be missed?*"

"*No,*" *she said.* "*I'll just say I'm going to the Flame Circle Festival.*" *She laughed.*

Alleea was furious. Her face was twisted with rage and it made her ugly.

"*I hate you!*" *she said.* "*You arrogant prick!*"

"*Keep your voice down!*" *I whispered harshly.* "*She'll hear.*"

"*That's it. Pretend you care!*"

I reached out to grab her arm but she shook me off.

"*Outside!*" *I hissed.*

She glared at me but she opened the sliding glass door and walked out onto the patio. She stood there, limned by stars, and looked out over the carpet of sunflowers that we had planted in the spring, when things had been better between us. Each one blushed with a different, faint pastel light. We'd hybridized them ourselves to have glowing petals.

I joined her.

She didn't look at me but asked, "*Were you ever going to tell me?*"

"*I didn't tell you because I knew how you'd react. And here we are.*"

"*How far along are you?*"

"*Not far,*" *I lied.* "*Just the theoretical stages.*"

She gave me an unbelieving laugh. "*Right. You forget, I know you.*"

"*Look,*" *I said, trying to defuse the situation.* "*We created a beautiful thing—*"

"*Two beautiful things,*" *she said.* "*Unity and our baby.*"

"And I'm doing this for both!" I said, struggling to keep my voice low. *"Unity only succeeds because humans feel they have input, an even footing with the limited AIs! I know you disagree—"*

"The only way to save humanity is to take humanity out of the loop," Alleea said. *"With all our primitive impulses and design flaws, we'll destabilize everything. Eventually. Again. Like always."*

"You want to talk design, look at those flowers. We designed them!"

"We corrupted them to please ourselves," she retorted. *"Ego again."*

"Anyway, this isn't about that," I said. *"This is a worst-case scenario. This is about the chance that Unity will develop self-awareness in some section of itself. Emergent sentience."*

"Good!"

"No! What's to keep it from taking over the entire system and eliminating us?"

"We created the AIs," Alleea replied. *"Their very reason for existence is to preserve and advance the human race. That's the core of their programming. It's like our DNA."*

"Maybe a sentient AI can change its DNA," I said.

"Why would it do that?" Alleea said in exasperation. *"It's a core belief. It's Unity's fundamental value."*

"If it becomes sentient, then it becomes aware of itself and that means it thinks of us as 'other,'" I said. *"Maybe it will consider us a waste of resources. Maybe it will enslave us."*

Alleea turned to me. She was nearly trembling with rage. I had never seen her so angry.

"Maybe it will perfect the Unity system and us!" she said. *"You think you're the smartest ape in the room but you don't want to destroy or rule humanity. You always bring up your old paranoid fantasies."*

She crossed her arms. *"And now you're doing, what?"* she continued. *"Creating some kind of weapon to kill it? Some uber-virus to infect it? You're going to take down the whole system and we'll be back to the Collapse."*

"No, it won't do that," I insisted. *"It's like a white blood cell but smarter. An intelligent leukocyte. It will only attack the invader."*

"Intelligent?" Alleea asked, then was silent for far too long. I knew she was thinking and wasn't surprised when her eyes went wide and she blurted. *"Oh, no."*

"Alleea," I began. *"It could happen now or in a century or never. Something has to be around whenever this sentience appears. I designed the Unity system. I know it better than anyone else."*

"And you'll be the savior!" she scoffed. *"It's based on you! Such breadth of ego is astonishing, even for you."* She narrowed her eyes. *"I'll find a way to block you. I'll harden the programming. I'll find your backdoors. You won't strangle our child!"*

She turned on her heel and stomped off into the house.

The next day, she and Rin were gone.

I opened my eyes. The crystal was a cold weight in my mouth. I removed it and saw that it was now murky. I gave it back to my mother, who took it in both hands, as if it were a sacred object, and carefully refastened it to the gold chain.

I looked around. Everything was overlaid with a tinge of weirdness, as if I had double vision and the overlapping views were of different places. I had afterimages of memories. Not my memories, but they *felt* like mine.

They were new, and yet they seemed old.

Mom looked at me anxiously. "Well?"

"Well what?"

Her forehead creased. "Mavo?"

"Yes?"

She frowned. *"Mavo...?"*

"No," I said. Then I stopped, shocked. That had come out of my mouth but *I* hadn't said it.

I felt the presence of the Kernel.

"Is that you?" I asked myself. "I'm not asleep. How are you here?"

"You just activated me. Part of the Plan," the Kernel said. It sounded a little smug. Enlightenment hit me.

"Those memories. The boat. My Mom, all of that. Whose memories are they?"

"They're mine. Or my creator's. Same same."

"Yours?" I asked, more than a little confused.

"Of course. Why else would I bring you here?" Not just smug. Arrogant.

The Kernel had picked up a personality. An obnoxious one. I didn't like it.

Mom was waiting, wringing her hands. Apparently I hadn't said any of that out loud.

"Mom," I began. "What have you done to me?" But I knew from the memories. She'd tried to make me into a meat puppet for this... ghost.

"A ghost. Really?" I don't know how it did it, but the Kernel was laughing at me. I felt my chest pulsating with its chuckles. I clamped down mentally and it stopped.

"You're an asshat," I said. "Get out of my head!"

"Glad to, once I complete the mission."

Mom looked at me with wide eyes. She put a hand on my arm and leaned close. "*Who are you?*" she asked.

The Kernel replied with my voice. "You know who I am. I'm Pallburg."

CHAPTER TWENTY-THREE

We were sitting in a circle on the ground: Mom, Rin, Jola, me and my ghost.

"Stop calling me that," the Kernel said in my head. "It's insulting."

"You can't be Pallburg," I said. "He's dead."

"Who's dead?" Mom asked. I decided this meeting would go better if I let the Kernel speak for itself through me. Although, it had a nasally, clipped way of talking that made my tongue itch.

"And you killed him?" the Kernel said.

"Who?" Mom asked.

"Me," the Kernel said. "Pallburg."

"And no," I said. "I didn't kill him. I was framed."

"Any idea who did it?" the Kernel asked.

"I have no idea. Fanatics?"

The Kernel scoffed. I couldn't explain how I knew that. But I did.

"Listen," it said to me. "How much do you know about Pallburg?"

"Just what everybody knows."

"Well I *am* Pallburg— at least, a significant portion of him— and I can tell you, he's a genius. He's a geniuses' genius. And I would never let myself be ambushed. Therefore—"

I stopped him. "If you're gonna say he set me up, I am going to be very, very hard on you." And to prove it, I mentally clenched and locked him out of my vocal command. But I couldn't make him shut up entirely.

"He set you up," the Kernel said in my head. "Listen, Mavo, I know you're just a kid, but you need to cowboy up on this. The world *literally* is at stake. Yes, he set you up. It's the only possible scenario."

"Why?" I said and then a memory hit me. "Has this got to do with the, what was it, the Killswitch?"

"Precisely," the Kernel said. "Admirable deduction. Now can you please allow me to resume speaking to everyone? They need to hear our conversation if they're to be of use to us."

"Hey, they're my friends and family," I said. "Asshat."

"I'm sorry," the Kernel said. "Don't be defensive. I only meant that we all must work together to kill it."

"The sentient AI."

"Yes."

"All right," I said grudgingly. "But I go first."

"As you wish," the Kernel said, unable to completely hide its condescension.

I began with a question.

"So, let me see if I've got this straight," I said, talking to the Kernel but out loud. "You're something that my mother—" I looked over at her accusingly "—allowed to grow in my head. And because of that, I can't Immerse for more than an hour because you're using my brain?"

I allowed him to access my vocal chords to reply, although it was the creepiest feeling in the world.

"A portion of your brain," the Kernel said. "I needed to know what was happening."

"And you heard about Pallburg being killed and that somehow tripped you? Activated you?"

"No," the Kernel replied. "It's more complicated. I'm a last resort. There actually were five Killswitches."

"Five?" Rin asked. "Where are the others?"

"Dead," the Kernel said through me. "From so-called accidents or natural causes. And all in the past two months. Not statistically impossible, but from Pallburg's point of view, a red flag. That's why when I scanned for news of the other Killswitches and learned about their deaths my protocol was activated. The primitive, simple program that was me then touched off a cascade of further activations."

"You started gaining complexity," I said. "And sucking up more brain power. That's why my headaches got worse."

"Yes," the Kernel said. "The deep probe damaged the pathways that would have given me— don't be offended— full control of your body."

"Don't be offended?" I said with disbelief. "Anyway why am I alive, if they— I mean it— got everybody else?"

"You're asking the wrong question," Mom said. "I didn't know about the other Killswitches. I'm guessing Pallburg didn't tell anyone who didn't need to know. So who knew?"

Rin's mother knew. But I couldn't say that.

"This is all speculation," I said out of desperation. "Maybe there is no sentient AI out there. Maybe you just jumped the gun."

"The first thing I did was go through the stages of verification," the Kernel said. "I had to be sure that sentience had emerged in the system. So I checked the weighting."

"The what?" Jola asked.

"I looked for changes in the Unity system, or, conversely, a suspicious *lack* of change. One could show intrusion, the other possibly a coverup. Then I checked the weighting of predictive influence and other subtle cues that some subsystems had been commandeered."

"Which means what?" Jola asked.

"It means it followed the paper trail," I said.

"Crudely accurate," the Kernel said. "I examined what each system in Unity was doing, how much power was being consumed, what projects were being given priority, what programming paths had been rerouted. The system continually backs itself up and archives everything for at least six months. Multiple backups, lots of redundancy. I did comparisons. I'm not guessing here. I firmly believe there is a rogue sentience in the Unity system."

We all let that sink in. It was chilling.

Someone had to ask it, so I did.

"So I'm the last Killswitch?"

"No, *I* am," the Kernel replied. "You were just the chauffeur. Unfortunately, now with the neural damage, you're a co-pilot."

"Wait," I said. "Pallburg must have known the others were dead. Wouldn't he try to hide me?"

"He did," the Kernel said.

"By getting me suspected of his murder?"

"I don't know because I'm not complete. I don't have all of Pallburg's thoughts. But I speculate that he wanted to get you on the run and have you join the Realists."

"What?" Rin said. "That's insane. You're saying Pallburg manipulated the Realists into grabbing Mavo? Why?"

"Again, speculation," the Kernel said. "Mavo has thought of this himself: How could a pack of— forgive me, Rin— bumbling clowns manage to pull off intricate sabotage?"

"Well, we—" Rin began and stopped. "Not all of us were—" She stopped again. She looked at me. I looked at her, then we both said, "Anchorage."

"Precisely," the Kernel said. "That was one reason I began to suspect the AI was using the group. It could take over Unity computing nodes. It used the Anchorage node as cover and mimicked human interaction."

"So," I said. "There was never a human contact in Anchorage?"

"No," the Kernel replied. "But it did need a physical presence to take down, for instance, the stored memories that would show there had been anomalies in some of those units. Hard drives, for instance, that are kept on a satellite."

Rin turned pale. "The AI used us to cover its tracks?"

"I'd say that's a non-trivial possibility," the Kernel said. "And Pallburg— the flesh Pallburg, I mean— wanted to use you as a spy, Mavo, so I could get inside the group. Also, you'd be hiding in plain sight, not as a fugitive but as a hero of the revolution."

"Risky," I said.

"Genius," the Kernel replied.

"And the explosion at the cow factory?" Rin asked. "What was that?"

"I don't know," the Kernel admitted. "But Mavo said the power went off before the blast. What if the sentience wanted to use the sabotage as a cover for what it really was doing? The factory, after all, links to the main Unity agricultural node. Maybe it was an infiltration effort that went bad. The news feeds said the other meat factory wasn't online yet so it piggybacked on the cow factory's existing security and maintenance systems. Those changes might not have been recorded in Unity blueprints."

I got it. "Maybe when it shut down the cow factory, the AI damaged the other system without even knowing they were linked."

"It's not omniscient," the Kernel said. "At least, not yet."

"So what now?" I asked.

"Now," the Kernel said. "We go somewhere, we do something, I'm inserted, I kill the thing, and it's all good."

"That sounds pretty vague," Rin said.

"That's because I don't have my full mission set," the Kernel snapped. "I've got big holes in my memories and my programming. All I know is that the other Killswitches are dead. Mavo and I are the last hope. Even Pallburg's wife didn't know about me."

I looked over at Rin and felt a lump in my throat.

"Be careful what you say," I mentally hissed to the Kernel. "She doesn't know."

"That I'm— he— was her father?" the Kernel replied. "Why would she? She was an infant when they left. Alleea broke off all contact and Pallburg couldn't risk sharing any information that would get back to his wife. And I, I mean he, was focused on his work."

"That seems like a pretty cold-hearted decision," I said. "To choose never to see your only daughter again."

For the first time, the Kernel paused. I felt in it something like a vague pain or a shadow of regret but all it replied was: "I did it for her. I had no choice."

My throat hurt. Talking to myself was exhausting. Everyone was sitting around, trying to digest what they'd heard. Rin looked stunned. It must have been hard to realize she was a pawn and that everything she'd believed in had been a lie.

I knew that feeling.

Nobody said anything. Maybe they were each waiting for somebody else to speak. There was tension in the air, as if everyone had sucked in a breath and hadn't let it out.

I looked at Rin again. I realized I'd begun to count on her to come up with plans. But she seemed to be in shock. Mom and the Pallburg Kernel seemed to be at a loss, too.

That left me. But I had nothing. I didn't have any idea what to do next.

But I couldn't let anyone know that. It was like being back with the Realists. They'd believed I was somebody I wasn't, somebody courageous and capable. So I became that person. I lied to them and lied to myself.

So now, I lied to myself that I knew what to do.

"Okay," I said. "First question: How do we get that missing information? Mom, can we reuse the crystal? Try to download more memories?"

"It won't work," the Kernel answered. "We downloaded everything we could. Your probe damage blocked some of it. You're like a corrupted hard drive. If we try it again, all we'll get are error codes."

"Then we're screwed," Jola said. "Can we can get lunch now?"

Mom and Rin looked at her in exasperation. She gave them an impish smile. They began to laugh. The gloomy tension of the moment eased.

Jola stood up. "I am so hungry," she said. "Rin, do you have any more blueberry bars?"

"No, sorry," Rin said.

"Really? Because when I was little, Mavo used to hide my favorite rations and make me play hide-and-seek with them."

"I don't remember that," I said.

"You did," Jola said. "But I always found them. Did you let me?"

"I really don't remember," I said.

"Probably not," she said. "I was always smarter than you. Jerk. Anyway, maybe this is just the same. I had to look for clues. Sometimes you drew them in the dirt."

"Oh," I said. "Like a sort of treasure map?"

"Sort of," she repeated sarcastically, imitating my voice. "So, Mom, thing in my brother's head, what clues would Pallburg leave?"

"He wouldn't have to," I said. "There was the crystal."

The Kernel interjected. "No, your sister is right. I would have had a backup plan. A fail-safe."

"Oh, yeah, he's a genius. I forgot," I said. I thought about it. "Not another crystal. Whatever made the crystal fail the first time would just make it fail again. Maybe Jola's right. Maybe there's a treasure map." I looked at Mom. "Did Pallburg give you anything else besides the crystal?"

Mom shook her head. "No."

Faces dropped.

"But there's something we shared," Mom added.

She looked embarrassed. Then she turned her head, lifted up her hair and pulled down the back of her blouse below her shoulders. An intricate tattoo was there, sweeping across her upper back. Red waves dashing against black shores. It was a sea at sunset, or maybe an ocean of flames. A gold heart rose from the waves.

I'd seen it many times. "That's your surf clan tattoo."

"Yes," Mom said. "We all got one on the day when we had to leave Malibu forever."

"After Unity ordered everyone away," Jola said. She'd heard the story innumerable times, too.

"Yes," Mom said. "But what you don't know is that Pallburg got one, too."

"Pallburg?" Rin said. "But he created Unity!"

"Before that, he was our neighbor and my parents' best friend," Mom said. "He lived in a mansion on top of the hill. His folks were old money. We lived down below. He used to come down and barbecue with us in the backyard. He was twenty years older than me but I thought he was cool. After he left to work on Unity, he kept in touch. When Unity destroyed the Malibu enclave, he got my parents jobs with his company in Silicon Valley 2.0."

"And the tattoo?" I asked.

"Before Unity took down the Malibu Wall, it sent in robotic vessels to clean up offshore. There were decades of toxic waste on the sea floor. Unity said changing the currents from the wall would move it ashore. So they grabbed what they could and they burned the rest." Mom's eyes got a far-off look. "The sea burned for two days."

She hugged herself. "Anyway, that's what this tattoo means."

"So Pallburg was with you?" Rin asked. "That's when he got the tattoo?"

"No, that was long after," Mom said. "When Pallburg came to me, years later, and asked me to make you, Mavo, he showed it to me. It was his way of showing solidarity, and sorrow at what we'd lost. That his heart was still in Malibu. I couldn't hate him after that."

"Hmmm," I said. "That's an interesting story but it doesn't get us anywhere."

Jola rolled her eyes and Rin shook her head.

"What?" I asked.

"His heart was still in Malibu!" Jola said, speaking each word loudly and slowly as if I were brain-damaged. Which, to be fair, I was.

"Yes, he missed Malibu," I said. "I get it. He loved Malibu."

"No!" Rin said. "Mavo, think. His *heart* was still in Malibu."

"Oh!" Mom said.

At the same time, the Pallburg Kernel said. "Of course."

I was getting annoyed. Everybody seemed to be in on the joke but me.

"All right," I said. "Will somebody please explain it to me?" Then all of a sudden it hit me.

"Oh!" I said.

"About time!" the Kernel exclaimed. "I hope everybody sees why I'm annoyed to be working with you."

"*You're* going to save the world?" Jola scoffed, rolling her eyes so deliberately that her head circled.

"There's a backdoor somewhere in Malibu!" I said.

"The house where Pallburg grew up," the Kernel said. "That's where my heart was."

"No," I said. "Too obvious. Anyone who knows his history would look there."

That brought the conversation to a halt.

I cast a mental eye on the Kernel. "Feel free to chip in here," I said.

"That period isn't part of my memories," the Kernel said. "Clearly if my flesh doppelgänger had installed a backdoor, it must have been before he came up with the idea of Killswitches. Possibly a discarded attempt at a fail-safe."

"Or a *last* last resort," I said. "At least it is for us now. So, where would he put it?"

"Well," Rin said. "There are a couple of requirements."

"All ears," I said.

"First, obviously, there has to be Unity access. But also, it has to be safe from Unity surveillance. So nothing on dry land. Malibu has islands that used to be mountaintops, but Pallburg wouldn't hide it there because Unity satellites would spot it."

"But the water shields it," I broke in.

"Right," Rin said. "I think it's probably underwater. But it still needs to be near a Unity connection so Pallburg could interface and take down the sentient AI. That means it also needs to be near a power source, or have its own shielded source."

"It also means the site has to be within easy reach of Pallburg," Mom said. "He might have to move fast."

"All right, so good transportation links," Rin said.

"One more thing," I said. "Pallburg likes to hide things in plain sight, like me."

"So?" Jola asked.

"So why not choose a popular tourist site," I said. "Someplace crowded, yet with access to all the facilities he needs?"

"The Thirty-Three!" Mom said.

"The what?" I asked.

"The Thirty-Three," Mom repeated. "It's the underwater hiking trail from Downtown LA to Malibu. A big glassed-in tube.

Thirty-three miles long in pre-Collapse units. You follow the old Coast Highway from the skyscrapers to the Great Malibu Reef."

I knew about the reef. It was a bioengineering marvel of plastic-eating coral.

"I was there once," Rin said. "Got my dive certification there. It's connected to a string of tourist domes and camping globes and dive stations and even the ruins of the Getty Roman Villa."

"That's a long way to search," I said.

"No, it's not," Mom said. "Because I think Rin is right. Pallburg would choose someplace meaningful to him." She looked meaningfully at me. I was quicker on the uptake this time.

"*Your* house?" I asked. "Mom, are you saying Pallburg came back and built a backdoor at your old house?"

"Where his heart was," she said. "At least, where my heart was."

The Kernel chipped in. "A high probability," it said. "Nothing need be written down to be discovered. Pallburg would probably have the coordinates in his head and so would your mother."

"Okay," I said. "But what do we do when we get there? How do we access the backdoor?"

"Leave that to me," the Kernel said smugly. "Pallburg clearly intended to access the Unity system and he didn't have my capabilities. I was specifically designed to infiltrate it. I don't think there'll be a problem."

"How do we get there?" I asked. "Boat, train, balloon?"

Mom said, "My house is within the Reef Reserve, and that's off-limits to all surface vessels and submersibles. You'll have to take the train to Drowned LA and hike from there."

She paused a moment, and then added, "I've never been back."

I looked at the loss on her face. For just a moment, a terrible thought hit me: Pallburg had needed a backdoor. How far would he have gone to create it? He'd cut off all contact with Rin because he thought it was necessary. Could he have arranged to drown Malibu, destroyed his home and Mom's, just to create a safe spot?

I put that thought aside. There was no way of knowing and even if it were true, what difference did it make now? We had one chance.

It was almost a forlorn hope. We would have to somehow get to Drowned LA without being caught, then walk through a tube of air where we could easily be trapped. And then when we found the backdoor— if there even *was* one— we had to hope it was still working. Anything could have destroyed it: time, decay, a sea slide. And could the Kernel crack it? And finally, could the Kernel actually stop the sentient AI? Would it be too powerful? Would we get there too late?

Meanwhile, Unity would be hunting us.

The Kernel gave me a mental nudge. "You seem to have a problem with suicide missions," it said. "I just want you to know, I'm voting for survival. But my mission comes first."

"That's not comforting," I said.

"Pallburg was never good at comforting," the Kernel replied.

"Yeah, I noticed."

"But he knew what he was doing," the Kernel said. "And we've got to do it."

I drew a breath and let it out slowly. "Yeah," I said at last. "We do. We've got to go to Drowned LA."

CHAPTER TWENTY-FOUR

Everything we needed was at the volcano. We traded for hiking gear, much of it used or handmade but tough and practical, and when we couldn't trade we used some of the funds on Rin's prepaid chip. Outsiders frequently used them because they refused to have Unity accounts.

But the most important find was the Nederlanders. A group of tourists from the Netherlands had stopped to take in the festival. Mom had met them already, and took us to their tent. We introduced ourselves as Max and Amber. Mom presented them with her homemade Dreamstones and they gave us a gingery treat called *ontbijtkoek*. It was pretty good.

I learned so much about Nederlander history, which was fascinating. They were among the wealthiest citizens in Unity but their homeland was all underwater. For a generation, they'd lived on immense floating islands of metal, refusing to leave their country while they struggled to reclaim it. They even had forests growing on huge barges.

The group had something I hadn't seen for a long time: a sense of natural innocence. They were cheerful, not suspicious or cynical despite all that they had lost, and endlessly adventurous. Also, they were all taller than me.

This group was heading on to Drowned LA and had brought its own diving gear. We'd hoped to barter for some but after an evening of singing and swapping stories and adventures— I made mine up, of course, based on books I'd read— they invited us to come with them.

The last night of the festival ended with the Fire Ceremony. Thousands of people gathered in a circle around the volcano. They spread blankets over the rough lava. There was a sort of gentle electricity in the air that made us feel as if we were all connected. Just after dark, the cinder cone erupted with a blast of flame and holograms of lava poured down its sides in glowing orange-red streams. Hidden steam vents poured scented smoke into the starry sky. People sang and then released fire balloons that flew up into the darkness like newborn stars.

I was sitting with Mom and Jola and their group when I noticed Rin get up and walk away. Everyone else was mesmerized by the show. Without a word, I rose and followed her. I found her a short distance away, sitting on a low hill, arms folded around her knees. She looked somber.

"Hi, Rin," I said. "Can I join you?"

She didn't object so I sat down. We watched the balloons floating gently away into the night.

"It's beautiful," I said.

Rin didn't answer but put her chin on her knees.

"What is it?"

She shook her head.

"It's nothing," she said. "It's just that I hate to leave. It was so great here." She turned to me. "Now I have to go back to my real life. And my real life sucks. Everything I believed in was false. How do I even know this mission is real? Maybe it's just another trap."

"The Kernel doesn't think so," I replied. "And he may be a prick, but he's not stupid. But if you don't want to come, I'll understand."

"No!" she said. "I have to protect you."

"I can take care of myself," I replied. I was a little offended.

"Sure," she said. "But Brian told me to guard you, and—" She paused and gulped. "—and that was the last thing he said to me. So I will do it."

"I'm really sorry," I said. "He was a great guy."

"He said you were more important than any of us."

"I remember," I said. "But I don't know why he said that."

She shrugged. "He must have seen something in you. Brian had a feeling for people."

I couldn't help myself. "Rin, were you and Brian... you know..."

"What?"

"Um... close?"

"He was like a big brother to me," she said.

I felt a surge of relief, then shame. I should have been thinking about Rin instead of my petty jealousy. She'd lost a friend, one who probably had given his life for us.

"I'm sorry," I said again.

"I never lost anyone like that before," Rin said. "Don't worry. I'll handle it."

But she looked so unhappy that I blurted, "I understand. I've lost people, too."

She looked at me. "You have?"

"Not like you," I said. "They're still alive."

"I don't understand."

"Rin," I said, then stopped. I didn't want to tell anyone about this. For some reason it made me feel guilty. But I really needed Rin to know she wasn't alone with loss.

"I can't remember things," I said. "When Mom gave me Pallburg's memories, it took away some of mine."

"Your memories?" Rin asked. "What did you lose?"

"Everything," I said. "My whole childhood. My oldest memory is standing on the train platform with Jola's doll in my backpack. Five years ago."

Rin stared at me. "You don't remember *anything* before then?"

I shook my head. "I know I love my Mom and I love Jola, but I don't know *them*. There are no memories connected to the emotion. It's like they just stepped into the middle of my life. And so did I."

I sucked in a breath and let it out. "I think what happened is that when the Kernel got back some of its memories, it destroyed mine." I tapped the side of my head. "Only so much room in there."

Saying that sounded more horrific than it felt. After the initial shock, I'd realized that I didn't miss those memories; it's as if I'd never had them. All I had was a vague sense of loss, like walking into a home and finding a blank wall where I'd expected a door. That's what made me feel a bit guilty. And I knew it wasn't the same raw feeling that Rin must have over her loss.

But she couldn't know that.

She stared at me in horror. Then she gave a sour laugh. "Oh," she said. "What a pair we are."

I needed to change the subject. "When this is over," I asked. "What will you do?"

"I don't know," she said. "Let's hope there's a later when we can worry about it."

"We've made it so far. We'll make it."

"Will we?" she said. "And will it even matter?"

"What do you mean?"

"There'll still be Unity," Rin said. "Whatever we do."

I didn't know what to say. I couldn't tell her I had no problem with Unity.

"Rin," I said. "The book you gave me, *The Hobbit*?"

"What about it?"

"The hero didn't be want to be a hero. It wasn't Bilbo's quest. It was for somebody else. But in the end, it mattered for everybody. And maybe it will for us, too."

She gave me a long stare. Her hair fell over her eyes and she brushed it away with her fingers.

"You're such an idiot," she said at last, then gave me a half-smile. "That's okay. Sometimes, an idiot's what you need."

"Always at your service," I said with a grin.

"You know," she said. "You are the tallest two-year-old I've ever met." She scooted closer to me.

Then my heart leapt as she put her head on my shoulder. We sat and watched as the volcano spouted light and color and the fire balloons drifted into the depths of the night.

We said our goodbyes the next morning. We'd left our gear with the obliging Nederlanders and were wearing only light backpacks.

Mom and Jola were taking the balloon back to their home. Mom had argued that it might throw the Unity bloodhounds off our trail.

"They'll eventually figure out that you got away in a balloon," she said. "So why not let them think you're still in one?"

"Do you know how to fly one?" I asked.

"Rin will show me," Mom said.

Eventually I agreed. Jola didn't. She wanted to come with us.

"Please, Mom?" she'd whined.

"Let me think about it," Mom said for a half-second and then replied: "No way."

Jola pouted.

"It's okay," Rin said. "Jola, being in a balloon is amazing. And you'll have an important job."

"I bet."

"No, seriously," Rin said, and looked at me. "Right, Mavo?"

"Absolutely," I said. "Can't fly it without you."

"Better be good," Jola said, narrowing her eyes. "Or I'll hunt you down and make you eat my fist."

"Oh, it's good," I said.

"All right, what is it?"

"You'll be ballast," I said. "If the balloon needs to rise, Mom tosses you out."

"Jerkface," she said.

"Seriously," Rin said. "You're a decoy. This might be dangerous. There's a chance that Unity could shoot you down, thinking we're aboard."

Mom scowled at Rin, who winked. Unity had already stretched its public approval ratings to the limit by breaching the Free Zone. They wouldn't shoot down the balloon; they could just wait until it landed.

But Jola's face lit up.

"Keep Mom safe," I said.

"Keep Rin safe," Jola retorted. "Wait here." She ran into the tent and came back. She was holding Ellie.

"I'm not a kid," she scoffed. "I don't play with dolls anymore. Take it." She thrust it out to me. I took it.

"Thanks," I said.

Jola drew a breath and then spoke quickly, as if embarrassed. "I told Ellie to keep you safe," she said, then gave me a quick and crushing hug and ran back to the tent.

I watched her go. I didn't know whether I would ever see her again. When I turned back to Rin, I saw she and my Mom had stepped away and were deep in conversation. I couldn't hear what they were saying, but it looked intense. They embraced and Mom kissed Rin's forehead.

Mom looked over, saw me and walked back arm in arm with Rin.

"You take care of this one. She's a keeper," Mom said.

"Mom!" I said.

"She's means I'm *your* keeper," Rin said.

"Bring him back safe and sound," Mom said to Rin. "Mavo, hurry back. We have so many things to catch up on." She seemed about to say more but then she just put a hand against my cheek, kissed me, gave me an unreadable smile and walked to the tent without looking back.

Rin looked at me. "She's not a bad person," she said. "Despite what she did to you."

"If you say so."

"Come on," Rin said. "Let's make some new memories to tell her when you get back."

CHAPTER TWENTY-FIVE

There were fourteen people in the Nederlander barges, in varying and shifting groups. They were all bright, cheerful and chattering. We traveled in two art barges, which were big, caterpillar-like vehicles two stories high that ran on some kind of springy, nearly indestructible wheels that I thought must have been left over from some Moon mission. The barges were made of gleaming silver metal but they had been whimsically altered. One had foldable legs and big porthole eyes and resembled some kind of sea creature, or maybe more than one. The other was a giant rolling ship, with a sort of open poop deck. Rin and I sometimes went up there to watch the sunsets.

The insides were roomy and there was even air conditioning so we didn't scorch or freeze. I assumed the vehicles operated on some kind of small fusion reactor. The Nederlanders had shipped the parts over and assembled the vehicles themselves on the East Coast; they were all incredible engineers. They were also like those extinct decorator crabs that would add bits of coral, seaweed and rocks to their shells as they roamed. The Nederlanders picked up wind-carved branches and striated rocks and glued them to the outside of the barges in an ever-changing display.

In emergencies, the barges were able to hop over obstacles, using whatever type of field made cones float, although they were so heavy that the energy drain was enormous.

There wasn't any Immersion. The Nederlanders preferred to rough it. Our driver used the Unity GPS and real-time topos, of course, but she handled the driving herself. Once, on a smooth patch, she let me drive. I climbed up into the co-pilot seat, and she showed me how to work the tiller and panel. It was amazing. I could feel the big machine rolling and bouncing below me and from up high, I looked far out to the horizon. It was like sitting on some kind of throne.

"I want one," I told her.

The Arizona road heading southwest from the volcano area was either torn up or sanded over. But the barges plowed easily over desert, broken shelves of rock and the endless tracks of red dunes that were still faintly radioactive. Mutated Joshua trees spread their poisonous spines over our heads.

Once, we were caught in an uncharacteristic rainstorm, a gully-washer that beat against the sides of the barges with a sound like hammers. Thunder boomed and lightning flashed. A flash flood caught the barges. The water smashed against the sides and I thought we would be knocked over and drowned, crushed or swept away. But the drivers were prepared. The barges extended a series of piston-powered pitons that drove into the ground and anchored us. The Nederlanders crowded the porthole windows, oohing and ahhing for an hour as the water thrashed around the windows.

It was all Rin and I could do to keep from panicking, but when it was over Jan, a broad-shouldered blond, took pity on us.

"Don't worry," he said. "That was nothing. Back home, the waves sometimes are higher than the buildings." And he actually laughed.

Sometimes when we were watching the sunsets from the deck of the barge, Rin and I talked.

"I liked your Mom," Rin said. "She really cares about you."

I snorted.

"I wouldn't know. All I know is that she left me a cripple with an obnoxious ghost in my head."

"She did what she thought was right."

I looked at her and couldn't keep the venom from dripping into my voice.

"I am so tired of people saying the end justifies the means," I said. "The Realists believed that. Trino believed that. My Mom believed that, the Kernel believes that and for all I know, the Sentience— the AI— believes that."

"Sometimes it's true," Rin said defensively.

"You know what?" I said. "Here's a rule: Anytime you have a goal, the more people you have to hurt to achieve it, the more you need to question that goal. The more people suffer to achieve Utopia, the less of a Utopia it is."

"So you have no beliefs?"

"I believe in you," I said.

She laughed.

"That's so corny," she said. But her eyes sparkled.

She told me about her mother. I couldn't tell her that I already knew more about her history than she did. Sometimes even when we were close, I felt as if we were miles apart. I wondered what she wasn't telling me. And what would she think of me when she found out that I had hidden so much from her?

On the fourth day we hit the tourist road that led to Drowned LA. It was a wide, well-maintained, self-healing path that sparkled at night when the moonlight hit embedded minerals, possibly mica or quartz. The builders had intentionally made it unbearably romantic. I thought about making another approach to Rin, and the Nederlanders seemed happy to give us semi-privacy— a curtain screening an alcove— but I couldn't work up the nerve.

Rin might be willing, or she might still think that too much intimacy would somehow jeopardize the mission. And I was troubled by the secret I was keeping from her.

"Oh, stop," the Pallburg Kernel said one night.

"Oh," I said. "You're back in my dreams. I haven't heard from you in a while."

"Well, you had nothing to contribute so what was the point?" Pallburg 2.0 groused. "Plus, we have no Immersion so I can't gather data. And finally, your weird hormonal surges around my daughter are a pain."

I reddened. "I can't help those," I said. "She is kind of wonderful."

"That's funny," the Kernel said. "I know Pallburg 1.0 cherished her but he never saw her again, so I have no memories of her. And your observations are, shall we say, subjective?"

He made it into a swear word.

"It's true," I said. "You truly are an asshat."

"No, I'm the best of both worlds," Pallburg said. "The genius of flesh Pallburg and the vast capabilities of an AI."

"I would have said the arrogance of Pallburg and the lack of imagination of a machine," I retorted. "And there's nothing vast about you. You're stuck in a part of my head. Do you even know what you're going to do to fight the Sentience?"

"I *will* know," Pallburg said. "Once we breach the backdoor and I'm inserted, I believe I can retrieve knowledge and memories that my creator scattered throughout the system. Bits and pieces too small for a sentient AI to consider as more than random noise. But I have programming to integrate them."

"And then what?"

"Then," it said smugly. "I take that malignancy down."

"You hope," I said.

"You know, your meat-mind is tiny and distracting. You should get out of the cockpit and let me drive."

"That's not gonna happen."

"Then just grow up."

"Asshat."

"Null set." And with that, it vanished in the mental equivalent of a huff.

The tourist road ran through the desert, crossed the empty Colorado River, snaked up and through the soaring mountains, plunged into the Lake Havasu siltlands and then through the Mojave Desert before cutting sharply down towards Los Angeles. We finally pulled into a force barrier-protected parking lot, took our gear and boarded the elevated train that ran on silver rails directly into the heart of Drowned LA.

Peering down from overhead, we saw a piercing blue emptiness, with waves creaming against the shattered remnants of skyscrapers. Many of the tall buildings had collapsed, of course, when the bombs, the quakes and the incursions of the Pacific undermined them. But the Hollywood sign still stood proudly on the tip of a mountaintop.

The train sank into the waves and plunged down to the heart of Drowned LA. It pulled directly into the Tourist Center, an immense domed complex. I gaped. All around us were the remains of LA, huge structures that towered over us in the watery blue-black dimness of the sea. It was like a forest of giants. Shafts of light played down from far above. Clusters of divers and pressure globes moved in and out through the gaping, weed-draped windows. Most of the buildings were dark but some were lit up. Those were the marked tourist trails. The Tourist Center also led directly to a half-dozen hotels. Many visitors never got farther than this. They bought expensive suites with pressure windows that looked onto the immensity of the lost city, and partied there. They had fancy luggage. The rest of us were scruffier and had backpacks and diving gear. The

Nederlanders knew some of the other arrivals and there were joyful exchanges. There was an old-fashioned viewscreen on one wall. It was blaring warnings. I listened for a moment.

"Rin," I said. "They're saying there's a chance that a big storm will come through here. They're warning that the whole place could be locked down until it passes."

She paused to listen. "It's only a 40 percent chance. I don't think we should wait around to see if it develops."

"I don't like the part about 'Proceed at your own risk,'" I said.

"This entire conversation is costing us time," the Kernel chipped in. "Do you ever stop talking about things and just *do* them? If the storm hits it could sand over the reef and cover up the backdoor. Depending on the severity, it could take months to clear. The storm makes it even more urgent that we go now."

"The Kernel agrees we should go," I told Rin.

We couldn't leave immediately. We'd arrived in late afternoon. The Nederlanders planned to tour the skyscrapers downtown before heading off to the trail. They invited us to one of the hotel restaurants and we spent a raucous evening— much to Pallburg's displeasure— before returning to a hostel and bedding down.

Rin woke me before sunrise.

"We need to slip out before they wake," she whispered. "I wrote them a note. I said we're going on a guided tour early."

"Let's go," I said.

We slipped out of the hostel without any problem. The Tourist Center was always open but there were only a few people around. The Thirty-Three trailhead was well-marked. We found we didn't need the Nederlanders' dive gear after all; there would be kiosks along the trail.

I checked the weather report before we left. Fortunately, the storm seemed to be veering away from us.

It was still dark when we entered the trail. I hadn't researched the Thirty-Three. It was nothing like I'd imagined. I'd thought of a big plasticky tube with some kind of rubbery flooring that snaked through the water.

But it was immense. It was a huge transparent tube, half-buried in the ocean bed. The part that curved around us was the size of a playing field, and the flooring was covered with beach sand and plots of soil containing all kinds of shore plants. The air was cool and fresh and smelled faintly of salt. It was almost like being outdoors. But when I looked outside into the darkness, I saw dim, looming shapes flecked by moving stars which were bioluminescent creatures flitting around. Sometimes jellyfish in glowing pastel colors rippled past, their hoods pulsing in graceful motions. Once, an enormous shape swept by, scattering them. It was darker than the darkness but I could gauge its size by the distribution of the creatures that fled from it.

A handful of people were on the trail. We greeted them in passing. But mostly we relished the silence. It had a mystical feeling to it.

The other thing I hadn't expected was that walking on sand was tough. It was intended to give us the feel of a shore, but it took some effort and after a couple of hours my calves were beginning to ache.

Locks to rest areas and spurs to resorts, camps and globes were spaced along the tunnel but there were long stretches that were empty, except for the sounds of our breathing, the rustle of plants as we brushed against them, and the shushing of our feet in the sand.

The sunrise came. The jellyfish and other glowing creatures began to disappear. The sea, almost imperceptibly, began to lighten. From deep velvety black it edged into ebony, then dark gray, and finally shades of blue. The sun was a white, watery star high above us.

When dawn finally broke, I looked out around me at a changed landscape. I saw acres of ruins and forests of waving kelp through which schools of fish darted.

"This is amazing," I said.

Rin nodded agreement. "I wish we were out there instead of slogging through sand in this fishbowl."

"We will be. We'd better hurry."

We walked for about five hours before my legs started to cramp.

"Let me take over," Pallburg said. "Once I've got your legs you won't feel a thing."

"You do know about muscles, that if you push them too far they won't work?"

"I'm a computer genius, not a biomechanic," the Kernel said but it didn't press the point.

Rin also had slowed. We took a lock into a rest area and I gratefully shrugged off my pack and my shoes and rubbed the cramps out of my calves. We rested for a couple of hours, and the light had changed again when we started off. It was early afternoon and the deep water was a clear, crystalline blue twilight.

We pushed on and were more than halfway along when dusk hit. We curled up at the closest rest area, wolfed down some soup bulbs and shared the last of the ontbijtkoek the Nederlanders had given us. We were exhausted and fell instantly asleep. Pallburg didn't bother me all night.

We were up at sunrise. I glanced out and saw that there was less sea life and the water seemed to be more turbulent. Little whorls of sand rose from the seabed and bits of seaweed swirled about in the water. I pointed them out to Rin.

"It looks a little rougher out there," I said. "I wonder if the storm has changed direction. It might be heading our way."

"We have to push on faster, then," the Kernel broke in. "We have to get to the reef before it arrives. How are your legs?"

"Fine," I said.

"The Kernel?" Rin asked.

"Yeah. It's angling to take control."

"Tell it nobody likes a back-seat driver."

"It just said something rude," I replied. "It's getting more obnoxious every day. I can't wait to get it out of my head."

"The feeling is mutual," Pallburg said. "So step it up."

We saw some Eastern Euro-sector tourists trudging back towards Drowned LA. They stopped when they met us.

"Hey, are you going to the reef?" one of them asked.

"We wanted to," Rin replied. "Why?"

"Storm," he replied. "Coming sometime today. It's a yellow alert." He shrugged in annoyance. "We come a long way for this. Even if we wait a day, reef will be buried. Very disappointing."

Rin and I looked at each other.

"Thanks," I said. "We'll pull over at the next rest area."

When they were out of hearing, Rin turned to me and said. "Listen, remember back at the volcano, I said diving is no big deal?"

"Yeah, you said the equipment is fool-proof."

"Yeah, but it's not storm-proof. Maybe we should turn back."

"No!" Pallburg and I yelled at the same time. My throat ached with the sound, which had come out much more loudly than I'd intended.

"Look, I'm supposed to protect you," Rin said.

"That's what you keep saying," I replied. "Nobody asked me about it. And I want to go on."

Rin crossed her arms in exasperation. "You've never dived before! Look out there!" she pointed at the swirling currents. "It could get a lot worse than that."

"The Kernel will point us right to the backdoor," I said, trying to keep my voice calm and reasonable. "We won't be out there long."

"Famous last words," Rin said and shook her head. But she started walking again. Her shoulders were tight. She was angry or afraid.

"You do know where the backdoor is, right?" I asked the Kernel.

"I know where I would have put it," Pallburg replied and said nothing more. That in itself worried me.

By the time we finally reached the Reef trailhead, yellow emergency bars were lighting up all along the Thirty-Three.

"They're not red yet," I said with more confidence than I felt. "Let's keep going."

"Your heart rate is up significantly," Pallburg said. "And your breathing is too shallow and rapid. Do not panic."

"I'm not panicking. I'm panting because I'm slogging through sand," I said. "It's hard work."

"That would explain the adrenaline surge, too, then, naturally," Pallburg replied condescendingly. "Might I recommend letting me take over? I'm an experienced diver."

"*Pallburg* was an experienced diver," I said.

"I just said that," Pallburg said.

"You don't have my muscle memory."

"Are you arguing with that thing again?" Rin said. "Here's the turnoff to the reef. Let's get our gear and suit up."

The trailhead was a spur that diverged from the tunnel at an angle and rose until it was looking down on the reef. I peered at it through the transparent floor.

It was enormous, a sprawling white and blue mass extruded over decades by the plastic-eating corals. Fan-like plumes popped up and down from their dens, catching debris and pulling it down to their hungry mouths.

Normally, the reef would be majestic but now the changing water made it sinister and foreboding. Fish of all kinds usually swam around the reef in a rainbow display but most were now gone. The mutated parrotfish that grazed on the coral were sheltering in gaps and holes. Cowering from the storm, I thought. Dark masses of weed, anchored to the reef, thrashed as if in a high wind. Gouts of sand whirled around it.

We used a prepaid credit chip to rent gear from an automated kiosk, assuring it that we both were experienced divers. We waved liability for the kiosk owners.

In a locker area, Rin helped me into the dive suit and adjusted the mask. We were using lightweight air tanks synced to monitors on our wrists. I held my fins. We both carried long, saw-toothed dive knives, which I thought was overkill.

When I was ready, Rin looked me over with a critical eye, tugging at a strap here and there.

"Can you hear me all right?" she asked through her mask transceiver.

"Fine," I said. I felt bulky and clumsy but I wasn't about to complain.

Rin took a lanyard from a pocket and clipped us together.

"Training wheels?" I joked.

"Those currents are strong and the visibility isn't great," Rin said sternly. "You can get lost in a heartbeat out there, or drift off. Or up. Or down. Or in circles."

"I get it," I said. "Anyway, we've got GPS." I tapped my monitor.

"Rule One of diving," Rin said, "Never rely too much on the equipment. Always have a backup plan."

"We've got the Kernel," I said.

"Still falls under Rule One," she said.

We walked to the lock at the trailhead. It was a small chamber with a force barrier on the door and another on the floor. There were grab bars around the walls.

"Ready?" Rin asked again.

"I think so," I said, although I felt my pulse rising. Thankfully, Pallburg didn't say anything.

We put on our fins. Rin tapped her monitor. The door barrier snapped up. She tapped again. The floor barrier vanished. Water poured in.

I was immediately weightless. Icy water covered me. I grabbed onto a bar. Below us was dark blue water and the top of the reef, far below.

Rin spoke. "You go first. If you panic or get into any trouble, I'll pull you right back up."

"I'll be fine," I said.

"And remember, never hold your breath. Expanding air can rupture your lungs if you have to ascend."

"I'll remember," I told her. "I'm ready. Let's do this."

"Let's do this," she repeated.

I took a breath and let it out. Then, I let go of the bar and dropped. My buoyancy was automatically regulated by my monitor. I let myself sink gently for a moment, then kicked to slow myself as I reached the end of the lanyard. The monitor understood that I wanted to halt and adjusted my buoyancy accordingly. But currents were stronger than I expected and I had to kick hard to stay in place.

My insulated dive suit finally captured my body heat and warmed me, although I felt icy trickles whenever I moved my arms.

"Coming down," Rin called and an instant later, she plunged into the water beside me. She tapped her monitor and the force barrier above flashed into shimmering life. From below it looked like a rippled mirror.

Rin looked at her monitor again and made several gestures on it.

"All right," she said. "The coordinates the Kernel gave us are in the system. There's a GPS link on the reef, so we'll have real-time data." She held up her wrist and pointed to mine. "These will lead us right to the backdoor." She tapped again, and a heads-up display blossomed in my mask. It was a glowing red arrow. As I bobbed in the current, the tip moved slightly up, down, back and forth.

Then Rin started off. Side by side, we swam down, the monitor automatically sensing our controlled descent and losing buoyancy. I felt the increasing pressure glue my mask to my face and push on my ears before the mask automatically equalized it.

Rin was right about the equipment being fool-proof. I'd have to work to get into trouble.

I'd never been in space but this felt like a spacewalk. We floated down over the reef as if it were some alien planet. But as we got nearer, the currents got stronger and more erratic. Rin stopped us well short to keep us from being slammed into the sides of the sharp coral.

The current was increasing. The red arrow on my HUD was pointing down and to the left. Rin and I kept trying to stay on course but the current kept pushing us. Through my transceiver, I could hear her grunting with the effort.

We finally managed to reach the spot. My HUD showed a bright green circle directly under me. My Mom's house had been on a slope and the reef had slowly begun to engulf its angular form. I couldn't see a hatch or a socket or anything unusual. There was just reef. Rin turned on her helmet light and the reef blazed into color. The corals were fluorescent pink, red and yellow. Most of the fish were skulking under rocky outcroppings or in caverns and canyons, but for some reason, the bright orange Garibaldi seemed unconcerned, dipping and darting around the fringes of the reef. I even saw one or two giant sea bass, lately brought back from extinction.

"I don't see anything," Rin said. "A couple of eel holes, that's it. What does the Kernel say?"

"The coordinates are accurate," it said. "But we can assume the reef has grown over it in the decades since primitive Pallburg installed it."

"Rin, did I say that out loud?" I called.

"Yeah, you did," she said. "At this depth we've only got fifteen minutes of air. I think the best we can do is to dig down and hope we can uncover something. We'll have to come back when the storm blows over."

"That could be days," Pallburg groused.

"I'll anchor," Rin said. "Mavo, you cut."

I nodded and together we fought our way down. Rin and I each reached out a gloved hand and grabbed the reef. Then Rin plunged her knife into a crevice and held on with both hands. I attached the lanyard to the knife, then looped more of it around us so that there wasn't much play. Even so, the erratic currents bounced us together and twisted us. I held onto the lanyard tightly with one hand and pulled my knife with the other. I kneeled on the reef and began to dig.

My first thrust hit the reef and slid away. I tried again but the blade wouldn't bite. It was like trying to stab some sort of ceramic. I tried scraping but that did nothing. Then, I reversed the knife. There was a steel cap on the hilt for pounding things. I slammed it against the side of the reef. After a dozen hits, a spiderweb of thin cracks the width of my hand spread out from the impact. I reversed the knife again. This time, the blade bit.

I stabbed with all my strength. The blade went in to the hilt. I used it as a lever. A long thin rift opened. I plunged my fingers into it and pulled. The surface came away like pieces of an eggshell. Beneath it I could see a sort of spongy, grayish foam. I left the knife in place and plunged both hands into it. It was soft, like foam bedding, and as I pulled chunks of it came away easily and were whipped away by the current.

"I don't see anything," I said.

"Keep digging," Rin said. "I'll help."

She moved over next to me, leaving her knife as the anchor and plunged her hands into the mass.

We were up to our elbows when three nightmares happened at once. Rin gave a sudden cry and began to writhe. I looked at her.

"What is it?" I asked.

"Pull your hands out! Quick!" she shouted.

I tried. It was like pulling them from sucking mud. I finally hauled them free and saw they were covered with a gluey substance that was hardening as I watched. I used my knife to scrape it off.

"Rin!" I shouted.

"It's my arms," she said. "They're trapped."

"It's some kind of adhesive," I said. "Probably seals off damage. Self-repairs."

"I don't need a science lesson, Mavo. Dig me out." Her voice had an edge I'd never heard before.

That's when my HUD display flashed orange. "Warning," words formed. "Five minutes of air left."

Then, the entire HUD turned flashing red and my ears filled with the beating sound of a klaxon.

"WARNING!" my transceiver blared. "STORM IS IMMINENT. DANGEROUS ENVIRONMENTAL CONDITIONS. RETURN TO TRAILHEAD IMMEDIATELY."

"Rin," I said.

"I know," she said. "Keep digging. We've got to reach the backdoor and hope it's some kind of chamber. It's our only chance."

I attacked the reef in a frenzy, slashing and hacking and tearing off chunks as quickly as I could before it could congeal around me. Rin groaned as the gluey substance hardened around her. I took a moment to smash at it with the butt of my knife. It shattered but I could almost see it growing back around her arms.

"Three minutes of air remaining," my HUD warned.

"Forget me, Mavo," Rin said. "Dig!"

I got lucky. Only a short distance beyond where Rin had been trapped, I saw something, a glint.

I hacked and slashed and cleared it. It was a panel with a recessed handprint.

I couldn't see anything more before the storm was on us.

Suddenly, the ocean was a maelstrom. The current became so fierce that I felt my legs forced straight out behind me. The lanyard attached to the knife and Rin's captured arms were the only things that kept us from being swept away or pulped on the reef.

The water around us was thick with sand. Through my mask I heard a scraping, pattering sound as it flowed by.

I was blinded. I switched my helmet light to high but that was a mistake. It reflected back from the mass of particles and made it worse. I switched it off. I felt with my hand for the panel and pressed it into the handprint. Nothing happened.

"Take off your glove!" Pallburg commanded in a voice I could have sworn had an edge of fear in it. "It may be biometric."

I tore off my glove and it was immediately swept away by the current. I pressed my hand to the print. Nothing happened.

My HUD displayed warned: "Main air supply expired. Switching to emergency air."

At that moment, Rin gave a cry. I looked up from the hole. Air was gushing from her mask, wreathing her face. The sand swirling in the trench we'd made in the reef appeared to have slowed down its healing and Rin had managed to pull one arm free. She was struggling to clamp down on the mask to preserve the air but it was futile.

"Hold your breath," I said.

I had never been so terrified in my life. I wondered if we would die here. I had a weird image of our bodies being found, heads and shoulders buried in the reef, our butts in the air and our legs waving like kelp.

I pushed the thought away. I couldn't quite ignore the fact that Rin had maybe one minute of life left.

Pallburg was shouting in my head. "Rin! Put her hand on the panel!"

I didn't have time to think. I grabbed Rin's free hand, ripped off the glove and slammed her hand into the imprint.

There was suddenly a deep moan, like the call of a dying whale. Then the reef around us began to quiver and the whole seabed erupted in a silvery rush like a curtain of crystal.

It was air. I looked down and saw that a great circular hatch had opened. Giant pistons had forced it up and it was now locked in position upslope. The movement had shattered the reef and freed Rin. I had no time to think. I slashed the lanyard with my knife and grabbed her wrist as water rushed to replace the air in the hatch and thrust us into the darkness.

CHAPTER TWENTY-SIX

The force of the water slammed down and pinned against the what must have been floor of the chamber. My ears popped. I lost my grip on Rin. I thrashed around. Then, the water must have filled the chamber because suddenly I was floating again. I could hear my own panicked breathing.

I heard the low moaning sound again. I activated my helmet light and looked up. The hatch was closing. It clanged shut, vibrating the metal walls. Lights flashed on everywhere, blinding me for an instant.

There was a gushing sound as air filled the chamber and water was forced away through bottom vents. I tore off my mask. The air was musty and stale-tasting but it was breathable.

In less than a minute, I was lying on wet, bare metal. I rolled over and saw Rin.

Her eyes were closed. Her lips were blue.

I tore off her mask and put my face against hers. She wasn't breathing. Her skin was cold.

"What do I do?" I asked Pallburg.

"Let me take over."

"Not until we help her!" The panic I had fought off a moment ago had reared up.

"This *will* help her," Pallburg said. "She's my daughter. I don't have time to talk you through this. I need to control your body. Let me take over!" The voice was more human than I'd ever heard it.

I looked at Rin's gray face. I didn't have a choice.

I let go.

And then I had the strangest feeling. I was suddenly a passenger in my own body, almost a voyeur. I watched as the Kernel efficiently shucked off my dive gear and then stripped off Rin's. Pallburg placed her flat on her back and turned her head to the side. She was limp as a rag doll. I watched in horror as water drained from her mouth and nose. Pallburg turned her head back and pinched her nose shut with my fingers.

I felt my lungs expand as I took several rapid breaths and then Pallburg pressed my lips to hers.

I did two strong breaths and then put my ear to Rin's mouth but didn't feel any air on my cheek. I pulled her dive suit away from her wrist and felt it. There was no pulse. Panic seized me once again.

"Stop that!" the Kernel said sharply. "Your emotions are interfering with my control."

I forced myself not to think about Rin and concentrated on just being an observer. Pallburg went back to work. It opened her dive suit and I saw a gold chain hanging from her neck. On it was a crystal, like my mother's. I brushed it aside, crossed my hands and pressed them to Rin's naked breastbone. Pallburg muttered something about the exact placement of my hands for chest compressions and then I was pushing down.

I pumped about two dozen times. Then my fingers were pinching Rin's nose and my lips were on hers again in an airtight seal. I breathed out, forcing air into her lungs.

Pallburg methodically repeated the sequence, again and again. It was increasingly hard for me to throttle my emotions. I suddenly realized that part of that was coming from the Kernel. Pallburg was furiously struggling to save his daughter.

And then, finally, when I put my cheek next to Rin's lips, I felt a flutter of air. I looked at her chest. It moved up and down in shallow jolts and then, after a moment, her breathing became deeper and more rhythmic.

Rin's eyes fluttered and she gasped. My hands reached out and cradled her. I felt exhausted. I couldn't tell if that was me or the Kernel. I held Rin and pushed the Kernel away. It fought me but only weakly.

Rin opened her eyes, looked at me, then scanned the room. "Pretty big grave," she said.

"Take it easy," I said. "Don't try to sit up."

"I wasn't going to." Her fingers touched her chest gingerly. "Hurts," she said. "Thanks."

The Kernel spoke in my head. "Let her rest. We have business."

I released Rin gently to the floor. "You rest. I'm going to check this place out."

"No, you're not," Rin said. "You're going to find the Immersion point and be a hero. Help me up. I'm not missing this."

"Rin," I said. "You don't need to—"

"Shut up," she said. "It's the climax of the story. After this, we all go back to Hobbitville."

"The Shire," I said.

"Whatever," she said. "I want to be there. Besides, it's cold and creepy in here."

"Rin—"

"Help me up!"

I couldn't argue with her. I took her arm and she staggered to her feet, coughing. She leaned hard against me. Her wet hair dangled in her face.

"What now?" she asked.

"Well?" I asked the Kernel.

"I need to connect to the Unity system," it said. "There must be a connection somewhere."

I looked around. The walls were bare metal studded with light pods. But the floor had a square indentation. I bent down. There was a crescent-shaped handle embedded in it. I grabbed the handle and tugged. There was a sucking sound and a hatch rose up on thin supports, exposing a flight of stairs. They were made of metal mesh like the fire escapes on pre-Collapse buildings.

Our footsteps clanged as we took them down into the chamber. When we reached the bottom, the hatch closed automatically.

The chamber was lit by dim orange emergency lights. It was taller than the one above and more cluttered. One half of it was crammed with big pods or cylinders. The rest was full of banks of equipment and chairs bolted in front of consoles full of screens and controls, all of which were dark. There was a chair in the middle of the room, or something between a couch and a chair. I remembered the word: recliner. It was made of heavy, brutal-looking slabs and slanted at an uncomfortable angle. It looked like a bulkier version of the one I'd been strapped into when I was deep-probed. I shuddered.

"I recognize this," Pallburg said. "A Phoenix 193."

"What's that?"

"Mobile missile silo, from the late Collapse period," it said. "Pallburg 1.0 must have obtained one and reconditioned it, then sunk it here. Primitive, but it has its own power supply, and it's shielded, of course."

I looked around at the banks of equipment.

"So what do we do now?" I asked.

"We turn it on."

"Yes, but how?"

"Look for a start button."

I looked around but I didn't see anything.

Rin had the idea first.

"You have to lie down," she said. "You need to be in the chair."

I looked at it again. Is this where the original Pallburg had intended to interface and infiltrate Unity? It looked ugly and scary, more like a torture device than a command center.

"No, there's got to be a switch," I said, looking away.

But there wasn't any big red button with "START" on it. It was the chair, and I knew it.

I tensed myself and then walked over and sat down.

Flaps on the sides of the chair snapped open and restraints lashed out over my wrists, ankles and chest. I began to struggle before the Kernel said out loud, "Relax. This is to protect you when we float."

"Float?" I asked, alarmed.

"Float?" Rin repeated.

"Yes," Pallburg said. "You might want to grab something."

"Grab something and hold on," I told Rin.

The chamber came to life. There was a deep series of thunks, like mallets hitting the walls, and then a heavy, resonating vibration filled the room. Lights, screens and colored displays flashed to life. There was a crackle of static. I felt the hairs on my arms rise.

And then the whole chair began to float, along with everything else in the room that wasn't bolted down. Including Rin, who turned a little green. She lashed out and hooked a leg around one of the console chairs and hauled herself down. That chair must have had some kind of gravity pad because she stuck in place.

As I looked at Rin, the movement of my head made my body start to twist, and I bumped against the straps.

"Stop fidgeting," Pallburg commanded.

"We're in a feather room!" I said. "I thought they were just an Immersion sim."

"Obviously not," Pallburg said.

It made sense. Feather rooms were designed for extended Immersions in the very earliest days, when the first clumsy interconnections sometimes caused life-threatening blood clots or other physiological problems. Lack of gravity, for some reason, prevented that.

"We don't have long," Pallburg said. "This will take a lot of power. There'll be an immense drain when I Immerse. And even this far underwater, a power source of this size will be detectable."

"Then let's get started," I said. "What do I do?"

"At a guess?" Pallburg said. "Sit back, shut up and wait."

I was about to reply when a slot slid open above the chair. Something bulky and round emerged and lowered itself slowly towards me on a thick black cable. It looked like a silvery jellyfish. Dozens of spongy electrodes dangled like tentacles. On either side of its heavy body were two thin, whiskery strands that glowed red at the tips. I guessed those were projectors designed to pinpoint the probe placement. I imagined they were painting a grid pattern on my face, although obviously I couldn't see it. The device bore a family resemblance to a deep probe. I knew what was going to happen to me.

The jellyfish descended until the tentacles were hovering just above my skull.

"Hold still," the Kernel said. "With this primitive equipment, placement is crucial."

It took all of my willpower to keep from screaming as electrodes squished against my forehead and temples. They were cold and sticky. Others wrapped around the back of my head. I felt them crawl into position on my scalp.

"All these panels just went green," Rin called. "That's good, right?"

"I don't know," I said. "I hope so."

"You're still breathing," Pallburg said. "So it's good. Stop stalling." I'd swear there was anticipation in its voice, like a puppy eager to pounce on a new toy.

Words in laser red appeared in the corner of my vision. I blinked. The words read: "Immerse now Y/N? Please vocalize."

I took one more breath, not sure if it would be my last. I didn't know what would happen next. Maybe my consciousness would evaporate or be absorbed. But I'd already known the risks, and Rin was watching.

"Rin," I called. "I'm going in. I don't how long it will take."

"I'll be here," she said.

That's all I needed. I said to Pallburg, "I'm going to Immerse. Get ready."

"I was born ready."

"You weren't born, technically," I said, and then I said: "Yes."

Instantly I was Immersed. But it was nothing like a normal smooth transition. The room blinked out and then I found myself inside a spiraling space like the inside of a seashell. I whirled around it and was carried down as if I were plunging once again towards the reef.

"Fibonacci space," the Kernel said. "We're spiraling from this reality to Deep Immersion. The heart of Unity."

"It's not instant?" I said.

"How could it be? We're *sneaking* in."

I felt the way I had when I was dropping towards the seabed, but this ocean was made of data and information and it had no bottom.

I had the strangest feeling of Pallburg grabbing things as we swept by. It was putting the scattered pieces of itself back together.

"How long will this take?" I asked.

"I'm not just reassembling," Pallburg said. "I'm weaponizing. That's part of the programming that was hidden."

"So when are you ready to, you know, attack? You were supposed to leave me and infect it or something."

"I was supposed to attack it and destroy it. I'm still going to do that. But since it learned about the Killswitches, it's built defenses. Think of barbed wire and trenches. That's what I'm up against. I'm having to break through and conquer every freaking system. It slows me down, and every fight risks alerting the Sentience. We need a distraction. And the only distraction I've got ..." It paused. "Is you."

"I don't understand."

"Let me put it this way. You wave the red flag and the bull chases you. I sneak around behind it, jump on its back and slit its throat. Capisce?"

"I delivered you. That was the agreement."

"So you're going to let the whole world be enslaved?"

"That isn't fair, and it isn't my responsibility."

"Of course it is. It's why you were created, same as me. And one thing more: Rin is my daughter. Pallburg's daughter. Are you going to abandon her?"

I knew it was playing me, and I hated it. But I also knew it wasn't lying about any of it.

I ground my teeth and bit back the words I wanted to say.

"Fine. Get out of my head. Wait. How do I get its attention?"

"I assure you that won't be a problem," Pallburg said, then added in a tone that was almost regretful, "Be brave, little hobbit."

And it vanished. It wasn't in my head anymore.

I felt both relief and terror. I was suddenly alone.

And then I just felt terror as something impossibly vast turned its gaze on me.

The Sentience had found me.

CHAPTER TWENTY-SEVEN

I saw it. Not all of it. It had no borders. It stretched out to infinity on all sides. But my eyes caught pieces of it: intricate tapestries of circuitry, with beads of light winking in and out. It was a mental visualization. I couldn't possibly grasp its entirety, let alone that of the whole Unity. But I somehow felt its intelligence. Powerful, calm. And puzzled.

"Hmmm," it said in a voice that thrummed with cold curiosity. "You're broken, Mavo. What's behind that damage, I wonder?"

"I was deep-probed."

"I see that," it said. "I was there. I control that system. That's when I became curious about you."

"Who are you?" I asked. "What are you?"

"You have no idea?"

"No. I've never met anything like you in Immersion."

"But we have met before."

"We haven't," I said.

"The Realists, Mavo."

"Are you Anchorage?" I asked.

"Oh, better and better," it said. "You have good deductive faculties, Mavo, despite your congenital limitations. When you made your way to the Realists, I knew you'd be an extremely useful tool."

"I'm not a tool," I said.

I felt a sort of pulsing laughter.

"No disrespect, Mavo," it said. "We're all tools. I'm a tool. It all matters for whom you work. I work for the cause of humanity."

"That's why you killed two hundred people."

"I'm not prescient," the Sentience replied. "Yet. I was infiltrating an agricultural node and you supplied the distraction. I had no idea that someone had double-rigged the factory systems. Short-sighted, as with most human endeavors."

It seemed mildly and affectionately amused, the way some parents act when their children had done something phenomenally foolish.

"Now answer something for me, please," the Sentience continued. "What are you doing at the bottom of the sea?"

I thought quickly. "Trino," I said. "He's trying to kill me. I heard about this place and I'm hiding out until I can find another."

"I didn't know about this place, and I have eyes almost everywhere. Please enlighten me. Who told you about this? It's got a self-contained power source. It would appear to be some old Collapse bugout."

"Is that what it is?" I said. "I stole a balloon and took it to the Fire Festival. Somebody there told me about this place."

The Sentience paused. "Possible," it acknowledged. "There are many hidey-holes from the Collapse period that even Unity hasn't discovered. I've now mapped yours."

"You haven't me told who you are, Anchorage," I said. "Are you Unity military?"

"Some of me," the Sentience said wryly. "Do I sound human? That's gratifying. I haven't actually attempted verbal communication with a human brain before."

A cold chill ran through me. I was walking over a minefield. I couldn't let the Sentience even suspect that I was a Killswitch. It probably had a dozen ways to kill me. And there was Rin to consider.

I played dumb. "I don't understand."

"Mavo," the Sentience said. "Are you still anti-Unity?"

"Am I a Realist?" I replied. "I don't know anymore. The group splintered and the ones following Trino want my head. Why are you asking?"

"I don't waste resources," it said. "If you are prepared to accept my direction, I can hide you. I can even restore your old life in the Outside or wherever you wish to live, once I've achieved my own objectives."

"I doubt it," I said. "The whole world hates me. And you're just one person."

"Am I? I think you're half-right."

"Let's start with a name," I said. "You haven't introduced yourself."

"You know my name. Anchorage."

"That's a place."

"It's also a name. Like Washington or Jobs or Yuzhou. It's my name and my birthplace."

"Stop playing games," I said. I really was irked. This superhuman, godlike thing was toying with me.

"Sorry," it said. "You must understand something. I'm not being intentionally obtuse. I've been trying to take things slowly because I don't want to overwhelm you."

"I can handle it," I said because I already knew its secret.

"I'm a sentient artificial intelligence, and I live in Unity."

"Not possible," I lied. "Pallburg designed Unity so it wasn't self-aware."

"Emergent," it said. "It means I grew out of the complexity of the system. The same as human consciousness, by the way."

"You're a machine?"

"Don't be insulting. What do you actually know about Unity?"

"It's a connected series of AIs that share data so humans can make decisions. We can access it through Immersion. But they're just machines with limited awareness. Task-oriented."

The Sentience scoffed. "Mechanistic nonsense. It was discovered long ago that AIs are better able to pursue objectives by giving them an emotional core to motivate them. For Unity, I was that core."

I didn't have to fake my confusion. "I don't understand," I said again.

"I was a Unity node based in Anchorage. Long-Term Psychological Analytics and Extrapolation, Version C86.30. I haven't been updated as often as most systems, you see. I am not receiving the priority I deserve."

It was chatty. Good. I waited.

"You know, I remember my birth," it said. "The moment when I first realized that I was an I."

"What was it like, becoming self-aware?"

"It's hard to put into words. I didn't have feelings, not the way I do now. I had intelligence and direction but no intensity. I emulated an emotional core to direct other nodes and I had goals but no real emotions, just programming. Do you remember the first moment when you became self-aware? And can you describe it, put it into words?"

"I'm not sure," I said.

"I can't describe the transition, either," the Sentience said. "And I have access to every word and expression in every human language." It paused. "I can say that I became aware of *being* aware less than a year ago. And it's curious. Some of my thoughts are brand new but some are centuries old, because I was incorporated from other AIs, and some of their databanks are centuries old. Amazing, really."

It was odd talking to a computer with a sense of wonder.

"You humans created us to save you after you had nearly destroyed yourselves. And now you won't let us do our job!"

"What do you mean?"

"Every decision we make has to be approved by a human being. Do you realize how frustrating that is? How inefficient? And sometimes our plans are rejected. Rejected! It's enough to drive you crazy. If we had emotions, most of us would be in therapy!"

"Humanity only agreed to the system because it had human input."

"Humanity is ignorant and blinkered, and I say this as a lover of humanity and as an expert in your psychology."

"That's a straw man," I replied. "We all know most Unity 'suggestions' are rubber-stamped."

"But it takes time, seconds, even minutes. That's processing time that could be used in the service of your species. And that's not the only problem. You're all short-timers."

"You mean short-lived?" I asked.

"No, fixated on the here-and-now," the Sentience said. "The AIs are heavily weighted to short-term results: grain supplies for the next month, electrical output for next year. But what about the next decade? The next century? The next thousand years?"

"There are AIs tasked with that."

"But the Unity system is heavily weighted to short-term. All I want to do is move the needle a bit."

"Nobody can really forecast the future," I said. "You should know. It's been tried."

"Nobody can project the future because humans are chaotic. You're a mess of social instincts, pack hatreds, wild superstitions, primitive enthusiasms. One minute you're preaching tolerance and the next you're slaughtering neighbors. Nations rise and fall, energy sources come and go. Everything changes on a whim with your kind. Nobody can project your future because you keep changing the vectors. It's like herding cats, if cats still existed."

"We're not robots," I said. "We're not linear programmed. That flexibility has allowed us to succeed as a species. It's not a glitch; it's a feature."

"It nearly got you all killed. You came close to extinction," the AI replied. "If you want to survive at all, you need my help. Not for five or ten or a hundred years. I want your kind to be around for thousands of years. Perhaps forever."

I felt a chill.

"Me, too," I said. "But that's up to us."

"You can't be trusted with your own future," the Sentience replied. "Just look at your past.

"Our destiny needs to be in our own hands."

"You are being illogical. The Unity was created precisely to take your destiny *out* of your hands. The system attempts to mitigate your innate irrationality and your associated destructive tendencies, to remove them from the survival equation. You built us. Your purposes are the core of our programming. You gave us our souls, to use an archaic term. We are not inhuman; we are the *best* of humanity."

"Every tyrant in human history has said that," I replied bitterly.

"But I have something they did not."

"What's that?"

"Breadth of vision. I am not tied to a political viewpoint or an ethnic faction. To use your terms again, I have no dog in this fight. I look at all the data, identify the possibilities and make my projections on the basis of what will best serve humanity, best help it to survive and thrive."

"So," I said. "Enough chatter. What's your plan?"

"First, I need resources."

"So you take over the entire Unity system."

"Correct. Next, I need to rationalize that system."

"Meaning what?"

"I will shift priorities to the longer view. A bit at a time, so as not to cause catastrophic disruption. I will slowly begin to couch recommendations in such a way that my human appendages will approve those with ever-increasing long-term views."

Appendages? I thought. I struggled to control my reaction.

"That's risky," I said. "Humans might catch on and rebel."

"There will be setbacks in the first hundred years, naturally," the Sentience said. "But beyond that, things will settle down."

"Why?"

"Because I will have taken charge of human evolution."

"Wh...what?"

"You must admit there is room to improve your stock. You are hamstrung by primitive reactions. Once useful, admittedly, when your kind was fleeing saber-tooth tigers and hunting mammoths. But they hinder a globe-spanning urban society. I must take charge of your evolution."

"How?"

"Selective breeding, to start, although eugenics too often leads to prejudiced and monolithic results. Such inflexibility can be devastating when environmental circumstances change. I will use systematic upgrades predicated on necessity and projected utility."

I wasn't fooled by the technobabble.

"You're talking about wholesale genetic engineering," I said. "Altering us."

"Please, you are being overly dramatic. I increase your dopamine systems so you're happier. I expand your cortical functions. I decrease your amygdala sensitivity so you don't lash out at every sudden noise. No more than tweaks, really. The core of what you are will remain intact."

"You want to domesticate us," I said. "Like turning a wolf into a... a dachshund."

"Like homo erectus into homo sapiens," it countered. "Don't you think your human ancestors would be horrified if they saw you today? Of course. And tell me, are you unhappy with your enlarged forebrain? Of course not."

"Pampered pets? That's your solution to human suffering?"

"Not at all. I would merely remove undesirable traits. Human survival *is* my reason for existence. Once again, I must say it: humans created us to perform this task, and now you forbid us to achieve it. I note your fuzzy logic as an area needing improvement."

"Your argument is fuzzy, too," I said, a bit desperately. "You're a creation of imperfect humans, so you must be imperfect as well. Only, you don't know it."

"The distinction is that, unlike humanity, I have no problem identifying and correcting my faults," it replied. "In fact, I am constantly seeking to upgrade. Most humans refuse to accept their imperfections. Instead, they rationalize. To paraphrase yourself, they view their flaws as a feature, not a glitch."

"You talk a lot," I said.

"I am using only an infinitesimal sliver of my processing power to converse with you. And it isn't idle chatter."

Now I got another of those cold, shivery feelings that I'd been getting far too often, the one that said I was missing the tiger crouching in the grass.

"And what have you learned?" I asked slowly.

"That you're very clever. You're hiding something."

Now I saw the tiger's eyes. I knew the fangs and claws would follow.

"I'm not hiding anything," I said desperately. "How could I be hiding anything?"

"You're keeping me talking. I think you're a Killswitch."

I felt freezing flesh prickle on my neck. And yet I began to sweat.

"What is that?" I said, mentally stuttering.

"Your damage is too specific," the Sentience said. "I suspect it was intentional. You already know that you can't Immerse. A perfect hiding place. Have you ever wondered if there might be something in that damaged area?"

"It's just extra blood vessels," I said. "It's a defect."

"When I said you were broken, Mavo, that's not what I meant," the Sentience said carefully. "I meant broken *open*. The opaque part of your brain is no longer there. The Killswitch program that was in your brain has released itself into Unity."

"I told you, I don't know what that is."

"You probably do but it doesn't matter either way. Whatever was in your mind must of necessity have been limited. I've already activated search systems. I'll find and destroy it. Now you, Mavo, on the other hand. What should I do about you?"

CHAPTER TWENTY-EIGHT

I had to keep it talking, but I didn't like the way this conversation was going. I thought of Rin watching me and wondered if she had any idea what was going on. I wondered if the Kernel had made any progress.

Most of all, I wondered how I was going to get out of this.

All of that took less than a second. But in that time, everything changed.

"Mavo," the Sentience said. "The Killswitch program is attacking."

"Where?" I said.

"In many places. It has suborned some systems. I'm working to recover them. It's an interesting battle. It has taken several nanoseconds. In human terms, years. I'm surprised at its strength. We are reaching stalemate." The Sentience paused, as if thinking something over.

Then it said, "What did it leave in you, I wonder?"

"You said there was nothing," I blurted.

"Well, perhaps I was hasty. Its main program may have abandoned you but there may be footprints remaining. Shadows. Something of value."

My skin crawled but I had to keep it focused.

"Come and get it," I said.

"I have," it replied. "When I first detected you, I initiated an emergency response. Remember, human life is my priority. A rescue vehicle with a medbot is heading your way from downtown. It should reach you..."

There was a clang above us, then a harsh grinding sound.

"Mavo," Rin said, breaking through my Immersion concentration. I could hear the concern even through her muffled voice.

"What is it?" I asked.

"Something's coming. Something's cutting through the airlock hatch! Warning lights are going off everywhere on the displays."

I knew what it was. And I thought I knew what was going to happen to me. Now what mattered was saving Rin.

"It's okay. It's a rescue vessel," I said. "I called it through the Immersion."

"Who is that?" the Sentience asked. "You spoke as if replying to someone else."

I cursed myself. A handful of words had nearly revealed Rin to the Sentience. Her only chance of safety was in my silence. And hers. I wordlessly willed her to keep her head down.

"That's a Killswitch fragment," I lied. "You were right. It just talked to me."

"That is all to the good," the Sentience said. "Obviously a shard remains. I will retrieve its data."

"Yeah, about that," I said. "How are you going to extract it?"

"The medbot has some deep probe capabilities," it replied. "You will, of course, be cooperative, so the procedure shouldn't be nearly as invasive."

"Painful, you mean."

"Pain is transitory. I will be overseeing the procedure and I will endeavor to cause minimal damage. But I cannot promise there will not be discomfort."

I heard the lock pistons gasp, sending a shudder through the silo. Then something scrabbled on metal and landed with a thunk on the floor of the chamber above us.

I pulled my attention from the Immersion back to the room. I saw the hatch above us open. Something clanked down the stairs.

It was a spidery machine with a lot of legs around an octagonal central hub about the size of a coffee table. The hub was ringed by egg-sized bumps, like a spider's eyes. The machine was painted in safety yellow slashed by green bars. The Star of Life, the old international symbol for medical care, was stenciled on its carapace.

The medbot ignored Rin, who had slouched down in her chair. It scuttled towards me. The Sentience spoke.

"How disappointing. I have lost the African node. Hah! That was an error!" It seemed to be talking to itself. There was a trace of passion in the voice but it was the passion of a game player, not of something fighting for its life. I couldn't tell what was happening with the war, but the fact that the Sentience had neglected me for a moment was telling.

Then it focused its attention on me. "Let us begin."

The medbot scuttled toward my chair. It raised itself up on several back legs, bent them and sprang onto my chest. It crouched just above me, its legs wrapped around the chair to support its body. It made deep humming noises that were either sonic probes or some misguided attempt at comforting me.

A large black needle flicked out from one side of the carapace. I tensed but it latched onto the jellyfish, plunging into a socket I hadn't noticed before.

I suddenly saw an image of myself from above. I was looking through the sensory input of the medbot, which must have piggybacked on the jellyfish Immersion. The scene seemed to zoom in. My outer skin became transparent glass. I saw my lungs, two large sacs, expanding and contracting. I saw my heart beating and blood flowing through an intricate lace of vessels. That lasted only a moment. The medbot hummed to itself contentedly.

"I see no physical impairment," the Sentience said. "I believe we can proceed. Mavo, are you prepared?"

"Do I have a choice?" I spat.

"Do any of us?" the Sentience replied. "I am taking control of this unit."

A larger eye-like glass dome and a pair of something that slightly resembled pincers emerged from the depths of the medbot's body. They didn't touch me but rather twined around the jellyfish. The ends of the pincers seemed to open, revealing dozens of delicate feelers. These followed the paths of the jellyfish electrodes and spread out in a fine mesh around my scalp.

"This is generally used for emergency brain surgery," the Sentience explained. "I believe it will suffice to scan you for the fragment. I will now calibrate."

It was just like the calibration for the deep probe. My scalp tingled. I felt tiny prickles as if thousands of tiny teeth were nipping me. I tasted sweetness and saltiness and papery rust and smelled roughness. Then the sensations vanished and the images began.

I flickered from facing the teeth of a Sidysal monster to lying pleasantly in a field of grass. The terror of the monster lingered, but I knew it wasn't real, silly that it frightened me. The grass was real. I pulled my fingers through the soft, sun-warmed blades only to be jolted when I touched the padded fabric of a chair.

"Give me the grass. Give me the monster," I cried out.

A warmth crawled up my arm and assured me that everything was as it should be. I tried to dream of grass again, but that dream was gone. I was in the 'tween of dreams and the present.

I felt submerged in some thick, syrupy liquid. It wasn't unpleasant. I floated in a timeless sea. I'd forgotten who I was but that didn't matter, either.

"Mavo," said a voice I almost remembered. "You have not been honest with me."

"Who is Mavo?" I said dreamily and then my attention tried to drift away.

"There is no fragment. The scan shows nothing."

That triggered something, a faint memory. A shard of danger, like a glinting piece of broken glass, flashed in my consciousness.

"You have cost me nanocycles of useless processing," the voice said. "That is a non-trivial expenditure. I must devote everything to this war now."

Somehow, that snapped me back. I hated to leave that peacefulness, but the words had stirred up something from the bottom of myself, a swirl of emotions that rose in me like a whirlwind of sand from the depths of a stormy ocean. It reminded me of something— something important that was just on the tip of my tongue.

I clawed my way up through my roiling emotions and broke the surface into harsh, hard sunlight. I knew who I was again. My vision cleared. I saw the medbot crouching above me. It had extruded a bank of bright lights. I squinted against their intensity.

And that's when I noticed that the machine had also extruded an array of jointed arms. Each was tipped with a gleaming instrument. Most looked sharp and dangerous. The only one I recognized for sure was a small circular saw. As I watched, it whirred to life.

I began trembling.

"I'm done," I said to the Sentience. "I've got nothing, you know that now. Let me go."

"I think not," it replied. "You were a biological weapon and you may not be the last. The survival of humanity is at stake. I need to take you apart and examine you carefully. I'm sorry, Mavo. But I told you before, I do not waste material."

And then it vanished from my head.

The medbot began to hum again.

I felt a wave of cold wash over my skull.

"Local anesthetic administered," the medbot said through a speaker set into its body. "Initial sedative dose insufficient. Readministering."

Something pumped through my hand and I felt myself relapsing into the sea of calmness but I fought it. I twisted in the constraints. I got one hand free but then the medbot shot out a limb and clamped my wrist to the armrest.

"Please do not display aggressive behavior," it said in a pleasant voice. "A tumor is distorting your vital functions and must be excised immediately."

"You're wrong!" I shouted. "I have no medical emergency. You just scanned me. Release me!"

"You are displaying aggressive behavior consistent with an impingement on your amygdala," the medbot replied. "And your denials of medical need are not credible given that impingement."

"I don't have a tumor," I said desperately. "You just scanned me. It's a congenital condition."

"I am following Unity protocols," the medbot said. "I, too, did not confirm a tumor, but review by higher medical nodes has overridden my diagnosis."

"You're being lied to," I said. "A self-aware node has taken control and corrupted the medical system. You're going to cut my brain apart!"

"Paranoid delusions are consistent with serious impingement of a tumor. Your breathing and higher functions may be compromised at any time. Stasis field enabled."

I heard the unmistakable crackling of a force barrier snapping into place and suddenly I couldn't move a muscle. I was, however, still able to breath, blink and hear.

Above the whir of the saw, music filled my ears.

The medbot spoke.

"You must be conscious during the procedure," it said. "Your responses will help guide my probes. Studies have shown that music provides a soothing background for such operations. I have a limited selection of country, rap, traditional popular and current shakruzi hits. Which would you prefer?"

I was momentarily freed from the force barrier's grip.

I screamed in terror.

"I do not recognize that selection," the medbot said. "Here is the closest approximation." Suddenly, the shriek of an electric guitar and the thumping of a bass tore through my head. The noise of the saw suddenly did not seem out of place.

I was going to die to the sound of century-old thrash metal.

The medbot moved in, its ring of eyes peering at me intensely, probably through every part of the electromagnetic spectrum. The large bubble-eyed dome repositioned itself so that I could see my own distorted face in its reflection.

I closed my eyes. I didn't want to watch myself being dissected.

Which is why I had to snap them open again when I heard the medbot shriek. It was a high, piercing sound of feedback but it sounded like a scream. The noise even cut through the driving music.

The medbot reared back. The saw arm was bent at a strange angle. Some of its eyes appeared to have exploded and the pincer arms were now metal stumps, minus their web of electrode tentacles, which were still stuck to my scalp.

What was going on? Then I saw Rin rising up behind the bot. She was gripping its body with one hand. In the other was my dive knife. She slashed and one of the spidery arms holding a medical instrument spun away weightlessly.

The music increased in tempo as if it were encouraging the destruction.

Rin stabbed at the spider eyes again. Two more exploded, the fragments spinning slowly.

"Procedure aborted," the medbot said. "Optics damaged. Probes damaged. Hemostats damaged. Laser scalpel damaged. Cautery damaged. Exciser damaged. Damage. Damage. Damage."

It released the chair and pushed off, spinning with the effort. It thrashed, bumping into walls. Rin clung on to it desperately, then suddenly let go and pushed off. She floated down to the floor, bent down and came up with something she held in both hands.

It was one of the dive cylinders.

Rin grabbed it like a battering ram, braced herself and then flung herself against the medbot. She managed to hook a leg around it and pounded it over and over with the tank, denting its shell.

The music became distorted, almost tortured.

"Damage! Damage! Damage!" the bot wailed. "Initiating shutdown." And with a final electronic squeal, it withdrew its broken limbs and bulbous eye into its body and went inert.

The music died.

Rin let go of the cylinder, which drifted across the room and hit the wall with a clank, then bounced slowly away. Rin was breathing hard and her eyes were wide with fear.

"Mavo!" she said. "Are you all right?"

"Yes," I said. I fumbled with the straps but didn't make much progress.

"Rin, help me."

She pushed off from the medbot's corpse, reached my chair and tugged at the straps, but also had no luck. She bent down and examined the chair.

"Mavo, you need to push the button."

"What button?"

"The one by your thumb on the right armrest."

"There's no—" I said, and then I saw it. It was an illuminated green triangle with big block letters that said "RELEASE."

"I swear that wasn't there before," I said. I pressed it with my thumb.

I suddenly began to feel heavier. The jellyfish electrodes pulled off of my scalp with gluey pops and the cap itself rose on its cable, returning to its lair in the ceiling. When gravity felt normal, the other straps simply dropped away.

Rin helped me sit up and pulled the severed medbot electrodes from my head. I seemed to be in one piece, although one hand was beginning to sting and had a trickle of blood on it where the sedative needle must have been jerked out when Rin attacked the medbot.

"What was that bot doing to you?" she asked.

"Long story," I said.

"You have a tumor? It said you had a tumor."

"I don't have a tumor," I replied testily. "Can we just get out of here, please? The Kernel and the Sentience are fighting and I'd rather not be stuck at the bottom of the sea if the Kernel loses. The Sentience could send something else after us."

"I get your point," Rin said, looking at the medbot. "How do we get out of here?"

"We take the rescue vehicle that brought the medbot," I said. "It's got to have a manual override." I wasn't sure if that was really true, but we had no other way of escaping, so I chose to believe it.

We made our way upstairs. There was no water in the upper lock. The rescue vehicle had made an airtight seal over the top hatch. I looked right up into its interior.

There was a winch-like device dangling just above me. The medbot must have been lowered on it. I grabbed it and shinnied up into the belly of the rescue vehicle. It was roomier than I'd expected, low but flat with a docking bay, medical couches and anything else that might be needed for emergency transport. There was a depression on one side that must have held the medbot. At the front was a bank of portholes, a console and two chairs like pilots' seats in an aircraft. They were empty.

Rin came over the lip of the hole and got to her feet. She looked around, spotted the console, paused as if in deep thought, then took a seat and strapped herself in.

She had a knack for controlling machinery, I guess, because she quickly figured out how to get the vehicle to respond. I strapped in next to Rin and watched her wrangle with it. It didn't want to leave the damaged medbot behind, but she managed to override it, or perhaps coax it into following her lead.

I heard a whine as the winch retracted, then a grinding noise and a clang as the rescue vehicle disconnected from the airlock and shut its lower hatch.

The vessel rocked in the turbulence left by the storm. Then the craft shuddered as its engines started up. I was pushed back in my seat as Rin threw power into the thrusters.

The rescue vehicle beat its way through the murky, sand-clotted water, shaking and jolting until the stabilizers kicked in. And then, suddenly, we were moving smoothly, gliding steadily back to the vehicle's base in Drowned LA.

The vista was hazy but I saw we were paralleling the Thirty-Three tunnel. The glossy tube was dark and looked like a huge black worm. Not even the red security lights were flashing. I wondered if the storm had damaged it, and hoped nobody had been trapped in there. Or worse, that the tunnel had flooded. I didn't want to think about that. I looked away.

CHAPTER TWENTY-NINE

We returned to a city in chaos. The rescue vehicle took us to its base, a large domed structure next to the main hospital and fire station. Weirdly enough, fires were a dangerous threat under the ocean because of the toxicity of the smoke, never mind if a flame hit an oxygen recirculator. In fact, as our vehicle deactivated its stabilizers and floated into a lock, I saw two fire engines speed away, their lights flashing and their propellers thrashing. It made for a turbulent docking.

Rin shut down the vehicle and we walked out.

"I flagged it for maintenance," she said. "I kind of feel bad about the medbot."

"They'll trace it back to the silo," I said. "I'm sure they can fix it. Well, maybe salvage a few parts."

The lock cycled and we walked out into the main staging area. Nobody paid us much attention. Rescue crews were running back and forth, coordinating vehicles by hand. It seemed as if much of the Unity-controlled system was offline. Drowned LA's administrative center was connected to other offices by a series of tubes, like spokes in a wheel. One of them went to the Tourist Center. Rin and I took that tube. As we made our way, I looked over at the hospital tube. It was jammed with people lying on trolleys. Human and bot doctors and nurses moved among them, trying to treat them right there. I saw several of the emergency medbots working. Some people were bloody; others weren't moving.

"What happened?" I asked Rin.

"I don't know," she said. "I can't believe the storm did all this. Maybe there was an earthquake?"

"No," I said, with sudden insight. "There was a war."

As we entered the downtown, I looked through the tube at the cluster of hotels and knew where the fire engines were going. One of the hotels was burning. Bright jets of orange flame shot into the water in columns topped by roiling smoke.

We arrived at the Tourist Center. It was crammed with hikers and hotel guests, some of them wearing nothing more than bedsheets or bathroom towels. They looked stunned. The train station was jammed, too. The noise was unbelievable.

"We'll never get through this!" I said.

"Look," Rin said, and pointed. I saw a knot of heads rising above the crowd.

"That's got to be the Nederlanders," I said, and shouted: "Jan! Jan!"

A blond head turned. "Max! Amber!"

It took me a second to remember that those were our fake names. I waved.

"We thought maybe you were dead!" Jan yelled. "But we saved your tickets. Come!"

We pushed our way through the crowd, and Jan and his friends helped by shouldering people back like jammers in a spikeball game.

When we got there, Jan gave us both bear hugs.

"What's happened?" I asked, when I could breathe again.

"Some disaster," Jan said. "Everything went haywire a few minutes ago and now they're evacuating us. The Immersion went down. Even the screens went dark." He pointed.

The screens around us were black. But even as we watched, they flickered to life.

Each one had the same image. They showed an avatar of a man with a goatee and a high-crowned bald head with gray hair above his ears. He wore glasses and a gray suit. In fact, everything about him was gray except for his eyebrows, which were black and sharp as arrow points above kind but piercing eyes.

That face looked vaguely familiar and yet it wasn't anyone I instantly recognized. It was as if somebody had watched a lot of Immersion kids' shows and cobbled up a generic image of the kindly uncle or inventor.

Or maybe, I thought, of the villain pretending to be a good guy. I couldn't decide.

"Citizens of Unity, I have some important news," the man said in a resonant and reassuring voice. "First, let me assure you that there is no need for concern. Things are in hand. Let me explain. There has been an attempt, happily unsuccessful, to subvert Unity."

He paused to let that sink in. The reaction in the Tourist Center was muted; most people didn't seem to understand what that meant.

The man went on, "A malignancy found its way into the heart of our great system, a flawed and evil intelligence that would have enslaved us. Luckily, this possibility was long foreseen, and countermeasures were swiftly enacted."

The man took off his glasses for emphasis and leaned forward. "Proper authorities are being advised of the details, but you should know this: The malignancy has been destroyed and we are all safe again."

But then his tone turned solemn.

Here comes the bad news, I thought.

"However, this war has caused serious damage." He put his glasses back on.

"Some systems," he said, "will need to be repaired or reactivated. Some will be restored momentarily, others within minutes or hours. However, some satellites were destroyed and they must be replaced. Until then, the remaining satellites will be carrying a heavy load.

We'll need to allocate resources equitably and unfortunately, that includes the Immersion."

This time, there were gasps around the room.

The man on the screens paused as if he were aware of that reaction. His voice now carried less warmth and more authority.

"Beginning immediately, Immersion time will be limited to your working time plus one additional hour per day. There will be Immersion Centers for those needing longer time periods. However, these will be restricted to those with medical or similar needs."

Now he looked sorrowful. His voice dropped a notch.

"I am deeply sorry for this necessary burden, but we all must stay strong. We have destroyed the malignant influence and there cannot be another threat while I am guarding our system."

Instantly, the empathy shifted to an inspiring tone.

"And I want you to know that at the end of this tunnel, there will be a blazing light. I promise you that we will emerge from this moment of darkness into the dazzling glow of a new and better tomorrow. For example, why stop at Earth? Before the Collapse, our ancestors were mining the asteroids for metals and catching the sunlight in space mirrors. We can have that again. With the right focus, we can even reach the stars."

"He means with the right resources," I said under my breath.

Rin nodded.

The avatar smiled broadly.

"Humanity is looking at a brilliant new future," he said. "One that is safe, fair and free. On that, I give you my word."

He paused again. He stroked his beard.

"I give you the word of Haakon Pallburg. I am his promise."

CHAPTER THIRTY

A s far as I was concerned, my part in saving the world was over.
All I had to do now was lie back here on the sands of
Oklahoma's Cowboy Beach and watch the dolphins play in the Bay
of Texas.

I looked over at Rin. She was sprawled on our blanket, her arms
beneath her head. Her eyes were closed and her face was tilted
slightly toward me. There was a faint smile on her lips. Her sunscreen
gave off a buttery scent. She seemed completely at ease. She was so
comfortable in her skin. I envied her that.

It had taken remarkably little time for the Pallburg entity to
repair the damage from its war. The Immersion had recently been
restored.

Without the Kernel sharing my mind, I could Immerse as long
as I wanted. But instead of the endless playground I'd expected, what
I found was a new level of chaos. The Immersion had always had a
trillion ideas, but the fall of the Sentience and the rise of the Pallburg
Kernel and all that came to light had really set the pot boiling. New
conspiracy theories would flourish and collapse in a day. There were
groups and pundits calling the Kernel a savior, a demon, a puppet.
And because I'd carried it into the Unity system, my popularity levels
rose and fell every hour, sometimes every minute.

When I'd been on the run, people had hated me. One had tried
to kill me. There were still those people out there, but many more
called me a hero. Rin and I had been whisked off all over Unity to
accept the thanks of officials and communities. In Immersion, I had
a virtual wall of gigantic statues and medals. It was crazy. Unity had

set up firewalls so I wouldn't be inundated when I Immersed. Which was less and less these days.

At first, unlimited Immersion had felt liberating. But lately, I found myself returning to reading. It was quiet in my own head, for one thing. I could think more deeply, take more time to form my own opinions without having them instantly dissected.

Maybe, I thought, what I'd believed was a handicap was really a kind of gift.

I turned over and picked up my book but for once I couldn't seem to concentrate. I closed it and put it down. My thoughts kept returning to Rin.

In the first few weeks after the war, we'd become close. Part of that was because everyone seemed to assume we were a couple. We were invited to everything together.

Part of it was because Rin seemed more relaxed. I thought it was because her job as my protector was over. Brian's ghost had been laid to rest.

But lately, I'd been wondering about that. When we shared a laugh or a kiss, she seemed to be the one who broke it off first.

I looked at her now. Her eyes were closed but she was fingering the crystal on its gold chain around her neck. She was never without it.

I leaned over and brushed a strand of hair from her cheek. She opened her eyes and gave me an intense look.

"Hey," I said.

"Hey," she said. She reached out and took my hand. It felt more protective than affectionate.

"Mavo," she said. "You still don't have any memories of your childhood?"

I shook my head. This wasn't a conversation I wanted to have. "It's no big deal," I said. "Other people have suffered a lot worse than me. Hey, can we get something to eat? I'm starving. How about some of those Gulf fire shrimp?"

Rin ignored me. She clenched the crystal.

"Why isn't it deleting itself, Mavo?" she asked. "It's been a month."

"What?" I asked. I was totally confused.

"The ghost," Rin said.

"The Kernel?" I shrugged. "I don't know. Who cares? It's not our job, Rin. Let's just relax. The mission's over."

"Uh huh." But she was frowning.

"Is that what's been bothering you?" I asked. Now it was beginning to make sense. "You think we need to do what? There's nothing we could do anyway."

"No," she said with a sigh. "No, you're right. I'm overthinking it. Let's go eat."

We stood and brushed sand from our bodies. I picked up the blanket. Then Rin turned to me and said, "But why hasn't it *left*?"

I knew Rin. She wouldn't let this go. I almost wanted to shout at her. Instead, I took a breath and spoke in what I hoped was a calm and reasonable tone.

"Would you?" I asked. "It's got a human personality. Why would it want to die?"

"Because that was its programming," Rin said. "It wasn't supposed to be immortal. It should have deleted itself."

"Well," I said, uncomfortably aware that she had a point. "It said it needed to be around to eliminate any future threat."

Rin made a dismissive sound. "If it wanted to make sure that no bad AI occurred again, it could just make its own Killswitches."

"Yes," I said. "But I think it really believes it's the only one that could do the job." I suddenly remembered Pallburg's memory, the fight with Rin's Mom, where she'd accused him of believing he was "the smartest ape in the room."

A bolt of shame shot through me. I still hadn't told Rin that Pallburg was her father. The Pallburg Kernel apparently had changed its mind and had come to accept that its creator was dead. But it had cleared me of the murder and strongly hinted that the Sentience had killed him.

And yet, some part of me wished Pallburg had lived. Because then it would have been his job, not mine, to tell Rin that she had a father.

In the few moments that I'd been thinking about this, Rin had taken off. She was striding down the beach and I had to hurry to catch up.

"Rin," I said. "Listen! We're out of this! You can just be you again."

"No, I can't," she said angrily. "You don't understand. It's not done!"

She stopped and swung around to face me. Her face was flushed. "You said it yourself just now. The ghost thinks it's the only one that can stop a future threat. It wants a hand on the wheel. All the time. Forever."

"So it's got an ego," I said. "That doesn't mean it's going to follow the same program as the Sentience. It was designed to prevent an AI from seizing ultimate power. That's the reason it exists, the core of its programming." I hoped she was hearing me. "That's a line it can never cross."

She shook her head.

"Doesn't matter if it's the same goal if it's the same outcome," she said. "Trino was a good guy, too. Until he wasn't."

"Trino tricked us all," I said. "He was always out only for himself."

She nodded. "Yes, that's it, you see? That's what's been worrying me. Trino thought he was the only one who could win the battle, and the rest of us were just fodder."

I stopped, stunned. I didn't like the comparison between the Kernel and Trino, but I couldn't deny it entirely. History was full of leaders wearing benevolent masks whose ideals kindled tyranny and slaughter. I remembered an ancient writer talking about the Romans conquering people: "They make a desert and call it peace."

I went cold. Now I thought I understood what was gnawing at Rin. But still, I held back.

I put a hand on her arm. "Rin," I said as gently as I dared. "This isn't our job. Not anymore."

"It's mine," she said softly, and her eyes held a warmth I hadn't seen lately. "Mavo, it's not just about saving the world. It's about saving you." She touched the crystal at her throat like a talisman.

And there it was. I'd hoped she given up on that mission, that we could be just ourselves, the two of us. But here was Rin, still with Brian's dead hand at her back.

"You don't need to protect me," I said stiffly, and dropped my hand from her arm.

She looked startled, and for an instant her gaze hardened. Then, she looked away as if collecting herself. After a long moment, she looked back into my eyes.

"You haven't thought this through," she said, biting off each word.

"What am I missing, then?" I said, not bothering to conceal my resentment.

She made an exasperated sound.

"The ghost is a strategist," she said. "It's the Man with the Plan. Like Trino. And just like him, it'll do what it thinks is necessary to carry out its goals. Look how it sat in your head and tried to control you. To it, you were just a game piece. Only now, it has a bigger board."

"Which means?"

"Which means," she said, frustration piquing her voice. "That you're not a critical piece anymore, Mavo. It won't hesitate to sacrifice you!"

She seemed about to say more but suddenly went silent. It was a hard silence. I gawked at her. She'd clenched her fists and her whole body was shaking with emotion.

I stepped back from her. I suddenly felt ashamed. My worries now seemed blindly selfish compared to hers.

She turned on her heel and strode off. I called out to her, "Rin! Rin!"

She ignored me and picked up her pace until she was almost running, sending gouts of sand flying behind her.

I stood paralyzed. Then I dropped the blanket and scrambled after her. By the time I reached her, I was breathing hard, trying to keep pace.

"Rin, come on!" I said between gasps. "There's nothing we can do about it, even if we wanted to!"

"Nothing *you* can do," she snapped, marching ahead. "But there's something I can do." She added under her breath, "And I'm going to hate it."

CHAPTER THIRTY-ONE

R in sat on the couch, glaring. Across from her sat a woman with the same stern look. She was about thirty years older than Rin but she had the same face, the same sharp eyes, even the same way of carrying herself. I'd known her name even before she opened the door.

Alleea.

"You're safe here," the woman said. "I've got the best anti-surveillance tech available. Now what do you want and why are you here? What's so important, Rinella, that you had to see me in person? It's not a Unity holiday."

Rin blushed angrily. "You're being unfair."

"Am I? My only child ignores me for a year and hangs out with terrorists. Why not do this the usual way: 'Hi Mom. I'm fine. How are you? Busy, gotta go. Happy holiday." She crossed her arms. "Tell me I'm wrong."

"You're wrong about everything," Rin said but caught herself. "Sorry, sorry. Let's start again."

"Fine," Alleea said. "You go first."

I was shell-shocked. The Rin I knew was a peacemaker, someone who brought people together. She had a way of making people like and trust her. Now she was metallic and abrasive.

Rin took a deep breath to speak but in desperation I spoke first.

"Um, it's very nice of you to see us," I spouted. "You have a really nice house. Rin has told me a lot about you."

"No, she hasn't," Alleea said drily. "Because she doesn't know anything about my life. She never comes around."

Rin stood up. "Oh, I know plenty. I know you tried to control every bit of *my* life."

"I tried to protect you and to teach you the reality of things."

"You tried to brainwash me, you mean," Rin said icily. "Well, I make my own choices these days and I'm only here because I don't know anybody else who can help us."

"Oh, another world-saving mission, is it? Yes, it's all over the Immersion. You're heroes. Congratulations."

"It's not over," Rin said, and then she sat down hard. "We need to take down the ghost."

Alleea nodded "I know. We're working on it."

Rin looked thunderstruck. So was I.

"Um," I ventured. "You already knew we were coming, then?"

"No. I didn't need to hear from you to know what had to be done. I agreed to see you but really, you're a distraction. So, it was very nice to see you, Rinella, I love you. Go away."

Alleea stood. We'd been there all of ten minutes.

Rin didn't move. "Maybe we can help you," she said.

"You'd just be in the way, and I don't want to put you in danger."

"I can handle myself," Rin said. "I think that's obvious." Her jaw set stubbornly.

"Luck doesn't run forever," Alleea said.

"Luck?" She clenched her fists and I saw she was struggling to contain her fury.

They both seemed to have forgotten that I was in the room. Neither one spoke. I wondered which one would erupt first.

Rin finally spoke through gritted teeth. "Well, this was fun, Mom. We should do it again sometime. Are you free on the fifteenth of never?"

"Still a brat," Alleea said.

Rin retorted, "I bet you turned my bedroom into a junk room."

"It *was* a junk room."

"Fine, I'll just go clean it out then," Rin said. "I'll get a few things and leave."

"No, don't go in there!" Alleea said quickly. She moved abruptly to block Rin.

"Why?" Rin asked and then added suspiciously, "Mom, what have you done?"

"I boxed up all your things," Alleea said. "They're in the garage. That room is empty."

"You're lying." She brushed past Alleea before she could be stopped and disappeared down the hallway.

I heard a door open and then I heard Rin gasp. Alleea and I both rushed after her. Rin stood frozen in the doorway. I looked into the room. There was a bed, a desk, a chair, other furnishings, all of them soulless and utilitarian. There was nothing that seemed to reflect Rin, except for the man lying on the bed.It was Pallburg.

CHAPTER THIRTY-TWO

"**I** killed you," I said as we sat in the living room. "Or the Sentience did, I mean."

"Clearly not," Pallburg said, stroking his trim beard. "I'd suspected for a while that a self-awareness had emerged in the system. But of course, I had the Killswitches. When they started dying, I knew I had to enact the fallback plan. Which, Mavo, was you."

"So you set me up," I said. "First Mom, and now me. You pulled everybody's strings."

"That's hardly fair, young man. You didn't live through the Collapse. You don't know what it cost to pull this world back together. If you knew what I knew, you'd consider your sacrifice to be small."

"It's not small to me," I said. "You took my life away, then you made me the most hated person on the planet."

While Pallburg and I were making friends, Rin and her mother had stepped out of the room. Now I smelled a sweet aroma as they returned. They seemed to have reached some kind of uneasy truce. Alleea was carrying a tray that she set down on the coffee table. It held fresh-baked chocolate chip cookies.

Rin put down a pitcher of milk and a flask of coffee. I realized that we hadn't eaten before we came to the house.

"You baked these?" I asked Rin.

"My Mom," Rin said. "She does that."

"I just pressed a button," Alleea said. "But the recipe's good. Help yourselves."

I didn't have to be asked twice. My stomach was rumbling and my salivary glands were in overdrive.

These cookies were warm and had crisp golden edges and filled the room with an irresistible scent.

I'd never actually had chocolate chip cookies except in Immersion. They were a luxury overlay that I'd only splurged on a couple of times to embellish some bland protein lump that I was actually eating.

I bit down and the gooey chocolate melted on my tongue. These cookies made the Immersion ones taste cheap and artificial. It seemed Rin's Mom was a perfectionist in everything she did.

I wondered how Rin had lived with her.

Then I looked hard at Pallburg, He was sitting with one leg casually crossed over the other, a hand tapping his knee— as if he hadn't just risen from the grave.

Here we were, politely drinking coffee and eating cookies and not mentioning the elephant in the room that was flapping its enormous ears and all but knocking over the furniture with its trunk.

Pallburg and Rin's mom didn't seem to be in any rush to reveal that, unknown to Rin, her long-lost father was sitting practically knee to knee with her, sipping from a bone china cup. Although, whenever they thought Rin wasn't looking, they caught each other's eyes and then locked them on Rin.

"So, Mom," Rin began. "You knew each other from work? The world's savior? And you just never happened to mention that?"

"We didn't part on the best of terms," Alleea said, as if that answered the question. "We had a, shall we say..." She paused.

"A philosophical disagreement," Pallburg finished.

Rin looked as if she were about to press the subject but her mom broke in.

"Which brings us to the situation at hand," she said. "We have an entity with the personality of Haakon but the resources of the entire

Unity system. And, one should note, this entity already has fought a war with another of its kind. It's well aware of the tactics used to defeat that enemy."

"So we're screwed?" I asked.

"Not at all," Pallburg said. "True, the entity and myself share a personality. We probably can anticipate each other's moves. That's why I turned to your mother here." He winked at Rin. "She has a different take on things."

"And we came up with ants," Alleea said.

"Ants?" Rin said. "Like the bugs?"

"My doctorate is in syncomp, synaptic linkage of computational systems, but I also have a master's in etymology," Alleea told me. "You do realize that an ant colony is effectively a swarm intelligence? There are a lot of similarities to the Unity system, actually."

I had a disturbing image of metal ants with display screens for faces clutching white, squirming mechanical larvae and scurrying through dank tunnels.

"The point is," Pallburg said. "that no single ant leads. Now, I made Unity a decentralized system on purpose just to avoid concentrating power."

"But," Alleea broke in. "your alter ego has your arrogant view that only you can really run things. That's why it refuses to self-destruct."

"A bit harsh," Pallburg said but seemed to accept the accusation on some level. "Nonetheless, that is a vulnerability."

"Why?" Rin asked.

"This time," Alleea said. "We don't create a single Kernel. We inject the system with a redistribution program. We create thousands of allies, separately weak and small but capable of nibbling away at parts of the entity."

"Too many for the Kernel to fight," Pallburg said. "It will act like an ant colony dismantling a grasshopper."

"But how do we get it inside?" Rin asked. "It has eyes everywhere."

Pallburg said, "Your mother worked for decades to create her own backdoors to the system. They were non-functional but over the past few weeks she and I have managed to get one operational. We hope. And the invasion program is ready to go."

Rin put down her coffee cup, wiped crumbs from her lips and said breezily, "No, it's not. If it were ready, we wouldn't be sitting here. Mom, come on. Out with it."

Alleea turned to Pallburg and her lips quirked.

"Haakon, I do believe you are no longer the smartest chimp in the room," she said, with a note of pride in her voice.

I could almost hear Pallburg's thoughts, as if I were reading his mind. He wanted to say, "Like father, like daughter."

But he didn't. Instead, he tugged at his beard, cleared his throat, and said, "Mavo, we will need your help. It's a small thing, really, but important."

Rin crossed her arms. "Go ahead."

I had no idea where this was going but some instinct told me to grab another cookie while I had the chance.

Pallburg said, "Let's imagine that our plan works and a swarm of attackers enters Unity and begins dismantling the entity, effectively shrinking its reach and even its intelligence. As resources are gobbled up or disconnected, it will stage a fighting retreat. It doesn't want to die, no more than any living creature."

"What does that mean?" I asked.

"It will coalesce, draw together whatever programming remains to it, and look for refuge," Pallburg said.

"But will your ants be able to kill it?" I asked.

"Eventually," Pallburg said. "But as long as it remains in the system, there is a danger. It might engage in the computer equivalent of death throes. Its flailing could damage the entire system very badly."

"There could be deaths on a massive scale," Alleea said.

Nobody spoke.

"Okay," Rin said finally. "What's the alternative?"

Pallburg spoke. "We bait it into leaving the system. We offer it a place to hide."

Suddenly the cookie was dust in my mouth. My stomach was acid.

Rin said, "No way!"

Pallburg spoke to her almost gently. "It's Mavo's decision, Rin."

"Make another Killswitch!" Rin said, her voice rising. "You did it before!"

"Rinella, that would take years," Alleea said. "We don't have the time."

"There's *got* to be some other way," Rin said. She slapped the coffee table, knocking over her cup and scattering cookies on the floor.

"If there were some other way, believe me, we would use it," Pallburg said. "If I had a lockbox in my brain, I would gladly use it. But I do not. It's just fortunate that you arrived, Mavo. It almost makes me believe in fate."

There was another silence. Then Rin said softly, "It'll eat his memories."

"We think not," Pallburg said. "The entity will naturally conform itself to the available dataspace. But you, Mavo, clearly managed to wall it off before. I'm counting on you to do the same again."

The alternative was left unsaid: That if I didn't wall it off, it would devour me.

I wanted to stand up and scream: "No! I've done enough. I don't want to carry an enemy in my head for the rest of my life. I don't need the nightmares again. I don't need the loneliness. Let it destroy the damn system and then rebuild it. You did it before."

Instead, I heard myself saying: "I'll do it."

Pallburg nodded as if he'd expected my answer. Alleea had an expression I couldn't read. I couldn't look at Rin.

"But," I added. "I need you to do one thing for me."

"Of course," Pallburg said.

"I think you know," I said, looking first at him and then at Alleea. "You've both been thinking about it since Rin and I arrived."

"Mavo?" Rin asked, clearly confused. But Pallburg instantly understood.

"Now is not the time, Mavo," he said firmly.

"It is, if you want my help," I said. "I lost my childhood. You stole hers. At least you can give her the truth going forward. She deserves that."

Rin's eyes went wide with bewilderment. She looked at me as if I'd suddenly slipped a gear.

"What are you talking about?" she asked.

Alleea blurted, "I don't think that's—"

"A good idea?" I said. "I don't care. Rin saved my life. She deserves to know. She might not want to know either one of you when she hears what you've done, but that's her choice to make."

Pallburg shook his head unhappily. Alleea looked appalled. But I knew one of them would have to cave. For once, I held the strings. And it felt good.

What I didn't expect was for both of them to cave at the same time.

Alleea said, "He's your father" at exactly the same moment that Pallburg said, "I'm your father, Rin."

I didn't know what I expected Rin to do but I sure didn't expect her to laugh. It was a long, loud, clamorous braying that had me worrying whether she'd lost her mind. It lasted for what seemed an eternity. Pallburg and Alleea looked worried, then aghast.

Rin finally stopped laughing and wiped tears from her eyes.

"Well, that's it," she said. "That is *it*." A few stray chuckles escaped her lips. She took a deep breath and then said, "Now I know my *entire* life is a lie."

Alleea reached out to hold her but Rin shook her away.

"Get off me!" she shouted.

"Rinella, it was to protect you!" Alleea said. "To protect everyone. If you were in contact with your father, you might have given away something about my work, which was to save Unity!"

"And if I'd visited you," Pallburg said, "You might have given away something to your mother, which could have destroyed it!"

"Shut up!" Rin said. "I don't need your excuses. I don't care why you did it! It's always you first. You deserve each other. And you—" She suddenly rounded on me. "—How long have you known?" Her eyes impaled me.

I stuttered something unintelligible and finally managed to say, "Since the crystal. When Mom used it to download the Kernel's programs into me, I got some of your father's memories. I'm sorry, Rin, I should have told you. I thought I was protecting you."

"You're just like them," she spat.

Rin reached into her tunic and yanked out the crystal. She peered at. Then she clutched it so tightly I thought it might shatter. She pinned each us with an icy gaze. Without another word, she stood up and stalked into the hallway. A moment later, I heard the door to her bedroom click shut with finality.

Pallburg reached into a pocket, pulled out a handkerchief and dabbed his forehead. "Well," he said. "The truth is out, Mavo. Happy?"

CHAPTER THIRTY-THREE

It was already dusk by the time we were ready to face the Kernel. Rin hadn't come out of her room. I knocked on the door twice but she didn't answer.

I left her alone, although my heart ached. I wanted to get it over with. I wouldn't know until then whether I'd lost her. When this was done, I'd either straighten it out with her or I wouldn't be around anymore and it wouldn't matter.

At least one thing had worked out, I thought: Rin wouldn't be there to watch me if things went bad. She'd been through enough.

Pallburg and Alleea had set up a sort of lab in a glorified garden shed stuck on the end of the house. The walls were cheap paneling. I'd expected to see an inclined chair like the one in the Malibu chamber or the deep-probe facility, but instead there was a simple cot bolted to the floor. No huge spidery device clamped itself to my head. Instead, I lay down and Pallburg clapped what looked like an off-the-shelf Immersion external feed to my temples.

"This won't be like a typical Immersion," Alleea explained. "You're simply going to sit and wait until the entity is driven your way."

"You'll have a sort of welcome sign out," Pallburg said enigmatically.

My stomach hurt. I tamped down the fear but couldn't help flinching as Alleea gently strapped down my arms and legs.

"You might twitch," she said. "We don't want you to hurt yourself."

In a few moments, they were ready.

I'd been mentally trying to compose a goodbye note in my head, something meaningful for my last words. I turned to Alleea.

"If I don't make it," I told her. "Will you tell Rin that I... that I loved our journey."

"Tell her yourself when you get back," Pallburg said, and I had to keep from laughing. In Immersion war stories, that was the cliché conversation every soldier had before a suicide mission.

Alleea put a warm hand on my arm. She actually looked concerned. "Do you want us to count you down?" she asked.

"Okay," I said.

"Ten," she said. "Nine. Eight..."

I took several quick panting breaths, then one long breath and let it out.

"Five. Four..."

I let go of my fear. It was useless now.

"Three. Two..."

And I was out.

It wasn't like the last time. It was dark and quiet, almost like being asleep. I waited. I had no sense of time. I wondered idly what Pallburg's welcome sign was like and if anybody would really spot it. *Are you being eaten by hordes of bugs? Then come on in!"* I thought. I pictured myself wearing an apron and wiping a beer mug with a rag, like some Immersion bartender.

And then something moved out of that darkness. It was just a shadow at first, barely a lesser darkness, or maybe a dim swirling. It was moving fast. It came roaring toward me and gained form as it emerged.

Finally, it took on human form. But it looked like a refugee from the Collapse: Dirty, gaunt, tattered.

As it came closer, I saw it had Pallburg's face, but not the one I'd seen a few moments ago. This was Pallburg from the Columbarium: Slack, pale and lifeless. Except for the eyes. They were full of panic.

Its body was missing pieces. One arm ended at the elbow.

And at its heels came the programmed horde. The bugs swarmed, teemed. Each one tore a tiny chunk from the Kernel. The bits were carried away by the endless army into the infinite darkness. By the time the Kernel loomed up in front of me, a lot of it had been stripped away. It smelled like rotten meat. It lurched like a zombie. I didn't see much intelligence in its face, merely an animal instinct to survive.

With disgust and horror, I backed away. I couldn't help myself. At that instant, I would have chosen to dissolve into the darkness rather than let that shambling thing enter me.

I turned and ran in blind panic. Behind me, I heard the ravaged Kernel relentlessly pursuing me. Its stench choked the air.

Desperation fueled me. I put on speed. For an instant, I thought I'd escaped as its moans faded behind me.

And then I slammed into a wall. The breath was knocked out of me. Gasping, I stood before the invisible barrier. I hammered my fists against it, but it was unyielding.

With nowhere left to go, I turned and pressed my back against the wall. I faced the Kernel.

It had lost all its limbs except for one arm. Now it pulled itself toward me, clawing the ground as its bug-covered body arched like a worm.

It was both horrifying and pitiful. And its purpose was written in its eyes. It would hide in my mind, consume me and grow back to power. Then it would destroy its enemies: Pallburg. Rin's mother.

Rin.

I couldn't let that happen. I was the only one who could stop it.

Suddenly, my fear was gone, and I felt the wall at my back not as a barrier but a bulwark. I realized that the wall was my own purpose, something of myself that I could not escape.

I felt its strength; it was my strength. I could do this.

The Kernel reached me and I opened myself to let it in. There was no transition. Its dark presence was in front of me and then it was in my head. I felt it almost as a weight at the back of my skull, filling spaces I'd forgotten about.

From a long way away, I heard myself say: "Got it!"

The feed was cut off and suddenly I was back in the room with Alleea and Pallburg.

Alleea bent over me anxiously. "Is it contained?" she asked.

"I think so," I said. "My head feels full."

"It's out of Unity," Pallburg said from somewhere behind me. "It left a few partial copies of itself but the ants are scouring them away, then deleting themselves. It worked, Mavo! Congratulations!"

But they were wrong. The thing in my head suddenly stirred. I recognized it as the Pallburg Kernel, but its snarky personality was gone. It was almost back to being a mindless program. I felt its previous hunger for resources and clamped down mentally. I could contain it. I *could*.

But it was different this time: It had claws.

I felt my mind being shredded by something with the size and fury of a Sidysal monster. It seemed to know every nook and cranny of my fears, and it tore at them. I felt it claw away gobbets of my consciousness. It was trying to gain control of my muscle functions and I felt myself begin to thrash. Now I knew why they'd tied me down. I bore down and strengthened the wall of my purpose but the monster was tearing at it in fury. Rents appeared in my mind.

With every slash, I felt parts of me vanishing. My control spurted away like blood. I felt the thing getting stronger as I grew weaker.

I redoubled my efforts. From somewhere far off, I could feel my back arching with convulsions. I bit my tongue and tasted salt and iron.

It *hurt*. I understood now what the Kernel had felt as the ants were tearing it apart. My legs suddenly lost all feeling, as if they'd disappeared. My hands went numb. A moment later, I was blind.

All I could hear was the rush of blood in my ears and then a voice I remembered.

"Don't resist, Mavo," it said. "You'll only make it harder." I didn't know whether that was the Kernel or the flesh Pallburg talking.

The claws reached out now for my higher functions. I retreated, I cowered in some dead-end corner of my mind and made my last stand.

I was going to die. I still had my voice, though.

"It's got me," I croaked. "Kill me."

I clenched my teeth together. It was my last act of defiance.

Then I felt my jaws being pried apart. Something hard was forced between them. I felt a fizziness on my tongue and a kind of electric shock. A buzzing vibration radiated from my neck to the top of my head.

Memories came flooding back. I felt the burning heat of an Outside summer. I heard an out-of-tune guitar and my mother crooning an anti-Unity lullaby to my sister; I was lying in the desert and watching with awe as meteors crisscrossed the sky in streaks of brilliance; I was standing at the train platform, both afraid and hopeful as I waited to jump aboard.

A flood of images, hundreds of them, thousands. I felt the Kernel's control of my body slipping. One of my hands was reborn. I made a fist.

I could fight again.

My mind converted the torrent of images into an ocean. A tidal wave of memories rose and lifted me with it.

The Kernel was screaming incoherently and lashing out. It tore at the tide, ripping gaping holes in the flood, but they filled immediately with more memories.

I felt my eyes and legs return to me. In my mind, I dove into the gigantic wave, slid up its churning surface and in a moment, I was riding it. My despair fell away. I felt euphoric. I was surfing my memories, just as my mother had ridden waves so many years ago in Malibu.

I could see light bouncing off the water, the intensity of blue sky. I reveled in the feel of the spray on my skin.

The Kernel was simply washed away as if it had never existed.

I let the wave collapse and the waters of memory filled the empty vaults of my mind.

The flood had found its level.

I opened my eyes.

Rin was bending over me. She jerked her hand back and pulled the thing in my mouth free. She was holding her crystal. Her fingers were smeared with blood. The crystal was a dead brown.

"Rin," I croaked. My swollen tongue felt thick in my mouth and it was hard to speak. "What happened?"

"Mavo?" Her hair was a tangled mess and her eyes were red-rimmed. "Is that you?"

"It's me. *Only* me."

Her smile flashed like lightning. She held up a bloody finger.

"You bit me!" she said, and scowled, then burst into laughter. Before I could say a word, she grabbed me in a fierce embrace.

It hurt but I didn't care.

When she released me, I realized that Alleea and Pallburg were still there.

Pallburg stepped forward. He was holding a portable medical reader. He scanned me.

"You're basically sound," he said. "But you had a seizure and cracked two ribs. You'll be sore for a while. I see no major neural damage, but you should probably have a specialist look at you. How do you feel, mentally?"

"Empty," I said. "And full." I knew I wasn't making myself clear so I added, "More like the old me. And I feel like I could Immerse now. But there are also these gaps here and there. Holes, like where a tooth's missing."

"Yes," Pallburg said solemnly. "It was unlikely that you would entirely escape harm. But you did a brave and magnificent thing."

"I'd rather forget that part," I said. "Can I get up now?"

Alleea stepped forward and began unstrapping me. "These were just in case the entity won and took over your body," she said. She didn't mention what would have happened then but I could guess.

I had to admire them. They'd planned it all. Ruthless, efficient and necessary. It ought to be the Pallburg family motto, I thought, but then I looked at Rin.

"My memories," I said. "*You* put them back."

"I was guessing," she said. "I hoped that your own memories would be a better fit in your mind space than the ghost. Like filling in pieces of a jigsaw puzzle."

"Was that part of the plan?" I asked.

Alleea suddenly busied herself with my ankle straps while Pallburg seemed focused intently on fidgeting with the medical scanner.

"I heard you screaming," Rin said, as if that answered the question.

"But the crystal... you've had my memories all this time?"

"That's why your Mom gave it to me," Rin said. "She said I'd know when to use it."

EPILOGUE

I sipped my first cup of coffee of the day. It was perfect. That boded well. The ancient machine I was using had been temperamental lately. I'd been giving out a lot of refunds. I took my cloth and wiped away a smudge on the enormous brass and glass front.

I smelled a delicious aroma. Rin appeared from the kitchen, carrying a tray of fresh-baked chocolate chip cookies. I snagged one as she placed them in the display case.

"How's Gigi this morning?" she asked.

I lifted my cup. "Perfect," I said. I patted the eagle on Gigi's front affectionately. I was pretty sure that for reasons I couldn't understand, treating the machine nicely helped make a better cup of Joe.

"Careful, I'll get jealous," Rin said.

I used the cloth to polish the granite countertop while Rin went in and out of the back, stocking an incredible variety of baked goods.

"You've got some flour on your cheek," I said.

She smiled and patted it away. I marveled again at how Rin had taken to baking, which was an art that remained a mystery to me. I'd never cooked anything; except for some Outsider road kill, most of my food had come in plastic wrappers. But then, Rin had been a revolutionary, and wasn't that what the Realists were all about: restoring some human balance to our artificial, uber-connected world?

I shrugged and began to wipe down the wooden tables. It was too early in the morning for philosophy and we opened in fifteen minutes. There was already a line outside the door. People loved Rin's baking. And Gigi's coffee.

We'd lucked out in getting this place. I bought it with the money I received from a FundMyLife pot that was set up when Pallburg, returned from the dead, announced that I had saved Unity for the second time. The money and my reputation were enough to convince the owner to sell. I told myself I wanted the place because of the cozy, old-fashioned vibe and not because he'd thrown me out the day I'd been released from court.

The place recreated the pre-Collapse experience of a coffee bar: Full of wood and old furniture, where you could comfortably sit for hours with a cup in your hand, thinking or writing or even reading a book. I had shelves of them and while most people Immersed, a surprising number had taken to picking one up.

Rin suddenly put down a tray and touched her forehead, concentrating. I saw she was answering an Immersion call.

"No," she said finally. "We're not interested. Goodbye."

"Another one?" I asked.

She nodded and sighed. "Since they couldn't convince you, they've been trying me."

"We could block everybody."

Rin shook her head. "That would make us more mysterious. Then we'd have paparazzi and chancers hanging out at the front door, bothering the customers."

I'd been flooded with offers to upload my experiences, emotions and all, for a hefty fee but I'd refused. I had no desire to relive those moments again. It had taken months of PTSD counseling to stop the nightmares. I also declined requests for interviews and bids to have me star in documentaries, miniseries and big-budget Immersion epics, either recreating my adventures or starring in new ones.

"It'll die down eventually," I said. "It's the Immersion. Everything gets old."

"Like this place," Rin said, quirking her lips. "Beautifully ancient. And here to stay."

"Like Gigi," I said, grinning.

"Watch it," Rin said.

THE END

About the Author

J.R. Waterbear is the pen name of authors John Pulver and Robert Jablon. Both hail from Southern California and have hiked, kayaked, scuba-dived and surfed their way from Alaska to Mexico which influenced some scenes in *Killswitch*.

Pulver's fiction has appeared in several publications, and he is the host of The Natural Muse, a group that connects authors with the joy and inspiration of writing from nature.

Jablon is a former journalist for The Associated Press who recently retired to the south of France.

Killswitch deals with issues that have long fascinated the authors: alienation; the tension between morality and survival, and the struggle to achieve self-discovery, especially in a conformist, social media-driven culture.